The Survival of the Fittest

BOOKS BY PAMELA HANSFORD JOHNSON

NOVELS
The Survival of the Fittest
Cork Street, Next to the Hatter's
Night and Silence Who Is Here?
An Error of Judgment
The Humbler Creation
The Unspeakable Skipton
The Sea and the Wedding

PLAY
Corinth House

NONFICTION
On Iniquity
The Art of Thomas Wolfe

PAMELA HANSFORD JOHNSON

The Survival of the Fittest

CHARLES SCRIBNER'S SONS · NEW YORK

To My Son, Philip

Author's Note

TWO CHARACTERS IN THIS BOOK, "BELPHOEBE" AND MAMONOV, MAY be recognizable as, respectively, a poet now dead and a writer now living.

The first is an affectionate though very slight sketch. The second is only suggested by the original, and in the novel is a much older man. No word of their dialogue has been taken from anything either of them ever at any time actually said, and the incidents surrounding them are invented.

Kit and Alison are composite characters, each drawn from three separate sources.

Jo, and all the others, are pure inventions: or, if they had their inspiration in the physique or in the mannerisms of any real persons, immediately took upon themselves individual beings of their own, and bear no resemblance in my mind now to any possible originals, living or dead.

P.H.J.

Contents

PART ONE
The Wild Life

Chapter One

"GOD," SAID KIT, "WHAT A HORRIBLE HOUSE YOU LIVE IN!"

Jo, too used to this kind of thing to resent it, merely looked at the house with fresh eyes and thought there might be something in the suggestion. Nineteen-ten had not been a good period for building, and the row of semi-detached villas on the west side of the common had that combination of the mean and the flashy so characteristic of it: a stained-glass panel in the door, some coarse scroll-work in plaster above the lintel, strips of blue and yellow glass set into the tops of the windows.

"When you come to think of it, I suppose I do." He un-latched the gate. Kit hesitated.

He said, "You're sure this isn't a bore for your mother?"

"Of course not. She's always saying she never meets any of my friends."

On the horizon, the last of the sunset lay in a single strip, pink and lucent as water-ice, behind the trees. The lamps sparked up in a wide parabola as far as the eye could see, and the bushes blackened.

"Anyway, I want you to see *my* pub. We can get away as soon as we've eaten."

The young men had been at the same school but then the four years' difference in their ages had separated them. They had met again by chance three summers ago at a circle for aspiring writers. Kit had written one short story, which had been published, and Jo four, which had not. Kit was halfway through a novel. Their ambitions had brought them close. Two or three times a week they met after work, and visited public houses in Chelsea or Bloomsbury, which gave them heady ideas of the artistic life: the smell was sweet in their nostrils. Jo had to be very careful afterwards to hold his breath when kissing his mother so that she should not detect the beer on it.

They went into the sitting-room, which was very hot and had a good deal of Benares ware scattered about. Before the fire, rubber-tipped sticks to hand, sat the fat woman, very white of skin, arthritic hands folded in her lap.

"This is Kit Mallings," Jo said. "My mother."

"Well, it makes a nice change for me to have a visitor." Her gaze noted Kit's curly black hair, his orange shirt, the checked sports-jacket a size too large, the corduroy trousers concertinaed over his suede shoes.

"It's more than nice of you to have me, Mrs. Upjohn," he said in his stateliest manner, bowing a little as if to greet a queen. Jo was nervous, wondering whether he could keep it up.

"I can't rise to receive you," she said, "because they have put a silly pin in my thigh. I think of it as something like a clothes-peg."

She had a strange, almost bow-fronted face, quite lean at the extreme sides of it, but then the cheeks swelled up towards the tiny nose, which hardly seemed to interrupt their progress. Her eyes, like her son's, were green and clear but her hair was fair with an apricot tinge, and she wore it in a net.

Kit said he was sorry to hear about her accident. How had it happened?

"Carelessness, pure carelessness!" she cried. "Silly old me. I was putting up some curtains and I fell off a chair." She smacked her hand sharply. "Serve me right. Only myself to blame. Still, I do manage to drag around a bit, don't I, Jo?"

"You're a marvel," he said, and touched her forearm.

4

Kit asked if he might smoke.

"Of course you may," Mrs. Upjohn answered, "I do myself. It's one of my little comforts. But I expect Mildred's nearly ready with supper."

Nobody smoked.

"And what do you think of the world, Mr. Mallings? Are you a politician like Jo? He thinks we should never have allowed that man Hitler to go so far." This was not so long after the re-occupation of the Rhineland.

Kit said he hadn't any politics, really: he supposed he was some sort of anarchist.

"Oh, you throw bombs, do you? I see we shall all have to be careful. Perhaps we ought to make you turn out your pockets!"

"Not necessary. No danger."

Mildred came in and was introduced. She was a woman of thirty, five years older than her brother and as dark, but her build was dumpy. "Supper's ready."

She and Jo hoisted Mrs. Upjohn out of her chair, put the sticks into her hands, and supported her inching progress into the next room, where the meal was laid. Kit's "Can I help?" was unheeded.

When Jo saw the table, he was dismayed. As a rule, their evening meal was simple. Now, on a lace-edged cloth which he did not recognize, was something very like a banquet: cold salmon, cold tongue, pickles, sausage rolls, salad, brown and white bread and butter, tinned peaches and pears, cream cakes, Dundee cake. The teapot was covered by a cosy of orange felt, quite new, decorated with floral cut-outs. Kit, he knew, ate very little indeed, but there must be an attempt made, at least, to diminish this pile of food, and it would upset his mother if they were to rush through it. This meant that it must be a full three-quarters of an hour before they could escape to the pub, and he could imagine Kit fretting.

Pretending to help Mildred, he followed her into the kitchen.

"She would have it," Mildred said, shrugging. "She said we must lay out the red carpet for any friend of yours. We'll be eating the stuff up for days." She added, "Don't blame me."

When they returned to the table, Kit was giving Mrs. Upjohn an imitation of a delighted schoolboy, preparing for a "tuck-in."

"I say, this looks marvellous! You'll have to forgive me if I can't eat too much, I've had a bilious attack. I only wish I could manage the lot, single-handed."

Mrs. Upjohn, smiling, piled a plate for him, adding a mound of pickles, which he hated. "Now, look here, young man, you're skinny enough as it is. Your clothes are hanging on you."

She did not know that Kit, displeased by the shortness and slightness of his build, had found it convenient to emphasize both. Thus, he was usually cossetted and made much of.

They were all seated now, and the cups had been passed, strong tea, steaming. Mildred described her day. She was a part-time schoolteacher, devoting the rest of her time to her mother's comfort. She was a dry, rather amusing talker, with a scratchy gift for enlivening some minor incident and little sensibility of subjects acceptable at meal-times. There was the child of good family who was discovered to have nits in her hair, and had fainted dead away. There was the little girl who got locked in the lavatory.

Joe ate and ate, knowing he would get indigestion later. Even now, he felt bloated.

"Now, now, Millie," said Mrs. Upjohn, "tell us something pleasant about somebody, just for once."

"I've heard the kids call me the old cat. Take me or leave me."

"Nonsense, you're not old! Don't you say that to your young man, or you'll have him believing it."

Mildred colored and said nothing.

Kit was making eating noises, and a great clashing of his knife and fork. "Quite delicious," he said. Out of the corner of an eye, Jo saw that he had eaten perhaps half a slice of ham, and had stowed the other half out of sight beneath the salad. It was skilfully done.

"Eat your pickles," Mrs. Upjohn said, "I bottled them myself. Tell me what you think of them." Her gaze was steady upon him. Bravely, Kit speared a walnut and put it in his mouth. His throat moved. His eyes filled with tears. Hastily, he drank half a cup of tea and washed it down. "They're wonderful. If only I dared, with my stomach—"

Jo hastily drew his mother into discussion of a programme they had both heard recently on the wireless. Meanwhile, he could see that Kit, handkerchief covering his face, appeared to be

6

shovelling walnuts into his mouth at great speed. Then he rolled the handkerchief up and stuffed it into a trouser-pocket.

Kit sighed with relief, beamingly accepted peaches and cream.

It was a quarter past eight before they could get away. Mrs. Upjohn was brave about their early departure and did not delay it too long. She held Kit's hand in both of hers. "Come ye again. It's a treat for me to see young people occasionally. Besides, I may surprise you. You're going to be a famous writer, I know. Well, I'm not an ignoramus about books. I used to read poetry by the mile."

"It's true," Jo said eagerly, "she knows an awful lot."

"Coventry Patmore," said his mother, "nobody reads him nowadays. *The Angel in the House.* Come ye again, Kit—I shall call you Kit—come ye again."

"Yes, do," said Mildred, who was clearing the table, "if you really think you can bear it."

The weather had turned chilly. The two young men started across the dark common, in the direction of a distant line of lights twinkling in the rising mist. Kit shivered, and said he hoped it wasn't too far. "It's like the steppes out here. Innumerable miles. Got any wolves in your ravines? I'd like to see the steppes."

Pausing under a lamp, he removed from his pocket a damp, dark-stained handkerchief. "God, I reek of it!" He stepped aside and pushed the handkerchief carefully into a bush. "I hope your mother didn't see me."

"She didn't, or she'd have had something to say."

"I like Mildred."

"So do I," said Jo, "but she has a poor life of it."

"Your mother mentioned a young man."

"You know the auctioneer's, at the bottom of The Rise? He's the younger brother. Nothing's going to come of it, though. Nothing ever does."

"I can see," Kit said delicately, "that things are difficult."

After fifteen minutes of hard walking, they came to Clapham Old Town, and to the little pub showering its colors over the pavement.

"Warm gules," said Kit.

"I wish you'd seen Mother at her best."

Chapter Two

BOTH OF THEM HAD DRUNK ENOUGH BEER TO FEEL THE EFFECTS. Kit had been proudly introduced to the barmaid and had gone through the ritual of gallantry. At a corner table by the window, which had fake mullions, they stared at each other in sentimental intimacy.

"Yes, I do like your pub. Too far away, though. How's Lucy?" This was one of Jo's current, and transient, girls, met only in a certain public house in Fitzroy Square, though she would occasionally go with him to the pictures. Not waiting for a reply— "You shouldn't look so sharp and stern. You could use your profile as a printer's guillotine."

"Better than to have no profile at all."

"Ah, but look at me from the front! All poetry. No, poesy. Yes, poesy. Lovely mucky word, enough to make a cat sick."

"Cats are always being sick."

"We never had one."

"We've got three," Jo said, "but they stick around the kitchen. Inverted snobs."

Kit got up to order two more pints. "You know," he said to

the barmaid, "you remind me of a girl in a Russian book, called Anna. I'm paying you a great, great compliment."

"I hope she was a nice girl!"

"Very nice. She only had a single lapse."

"Well, I don't lapse."

" ' 'Tis true, 'tis pity, pity 'tis 'tis true.' "

"Tell that to Jo, there," said the barmaid meaninglessly.

Kit drank deeply, leaving a moustache of foam on his upper lip. After a while Jo asked him how the work was going. "It's not half bad. Did you ever read Djuna Barnes? A bit like that, but much, much better. Very obscene. What about you?"

"I haven't done much. I've got stuck."

"Better let me see it."

Then Kit said, "I want you to meet someone. How about to-morrow night?"

"Can't. Mildred's got a date."

"Friday, then. Six Bells?"

"Who is it?"

Kit seemed excited. His large eyes glowed, and under the beer froth his lips widened. "Alison Petrie."

Jo exclaimed in reverence.

This was a girl of twenty-three, whose first novel had made something of a sensation, and was even said to be selling quite well. It was fashionable at the moment to have read it. She seemed to have come out of nowhere, a typist in a City office who, in slack periods, had written a vigorous, tart, adventitiously realistic book about a neophyte prostitute in Paris, a city she had never visited, and a subject she was said to know nothing whatsoever about.

"I met her last week," said Kit. "We're getting along splendidly. She wants me to stop smoking and drinking, which is a very good sign. I'm rude about her stuff, and she doesn't mind, and that's fine, too. She is dark, small, her chin is hard, she has blue, blue, blue eyes with a broken vein in one of them, which oddly enough is very pretty. She is shy and shrinking, literary parties scare her stiff. She glowers at people, except at me. I think I'm in love with her. I don't mind you meeting her. I trust you."

Since Kit liked to keep his friends in separate compartments, Jo was deeply flattered: then, a second later, not so flattered. But he expressed pleasure.

"O.K., Friday, six o'clock, usual corner."

"I've got some news for you, too," Jo said, but it fell flat. "I've joined the Labour Party."

" 'The People's Flag is Deepest Red,' " Kit sang, so suddenly and so loudly, in the vast deep voice too strong for his body, that everyone in the pub turned to look at him and the barmaid cried, "No singing here, we've no licence."

"More fool you." He returned to Jo. "And what will your mum say?"

"What should she say?"

"That'll mean more nights out a week, when you don't come home."

"Only one more."

"Rough on Mildred."

"Oh, shut up!" Jo cried. "You leave my family out of it."

"Poor bloody auctioneer."

"I said, 'Shut up!' "

"You asked me to your house. You can't expect me not to be interested now."

"We love Mother." Jo's eyes, pale as peeled grapes, the lashes thick, short and dark, were clouded with tears.

" 'There is no one like a Moth-er—' " Kit was singing again.

Jo clamped a hard hand on his arm. "This is *my* pub. Don't you bleeding well spoil it for me."

"Nothing can spoil anything for you but yourself, you damned John Knox. I'm going to be sick."

"No you're not."

"How do you know? I *shall* be sick if I want to. When I think of those pickled—" He gagged.

"Mother and Millie went all out for you. What sort of bastard are you to sneer?"

Kit seemed to be thinking. He said, "No, I shan't."

"What?"

"Be sick."

"Time, gentlemen," sang the barmaid, in a voice penetrating as a solo choirboy's.

The night air unsteadied their feet, but cooled their temper. The mist had thickened, and over the roof-tops the moon was like a mandarin orange. There was a stinging scent from the mist, a sweet one from the grass and the budding hawthorns.

"You can take the tube from Clapham South," Jo said. He

10

was feeling the effects less of drink than of the indigestion anticipated. "Why you had to go and live in Putney—"

"There's a river at Putney. It stinks at low tide. Last week on
the foreshore there was a dead and headless dog, swollen up like a
balloon; it was a lovely pale-blue. You know I love you, Jo. Not
like a mother, like a brother. You get some sandpaper for that
sharp nose, and I'll love you more than ever. You and me, we're
friends."

"Friends," said Jo, and when he had seen Kit to the station,
walked slowly home alone, his steps becoming firmer as he went,
by the longer route, by the lighted road. He was hoping that by
the time he got in, they would be in bed.

They were not. They were sitting over the fire, listening to
Henry Hall's band. Mildred switched off the set. She said: "I liked
your arty friend, but he oughtn't to put good pickled walnuts in
his handkerchief. Did they make him smell?"

"Yes," said Jo, "somewhat." He was relieved.

"He is very artistic," said Bessie Upjohn, "isn't he? Does his
mother like him to go about dressed up like that? Give me a cigarette, I've run out."

"Where did you find that horrible tea-cosy? You needn't have
made so much fuss."

"Is that all I get for my pains?" Mildred looked up from her
knitting and faintly grinned. He was well aware that the fuss was
not her fault.

"His mother doesn't give a damn what he wears or what he
doesn't."

"But will he do anything?" Bessie inquired.

"He will."

"So often people like that just splutter out. How can you
tell?"

"I have a sharp nose," said Jo, too late remembering the
sandpaper. Mildred giggled.

"And if his mother doesn't give a damn what he does," said
Bessie, "I give a *damn* what you do." She took upon her the look
of authority he admired and dreaded. "Now I know I'm a burden
on you both. But since I can't help it, I don't care. You're young,
you must saddle it. There's plenty of time ahead of you. And,
Joseph"—this was the solemn use of his name and therefore alarm-
ing—"you must admit that I'm not greedy where you're con-

11

cerned. I like you to go out and about. I should like to see you marry a nice girl."

"I don't know any nice girls, and I couldn't afford it."

"There is plenty of room in this house. Jo, you've been drinking."

He yelled at her—"What else do you think I've been doing, when you know I've been to the pub?"

"Well," said his mother, "let's make it a general celebration, in honor of your friend, and have a nightcap together." She told her daughter that, if she looked in the sideboard cellarette, she would find a bottle of sherry. It was news to Mildred.

"Where did this come from?"

"I asked Mrs. Warren to buy it for me. I thought perhaps Jo might bring his friend back after their expedition."

"He had to get home."

"Well, then, all the more for ourselves. And Jo, don't shout at me again. It sounds so funny."

The three sipped at their glasses gingerly, since this was so uncommon a thing to do. Jo felt an atmosphere settling, half-Christmassy, half-funereal, and because he disliked the unusual, he felt ill at ease. It was plain to him that Kit's visit had acted as some kind of catalyst, and he wished he had never brought him home. His private life he liked to keep to himself: it had been an impulse of vanity which had persuaded him to show his friend that he, too, had a place of his own—not the home, but the pub: the home part of it had been necessary since he, if not Kit, needed to eat before an evening's drinking, and anyway, it killed two birds with one stone—"I never meet your friends."

He had not been shaken earlier by Kit's frank remark that the house he lived in was ugly. Now, already too full of beer, the sticky sherry feeling its ungracious way down to make concave the existing liquid surface, he was shaken a little. Yes, it was ugly: most people's houses were, outside. But it did not pass muster inside, either. His mother and Mildred, neither of them ordinary people, were commonplace in their tastes, and Bessie sentimental in hers. Her husband, his father, had been an accountant in the Indian Civil Service: hence the Benares ware, the writhing lamp standards. His photograph—dark face, Kiplingesque moustache—stood on the sideboard. But he had not been responsible for that terrible tea-cosy. Mildred had bought that.

12

Bessie Upjohn allowed her glass to be refilled.

"Now," she said.

They waited upon her.

She said, simply, "I should be very frightened at over-burdening you both, in my present condition, if I thought I had another twenty years to run. But my heart's weak, as you know, and I don't expect to make old bones. Mildred knows I love her, but she also knows I am old-fashioned enough to give precedence to boys. So I won't keep Jo on a string. If we'd all got more money coming in, I'd keep nobody on a string. As it is, Mildred has the worst of it."

Mildred regarded her with sardonic eyes, unblinking. She did not love her mother, though every Sunday morning, in church—this was Bessie's sole compulsion, that they should go together to Clapham Congregational, a business entailing a bath-chair—she prayed fervently that she might come to do so. Having no belief in hell, she yet did not desire to qualify herself for the place.

"Oh, not so bad," she said, "not so bad."

"But I'm not going to blame myself for what I can't help. I gave you both much: you can give me a bit for a while longer."

"For Christ's sake," said Jo, "what's started all this?"

"I've had time to think."

"I'm going to bed," Mildred said, and she went.

Alone with her son, Bessie took his hands in her own. "Are you very tired of all this, Jo?"

No, he replied, he didn't feel tired, or tied down.

A nice girl, perhaps?

He repeated, as he had done earlier, that there was no nice girl.

"What about Millie?"

He said that if Mildred ever wanted to get married, she must do so.

"Then what would you do?"

"Me, and Mrs. Warren, we'd manage between us." He added that she must not fret herself, nothing was fretting anybody, everything was fine.

"Your Kit, do you think he's ever heard of Coventry Patmore?"

"He's heard of everything."

"He didn't answer me about that."

"He's up in the clouds."

She said with fervor, "I wish you were! I wish you could be!"

She meant it, too, and he knew it. As he had told Kit, he loved her.

"I shall go to bed, too," she said. "Help me." Her room was now on the same floor. There was no need to disturb Mildred, since she could still manage to undress herself.

Chapter Three

IT WAS MILD ENOUGH TO SIT IN THE GARDEN OF THE SIX BELLS, WHERE the small fountain dribbled rather than flowed, and where, beyond the hedge, the ribs of late sunshine lay level on the bowling green, and gilded the faces of the players to masks of Agamemnon. Jo was talking to Clement and Georgina Maclaren. There was no sign yet of Kit.

Clement was a big man of thirty, with wide blue eyes and much wavy fair hair. A successful free-lance journalist, he had an air of bullying nonchalance that made him a figure in Chelsea and Bloomsbury; he was not exactly liked, but he was popular. Georgina, his wife, was also tall, and as offhand as he. Nobody expected the marriage to last long.

Jo felt, in this company, a privileged outsider, which was the light in which they did, in fact, regard him. Kit had gained full admission, partly on the strength of his short story and partly because he was Kit. He was a natural insider and dressed the part, which was something Jo did not dare to do: in any case, he would have felt ridiculous. His only concession to what he thought of as

15

"the wild side of his life" was to wear, with his best blue serge suit, now badly rubbed in places, a bright-red tie.

"King Farouk will become as fat as a house," said Georgina, glancing through the evening paper which announced the Accession, "but at the moment he is not without allure." Her long brown eyes moved sideways towards her husband, and she smiled to herself.

"Yes," said Clement, "you'd fancy yourself in some bloody great harem, wouldn't you? Queening it."

"I should have to be Head Girl," she replied demurely. "Yes, certainly Head Girl."

"It's about time the other Head Girl showed up. Why can't Kit be punctual? He drags us along here, when he knows I'd rather be at the Fitzroy or listening to Vincent d'Indy"—this was a new craze with all of them—"and then he's half an hour late."

"I thought her book was a bore," said Georgina.

"What do you know about it? *Can* you read? I've often wondered."

"And I hated that awful *Murder in the Cathedral.*" Georgina gave rather a good imitation of a "poor woman of Canterbury" complaining of the bitter ale.

Jo, who had thought the play wonderful, did not dare say so.

"Have you seen Kit's book?" Clement asked him. "He showed me a couple of chapters. It's bloody good in a wild, contorted sort of way. It is all about a girl with a very fat bum. Believe it or not, that is the *clou* of the whole affair."

Jo felt jealous. He himself had been shown nothing of it. He did not reply.

"It can't be," said Georgina. She waved brightly to a young man who had just come out of the pub. He waved back, and went across to the side of the terrace, froth slopping down from the four beer mugs he was trying to carry simultaneously.

"Who's that?" Clement said sharply. "Another of your buddies?"

"No one you know."

"Well, who is he?"

"Oh, he just paints. Not very well."

"Where did you meet him?"

"Somewhere. I forget."

16

The young man, seated with other friends, raised his glass and silently toasted her. She raised hers in return.

"Why the graveyard silence?" Clement asked Jo, in a hectoring tone, as if something were his fault.

Jo said he didn't know why, and it wasn't graveyard.

Georgina smoothed his sleeve, and her eyes invited him. "He's a sexton. He is calculating how far down he's got to dig."

"Don't start on Jo," Clement said, with a fair assumption of equability, "he's not for the likes of you."

At that moment Kit joined them. His arm was round Alison's shoulders, and he was radiant. He might just have created her out of clay.

She said nervously, "Hullo."

She was as Kit had described her, but smaller than Jo had expected her to be, and rather full-breasted. She wore a neat black dress and a little string of pearls.

"The Head Girl," said Georgina, who did not often like women much.

Kit introduced her. "This is Alison, who is going to be very great. This is Clement, who is great already in his own way, and gets paid thousands of dollars by huge shiny American magazines. This is Georgina. And this is my friend, Jo."

"Hullo," she said again, and sat down rather abruptly on the edge of a wooden chair, as if ready for retreat at any moment.

Jo was warmed by the style in which the introduction to himself had been made. He felt very happy all of a sudden.

"Beer," said Kit, "you shall have some. Make chums while I've gone." He darted back into the building.

Alison fiddled with her pearls. Then she looked straight at Georgina. "Why am I the Head Girl?" Her voice was strong and deep.

"Well, aren't you *the* lion of the moment? Is it wonderful?"

"In so far as it's even true, no. It's terrifying."

Georgina said casually, "I'm afraid I haven't read your book," to which the other girl unexpectedly replied, and firmly, too, "That is something which can easily be remedied."

Clement laughed aloud, tossing back his buoyant hair.

"So sucks to you, Georgie."

"I only meant," said Alison, uncomfortable again, "that it

17

could be." She turned to Jo. "I'm glad we've met. Kit's told me so much about you."

He answered, in a way he knew to be silly, "Not too much, I hope."

"All of it was good."

He noted the broken vein in the eye, a mere thread of scarlet, which intensified the blueness; the small, well-shaped mouth; the straight black hair cut very short and swept behind lobeless ears. He was awed by her, and he was delighted. It seemed to him wonderful simply to be talking to someone who had actually published a book, but even more wonderful that he should not be afraid of her, as he had expected to be.

Georgina rose—"I'll be back soon"—and crossed the terrace to join the group there.

Alison said to Clement, "Did I say something to upset your wife? I'm afraid I sounded rude."

"It's nothing to do with you. In fact, it couldn't be more remote. We had a flaming row just before we came out, and I belted her with a hair brush, bristle-side down. She's just trying to pay me back."

Kit reappeared with the drinks, drew up a seat at Alison's side, and kissed her cheek. "She's in love with me, and I am with her."

Jo saw her face soften, the color of her eyes grow darker by a shade. She blushed and was beautiful. He had seen the blush of embarrassment before, but never the blush of love, and he wished it were for himself.

"Now you tell your side of the story," Clement said to her, as if he were about to pull out a shorthand notebook and jot it all down.

"It's quite true," she said.

"But of course, Clem, she will get more and more famous and grow away from me. When she's riding in her carriage and pair, and I am holding out my little tin cup in the gutter, she will halt her coachman and ask him to give me a silver sixpence."

"You idiot," she said. "Anyway, I'm not famous now."

"No," said Clement, "and you're a wise girl to see it. But people know about you. Think how nice that is!"

She said she didn't enjoy that part of it, people knowing. "I

18

shall never grow away from you," she added to Kit, as if she had taken him seriously.

Jo felt an outsider on more counts than one. He was not aware of being physically attracted by her, yet he would have liked her to love him. The sun was sinking now and the bowlers had departed. The trill of the fountain was magical, and so was the springing up of fairy-lamps in the branches of the trees.

"All these 'nevers,'" said Clement. "Never is a bloody long time." He would not turn to see what Georgina was doing, but the whole poise of his body indicated that he was aware of her at his back. His ears seemed to flatten like the ears of a horse when it listens and is afraid.

"She won't sleep with me, you know," Kit said tenderly, his arm stealing round Alison's neck, "because she is very pure. You would never think it from her book."

"Shut up," she said, "that's private."

Clement grinned at her. "You must take an 'ahem, ahem' for granted before hearing me further. Do I understand that yours was a work of the imagination?"

"Aren't I supposed to have any imagination? It's getting cold out here. I want to go inside."

"We'll all go in," Kit cried, "and then we'll all go out again. We'll go to the Fitzroy. Clement is rich, and will take us in a taxi."

"No. You know I don't like it." Alison was sharp.

She wanted to be alone with him. Ill-fitted for the company into which he, and her small success, had led her, she felt driven.

"Oh yes, tonight you'll like it. And Jo will be at your right hand. He will keep off all the horrible people you hate."

Georgina called, across the gathering dark, "Clem! Come here," and he went to her.

"I love her very, very much," Kit said seriously to Jo, "and she loves me. She believes in me. We are enormously happy. Stay and keep her company, I need the Gents."

"Are you very cold?" Jo asked her, when they were alone.

She relaxed. "A bit. Not much. But it's getting dark. I'm still feeling bad about Georgia."

"Georgina."

"Georgina. I rather like her. Jo"—she spoke his name easily

19

—"does Kit drink too much, or is there a bit of pretending about it?"

"A bit of pretending." He saw that she was shrewd. "But not all."

"The trouble is, he can't, really: and I can. I'm afraid that sounds an unwomanly admission. Can't we do something about him?"

Jo replied that he wouldn't try, if he were she. Kit didn't like interference, even for his own good; in fact, he would hate it more if it were for his good.

"He's very young. Over a year younger than I am."

"Which makes you Grandma."

"So you can make jokes!" She smiled widely.

"I suppose so," he said, after some hesitation, "of a sort. I don't think that was a very good one."

It was too dark now to see faces clearly. Georgina and Clement were going back to the bar. On their way they paused and kissed, glued together like the bodies of flies on a window-pane. Kit came out, doing up his trouser-buttons.

"Come on, now, or we'll never stick Clem for that taxi."

Clement, in fact, paid for two taxis, since Georgina insisted that her other friends should join them. They were now a party of nine in all. As the night went on, Alison seemed to grow more restless than she had been in the garden. They had not been long in the Fitzroy, Georgina's friends still unintroduced, when Kit found a host of acquaintances of his and Jo's, so he wandered from group to group, hailed and treated, his splendid voice upraised. Clement and his wife began to quarrel again. Jo did not make the rounds with Kit, as he would normally have done, but stayed beside Alison who, though several people greeted her with open awe, or with awe disguised as indifference, would not move from her chair. Helpless, beautiful in disappointment, she seemed to take comfort from him.

It was only ten minutes before closing time that Georgina left her friends and came to sit with them. Her eyes appraised Alison, not coldly.

She said, "Why don't you strike out and make the splash they all expect? This sort of thing may not come to you more than once."

"I can't."

20

"Why not? Why the decorum? Why the pearls? You ought to look like a writer."

"Why should I look like one, when I am one?"

"Relax," said Georgina, "relax," and she was not being unkind.

Jo felt himself forgotten. Something had sprung up between the women, sympathetic, arcane. This had nothing to do with him. Nevertheless, he listened.

"Do you really want to know why? These people"—Alison made a circular movement with her left hand—"they make me feel inferior."

"For Christ's sake, why should they? You've done something. Don't you realize that at least three-quarters of this lot never will? They only talk. It's *better* to talk about the books you're writing than to write them. Talked about, they sound like genius, but when you see them—ah, my little one, then comes the let-down."

Alison said, stubbornly, that they all seemed cleverer than she was. Anyway, she felt that they were.

"If you believe that, you'll believe anything. But if you really want Kit, who will outclass you one of these days, you'll do things as he likes them."

"I'll do them as I like!"

"Then God help you," Georgina said dramatically—she was not sober, which was why she had had a sudden upsurge of affection for Alison—"because Kit never will. Take a tip from one who knows."

"Was Kit ever—?" This came from a lapse of control.

"One of my boy-friends? No, Lioness, he wasn't. 'Out of the cradle, endlessly rocking'—I don't snatch them."

She got up and returned to Clement. Then the bar was cleared, and they found themselves on the streets, lights going out all around them.

Kit took Alison home, promising to appear at Clement's flat later. Jo, Georgina, and the anonymous persons, who had now added two more to their number, did go there. The married couple left them in possession of a good deal of gin, and went to bed. The others, after expressing some derision at the comparative sumptuousness in which Clement lived, took full advantage of it. Jo found himself sleeping with a German refugee girl who, when he awoke from a short and efficacious nap, frowningly pinned up her golden plaits before the glass and told him of horrors. Kit did not reappear.

Jo walked home, a long walk by starlight, reaching his house at a little after five-thirty. He was skilled enough to awaken nobody.

Chapter Four

THE DIVISIONAL LABOUR PARTY, WHICH EXISTED IN A TORY STRONG-
hold, had acquired new premises, the ground floor and basement
of a derelict shop. Jo, in borrowed overalls, was giving the walls a
coat of hysterical yellow paint. Sybil Rainey was scrubbing the
floors. She was a sour, handsome woman in early middle age, the
rebellious daughter of an Irish landowner. She did not care to talk
much. Downstairs, other members were whitewashing brickwork
and repairing broken floorboards.

"It will look all right when we've got some posters up," Joe
said.

"It had better," said Sybil.

The Spanish Civil War had strengthened the local party in
numbers, though the newcomers most concerned with it were
nearly all semi-intellectuals of the middle class. The trade-union
members were much more concerned with home affairs; this had
already begun to make a breach in the ranks, though all were preparing enthusiastically for the next public demonstration.

It was August, five o'clock on a stuffy Saturday afternoon. Jo, as he worked, found his thoughts swinging between politics and personal guilt. It was true that he was becoming increasingly involved politically: but also true that he might well be trying to write again, instead of painting walls. He was still getting nothing but rejection slips, was only too well aware that his work was influenced by Kit's, and would have given a great deal to free himself of it and find his own style.

Kit's novel was finished and had been accepted by a publisher. Only last week had he allowed Jo to see it, though, and this was hurtful; everyone else in London seemed to have done so. Jo was by no means sure what to make of it. It did, indeed, have a steatopygous heroine, though her build was not, as Clement had suggested, the central theme. She was a girl of immense sexual drive who had a death-wish: she was half-woman, half-myth, and the world in which she moved was half-real, half-mythical. The style was dense, over-laden with startling imagery, and by no means easy to read: yet there was the promise of power behind the novel as a whole and the sense of a rare literary personality, a personality not yet fully crystallized.

Kit and Alison seemed happy, and talked of marrying. She was a patient young woman, apparently used to being let down when he broke engagements with her. On these occasions, Jo had often filled in; and he and Alison had talked earnestly together, mostly about Kit. The immediate stir created by her own book had subsided, and she was worrying about what she could find to write about next. Unlike Kit, she was generous about the stories Jo showed to her, though perceptively critical. She had the trick of loading her entire attention upon one thing at a time. Always reluctant to go on "wild" expeditions to the intellectual pubs, she had become more so: to an extent, her own position as a cynosure of attention had made such expeditions tolerable. Now, though Kit had published nothing but that single story, he was becoming more of a cynosure than she. He loved to talk of work in progress, which she did not, and he did it so well that he created an atmosphere of excited anticipation wherever he went. Slowly, he was acquiring a kind of nimbus, one which Alison perceived clearly enough, but was not dazzled by. Her concern was solely for him as a man: Jo was afraid it might become too overtly motherly a concern to do her any good in Kit's eyes.

24

Up from the basement came Bobby Price, spattered with whitewash.

"Well, Jo *bach*, I'm through for the day and the sun's over the yardarm. What about it? What about it, Syb?"

Sybil replied that she wasn't through for the day, and wouldn't be for a couple of hours to come. She had found in her own house a roll of forgotten linoleum and proposed to lay it.

Just as Kit was becoming a star of bohemian London, so Bobby was already a star in more specialized circles. The son of a Welsh miner, he had written two proletarian novels, both worked over—to an extent he sedulously concealed from all but Jo—by his publishers. He was a near-Communist, and the trade-union faction thoroughly distrusted him. He was a sharp-eyed man of twenty-five, who would have been good-looking if his nose were not slightly askew, giving a warning quality to the whole face. In personal relations, he could never quite be trusted: in political ones, his integrity was absolute, at least in his own terms, and they were not the terms many people liked.

"I can't," Jo said, "I promised I'd be back early."

"Your way's mine. I'll walk along with you."

Recumbent lovers strewed the fields, the bolder ones couched between the little hills under the may-trees. An irritable girl was trying to restrain her dog from sniffing at them. The grass was powdered with the dust of August and the leaves were dry. Flies murmured around a mephitic hollow in the scrub which had been used as a public lavatory.

"We've got to get rid of Hatton," said Bobby, "somehow."

Hatton was the chairman of the party branch, and was suspected by sophisticated newcomers of Trotskyism.

"Yes, but how?"

"The A.G.M.'s not so far off. We've got to strengthen our forces. Pack the meeting, if we have to."

Jo was worried. Bobby, seeing this, laughed at him. "The end justifies the means. What happens to the world in general is more important than a wound to the pride of Mister Hatton. If we don't watch out, we are going to be at war in five years."

"I don't see how getting rid of him's going to stop that."

This was still a time when such words could be spoken airily, at least by people like Jo. War was in their minds: but not yet *their* war, nothing that immediately threatened them. Things would be all right if Franco lost his war: and, anyway, there were pacts existing or to be made, protective as an infinity of minefields.

"It's a drop in the ocean, but the ocean's made of drops. I'll be in touch with you."

"Are you writing?" Jo asked him, to change the subject.

"Trying, I'm trying. I want to write a novel about the unemployed. This blackening world," Bobby added softly. He began to croon a song Jo did not know, and was at once attracted by:

> "Whirlwinds of danger are raging around us,
> O'erwhelming forces of darkness prevail.
> Lo, in the fight, see advancing before us
> Red flag of liberty, that yet shall prevail."

It was a strong tune, in a minor key, a marching song, and implacable:

> "Then onward, ye workers, freedom awaits you
> For all the world on the land and the sea:
> On with the fight in the cause of humanity,
> Forward, united, and the world shall be free."

"What's that?"

"It's going to be a great demo piece. Only there will be a row about 'united,' because that implies the idea of a United Front, and it makes Hatton and the T.U. contingent go green."

They had come to Jo's door. They lingered for a few minutes outside the gate, outside the ragged privets, grey from the dust of the road.

"I'm going to the Soviet Union," Bobby said. "I've been invited."

Jo exclaimed.

"They read my books there, *bach.*"

"When do you go?"

"End of next month. You know Kit Mallings, don't you? I'd like to meet him."

"To Russia! You lucky bastard!"

"Can you get me and Mallings together?"

"Why?"

"That new story of his." He mentioned a Communist literary paper, new, with a minute circulation. "It's interesting."

26

Jo, who had not been told of the story, felt the worm of jealousy moving inside him. It seemed to him suddenly that he was being used, though for what purpose he did not know. Used by Kit. His emotions, for a fleeting second, were those of a lover from whom secrets that are common knowledge to everyone else are being deliberately withheld.

"I can fix it," he said, "if you come to Chelsea one night."

"Any old night. You name it." Bobby waved and went away, with his usual cocky strut.

As he let himself into the house, Jo pondered on a mystery. What on earth might Kit have written that could conceivably interest Bobby, and be printed in such a magazine? Surely not about fat girls, worms, graves and epitaphs. His resentment grew.

He found Mildred ready to go out, face powdered and lipsticked, hair tightly waved. She looked elated and he thought she was, luckily for herself, an incurable optimist. Nothing would ever make her pretty. What sort of image did she see in the glass? He was fond of her and could not abandon the hope that one of these days some man not interested in prettiness would desire her. Yet with the hope, some fear was mingled. Suppose that, by an outside chance, she did get married? It would be the end of such hopes for himself, because the shadowy figure of his ideal, who as yet had no face at all, would not want to live under his mother's roof.

He cried, "The relief has arrived!" and struck an attitude.

"I wondered when it was going to. Even *if* it was."

"Have I ever let you down?"

"Not that I know of. But my gallivantings are so few that I fear for them."

He asked after their mother.

"There's a steak and kidney pie in the oven, and baked potatoes. You don't have to wash up."

He knew he would do so. What could an evening out be to her if she had to return to dirty dishes? He smacked her bottom lightly.

"There are worse men in the world than you," she said. "I'm going out with a worse, in fact."

"Same one?"

"The same. Do you suppose my choice is wide and various?" She paraded up and down, surveying imaginary ranks of suitors. "To whom shall I toss my 'broidered sleeve? Not that one. Cross-eyed. No, and not you: your breath smells. Not you, either: too poor." Her plump body assumed a military strut. She could be quite funny, could Mildred.

"You get out," said Jo, "while the going's good."

Already a voice was calling—"Millie!"

He found his mother brooding over a photograph album, the contents of which he had been shown many times before, and would be shown as often again. Mildred had laid the table in the living-room: the dining-room was used only for visitors. Bessie Upjohn seemed to ruminate those old snapshots, rapidly becoming saffron-colored with time, like a cow in a lush pasturage. She looked entirely happy: a state which, Jo believed, came to her—if fleetingly—more frequently than it came to himself.

"Look, that was me the very day I became engaged to your father. Not a bad-looking girl, eh?"

Obediently, he looked over her shoulder. Her flesh had a curious smell, something between hay and honey.

"What neither you nor Millie will ever understand," she said, "is that I feel the same *now*. Inside me, there's a young girl. It's awful, isn't it?"

Touched to pity, he said that he understood.

"I feel my life stopped when I was about twenty-five. Since then, my body grows old, but my mind doesn't age. I wish you two would try to imagine that."

Jo slammed down the pie, the potatoes, the plates. His pity was dispersing. "Come on," he said, and helped her to the table.

"A boring old woman, yes. But what I say to you is true."

Yes, it was boring: and yes, it was true. It would be true of himself if he reached old age. The clock was stopping for him also. Twenty-six, nearly, and he would never feel so different from that. "Don't be silly, you're not even sixty yet."

They ate, and Jo washed up.

It was a quarter past eight when the telephone rang. Kit spoke to him, sounding defiant and excitable. "Bet you won't guess where I am! I've taken Alison to see *your* pub. Come along and join us."

Jo said he couldn't, it was impossible for him to leave his mother alone.

"Well, we'll come and call on you."

28

"We've nothing to drink in the house."

"Alison and I will come loaded with bottles. Will your Ma object?"

"No," Jo said, though he could not be too sure.

She did not. The idea of a party cheered her, and she kept Jo busy running to fetch glasses, to bring her new shoes and the pink cardigan, to put out cake and biscuits, to plump up the cushions, to straighten a couple of pictures on the wall, even to bring out and put on the mantelpiece a bronze Siva which was usually kept, in reverential wrappings, at the bottom of her wardrobe. She was nervous at the thought of meeting Alison, of whom she had heard much—"I hope she won't think I'm silly."

"She won't," Jo said, "she's a humble sort of girl. Too much so for her own good."

They came within half an hour, laden with quarts of ale, which they dumped with relief in the hall. Jo wished they had not brought so much: this looked like preparation for an orgy, and he was quite certain what his mother's reaction would be to anything like that. "Look here," he muttered to Kit, "don't bring in more than two for the time being."

Alison was wearing a dress of blue cotton, and to his eyes looked beautiful and not quite happy. Kit, dressed glaringly, was in high spirits.

"Mrs. Upjohn, let me give you a kiss! This is my girl."

"I'm sure," Bessie said stiltedly, "that I'm very honored to have you here, Miss Petrie. I've begun to read your book"—this was untrue—"but my eyes are so bad these days that I have to go like a snail. Make yourself comfortable—no, try the big chair."

Alison murmured something courteous.

"Now, Jo, do the honors!"

"That's my job," said Kit, "he can't even get the top off a bottle without Vesuvius erupting."

"Jo, give your friends some cake."

"I'm awfully sorry," said Kit, "but I can't manage cake with beer."

"I would love some," Alison said, with polite enthusiasm.

"Mrs. Upjohn," said Kit, "you'll join us, won't you?"

She hesitated. "It's a long time since I've tasted beer. Perhaps a thimbleful, just to keep you all company." His mother's emphatically inclusive "all" irritated Jo. It was a reflection of her thoughts about her own inner youth and it made her seem rather absurd. She should wish to be an outsider, he felt, realize that was the position she could hold with dignity. He did not wish Kit and Alison to smile at her in secret.

Kit drank off his own beer without seeming to swallow; poured himself another and sank down on the hearthrug at Alison's feet, with the air of one who means to make a night of it.

"Now, what about *your* book?" Bessie cried jovially, not having observed these ominous signs.

"Ah, that's where this girl's nose is going to be out of joint. Mine comes out in March next year. You'll be nothing then, me proud beauty."

Alison laughed, but did not speak immediately. Jo saw her push the cake away behind a framed photograph of Mildred as Captain of the School.

Her reply was delayed. "I never said I was anything."

Jo asked him what on earth he had been writing for the left-wing magazine. Oh, Kit explained, that was an experiment. He had wanted to do something in a style quite unlike his own, sharp and unadorned. It had been nothing more than a sketch of boozers in a pub in the stockbroker belt—the local tart, the local Fascist, local drunk, and so forth. No moral to any of it, though the magazine had found one. "Horrors of the bourgeoisie."

"Bobby Price wants to meet you."

"Why? His stuff's terrible. But I don't mind, if he sees any point in it. I'll be at The Bells on Tuesday. Tell him to drop along." Kit turned to Bessie. "I don't think I said anything that other night when you mentioned Coventry Patmore. Jo says I didn't. But I just didn't catch the name. Listen: I shall recite to you."

In his organ voice he recited "The Toys." He did it beautifully: Bessie went softly into tears. But it seemed to Jo that there had been an underlying irony about the whole performance, just the faintest overstressing where no stressing was necessary. He felt a touch of anger—not precisely for his mother's sake, even though he felt she had been the subject of condescension: Kit had given her a whale of a time. He looked at Alison, who was drinking with

30

a kind of unnatural, almost masculine abandon, looking at the wall beyond Kit's head. This anger, was it even fair? Kit really loved to give pleasure and knew how to do it. He had spent hours patiently reading to a girl of their acquaintance, recovering in Moorfields from an eye operation. She had liked romantic novels about doctors and nurses. And she had meant nothing to him at all.

"Thank you," Bessie said, "thank you. That was lovely. Wasn't it lovely, Miss Petrie?"

"It isn't," said Alison, in a tight voice, "my kind of poetry. But Kit can make anything an experience."

"Hah!" Kit cried, "it's coming out."

"What is?" Jo was bewildered.

"The cat from the bag. She's taking it out of me. We were fighting, in your pub—weren't we, darling? That's why we decided to ask you over, so that you could help keep the peace." He took Alison's hand and kissed the palm of it. She drew it away. "No, no, no, darling, you mustn't rebuff me. I'm sorry, I'm at your feet."

Bessie looked at all this as if she were witnessing some recondite play.

"Look, I'm actually kissing your feet!" Kit did so.

"Don't be a fool," Alison whispered, "get up, get up. Don't do it. Please, Mrs. Upjohn, pay no attention to him. He's only clowning. Kit, you are embarrassing me."

"I mean to be. I intend to embarrass you. It's your punishment." He refilled Jo's glass and his own.

Alison got up. "I'm going."

"No, no, no, the night's young. You don't mind us, do you, Mrs. Upjohn? Please say you don't."

She was nonplussed, and now, uneasy. "You young people. . . ."

Kit swivelled round so that he was sitting confidentially by her knees. He smiled up at her. "You see, this girl of mine is so conceited. She pretends not to be, but she is. She was huffy with me because I was telling her that her little day was done, and my great sun was going to rise like a gas-filled balloon, higher and higher—"

"In which case," Bessie said, with one of her tart upsurges, "we should all lose sight of you again pretty quickly and that would be the end of you!"

Kit burst into a roar of laughter. She was marvellous, he had always suspected it, she was quite marvellous. "Jo, go and bring in those other quarts, there's a good chap."

Jo looked at Alison, who had sat down again, but whose eyes were magnified by tears only with difficulty held back. His mother looked at the girl; then, lingeringly, at himself. He felt as though she had touched him on bare flesh.

He said, "No. Mother's tired."

Kit wheedled. "You're not tired, say you're not. Let us stay for a little while longer. It's so nice and comfortable here. Please." Before she could reply, he jumped up, darted out of the room and returned with another bottle. "Isn't this fun, really? You must have had fun like this, once upon a time. Fights with your sweethearts . . . didn't you? And you're still young, and it's so hard for you to be tied here as you are."

"I know we never drank like that in my day," Bessie said, struggling now to sustain a degree of severity and failing to succeed.

"One more only, really and truly, only one! You, too. Be daring, now!"

She accepted a very small drink, as if this were daring indeed. Then she began to talk to Alison, more easily than she did to most people, and the girl gratefully responded. Where did Alison live? With another girl in a flat? But did her parents like her doing that?

"They live in the country," Alison said, "in Wiltshire. I have to be near the center of things."

"They live in the country," said Kit, "in a damned big house, all white rugs and servants who shimmer, and I can never get across the hall without feeling someone's set up invisible trip wires."

Jo knew, by the tone of his voice, that it was recent news to him, and that he could only have been let into this part of Alison's life less than a week ago. If it had been before, Kit could not have kept it back.

"Oh rot, what rot! There's only a man and wife, and Daddy's too busy with the farm even to notice you, and Mummy's too vague."

"And she left it all, so she did," Kit said dreamily, "to be *independent,* and work in an office, and become a great writer. But she's always got somewhere to go home to, though she's concealed it for ages and ages because it looks bad. She's lovely rich Alison, and I love her very much, even though she's not believing me at this moment."

"Well," said Bessie, "I'm old-fashioned and I may be dense, but it doesn't seem to me that you're being very kind to her tonight."

He changed his mood utterly. "I'm not being unkind, I swear it. I'm only teasing her. She knows that. Now I'll stop, and sit nicely on a chair, and Alison will forgive me and it will all be fun." He rose and kissed the girl very gently on her forehead and her lips. Then, as he had promised, he did sit nicely on a chair.

Alison looked at him. Her lips trembled. She smiled with absolute love.

Kit began to talk about Jo, of how much he admired him. "He's the best-read man I've ever met." Both young men were voracious readers but Jo genuinely the more so. "It's an awful pity he couldn't have gone to a university."

"There was no money for that," Bessie said briskly. "I suppose there wasn't for you, either."

"No. But it wouldn't have done so much good to me. Jo would have made a wonderful teacher."

"He's not doing so badly as he is. He's got excellent prospects."

"I think," Jo put in, "that you two had better stop talking about me as if I wasn't there. I am here. Please notice, Alison, that I am here."

"Ah, but *I* wasn't talking about you. Because I knew quite well that you were."

It was at this moment that Jo, for no reason he could clearly describe to himself, was taken by the terror he had, without realizing it, been dreading for so long. *He must not fall in love with Alison.* There could be no happiness in it, only misery of a dreadful and aching sort. He made a violent effort to shut the thought right out of his mind, an effort so violent, in fact, that it must have changed his expression, for Alison said quickly—"What is it? Are you all right?"

They were staring at him.

"Yes. Why not? Of course I'm all right."

"Drinking," said Bessie, "you know it's bad for you. And

now, good people, I'm going to my bed. If you take my advice, you won't be long out of yours."

As Jo helped her away, they thanked her for the evening. She said, rather muzzily, "Come ye again," as if her mind were elsewhere.

"Let us finish the night," said Kit. "There's still more in the hall."

Alison said, "No. I've got to be going."

"I think you'd both better," said Jo, "though I hate to seem inhospitable. But in about ten minutes Millie will be back, and she'll open all the windows and flap the curtains about, and empty the ash-trays, and make general hay of the party atmosphere. She won't mean it in any censorious spirit, but she won't be able to stop herself."

It soothed him a little to feel, even for so brief a moment, in command of the situation and able to enforce his wishes. Kit, when he came to the house, seemed to take possession of it; Jo was going to see to it that he didn't come often.

They left cheerfully enough, making him a present of the two remaining quarts of beer. As they went off down the road, he heard them laughing, the intimate laughter of passion, and of relief after tension. They would marry soon, they would be happy.

Jo went back to the living-room and aired it thoroughly, as Mildred would have done. He had only just finished when she came in.

Chapter Five

IT WAS A SUNDAY DEMONSTRATION, WITH A MARCH FROM THE Albert Memorial to Trafalgar Square. It was September, and windy. Jo was proud to have routed all his friends out: Kit, Alison, Clement and Georgina were with the Left Book Club contingent, and the two women, at least, were stimulated by it all. Spain had captured the young imagination strongly: the beautiful Spanish flags, gold, red and purple, whacked against their poles and billowed out upon the grey skies. It was a satisfactory turnout, rigorously herded by the mounted police, who could always be infuriated by steady chanting of "The Policeman's Holiday." There were some jeers from black-shirted Fascists on the pavements: but on the whole the watching crowds seemed sympathetic.

Jo himself was not in too happy a position, since he was at one end of a banner carried, at the other end, by the chairman of the local party, Hatton; because Jo was tall and Hatton short, the banner persistently slumped at an angle of forty-five degrees. Hatton had red hair and a prognathous chin. He and Jo disliked each other.

The singing was strong, if various: the Left Book Club group

35

were rendering "Riego's Hymn," the Communists "The International," Jo's party "Whirlwinds of Danger," which was being led by Bobby Price. There were occasional chantings of "Red Front! Red Front!"

"There's going to be no front with those Communist bastards so far as I'm concerned," said Hatton, who was quarrelsome by nature.

"Whirlwinds of Danger" presented its usual difficulties.

"Forward *united* and the world shall be free—" sang the intellectuals.

"Forward, *ye workers*—" sang Hatton and the Trade Unionists, all, with the exception of the electricians and the miners, determined to have no truck with the extreme Left Wing element. Jo, whose singing voice was not strong, lost to Hatton in the struggle: but Kit's voice rose, rich as Chaliapin's, from the group immediately behind.

The square was already filling up, and the pigeons were wheeling in panic, their lime dropping like snow. Spectators packed the terraces of the National Gallery. On the plinths, speakers had set up their megaphones. Jo and Hatton, with mutual relief, stacked their banners against a wall, and parted.

"Good demo," said Kit, "most excellent. What a good boy am I!"

"Look," Alison said, "this is serious. Do you realize how serious it is?"

He hesitated. "Yes. Of course."

"You're all going to be sorry if you don't realize it," said Georgina, drawling. "For my part, I'm half-elated, half-sick."

"The only time she's been really moved by anything but herself," Clement said. "It makes a wonderful change."

"You! You're simply out for the day. That's all it means to you."

"I don't wear my heart on my sleeve."

"You would if you had one at all, just to show it existed."

Harry Pollitt was speaking: more, he was reciting:

> "And trample on their palaces
> Until they break like glass!"

A lawyer followed, a long-jawed, austere, respectable figure; and then a woman with hair almost scarlet. Someone heckled, and the police took names.

36

It all had a partyfied air, the air of that "day out" with which Georgina had charged her husband: yet to most of them it was deadly serious. People of all ages, though the majority were young, were stricken by a generous rage that they could not, and did not wish to, control: they were also beginning to feel the first personal touch of fear. The world was darkening, and they knew it.

"Is it going to end in a rumpus?" Kit inquired, looking hopeful.

"Probably," said Jo, "if we don't let them divert the march back, which they'll try to do."

Bobby Price came between them. "Listen, comrades, a tip in due season. If the Cossacks are trying to stampede you, get behind the tail of a police horse. It may fart a bit, but it's safe, because the horse behind won't charge the one in front of it. *I* know."

"Thanks for those kind words, Bobby," said Kit. They had struck up some sort of a friendship, without any depth to it. "But I shall beat it for the tube station if trouble does break out. I am small, I am a coward. And I should be afraid that my bloody protective horse might take a backward kick." He added to Jo, "Let's get out of here as soon as possible. I've got a piece of news for you."

There was, however, little trouble that day: the rage, the fear, had not yet begun to reach a climax; a climax that was to be reached when altruism, comradeship for strangers, had given way to fear for the menaced flesh.

Hatton and Bobby carried the banner home: Jo went off with Kit and Alison to a teashop. Clement and Georgina had left some time before, because they were going to a party in Highgate and it took an hour to get there.

The wind had dropped and the rain had come, streaming down the window-panes. Along Whitehall, down Villiers Street, along the Strand, the crowds were dispersing. Here and there flags bobbed like yacht-sails on a grey, heaving sea.

"Well," said Kit, "I am leaving home and Georgie is leaving Clement. Today you witnessed their Last Ride together. How's that for a start?"

Tired of Putney, bored by his parents, he had gone in with Clement and some young poet whom, he said, Jo didn't know, to take two rooms in Chelsea. Two rooms, with covered bath in the kitchen, which would make a nice table, at the corner of Tedworth Square, thirty shillings a week. "It'll be a comedown for Clem, but he doesn't mind. He's going to pay a quid, and Phil and I will share the other ten bob between us. Room for you, Jo, if you like to come."

"You know I can't."

"It will be the *vie de bohème,* for which, in my naïve manner, I have longed. Allie here is going to find us lots of lovely furniture, and curtains and dusters, and pots and pans."

Jo had never heard him abbreviate Alison's name like this. He glanced at her sharply: she was silent and expressionless. He knew why, and knew what all this meant to her. There would be no immediate marriage. By this maneuver she had been pushed out—for the time being, at least.

"Allie's going to be our muse," Kit said enthusiastically, slopping the tan-colored tea into his saucer, "our presiding goddess. Won't it be wonderful?"

"It should be fun," she said.

Jo's heart hardened against his friend, though he knew that whatever happened he would not always feel like this. He was frightened of loving Alison: he knew he loved Kit.

"Fun for you?"

"Oh yes, fun for me. Though I shan't be able to supply them with Bayeux tapestries and Georgian silver. Mummy would be sure to miss them." She spoke lightly.

"You see," said Kit, his eyes innocent, "this is necessarily pro tem. Alison and I can't marry till I'm a bit firmer on my own feet, and I won't live on hers."

"Heroic," she said, and still she smiled.

"I'll have to give up my clerking, anyway. I get quite a bit of reviewing here and there, and when the book comes out—"

"Listen," she said, "if you sell a thousand copies, you'll have had a great success. This sort of thing I do know about. You're not going to be a great best-seller, you know."

He said, still looking amiable, "I hate you for saying that."

"Why should you? You must have some idea of what all this is going to cost. Food, light, heating—"

"Allie," said Kit, "has a soul devoid of romance. It's odd when you come to think of it, because her work reeks with it. Come, come, don't look so cross. I'll get myself established, and you can play Egeria, and about this time next year we'll trot off to

38

the register office like two dear little brown mice and live happily ever after. Well, I've got to go." He mentioned an appointment with a writer of startling eminence.

"Then for God's sake wash yourself first," said Alison, "you've got a tide-mark."

He kissed her lavishly, drawing public attention upon them both, and went away.

"So you see," she said.

"It may not be as bad as you think."

In the coarse light that changed the tones of her hair and flesh, she looked more vulnerable than Jo had ever imagined she could. Her tea, untasted, was forming a papery skin. "It will be all right next year. Who is this poet?"

"Philip Christie. I loathe the sight of him. He sneers at me."

Jo, too, instantly loathed him, even without the sight. He said, "If I told you I loved you very much, it would be the wrong time."

"Even if it were true, which it isn't, it would be the wrong time. Don't dare to pity me!"

They were silent for a few moments. Jo said, "It was a silly thing to say. Anyhow, you know Kit. He gets wild ideas, he has to act on them. Then they all fall to dust, as everything does for him, except his writing. And you."

"Except his writing. Just that."

"No. And you."

"If I had the guts, I'd leave him now. God damn him, does he seriously think I'm going to set up as some fake muse, or Cub Mistress—which is what he wants?" Her eyes were blazing, the red vein very apparent. "If only I could have the guts! If only I could!"

Jo, her very anger and grief restoring his own control, counselled patience. He had never seen Kit show the smallest interest in any other woman. She had only to play, for a very short while, whatever role he chose to cast her in.

"Why should I? Do you think I *haven't* done that? Do you think I haven't put up with his envy, his running me down, till I could murder him? But up to now it's been worth-while, because I, because I—"

"It's still worth-while."

"You've seen it, haven't you, what he's tried to make of me?

He's invented some stuffy image of me and he's forced me into it."

"Things haven't been easy for him, and you've helped him a lot. He's very ambitious."

"You've seen it all."

"Yes," said Jo, "but I always thought it was a kind of game you both liked playing."

"That's what I meant him to think. Now—"

Again he counselled patience.

She said, piteously, "You know him as I don't. Oh, he's loved me, but he's never really let me come near him. Do you believe, honestly, *you,* that it may come right for us?"

"I'm sure it will."

Her violence passed. She looked steadily into his eyes. "I'll try. Now let's leave this awful place."

"It's pouring cats and dogs outside."

Nevertheless, she insisted that they should leave. They walked aimlessly in the drenching rain. Her hair hung in rats' tails, and she did not care. "You can come to my place," she said, "it's actually not a stone's throw from here, in Charing Cross Road. And Edna will be out, she always is, at weekends."

She lived several floors up, above the offices of a lawyer and a theatrical agent, in three well-furnished rooms. To Jo it seemed very smart, in a way that would have made his mother and Mildred wonder how anyone could live in a place so bare: for nothing was at all elaborate. White walls, dark carpets, one or two pictures, several small lamps, all with different-colored parchment shades. It was not at all the usual flat shared by business girls, yet it was not a rich girl's flat either. If he had known nothing about Alison's background it would have puzzled him, and told him little.

"Your friend must be in luck," he said, as she switched on the fire and brought out a bottle of whiskey, "coming in for all this. Have you known her long?"

"No, I just advertised for her, and the luck was mine. She's a fully fledged secretary, much grander than I am."

Jo asked jealously if Kit came there often. Yes, she said, quite often.

"If you got married, wouldn't this be a good place for you both?"

"If I turned Edna out? You'd think so." Her voice was hard.

40

"But he'd hate it here. He likes squalor. This sort of thing would let him down in the eyes of his friends."

Despite himself, he had glanced past her into the bedroom.

"No," she said, "it's true that we don't. I won't. If we're going to get married, it would spoil things. Also, if I did, I don't think he'd marry me at all. And I want that. I'd be good for him."

He found himself thinking that here she was wrong, and had, all along, been wrong: she would be very bad for Kit indeed, in a way she already partially understood but would never admit to herself.

"Also," she said, and her face softened into amusement, "that is all right for the kind of girls he meets most of the time, but it . . . . None of my friends, the ones I grew up with, do, you know. 'Keep yourself for your husband,' my mother says. She's said it so often that I can't help it becoming an article of faith with me. I don't know whether it's virtue on my part or a sense of my commercial value, where Kit's in question."

"Don't," Jo said.

"Do you think, if I'd let him sleep with me, I'd have held him even so long as this?" She sipped thoughtfully at the whiskey.

"Isn't the trouble because you don't?" He had nerved himself to say this.

Alison said sternly, "I don't believe that's the trouble at all. First he was proud of me because I had some success, but that he couldn't really bear. Now I'm out of things again—anyhow, for the time being—he's suddenly ashamed of me because I'm not in them. We can't"—she paused—"we can't quite get in phase."

"You're not giving him much of a character."

"No, no, no, there's sweetness in him. He's generous, he loves like a child; he's sorry for people who are weak. But not for people who are strong."

"And you are strong?"

"My tragedy."

She leaned against him, and put her head on his shoulder. Her eyes closed, and tears ran under the lashes. Holding her in his arms, his heart thundering, he kissed the salt of her cheeks. He was terribly excited, and afraid of himself, so he spoke words of comfort, of reassurance, all of them about Kit. She seemed content not to move. He tried to hold time back, not to think beyond the immediate moment: that was the way to make an hour last for a year.

But he knew he must soon draw away from her or she would know what was happening to him; and when it happened, he was both relieved and ashamed. He put her from him, now, closed her hand around the glass. He felt exhausted and very cold.

"You'll see," he heard himself saying in a strange, avuncular voice, "everything will work out as you want it to." Rising abruptly, he went to the window, where he stared down at the head-lamps rushing through the pouring rain, each with an iris around it. The noise of the traffic seemed very loud.

"Thank you, Jo," she said. "I'm sorry I made an ass of myself like that. You've been very kind."

"You meant nothing by it, I know."

"Just that I trust you."

Suddenly he was furious. How dared she trust him? Couldn't she see that her trust humiliated him? He managed to answer equably, "Good. You can, you know."

"Come, finish your drink. Sit down beside me."

Bloody fool of a girl! Hadn't she the slightest idea that he was frightened of what she would see? He felt the heat, the dampness, in his clothes.

"I've got to go now."

"Don't. I'll make us some eggs or something."

He couldn't stay, he said, Mildred was waiting to go out. He had to be back. Keeping as far beyond the lamps as he could, he edged towards the door.

"I didn't mean to upset you," she said. "Tell me I didn't, or anyway, not much."

"No, of course you didn't. Cheer up. I'll see you next Thursday, with Kit."

He was out of the flat so quickly that he scarcely heard her astonished good-bye. He thought she was the most innocent girl he had ever met in his life, and told himself that he did not, could not, love her. He was sorry for her, but perhaps sorrier for Kit. Poor old Kit! He hated to give pain, but he would have to give it. Quickly, Jo hoped.

As he went into the tube station, the fears, the shames of the past hour forsook him, and only the marvels of it remained. He sat half-dazed in the hideous light, unaware of anything but the motion of the train, and of the image of her beautiful stern face, the face he had kissed and tasted.

42

Chapter Six

FOR SOME TIME AFTER THAT, THINGS SEEMED TO GO NORMALLY FOR all of them. Alison and Kit were at ease with each other, and he and Jo, on the nights she was not with them, went on their rounds of the pubs, being as orgiastic as their incomes would allow them to be. One night Kit broke two front teeth by attempting to slide down the bannisters face first, when in no condition to attempt the feat. The lease of the rooms in Tedworth Gardens was signed, and Jo had met the poet, a little, manic-spirited man of twenty-four. He did not like him.

At the beginning of November the move took place, Alison, as she had promised, providing the essentials. "The van's gone there today," she told Jo, over his office telephone, "three divans, not in mint condition but good enough, two sets of curtains and an infinite number of odds and ends. They want us to come on Saturday to see how they've settled in. Kit wouldn't let me help at all. It's to be a surprise. We shall have to be passionately admiring, no matter what sort of mess they've made of it."

Her voice was gay. She was, she told him, working again: an idea had come to her at last, and she was writing for three hours every evening. If the new book were successful at all, she would give up her job and accept a minimal allowance from her parents if she should need it.

"Why haven't you taken one before?" Jo asked, curious. "Don't you get on with them?"

She replied that she got on with them very well, but that she liked her independence and they were proud of her for having achieved it—even though they did find it hard to understand why she was willing to type in an office in Gracechurch Street between nine and five. "I don't deceive myself," she added, "I have things both ways. When I want luxury, I go home for the weekends." She spoke with her usual rather cold honesty: more than most people she wanted to be known as she was, warts and all. This was perhaps, Jo thought, due to a fear of being found out even in the smallest thing: to disappoint. What there was in her to dislike, she would rather have disliked at once. She was hungry for affection, yes: but not in the same way as Kit, who was so hungry that he would go to any lengths to conceal—from acquaintances, if not from friends—any element in his nature less than charming, less, Jo would have put it, than *cuddly*.

When they got to Tedworth Gardens, Kit was standing on a first-floor balcony, shouting and waving. He had left the front door open, they were to come right up. He called down to Alison, "I like the get-up!"

It was only at this moment that Jo noticed it. She was wearing a scarlet coat, a yellow head-scarf. She looked far more the girl at home in the "wild life" than she had ever done before.

"All for your benefit," she called back.

They went upstairs and into the front room, where the three young men now silently awaited them, Clement, Phil Christie, Kit. They stopped dead. Kit cried, "Sing, Muse!" and the other two burst out laughing.

In this room were two of the divans Alison had given them, but laid on the floor upside down, so that the stumpy legs prodded up into the air, all eight of them painted a bright orange. Beds had been made up very roughly on mattresses transferred to the stretched sacking. All over the walls, yellow dusters were stuck with drawing-pins. "Because they're a wonderful color," Kit said, coming forward to hug Alison and kiss her, "far too beautiful to

44

be used for cleaning up dirt. Don't you love our beds? They're baby four-posters. Clem's is in the other room, but his is right-side up."

"It's dazzling," Alison said, laughing too, but Jo could see she was aghast. Somehow they had made fun of her gifts, her parents' gifts. "Most ingenious. But where are the curtains?"

"The lady has no eyes," said Phil, sparkling his own at her. "What should we poor devils do without bedspreads? We have to have the niceties. Come, come, don't look appalled—you do, you know."

It was true: the curtains were draped over the army blankets upon the upturned divans.

"I'm not," Alison said, "I'm just staggered. Didn't you think I should be?"

"That's not a very Muse-like note in your voice, Allie."

She said, "Don't call me that, it's hideous."

"Come, come, don't be cross. You know *me*." Phil meant that she did not, and he did not mean her to. He was a short, small-featured but stocky young man, his eyes pale-grey, and so wide-open that the white was visible all round the iris. He had flaxen hair, fluffy, almost like a baby's.

"You must see the rest of the establishment," said Kit. "I don't think I'll show you Clement's room. It spoils the effect."

"I'm a neat young man," said Clement, "and I can't disorient myself quite so quickly from my former grandeurs. But I'll learn. Come on, Alison, you shall see my room, where the curtains are where you would expect curtains to be."

His room was neat enough, ordinary enough, though the paper was peeling badly. "I've pinched the vases," he added to her, meaning to be kind. She had thrown into the crate of kitchen-ware two large ginger-jars, which Clement had neatly disposed on the shelf above the shilling-in-the-slot gas fire. "They lend me my own kind of tone."

The kitchen, covered bath now laid out with beer bottles, glasses and cheese, was a cramped and shabby room with a long crack in the ceiling. The stove was rusty, the pots and pans still in their wrappings of brown paper. Everything was dirty.

"I would far rather," Alison said in a bright, unnatural voice, "be an Egeria to you all than disseminate sunshine in a more prac-

45

tical way, but I should like to bring some order into chaos right now, if someone will find the pail I sent you. There's a scrubbing brush inside it. And a bar of yellow soap."

"Good God," said Kit, "you stick to your new role and we'll stick to ours. Besides, you haven't heard the best of it. Who's going to tell?"

"Not me," said Clement, "I'm too old-maidish. Also, it makes me feel sick."

Phil sidled up to Alison. "Do you know, you're one of the prettiest girls I've ever met?"

Pretty she was not; knowing it, she frowned.

"And also, much too nice for all of us. Kit says the ancestral home—"

"It's a medium-sized farmhouse, that's all."

"—is a sight to behold. And spotless."

"You could see your face in the po," said Kit, "if there was a po."

"Oh, shut up!" Alison snapped at him, inadequate disguises falling away. "What *is* the matter?"

He smoothed her breasts, snuggled against her. "You'll be shocked."

"When have I been shocked by anything you could do?"

"We haven't done anything. It's been done to us."

Phil bowed his head as if in prayer, raised his right hand. "Tomorrow," he said, "we are to be fumigated. In short, we have bugs."

Jo laughed at last, not so much at Phil's antics, or at the substance of his revelation, but from a relief he could not understand.

"I am not," Alison said, "surprised."

"So keep well away from the walls, darling—look, here's one of your lovely chairs to sit on—and you'll be all right." Kit seated her with old-world courtesy. "We have only one night more of terror, picking them out of the wallpaper."

Jo said, "It happens to the best people. We got them once, from some people next door, and Mother collapsed. But there's a lot of unnecessary prejudice against them."

"Why so?" Clement inquired with interest.

"Jo is vocal today. How nice. Why so?" said Kit.

Even Alison was smiling naturally now.

"Because, when you squash them, they smell of camellias."

Kit slapped him approvingly on the back. "Christ, that's a contribution! And it's dead true!"

"Cats' pee would smell nice," Jo went on, "if we weren't prejudiced against that. It smells of cat-*nip*."

"Allie shall give us a pussy-cat then," said Phil, "a lovely leaking Tom—now, now, now, you know me!" He dodged away, pretending to be afraid she might hit him.

"The irony of it all," Kit said, "is that Clem's room is the worst infested. This is the least. So we'll drink to all of us here."

Slowly the strain seemed to leave them, and Jo felt that his own unexpected contribution had added to the release of tension. They were drinking more than usual. Clement left the flat, and returned with a bag of sausage rolls and pork pies. Kit pulled a chair up close to Alison's and made love to her in whispers. Sometimes he spoke of her to the others—"Doesn't she look lovely?" or "Now she's one of us."

It was half past eleven when Alison said she must go home, and she looked to Kit.

"Sorry, my love, but Jo will see you safely on your way. I'm going to do something grave and reverend, which is to join this crowd in a cleaning orgy. Truly."

Alison said she would willingly have done that. In fact, once the fumigation was over—her smile was open and happy—she would come in the following day after work and spring-clean. She would probably bring Edna.

"Ed-na?" inquired Phil, as if pronouncing, with the maximum of moral courage, some word of unguessable horror. "I'm sure we don't want Edna, whoever she is. Only you, Allie." He flinched again, pretending she had taken a swing at him. "Be nice, be nice, you know me."

Kit said she was not to worry. They had to learn the domestic arts some time, hadn't they? Besides, there was more news. The telephone was to be installed.

"When?"

"You'll be the first person we shall ring."

"You mean that—"

"My darling, my beautiful, possess your soul in patience. When I ring you we shall be all clean, all shipshape. Until that time, we shall stay *incommunicado*."

She had forgotten the audience. "You mean that I shan't see you until you ring? Do remember, you were so keen on having an Egeria."

He sat on the bath-board, swinging his legs. Behind his eyes something stirred like a bird in a bush, an unease, a compunction, a sadness. "Of course we're keen. Everyone knows about you and me. Tedworth Square, London, the world, the universe. But we are going to find our own feet."

She was so quiet that Jo was alarmed. She said at last, in a steady, reasonable voice, something unreasonable. "I have done a lot for you."

"And we're grateful, so grateful!" This was Phil, still ducking imaginary blows. "You do know we adore you? We're bursting with thankfulness!"

Clement said, "Alison, you are the best girl I know. Even Georgie praises you, damn her and her piddling painter."

She paid no attention to him.

Kit swung down to the floor with a bounce, staggered, regained his footing. "Bedtime. Anyhow, bedtime for lady visitors. We shall soon be in shape to receive you as you deserve."

They were all standing now.

"A bit more bedtime from you," he went on, enunciating clearly, "and you would not have to sit by the telephone palpitating, as in Dorothy Parker, you would be allowed to come in with your little swab and bucket, but despite those pretty clothes you are still the same adorable Alison, far more fitted for old John Knox here than for dirty old me—"

Jo knocked him down.

It was not a hard blow, and Kit fell easily, breaking his fall by gripping at the leg of a chair. He lay on his back, starry-eyed.

"Ah," he said, from his prone position, "now, my darling, you perceive the truth. It is not you he loves. It is me. Otherwise, he wouldn't have bothered."

Jo was filled with a kind of horror, not by what Kit had said, which he knew to be ridiculous, but by his own action, so out of character that he felt as if he were glued to the spot, incapable of movement. He did not know what to do next.

Clement knew what should be done. He heaved Kit up, shook him and bumped him down rather hard into a chair. "Get up, you damned fool, you know you're not hurt. Stop pretending, it makes me puke."

Phil declaimed:

> " 'Ah! what avails the classic bent
> And what the something word,
> Against the undoctored incident
> That actually occurred?'

I may have it wrong, but it's apposite. Could we possibly have christened the place better?"

"See you next Thursday, Jo," said Kit. "Fitzroy. About seven."

Alison was running down the stairs. Jo followed her. At the corner of Radnor Street she saw a taxi and raced to it, forgetting him completely.

When she had been carried away, he stood in the sharp starlight, uncertain whether or not to go back to the flat. He was wretched for her, but not so for himself. He would be meeting Kit in the usual place, within two days. Above him, the front-room light went out. Clement? He would be the only one of them used to watching the electricity bills.

Jo walked up towards the King's Road, and as he did so, a certain pride entered him. He had knocked a man down, and for the first time in his life. He refused to admit the thought that Kit was smaller than he, more drunk, and in any case unhurt. Also, he thought for the first time hopefully about Alison. For her and Kit, this must be the end: during the whole of that evening, *the end had been intended*. She would be miserable for a long while, but comforted to have him with her. After that, who knew? Anything might happen.

Chapter Seven

HE NEVER MET KIT ON THURSDAY, SINCE ON THE PREVIOUS DAY HIS mother had a slight stroke, and he and Mildred were both housebound. Then Mildred went down with influenza, and Jo had to get leave from his firm to nurse them both. During this miserable period, which occupied a fortnight, Kit wrote affectionate letters of sympathy, making a slight joke about the scene at the flat, but not mentioning Alison at all.

After that, Jo was able to return to work, but did not feel he should go out in the evenings, not to the Party rooms, nor to the pubs. Such company as he had, came to him: Clement one night, bringing beer, and Bobby Price bringing news of his visit to Russia, which had wildly excited him.

"Not all that Zinoviev crowd can have been guilty," Jo said, "it's against statistical chance."

"You've read the trial reports, or you ought to have done."

"And people disappear."

"I never met a single soul, *bach,* who knew anyone who had *ever* disappeared."

"Statistically. What with treason trials and purges, at least two-thirds of the Centre Committee of the C.P. here must be traitors."

"Bilge," said Bobby.

"Mathematics."

Jo would have liked to talk about the crisis over the King and Mrs. Simpson, but Bobby was not interested. "That lot have nothing to do with us."

Then Alison telephoned him. Would he care for her to come and see him, or was he too busy? Was there anything she could do for his mother? For a second he was too excited to answer her, and this she took for reluctance. "Don't mind saying no, if it's difficult for you. Actually, I thought it might be."

Eagerly he assured her that it was not difficult at all. His mother was much better, not out of her room yet but sitting up in a chair.

Alison said she would come about eight-thirty.

Waiting for her, he was consumed with a frightened pleasure. To have her here, in his home, for once not Kit's girl: to know what he would never let her know, or perhaps one day he might, that on his bedroom wall hung a huge photograph of herself, which he had had enlarged from a seaside snapshot she had given him casually one evening a few months ago. The enlargement had brought to it both clarity and mistiness: her features were sharp behind what might have been a very light veiling of rain. She was real and she was a phantom. Jo's phantom, not Kit's: his own.

He told Mildred and his mother that she would be coming.

"Well, I shall be out of your way," Mildred said, "I've got enough to do in the kitchen."

"Bring her in to see me, just for a minute," said Bessie. "It will make me feel quite gay to see a new face again."

Alison arrived punctually, carrying a bunch of huge-headed chrysanthemums, tightly curled as renaissance Davids, yellow and white, and a basket of fruit. She was wearing one of her dark dresses and the pearls.

She said quickly, before Jo could speak, "I know all this looks very ostentatious, but it's more fun for invalids when people are."

"Is that you, Alison?" Bessie called out.

"Come and see her first," said Jo.

Bessie exclaimed over the bounty dumped upon her bed, and

at once sent Jo to find a vase. When he came back, she was holding Alison's hand, and her bow-windowed face was flushed with meaningful, deliberating pleasure.

"I was telling her, Jo, the nicest present she's brought me is herself."

Oh God, he thought, I shall never get Alison away.

His mother rambled on about her illness, how bad it had been, how good her children had been. "Saint Joseph and Saint Millie, that's what they ought to be made, one day. Not a grouse out of either of them, not even the littlest groan they thought I might not hear!"

Alison said she had not expected to see her looking so well.

"I'm going to get up properly soon—perhaps tomorrow. It's so dull staying in a bedroom week after week. I believe if I tried, I could even manage it tonight!"

"No you don't, Mother," said Mildred, who had just come into the room, "not until the doctor says you can. If you imagine Jo and I are going to cope with some awful set-back, you can think again. Anyhow, I've come to get you into bed right now, so Jo and Alison can clear out of here and talk their heads off."

She winked at Jo, very slightly, and he was filled with gratitude.

At last he had her to himself, facing her across the fire. Upon her living face he superimposed the spectral face of the photograph. It was like a miracle to behold this blending, to hug the knowledge he would not give to her.

"It's been a hell of a time." Then he did not know what to say next and longed for her to speak, to help him out.

"It must have been. Nursing is always awful."

"I didn't mean that. I meant, since I last saw you."

"I haven't been much to see, these past few weeks. In fact, I haven't seen anyone."

He dared to ask her about Kit.

"Oh, he telephoned, as he said he would. He asked me round. They were all going to be there. So I said I couldn't come. I never thought I should rise to such a peak of moral courage. After that, nothing: until"—she paused—"something odd happened. Two nights ago. My telephone rang, and a voice like Kit's but rather fudged and muffled, if you know what I mean, said was I going to be alone because he wanted to come round. I said yes, and he—it—said, 'I'll be there in half an hour. An hour, anyway. Wait for me.' It was ten o'clock then. I waited till eleven, twelve, one o'clock. I even rang the flat, but nobody answered. He never came. Of course, I know now that it couldn't have been him at all, but one of his filthy friends playing a joke on me. Phil, I suppose: he's a good mimic. But it was an undesirable joke, don't you think?"

Jo, sickened, promised that he would get to the bottom of it if it killed him.

"No, you mustn't. I am recovering a little, I think, and it would make it all so much worse. I'm learning to do without him. The only really bad times are in the middle of the night." Her voice shook. "I thought of Sappho: 'The moon has set and the Pleiades: it is the middle of the night, and time passes, time passes. . . .'" She stopped.

You have always lain alone, Jo thought. But it was only in the body that she had done so.

"This is no way to behave," Alison said severely, addressing herself, and she began to make up her face fussily, conscientiously, as though this were something she had contracted to do an hour ago, but had forgotten. "Give me a month or so and I shall be out of this. In the meantime, let's go out occasionally, when you're off the chain again. But to quiet pubs in side streets, where there are only plumbers or businessmen. I don't want to meet any of our friends, or not just yet. Only you. Perhaps Clement. He's a very kind man really, though he would hate one to think so."

Mildred made rattling noises outside the door, to warn them that she was coming in. She brought coffee. "I've got Mother settled, and as soon as I know she's asleep I shall go to Eileen's for an hour." This was a friend who lived next door. "Will you be able to cope, Jo?"

He was afraid Alison might think Mildred was leaving them alone to give them a chance of love-making. He knew his sister as she could not: it was not that at all. He had told her of Alison's loss, though not of his own passion. She would feel it only right that the loss could not comfortably be spoken of in her presence.

"We'll keep an ear out," he said. Mildred went back to her work, and within half an hour had left the house.

For a while they talked about Spain, Germany, the King. Alison's political interests were deepening, and her fears were more immediate than his own. She attended Left Book Club groups and occasionally appeared on platforms for Spanish Medical Aid. She was a good speaker, she told him, not boastfully, but simply as a fact; she found it easy to speak in public about anything except her own work. "I could have been an actress, I think, if I'd wanted to."

She was over-warmed by the fire. One of her cheeks was redder than the other. Her dark hair, Indian-straight, had grown a little and now covered her ears: it made her look older, less insecure. Yet he knew she was painfully insecure, that there was desolation in her, that she cried in the night. She would be desolate so long as she clung to the belief that there was hope: and when she referred to Kit's work, which she did with an appearance of sangfroid, he knew that she had not lost it. One night there could be another telephone call. This time it would be from him.

Delicately, she began to probe Jo for what he might be able to tell her. "He writes to you, I expect."

"The odd note."

"Any news of any sort?"

"Not really."

"No new friends? He picks them up as if he were a flypaper, doesn't he? And most of them are bluebottles." She could not restrain the replacement of airiness by more than a touch of contempt. She was a proud woman: she had been cut down to a size not her own by people less than herself.

"So far as I know, just the old crowd." He sounded as if he were fencing, though he was telling her no more than the truth.

She cried out, "You'd know if there was another girl!" She sat up erect, arching, then straightening, the one cheek scorched, the other white. "But if you did, you wouldn't tell me."

He said slowly, "If I did know, I think I would."

He had just become aware that, without intending it, she was *using* him as Kit had used her, and that he could not bear it any longer. Her presence was disturbance enough, but the fact that the selfishness of her misery caused her to be unaware of this made the disturbance a hundred times worse for him. Hardly knowing what he meant to do next, he put out a hand and pulled her to her feet.

"Come on. I've got a picture I want you to see."

"What picture?"

"Come on."

He took her upstairs to his room, which was bitterly cold. The curtains were still undrawn and the trees were shuddering in the wind, the stars flashing between them as the leaves shifted violently. He turned on the light, closed the door. "Look."

She stared at the photograph of herself, then at him.

"How silly of you!" She was hesitant, not knowing what to say.

"Maybe. But I pretty well say my prayers to it. I told you how I felt, before, but you were hardly listening. I know you don't love me, I don't suppose you ever will. But you've got to understand how *I* feel, and what it's like for me when you can't see me at all because Kit's there. Yes, I'm selfish, I'm bloody selfish. I ought to stand by and let you cry at me, but I can't bear it. I'll go out with you, I'll let you talk about anything but that. I won't be used."

She did not speak.

"I pretty well say my prayers to that," Jo repeated, his heart thumping, a compression round his forehead. He went to pull the curtains: this was prescience which he was afterwards to think about. Why had he done it? He could not have anticipated what would happen.

She said, "Yes, you're right. In every word you say. You are selfish, too, but so am I." She opened her arms to him and he let her hold him, feeling that he might fall. After a moment he twisted her head round and kissed her lips.

"Let me go," said Alison, "just for a moment." She went to the door and turned the key in it. "I won't use you any more. That's over."

Shivering with cold and tension, she began to undress, slowly at first, then with tearing haste, and he did the same. Before he could catch more than a glimpse of her full breasts, her narrow hips, she had plunged like a diver into the chill of the bed and now stared out at him over the sheets, her eyes glittering, her nose projecting.

He came to lie beside her: her teeth chattered. "Yes," she said, "yes."

At any moment his mother might call out, or Mildred return. He was going to take Alison, whom Kit had been unable to take, without her love. He tried to be gentle, but gentleness was impossible, urgency too great. He looked into her set face, the eyes still wide and sparkling, lips parted in a hard smile. Then she gasped and cried out, not loudly, once; and after a little, took his head on her shoulders, smiling down at him as if she were content and bounteous.

"You didn't want it," Jo said.

"For you I did, very much. And for me, too. I'm glad. You must believe that. I'm more glad than I can tell you."

He had to say, "We've got to hurry." It seemed a major absurdity that he was forced to care about Mother, sister, the click of a key in the lock.

She laughed. "Yes, we're in mortal peril."

They dressed again, not looking at each other, went back downstairs to the hot room. She glanced at her watch. "It's late."

"How will you get back? Wait till Millie comes, and I'll go with you."

She would not have this. If he would ring for a taxi, it would take her to the station.

He went into the hall to telephone. His mother heard the bell. "What are you doing, Jo?"

"Getting a cab for Alison."

The sleepy voice: "What a pair of night-owls!"

"Do you want anything?"

"No. Goodnight, dear."

He returned to Alison, who was kneeling before the fire now, as if she could not get warm again. They did not talk very much while they waited.

When she was ready to go, she kissed him, pressing her open mouth against his cheek.

"Thanks," Jo said, "and I understood that it wasn't forever. Don't you think I didn't."

"No. But thank you, too."

"When shall I see you again?"

They would meet in Chelsea, seek out the back-street pub, where nobody would come that they knew. All would be as it was before. They would be friends, they would talk about politics and books and fame, and later, perhaps, they would talk of Kit as if he were any friend, no particular friend.

"Because you do love him best," Alison said, "and I think you realize it."

56

She was gone. Jo heard the swerve of her taxi as it made the U-turn.

If Mildred had come in then, and not stayed out half an hour later than she had anticipated, he would have fallen asleep and done no thinking whatsoever. As it was, he made up the fire, turned out the lights, and sat before the blaze, now and then turning as if to catch, as one might catch sight of an intruder, the shadow of his knife-like profile on the wall. At first he felt only humiliation: she had *used him* yet again and, having no strength, he had let her do so. Then he began to believe that he had helped her to the shadow of an idea in her own mind, less strong than the shadow etched by fire that flickered as the flame spurted up the chimney: the idea of completion, or, perhaps childishly, the idea of being grown up. Did she now hope to meet Kit with new confidence, no more a shy, celebrated girl scared of noise, bombast, confidence, experience? Those hopes of hers, however absurd, were still as high as the skyscrapers of New York.

In his ugly house, in the red glow from the hearth, with the winds yelling outside, the reality of the night faded, the real face was again superimposed by the photograph. His understanding of her, in itself so flickering (he turned his head sharply, nearly caught the whole silhouette), began to fade. He could not comprehend her humility: for he, despite what his friends thought of him, was not by nature humble. He could no longer have endured to be a mere accepter of her grief, a kind of human towel for tears.

Mildred came in, glowing from the cold and the gale, and she turned on the lights. "For God's sake, Jo, don't you know coals cost money?" She set to raking them out onto the fake Dutch tiles, letting them die. "Any outcry from Mother?"

In the freezing bedroom, the physical proofs of a dream, or a nightmare, confronted him: the touselled bed and, on the lower sheet, a scattering of drops like geranium petals. He had to consider what he was going to do about it. In the bathroom, he found a razor blade and took an experimental prod at his forearm: with no result. Closing his eyes, clenching his teeth, aware now only of being clownish, a failed Seneca, he tried again: and this time the blood emerged meagerly. Well, it would do for an explanation.

What he could not bring himself to think about, after all this thought, these antics (now, in a moment's retrospect, entirely ludicrous), was Alison. Even her name meant nothing, though he was still in love with her. He could not imagine any other condition for himself for the rest of his life.

Mildred came up and spoke from behind the door. "Want any cocoa? I'm making some for myself."

Jo thought: cocoa! Some lives may begin and end with it. He called back, "No, thanks."

He had the rare and exquisite knowledge of falling slowly into sleep, as a patient who enjoys the dentist's gas may experience the diminution of consciousness. He had sat in that chair, the fat triangle of rubber over his mouth, watching the window-pane. "As unto dying eyes, the casement slowly grows a glimmering square"—the perfect lines for the dental experience, and the beautiful hectic dream to come, the underwater swim in pale-green, Nilotic seas, buoyant and warm as bath-water, and far, far below, clean-washed pebbles glittering like moidores, swarmed over by angelfish. Heaven lies about us in the seas of our infancy. What swimmers we are! Between ourselves and the fish nothing, except a visceral enjoyment, an athletic sensuality.

Then: "Spit out, please."

PART TWO

Young Men in Love

Chapter One

KIT HAD BEEN WORKING WITH HIS USUAL DRIVING CONCENTRATION. Since he had left his job, he no longer needed to labor into the small hours and with Clement and Phil out all day he was able to write in the mornings while he was still fresh. He had had enough experience of writing when he was tired and half-drunk to abandon the last vestigial romanticism about midnight oil.

The flat, though far from clean, looked more or less normal these days, for Clement, having somewhat fractiously endured a month or so of the bizarre, had shouldered his way through protest, humped the divans the right way up, and brought some kind of order to the kitchen. The yellow dusters had been removed from the walls; in their place were reproductions of Picasso and Klee. Kit pretended to regret these changes: but secretly he was glad to work in conditions less distracting and to sleep in a proper bed.

Next month his first novel would be out: he was hoping for —even expecting—fame. He had spent much time in the pubs cultivating people who might be helpful. Several more of his stories had appeared in literary magazines unable to pay their contributors, but offering valuable shop-window space. Even now, he was a little lion, a lion cub: but the day was coming when he would roar. The story on which he was laboring now, for he was trying deliberately to restrict a natural fluency which he believed to be dangerous, was going well: again, this was one for Left Wing consumption. Aware of the growing dangers of the world, but able to see them only as behind a smeary screen of plate glass, as through the window of a hotel kitchen, he felt that by this activity at least he was doing what he could to help. It salved his conscience.

It would not be right to think that he had no conscience, though many people did think that. The business over Alison had become common knowledge and some of his friends thought he had behaved badly. He thought so himself, when she entered his mind at all, and he felt unhappy; though it all seemed to him to have taken place years, instead of months, ago. There were dog-in-the-manger times when he felt jealous of Jo, whom he knew she did not love. There were times when Jo's grape-green, solemn eyes, seen through a fug of smoke in the pubs of Bloomsbury, seemed too accusatory for comfort. He would never, he knew, have a closer friend, but he sometimes had to resist the impulse to pick a quarrel, to make a clean break.

Had he known that Jo had slept with her, he would have been utterly incredulous. Somehow, Alison still belonged to him: or if she did not, then it was unthinkable that she should belong to anyone else. As a man who has sold a painting or a house cannot see either without feeling the old superior sense of possession, so Kit felt about Alison.

Pouring his fourth cup of coffee, he sat down with words again, his mind quite clear of everything else.

In the side street below the window, a young man was teaching himself to reverse a car. He jerked back and forth, every time bumping the curb, crashing gears. It was a bright, sharp morning with a crystalline sky. On the leads of the house opposite a woman with a pink duster round her head was hanging out a line of washing. The car skidded across the road with a high, protesting screech and mounted the pavement, only just missing a collision with the wall. The driver got out and inspected it, first taking off and wiping his thick glasses.

Kit flung up the window. "Will you stop that blasted row?"

The man blinked up at him, sun shining on his stiffly curling ginger hair, which had the texture of the stuffing in a mattress. He called back, mildly, "I beg your pardon?"

"I'm trying to write. I can't stand that filthy noise."

"Oh, I do see that! I'm so sorry. I write myself. But this is such a safe street for practicing in."

"It won't be a safe street for you much longer, if you don't go away."

"I really am very sorry. I'm through now, anyhow. Did you say you wrote? I try a little poetry myself now and again."

"Damn you, clear off!"

Kit banged the window shut.

The young man got back into his car and drove it, at a snail's pace, out of sight.

Kit's mood was now destroyed, and with it his concentration. He telephoned to Jo, suggesting a meeting in the King's Head & Eight Bells that evening. When he had scraped together some lunch, he went to walk in Battersea Park, where the crocuses were just beginning to flower, the bare boughs had a mossy softness against the sky, and the earth smelled strong, sweet and masculine.

God damn the oaf who couldn't drive a car, who had ruined his morning. "I need more than I've got," he said aloud, "much, much more than I've got." But he did not know what it was that he needed.

"Whadja say, mate?" inquired the sinister park-keeper with his brown uniform, his pronged stick, so carneying to the grown-ups, so violent to the children when he found them playing alone.

"Talking to myself, mate," said Kit.

"Bad habit. Drives you barmy."

"I am barmy," Kit replied with dignity, "so there is nowhere I can be driven."

The weather began to blacken. As he came out of the iron gates, the newsboys were crying with voices desolate as the voices of gulls. Malaga had fallen.

"Tell me everything that's happened," he said later to Jo, in the King's Head, "about your ma, and Millie, and Alison, and old Uncle Tom Cobley."

The pin-table cracked and rattled. There was a mob around the bar, but nobody whom they knew.

Jo, heavy with secrets and love, said that his mother was all right, but that Mildred had lost her auctioneer. "So it's part relief and part gloom." Of Alison he did not wish to talk at all, so he merely said that she had finished another book. If you knew, he thought, if only you knew!

"She can't have!" Kit exclaimed.

"Yes, she has. Ever since she left her job she's been writing five thousand words a day."

"God stone the crows, what a girl! Have you seen it?"

"Some of it."

"Good?"

"I think it's damned good," Jo answered, and heard the attacking note in his own voice.

Kit looked at him with some surprise. "All right, I believe you! What about you, anything to show me?"

It was with reluctance, in his present mood, that Jo admitted this. He wanted to keep his story to himself, yet could not resist seeking the advantage of Kit's vigorous, sardonic criticism. He pulled a mass of greyish typescript from his bulging pocket.

"Yes," said Kit, "I guessed you had. Otherwise, I'd have thought you were kittening."

"But don't read it now."

"In this light, I couldn't. Is she happy?"

Jo said, "If you mean Alison, I don't think that's your worry any more."

"Snubbed." Then Kit said lightly, slyly, "Is she fretting after me?"

"Do you want me to tell you that she isn't or she is?"

Kit was disturbed. Once he had held his friend in the palm of his hand: now Jo was getting too independent, a Hamlet who had decided to take a firm line in Elsinore. He said cautiously, "You haven't got to tell me anything if you don't want to."

"I don't think I do. Anyway, there isn't anything to tell."

"Well, I'll give you my news." Kit announced that he was going to get rid of Phil—"About time, too"—because he'd had enough of him. Georgina was bored with her painter and had several times been seen with Clement. If they made it up, Clement would leave the flat, and then who would pay the rent? "If you could only get somebody in to help with your ma, you could come and share with me. We'd soon find some more or less prosperous third party."

"I can't afford to get anyone in," Jo said, irritated as he had

64

always been with Kit's blindness to all circumstances that did not suit himself, "you know that."

Kit retorted that even if Jo could, he wouldn't. He was a self-appointed martyr, bent on ruining his own life. "You wallow in defeat, don't you, like a hippo in a great steamy pool full of cabbage-heads?"

"I may be a martyr, but not self-appointed. Your trouble is that you never see there are things that can't be cured." He made himself speak philosophically, without heat. Kit admired him, and was more sorry for him than ever. It was true that they had heard the chimes of midnight: but would anyone, when Jo was old, ever remember him as Mad Upjohn? He said, meaning it, "I'm sorry. I'm in a bastard mood tonight, though you are too, so don't gloat. I only wish I could help."

A tall figure loomed above them, eyes magnified by thick glasses.

"I *think* you are Christopher Mallings. I'm afraid I disturbed you with the car this morning. I'm Nigel Dobson."

"Jo Upjohn," Kit said, making a surly introduction. "Yes, I'm Mallings."

"May I sit with you? Do you mind?"

"Do, if you want to."

Dobson plumped down his tankard and sat on the bench beside them, crowding them nearer to the wall. He had a jovial, enthusiastic manner and was very heavily built.

"I've seen your work," he said to Kit, "and I find it has a strong poetic quality. Naturally that appeals to me."

Kit murmured that he was so glad.

"But that last story, in *Miscellany*—I do think, Mallings, that you can do better than that."

"Oh, you do, do you?"

"I don't know you, of course, as yet, but I've always taken an avuncular interest."

"And how old, if we may ask, is uncle?"

"Alas," said Dobson, with a sad-sweet smile, "twenty-eight."

"The final stage of decrepitude," said Jo, joining in what seemed to him a game. "You have our sympathy."

Dobson looked hurt. Polishing his glasses, he said he was afraid he was in the way, had interrupted a private conversation. The last thing, he added, that he had meant to do.

"I wonder what the first was," said Kit. Then he felt sorry he had been rude, and his heart warmed to the motorist whom it was so easy to outface. "Have another on us. Go on, Jo, you get them."

"No, no, no, I couldn't," Dobson said, brightening. "This must be my round."

Kit, feeling that the pleasure of his own company might reasonably be paid for, did not demur to this further than courtesy demanded. Dobson shambled up and made his bear-like way to the bar.

"What the hell do you think you're doing?" said Jo. "He'll stick to us all night."

"No, he won't. Anyway, I rather like him. He's touching, and too fat."

When Dobson returned with the mugs, he had completely regained his confidence.

"Poetry," he said, "I do know about. Of course, I'm only feeling my way as yet. I'm an articled clerk by profession."

" 'The law is the true embodiment,' " Jo sang, " 'of everything that's excellent.' "

Poor old Jo, Kit thought, no man will ever be a highbrow writer who quotes Gilbert & Sullivan. But he grinned.

Weak eyes blinked. "Well, I think so. I doubt whether there's a better juridical system in the world than our own. But the law's not my first love."

"No, poetry is. You implied that pretty strongly."

He looked at Jo for a second in silence, then turned away from him.

"If you want to know why I found your last story disappointing, Mallings—"

"If you're going to insist on telling me, you'd better call me Kit. Otherwise I shall feel like a naughty boy holding my hand out." This last phrase gave him an idea for a new kind of amusement, later on.

"I don't want to offend you."

"You won't."

"But I do feel that absolutely objective criticism from an outsider is always valuable, don't you?"

"That depends," said Jo, "on the outsider."

"You shut up." Kit kicked him, under the table. "I want to listen to Noel."

"Nigel." He paused. "Dobson."

"Nigel. What a nice name! Dobson is nice, too."

Jo was puzzled by an unfamiliar jolt in Kit's voice, which had risen by half a tone. Still, he thought, he must continue with his own role.

"Well, I did feel the story had been hurried. I mean, it's a bit superficial, don't you think? It hasn't been properly worked over."

Kit, who had worked at every word of it with frenetic devotion, was nonplussed. "You think not?"

"I have an instinct for things like that. You had an original idea, you have considerable poetic feeling, but one senses that you're not sufficiently involved. To anyone like myself, it sticks out like a—like a"—Dobson sought for a simile—"like a pylon in a wilderness! Flaubert taught us *how* to work, don't you agree?"

"Stuff Flaubert," said Jo.

Kit tried to look shocked and stern. After an evening that had been heavy with overtones, a worrying evening, he felt glee returning to him. "Please! Nigel is being very interesting. I want to listen."

Thus encouraged, Dobson gave a longish lecture on Flaubert and his working methods. Kit, he said, was at the beginning of his career, and to think of these matters now might be of inestimable help in the years to come. Did Jo write?

"No," Jo said, not wanting another lecture all to himself.

"You should try. You never know until you do. I didn't. I hadn't the least idea."

"And you find you can?" Kit put his chin on clasped hands and gazed at Dobson in a manner bright-eyed and guileless.

"I find I can," said Dobson trenchantly. "It is only a matter of having the perseverance, the guts, never to think as you did, Mallings, when you wrote that story, that it was 'good enough.' A thing must be *absolutely* good." He added, "I haven't published yet. All in good time."

"At your age," said Jo, now thoroughly enjoying himself as the villain of the piece, and guessing that it fitted in with Kit's ideas, "have you got much time left?"

Kit said, "Don't mind him, Nigel. He's only jealous. He hates me to have all the attention." He was not only guileless now but girlish, fluttering his lashes, squirming on what little of the bench was left to him. "Now be quiet, Jo dear. Do go on, Nigel. I'm adoring every moment of it!"

However, Dobson refused to go further. When he had finished his beer he said goodnight to them shortly, and left the pub.

"Oh God, oh God," Kit cried, "he thinks we're pansies!"

They laughed until laughter became painful.

"I do love Nigel! I love him so much. Why were you so brutal to him, Jo? I thought you had a heart of butter."

"I thought I did it beautifully."

The incident had taken from them the last tinge of constraint, and they were together as in the old way. "Let's go to Kleinfeldt's," Kit suggested, "and make a night of it. A really lovely, wild night!" Everything around him had a panchromatic beauty so sharp as to be almost unendurable, the pink faces beaming soft as marshmallow through the wreathing smoke, the fairy-lamps like oranges and lemons round the bar, the whizzing of the silver balls in the pin-tables, the residual golden foam forming a Fujiyama on the sides of his own empty mug. He felt *ready for something*, though he did not know what. "Come on, we'll take a taxi. I've just had two quid from home."

Jo said it was too far and too late, but that they might go up to the King's Road.

"Tell me about Alison," Kit coaxed him, as they walked up Cheyne Row together. "I do worry about her."

"There's nothing to tell. Nothing at all."

When they went into the bar, she was the first person they saw. Jo's heart turned over. Though he had met her in one of the back-street pubs only two nights ago, it was quite another thing seeing her here. She was sitting in a corner with Clement and Georgina, and she waved to them as if she had not a care in the world. Kit halted in his stride, hoped this had not been perceptible, and came to join her, Jo behind him.

When they had greeted her she said lightly, "We're celebrating because I've finished my book, and Clem and Georgie are reconciled. This is a great occasion."

"Are you really?" Kit asked Clement. He was fond enough of them both to hope that they were, anxious enough about the fate of the flat to hope they were not.

"You asked her. She's the boss. I only stand and wait."

Georgina said she wasn't sure, but it seemed in the cards. She

68

found her husband, she added, with a liquid flicker of her brown eyes, more interesting than most people.

Clement grinned. "I know what she means."

"You do not know what I mean." She looked at him with sarcasm and sensuality. She had ease of nature, was totally amoral and totally relaxed. Kit would have wished to be like her.

Jo noticed that Alison kept glancing across the room to a curtained doorway. "Who are you looking for?"

Kit was interested in the apparent reversal of intimacy, expressed by the tone of their voices. To himself she had spoken as to some amiable acquaintance: to Jo, as if she might have been his wife. Well, she never would be.

"My friend," she explained, "has been an ominously long time in the lavatory. But as she hasn't drunk anything but tonic water, she can't be ill."

Alison did not merely seem light-hearted: by an effort of will, she had forced herself to become so, even if it were only for an hour or two. It had been a worse effort to come to the pub at all, and one she would probably have made for no one but Clement, of whom she was very fond. Kit, near to her for the first time in months, gave her no more pain than seeing his picture would have done. She had not been sure of seeing him at all that night, but had braced herself to take the risk. She was comforted by Jo, dark, at her side, a cherished familiar. Jo made all things easy for her. She knew how much of a wonder it was that he should do so, with the knowledge that never again could she let him become her lover.

"Here she is!"

Coming towards them was a small, narrow girl, rather short-legged, in a dress between the prim and the arty, her face half-hidden by falls of mouse-colored hair that swung just above her shoulder-blades.

"Sorry," she said, "I laddered a stocking. I've been trying to repair the damage with nail-varnish, and I got the stuff all over my hands."

Clement, whose manners were officiously formal, stood up. Kit and Jo half rose, each with a hand to the arm of a chair.

Alison said, "This is Polly Reston. She works for my publisher and writes my blurbs. Polly—" She performed the introductions.

69

"Hullo," the girl said, in her small, amiable voice. Her eyes rested on Kit's, and his on hers. At once he knew that he dared not, for the moment at least, look at Alison, for fear she would have understood what had happened.

Jo saw. He began to talk energetically, fussing over the company like a parson at a church tea. He, too, was frightened.

The girl had a pale face, not immediately pretty, then very much so: oyster-grey eyes and a charming cockled mouth, pink as a cat's. She had great composure. Taking the chair Clement held for her, she crossed her legs and surveyed them all with happy openness. "Now," she said, "I meet legends. Alison has talked of you exhaustively."

Kit and Jo were simultaneously aware that she came from a different social stratum from theirs, even from Alison's, with her farmhouse, her horses, her green fields. They could not tell how they knew. All of them spoke standard English and this girl did not speak the betraying Cockney of the upper class. Simply, there was something different.

Kit fought against this troubling aspect of her in the only way he knew: by what sounded, in his own ears, like insolence.

"What's your real name? Mary? Nobody was ever christened Polly, except a parrot."

Georgina laughed. "Rude man. Go away."

"My father was a Shakespeare fan," she replied, "and christened me Paulina. But that I found hard to bear."

Now he dared look at Alison, and saw that her eyes were very bright. "You're particularly splendid tonight. Why?"

"Dressed-up," she said, "but I can't help it. I've been to a party." Her voice was steady. Jo thought, she hasn't seen.

Both of them were small girls, narrow of hip, but Polly's breasts were small, too, like the breasts of a Cranach woman. She tossed her head, and her hair, very fine and cleanly, caught prisms from the lamps. "We've both been," she said. "But cocktail parties mean such a let-down afterwards, so Clement suggested we might continue with the convivialities."

"Were you there, too?" Kit asked.

"Certainly I was," Clement replied. "I'm a host and a guest in myself. Didn't you know?"

Polly asked whether anyone would be kind enough to fetch her something to eat. "A sandwich, or a couple of sausage rolls. I

70

don't mind paying for my supper, but I do mind fighting for it."

Kit got up and went to the bar. He was planning how he might find out much more. Obviously, only Alison knew all about her, but could he possibly ring up Alison and ask questions? No, he couldn't. But Jo could find out, and then tell him. Jo would have to.

He returned with a large ham sandwich, a Scotch egg and two Cornish pasties. "Allow me," he said solemnly, putting the plate before her. "On the house."

She thanked him. "But I can't eat all this. Alison, will you share?"

"Of course I shall share. I supposed I was being left to starve."

That was what she was being left to do, Jo thought, and again felt a hard, unpleasant clenching at his heart. Tonight she looked beautiful, hilarious, a party-goer, and most of the attention was for herself: but he knew that her ears were pricked for Kit's voice, and that beneath her gaiety was an undertow, dark and sour, of unbearable disappointment. Even so, he believed she had not seen what he had seen. He looked up, to meet Georgina's syrup-colored, nothing-missing eyes.

"One doesn't know what to do, does one?" she said.

"About me, poppet?" Clement put a meaty hand on her shoulder. She shuddered, but the shudder was histrionic.

"About anything." Still she stared at Jo.

He said he should be thinking about getting home: no, he couldn't make a night of it.

Alison cried, "Don't go! Please!"

The young men were wrong in thinking that worse suffering had not come to her that night. The spy-sense of love betrayed was acute in her. She had missed nothing. She could only pray she had been wrong, pray, at least, not to think about anything but the moment, the brightness, the mere energy of being young.

But Jo could not bear to stay longer, still less bear to find himself, by chance, alone with her. He said goodbye to them all with his usual gravity, which, on occasion, especially when he was unhappy, could be something like a Spanish grandee's.

"I'll see you out," said Kit.

They stood on the pavement.

"Look here, find out what you can about Polly Reston."

71

" 'Sits the wind in that quarter?' " Jo faintly sneered, but he was trying to stall.

"You know bloody well it does."

Jo said he didn't feel particularly concerned. Alison was all he cared about.

Kit said, energetically, "If that wasn't hopeless for me before, it is so now."

"Well, I don't care what harm you do to *her*." Jo meant, to Polly.

"I'm glad I'm not spending a wild night out with you. I'd rather spend it with Spurgeon."

"Spurgeon was a livelier chap than I am."

"You'll find out, anyway?"

"Oh yes, if that's really what you want. But I wish you'd leave me out of it."

"I can't. This is the most important thing that's ever happened to me. Jo, you must!"

Jo walked away without speaking. They had not quarrelled, and they would not: but there were moments when there was hostility between them stiff as a ghost and as dividing.

When Kit went back to the party, he heard the call of Time. He asked the girls back to the flat, expecting them to refuse: which they did. Clement and Georgina went off together, though Clement said he would be back not much after midnight. Alone, Kit sought other company. After all, he knew everyone. There was always a party in progress, somewhere.

Chapter Two

JO WAS NOT RESOLUTE ENOUGH TO OCCUPY ELSINORE COMPLETELY.
A week later, in Alison's flat, he asked her what Kit wished to
know. She replied freely enough, but her mouth looked frozen, as
after a dentist's injections.

Polly was the daughter of a derelict peer, and could be
styled "the Honourable," though this she thought ridiculous
and resisted. She was working because there was little money to
be had from her father. She was twenty-three years old, six
months older than Kit. She had been to a university and had
taken First Class Honours: to this she owed her job. She was extremely competent and, Alison added, with the same awful stiff-
ness, extremely nice. She shared a flat with two other girls. So far
as anyone knew, she was unattached.

"So you may take all that back to him, like some bloody
Cyrano de Bergerac."

"It's not quite the same case," Jo said, and tried to smile.

"I hope he doesn't hurt *her*. No, I hope he does. Then she'll
know what it's like—Jo, don't let me say that! You know I

73

shouldn't. I don't really mean it, or perhaps I do. What do you think?"

He put his arm round her. He could do so easily these days, just for her comfort.

He said thoughtfully, "I think I might mean it. But you don't. You're too splendid for that. Look, it may not come to anything, after all."

"Ah," she said, "but nor shall I. So really, it makes no odds." She jumped up. "I can't just sit here, with my thoughts going round like mice on a wheel. Let's go to the pictures."

Next day he saw Kit.

"Reporting back—suh!" He saluted, clicked his heels.

Though he was in many ways hypersensitive, he had that streak of callousness peculiar to young men, the callousness which permitted Claudio and Don Pedro to talk so gaily after a real treachery and a presumed death. Loving Alison as he did, pitying her as he did, he could not help feeling a touch of glee at being with Kit in an amorous conspiracy. This was an affair for men, in which Alison had no part at all, in fact did not exist: so she could not be hurt.

Kit listened to the report and he smiled. "I guessed some of that."

"Have you seen her again?"

"Yes. She's as clean and sweet as a new nut, and I'm head over heels in love with her. She smells of clover, and she's gentle as a lamb. She's my Polly, she knows it, and she'll tell me so pretty soon."

The world sang to him. Polly! Paulina! He explained this to Jo, looking as he did so a cross between an infant saint and a koala bear. He was half-acting his exultation, yet it was real enough. Acting reality was one of Kit's peculiar skills: he knew that by doing so he would always make himself a little harder for others to understand. He had lost the feeling of inner cold which occasionally troubled him: for the first time he knew love coupled with enormous tenderness. Yet he did not mean ever to lose his essential secrecy, for this had something to do with his writing. Even now, he did not mean that Polly should find this thing out, the thing of all most deeply buried, this burning core that even Jo would never suspect, or if he did so, never comprehend.

It was a fine Saturday morning, the almond trees prematurely in blossom. They swung together up the King's Road, rejoicing in the noise and glitter of it all. They were passing by the headquarters of the British Union of Fascists when they heard a young Blackshirt, no more than a boy, on amateur guard duty, swear at an elderly Jew, who gazed round him for a second or two with a look of shock and terror, then bolted down a side turning at a pace that made the Blackshirt roar with laughter.

Kit said to Jo, "He's not getting away with that." His eyes sparkled. "Come on." He rounded on the boy. "You silly cruel little bugger!"

The boy dodged back into the doorway, and Kit and Jo pursued.

"You dirty, stupid, snotty-nosed, brutal little sod!"

"Don't you talk to me like that!" The boy shouted something behind him, and two of his friends came out of the building. They were large men.

"Don't be a fool," Jo said to Kit, "we can't fight this lot."

"I am going to try," said Kit, and went for the three of them with flailing arms. As Jo intervened, he saw what they meant to do: they had Kit's arms pinioned and were trying to drag him into the headquarters. Realizing the dangers of this, he hung onto Kit's legs, while blows, hardly felt, rained down on him.

A crowd was gathering, and someone was calling for the police.

"No bloody police," Kit yelled, "the last thing I want! God, you'll have my legs off!"

Luckily, at that moment, he got an arm free, and hitting out at random, caught one of the men under the chin. They dropped him and Jo pulled him clear, hauling him to his feet. "This is where *we* run. Don't be a fool"—since Kit seemed about to charge again—"we haven't a chance. Run!"

They ran at top speed till they had reached the Royal Hospital gardens and here, in safety, they inspected the damage that had been done to them. It was lighter than it might have been. Jo had a black eye and his nose was bleeding: Kit's lip was cut and his arms were swollen.

"Dear Lord," he said happily, "I went berserk! It is love, it is love!"

"You damned fool, if they'd got you in there they could have filled you up with castor oil and you'd have got no help from our wonderful policemen."

"I've fought for Polly," Kit said, turning his eyes up like a knight at vigil.

"Is that what it was for? Then don't involve me again."

"You know you loved it. Let's go to the flat and clean ourselves up. Uncle Clement's bought us a first-aid kit."

Somehow, even for Jo, it was a wonderful day, the first really happy one he had known for months past. They felt like hero-warriors, they felt like brothers. When Clement came in, even he was constrained to admire them.

"All the same," he said, "they'll lay for you. You'll be a marked man."

"We are marked," Kit said proudly, a strip of pink sticking-plaster across the corner of his mouth. "And not with acne, like those B.Fs."

To Clement, not so much older than they, both of them seemed like children: even Jo. Their joys, their miseries, were so apparent, so openly on display. Neither of them, he thought, had given a flick of their imaginations to what he had been through since Georgina's leaving and her return—because he had not cared to make this apparent. He was happy again: he believed she meant to stay with him this time; and though he was aware that he would never be able to trust her, he wanted her on any terms. He knew the reason for her sensuality: she found the sexual life so difficult that she could not resist the quest for some man who might make it entirely easy for her; this was her dream, the end of her rainbow. He knew that he himself came out best from her experimentations and also that she had been telling the truth when she said she found him more "interesting" than other men: more interesting merely as a companion. She was not easily seduced by obvious charm, obvious beauty. She was one of the few women he knew who was not charmed by Kit. All the same, he would watch in anxiety for the sideways slide of her eyes, a certain ominous freshening of her voice when greeting someone whom he had not met, a certain jauntiness of step, like the sudden skip with which a child prepares to spring off across a park.

He was far more appalled by the state of the world than most of his friends, more instant in apprehension. As a journalist, with increasing responsibility, he knew more. Though he never minded a fight, though he was aware that within a year he might welcome a war with Germany rather than the alternative (which could only be gradual conquest without one), he was sickened by physical cruelty, and by the degradation of the individual. He had been in Germany and had seen some of this for himself. To other press-men he talked freely of these things: but to Kit, Jo and his pub acquaintances he said little, unless they urged him to do so. Vague-ly, he felt they were too young for it. Yes, even Jo.

Phil came in and admired the fighters with manic enthu-siasm.

"You always say you're a coward, Kit, but you're a bloody hero! Me, I'd have run a mile—I swear it. You know me. I'd always pass by on the other side."

"You'd better let me look at those arms," Clement said to Kit, who was wincing in a blue bath-towel. When he had done so, he said Kit had better go round and see the doctor. "I'm not sure that shoulder isn't dislocated."

"Wouldn't I know if it were?"

"I've no idea. But get dressed, and I'll take you."

They returned half an hour later, Kit more martial than ever with his arm in a sling. Clement had thoughtfully bought a small piece of steak for Jo's black eye.

"Do let me have a sling, too," said Phil, "you'd never give me away. Or at least, some sticking-plaster!"

"Not a bit of it. This is for Jo and me. Polly is going to love my sling, but you must all assure her it wasn't done in drink."

Within a fortnight, Kit and Polly had decided to get married and had put up a notice in the register office. What they would live on neither seemed to know nor to care; Clement had gone back to live with Georgina, Phil had been pushed out, and was angry about it. Polly would manage Clement's share of the rent and find Kit some publisher's reading. In the meantime, she said, she would make the place habitable. "You realize that I shall have to clean you up? I couldn't live in a pig-sty."

"Not even with me?"

"Not if there's not the slightest need for it. If there were, I would."

"I knew from the beginning," said Kit. The light in the kitchen was hard, beating down upon them as if they were actors in a play.

"So did I. It is most remarkable."

They returned to the living-room, where they held each other gently, in the grip of an emotion almost too deep for sexual passion. She told him, in a matter-of-fact way, that she had had two lovers: which brought him not the slightest sting of jealousy.

"And soon you will have had three. When we're married. I want it to be like that."

She asked him gingerly about Alison, if it were really all over. Yes, he said: over and dead.

"You hurt her very much. That makes *me* feel guilty."

"You needn't. She will marry Jo," Kit added, as if that settled everything, though he knew it to be untrue. He needed the whole affair out of their way, bundled out of sight. "They'll get along like a house afire."

He heard the sudden change in his own voice, and he got up. "Come on, we're going out. If we stay here I shall break my good resolution and I won't do that."

They walked down to the Embankment. The night was still and starry. They breathed the river smell, watched the lights switch color beneath the bridges.

He said, "We are quite secure. Do you realize that? Nothing will ever change for us."

Chapter Three

HE AND JO WERE SITTING IN THE PIER HOTEL, PLANNING THE WEDding, which was to take place in the following week. This was not one of their usual haunts; they had chosen it because they wished to be undisturbed. Polly would join them later.

"Just you and me and Clem and Georgie," Kit said. "It seems awful not to ask Alison, but it would be more awful if I did."

"Of course you can't ask her," Jo said, and again felt a touch of the old anger which had been subsiding.

Kit was staying with the Maclarens, since Polly had brought what seemed to him an array of painters and was ordering the flat to her liking. Jo often wondered whether he had perceived, in her neatness and resolution, a resemblance to Alison: though Polly always appeared sunny and sweet, and to have nothing of Alison's violence of nature.

"I met my future father-in-law yesterday," Kit said. "We had tea in the House of Lords. God! I was terrified, and so determined not to show it. I was awake half the night before, wondering whether I should offer myself just as I was, her own to be, or borrow Clem's best shirt and present myself suitably altered for the

79

occasion. But Polly said her father might as well know the worst at once, and that provided I washed properly, I wasn't to begin with fruitless deceit. Her very own words."

"What's he like?" Jo felt, despite his radicalism, a twinge of envy. He had never seen a Lord, except for a Red one or so, on public platforms.

"Abnormally tall: I hadn't expected that. Shabby as I am, but lordly-shabby. Weak eyes, no chin. Polly must have taken after her mother. Weak voice, as though he'd got laryngitis; perhaps he had. Very casual. Looked at me with only momentary horror—I did see him blink—said, 'How'd'do, hope it all works out for you both,' and then led us through that awful, muffled, crimson place, like a whale's gullet, to eat crumpets. He didn't offer us any cakes, not that I wanted any. I suspect him of being a miser, anyhow I do hope so, because one day Polly might find ten boxes full of doubloons under the floorboards. He rambled on about taxis, repairs to the roof, not being able to do much for us. His lordly name is Wantage, but he lives in Suffolk. We're to go down for a couple of days after the wedding."

Jo was jealous, afraid that his friend would be translated into a different world where he could not follow. He had a vision of Mildred and himself pushing the bath-chair across the common on a bleak Sunday morning, his mother in her best hat, grey felt, with a salmon-pink cockade.

"I keep brooding," Kit said, "on the word 'much.' "

"What do you mean?"

" 'Afraid I can't do *much* for you.' So it stands to reason that he might do just something, though Polly's dubious. Yes, he did say 'much,' " Kit mused.

A large shadow fell across them.

"I say, you fellows!"

It was like the opening of a boys' school story.

Deeply reproachful, a red-shaded lamp reflected in each of his lenses, was Nigel Dobson.

"You two were having me on a string that night we met. I've heard all about you now. Was that a thing to do?"

"Oh lord," said Kit, "you do draw the most extraordinary conclusions. I don't remember any string, cross my heart I don't."

"Well," Dobson said, sitting down heavily, "I hope I can take a joke as well as anybody else." He laughed rather mirthlessly. "What'll you have?"

Kit, who always repented his jokes a little and sometimes repented them quite deeply, could see no way of getting rid of him.

Jo, who did not repent this time, said that as a matter of fact they were talking business and hadn't finished yet.

"What sort?" Dobson asked simply. "Not, of course, that it's anything to do with me."

"Kit's getting married. We were discussing that."

"Oh. I see."

Dobson rose. They thought he had really left them, but in a moment he returned with drinks: double gins. "We must celebrate. But I say, Mallings, are you really sure of what you're doing? I'm always coming to the brink myself, then drawing back."

"Or perhaps the others draw back," said Jo. He had slipped back into the villain part which, combined with Kit's different approach, had brought them relief from an evening of remembered tension.

The big man looked at him. "You know, you do seem to me on the hostile side. What have I done? Have I upset you in any way? Do say straight out if I have."

Kit, resigned, replied for Jo that there had been no offense given—"And none taken," he added loftily.

"Oh, good." Dobson was easily consoled, since he was always ready to be. "Well, down the hatch! Yes, about getting married. It's a step to take."

Polly came briskly through the swing doors, bringing the night air with her like an invisible train.

"This is Nigel Dobson," said Kit, "a poet. Dobson—that is, if you persist in calling me Mallings—this is Paulina Reston, whom I am going to marry."

"In that case," Dobson said gravely, with a deep bow and a sacerdotal air, "there is nothing more to be said."

"Why is there nothing more to be said?" Polly sat down, in her usual firm and dainty fashion, her back straight.

"Not now that I have seen you. May I offer you both my sincere congratulations?"

She thanked him and accepted a drink. Laying her hand on

Kit's she said, "Father seemed to like you as much as he likes anyone, but he thinks we'll come to no good."

"The problem about marriage," Dobson said, "is children."

"Not necessarily," said Jo.

"Oh yes, eventually. In your shoes, Mallings, I wouldn't rush
into a family too quickly. Not in the present state of the world. Or
until you've found your literary feet."

"We heed the advice," said Polly, who had rapidly summed
him up, "and of course may take it. It does, of course, depend
quite a lot on Kit's literary feet. What poetry do you write?"

He blushed. "It would sound pretentious if I offered to read
one of my things to you, I suppose."

"Some other time," said Jo, "we'd enjoy it." He looked ostentatiously at the clock.

Kit, soft-hearted in matters of casual friendship, felt quite
ashamed of him. He was going too far. His own heart was filled
with pity for Dobson: would it have been so pitiful if the man had
not worn such large glasses? "I'll tell you what, read us just one,
but not a very long one, because we really have got a lot to talk
about."

"Mine aren't long." Dobson took a sheaf from his pocket.
"I'm a lyric poet, in the manner of Heine." He hesitated. "Or, possibly Rilke."

They listened politely while he read them six pedestrian
quatrains about the coming of love in the spring. When he had
finished, he took off his glasses and polished them with a piece of
chamois-leather. His work had moved him deeply.

"Fine," said Kit. "You keep it up."

Polly said she liked it very much indeed, and she thanked
him.

Jo announced that he was an auctioneer and estate agent, and
didn't know one poem from another.

"That's a taste which can be developed," said Dobson, "if one
really puts one's mind to it."

Again Polly thanked him for the reading, but she thought
they had better go now.

As they rose, Jo knew that he would come to like her, even to
champion her against Kit if ever she should need it: but he could
see in her, as yet, little but her freshness which, he thought, had
something of Kate Greenaway about it. Also, he knew the usual

82

ache of a young man whose closest friend gets married and must always, in a fashion, leave him.

Dobson went with them to the door. Just as they reached it he said to Kit, "I'll tell you who I met last night—Alison Petrie, the novelist. I think she's superb. Now, you ought to take a leaf out of her book, Mallings. That last story of yours—"

They left him standing in the doorway, any further words borne away on the soft and rainy wind.

"For God's sake," said Jo angrily, "if ever I meet that oaf again—"

He was angry, all of them were embarrassed. Yet suddenly they began to laugh and could not stop, the half-rapturous, half-agonizing mad laughter that is sometimes the only possible response to the impossible situation.

When they had managed to calm themselves a little, Kit said, "A week's time, my girl! We are in the very fury of love, clubs cannot part us—don't mind Jo, he's not really listening. We are, aren't we?"

She smiled at him, and he put his arm round her waist.

"But one thing I'm going to insist on. I'm going to have the old, traditional bachelor party, and you're not going to stop me."

"I'm not trying."

"All traditional, I want everything traditional. I only wish we were getting married at St. Margaret's, fully choral, you in white with sixteen infant bridesmaids all wanting to piddle at once."

"I don't," said Polly. "For us it would be quite inappropriate. But do let your party be a fairly respectable one. I refuse to marry some green, staggering, shaking wreck on the following day."

"You'll marry when I please and whom I please," said Kit, masterfully, "and the whom will be me."

Jo left them, feeling a little desolate.

When he got home he found his mother walking about inside a contrivance like a small steel dock with rubber heels.

"What do you think about that?" Her face was bright with exertion and pride. "Millie got it for me today."

"Where's Millie now? Ought you to be trying it by yourself?"

"Oh, I'm here," said Mildred, coming in with a tray. "Not so far away. Go on, tell us the gossip of the big city."

This request irritated him for the moment, in the way he

had been irritated as a child when, coming back from a party, he would be interrogated as to precisely what he had had to eat. Yet this was a momentary fret, after which compliance came easily. After all, where was he more at ease than here, with these two women, in this atmosphere that even now bore the smells of his childhood, cocoa, brass-polish, York ham, Bovril, biscuits, lavender-water, and a peculiar kind of pink face-powder scented like cachous? Whenever he came home to it, "the wild life" faded a little and he knew earth solid under his feet.

He told them Kit's wedding-day was fixed, a week from that day.

"Well, well, well," said Bessie. Abandoning the contrivance, she asked Mildred to help her to a chair.

"A little dock," said Jo.

"No harm in that. I'm before the bar of heavenly justice, or getting on that way." Bessie was jovial. "Not guilty, m'lud! Well." She folded her hands in her lap. "So it's all settled."

"I'll be at the heavenly bar before you will, at the rate you're going," Jo said.

"So they're settled. Yes. Good luck to them both, I say, if they want to take the risk. When they're through their first raptures, you must get them to come and see us. I miss my little Kit," Bessie added tenderly.

"He comes here out of charity," said Mildred drily, "though I wouldn't say there wasn't niceness in it."

Yes, there was niceness: otherwise there would have been no charity.

"And Alison. What's happened to her these days? Now that's a thoroughly good girl, no side to her." Bessie nodded.

Jo said that she had taken her annual holiday early and had gone to her parents in the country. He did not tell them she had gone because she could not bear to be in London while Kit was being married.

"I don't suppose we're such englamored company that they can't help seeking us out."

"Now, Millie!" We're good enough company for most people, I should have thought. At least, we try to keep our end up."

"Jo's friends keep their ends up without trying."

He thought, for a depressed moment, that it was true; then he thought: But I don't have to, either. His spirits rose.

84

"You're as sour as a lemon tonight, Millie. What's got into you? The kids trying?"

No more trying than usual, she said, adding that she hated children, poor little beasts.

With Mildred, as with Clement, suffering was not apparent. Perhaps this was her misfortune. They had all joked about her auctioneer, and she had, too: when she lost him she was for a while what her mother called "grumpy," then had appeared to recover herself. She had not. Her nature was not so strong in love as Jo's, but it was strong enough for her to feel the dull ache of rejection, of deprivation. That day she had seen the man again; he had talked to her idly at a bus stop, and had gone away without the word of another meeting for which she had, against all reason, hoped. It seemed to her a positive ending, which the last one might not have been—quite. She was sore at heart, and trying to restrain the rough edge of her tongue.

"Come off it," said Jo, putting his arm playfully around her shoulders. She pulled away from him as if he had made an incestuous advance: then, realizing the exaggeration of her gesture, lightly smacked his head and went away, saying she had more to do than chat half the night.

Bessie put her tray aside. "Chuck me a cigarette," she said to Jo companionably, and his heart sank. When she was slangy, it meant that she intended to be confidential. For a second the years seemed to fall away from her: he saw the mythical girl she was always claiming to have been, and in whom he found it hard to believe.

As he lit her cigarette and his, he tried to tell her that he was tired, did not want to stay up late, had a heavy day tomorrow; but the sultry pressures of her will, of his family's will, overcame him. Like a drugged man, he sat down in the chair nearest to her own.

She said, unexpectedly, even though it was something she had said in some form or other many times before, "I suppose you know you're my favorite." She smoothed his soft hair, down to the widow's peak where, for a second, her forefinger rested. "People will tell you that mothers should have no favorites, but, I tell you, that's not in human nature. I love Millie, but she's not you. So I want everything for you." She stopped. "I want Alison for you."

He could not check his involuntary revulsion away from her.

"After all," she continued peaceably, "our Kit is out of the way. I know he was a rival before."

He did not speak.

"I'm putting my foot in it? But, dear, there are times when perhaps mothers must. I see most things, you know, tied as I am."

Yes, he wanted to shout, go on, go on, rattle the tin can! "Tied as you are!" But still he said nothing.

"I knew," said Bessie, "that you were always soft on her— Touchy? Perhaps I don't put it in the modern way. Don't be touchy."

"Mother, just stop it. Isn't it my business?"

"But you must see, now he's out of the way, that things are going to be far easier for you."

"For Christ's sake, even if you were right, Alison would never marry me!"

Less at his words, more at the note in his voice, she bridled. "Aren't you good enough for anybody?"

"No. Or maybe I am. Anyhow, she'd never think so."

Often she had him at her mercy: and when she accomplished this, it was by the deliberate reservation of speech. He could visualize her thoughts, flying around the room like a gathering of great, thick, khaki-colored moths, crowding out the brighter air. They beat upon him, were battering him down. What was more, he believed that she knew it; and so, surrendering, he spoke again.

"Leave her out of it. I'll find someone else, one of these days."

Still the silent moths beat upon him.

He jumped up. "I'm going to bed."

Now she relaxed, and smiled at him quizzically. "So I've failed, have I?"

"I don't know what you're talking about."

"If only confidence were a bit easier between us, dear. You're not happy."

"As the day is long. Come on, let me get you to your room."

She sighed hugely, and let him raise her up. "Give me my little dock, dear."

No you don't, he said, there was to be no more practice that night. Too late. Putting her sticks into her hands, he supported her.

86

"'I once had a dear little dock, dear,'" she parodied, in reminiscence of some old song he had never known, "'The prettiest dock in the world.'" She added dreamily, "Don't accuse me, Jo. I am only trying to help, and making myself a nuisance, as usual."

When he kissed her goodnight it was with a resurgence of affection, though he thought he knew precisely the degree of truth in her, and precisely the degree of fraud. Aging, fat, crippled, plain, she could still surprise him, jerk him out of one mood to another. There were times when he believed she was one of the most obtuse women in the world: at others, that she was one of the most acute.

Chapter Four

KIT AND POLLY WERE MET AT THE STATION BY LORD WANTAGE, WHO was driving a battered-looking Daimler with the glass missing in one window. It was a blowy day.

"Your train's late," he said, "lucky lunch is cold. Don't you expect Voisin's, anyway. I've only one man to do for me and his cooking is rudimentary."

Kit, who did not know what Voisin's was, said something polite.

"Why don't we go to the Blue Lion?" Polly argued. "I'm starving, even if Kit isn't. I want steak and kidney pie."

"That's just what you're getting," said her father, "cold, from yesterday. The meat's good, but Bareham hasn't a light hand with pastry." His voice might be weak, but his manner was not. It was that of a man accustomed to making arrangements and of permitting no alteration in them. He was, as Kit had told Jo, very tall: he crouched in the driving seat. There was nothing about him to scare anyone: if he had pride of lineage, he did not display it. During the very short drive he merely complained: of the price of petrol, the rottenness of the railways, the petty difficulties of getting one's shoes repaired, or an electrical fault righted, in anything resembling a decent space of time.

He drew up outside a long, yellow, half-timbered manor house fronting onto the wide main street. It had been beautiful and was so still, but with the beauty of an old woman to whom nothing is left but the bone-structure. There were great gaps in the plaster where elaborate pargeting had once been, and a long crack in the front door. The grass in the narrow front beds had not been mown. Wantage ushered them into a hall, stone-paved, bitterly cold, from which a fine broad staircase led to a gallery. All was shabby, dusty, run-down. Everything moveable had once been fine, from carpets to furniture.

"Throw your coat down anywhere. Polly, get Whatsit, Kit, a drink."

Kit thanked God for this remark, but Polly looked suspicious.

"What drink have you got?"

"Go in there and you'll find out. I'll hurry Bareham up. See if the potatoes are done."

"Since we're late, they should be," said Polly.

On top of a piano, in the moldering drawing-room, was a bottle of Irish whiskey.

"Father really has done us proud! I think he must like you after all, I really do. Otherwise, I can't account for it."

Kit tried to tell himself that he did not care whether his future father-in-law liked him or not, but did not really succeed. He still felt, even in these casual and grimy circumstances, like a fish out of water: but not so far out of the water that he could not easily wriggle back into it.

Like many mean and lonely men, Wantage occasionally displayed a burst of hospitality, and was always elated when he had made the effort to do so, as if it had transformed him into the man he had longed to be. Kit drank gratefully, and was equally grateful that in this house he had no real sense of hidden trip-wires. It was quite unlike Alison's, though it had the ghost of a grandeur that hers could never have.

"Well, look around you," said Polly. "I know it's a shambles, but we have one or two nice things left. That's an Allan Ramsay."

It was a large, splendid, dashing portrait of a young Scots girl, her nose faintly reddened by the winds, one hand upon a riding-crop, the other to her feathered hat. The feathers were pink, her cloak moss-green. Her back had a Grecian bend, and stormy clouds, half-fluff, half-crêpe, blew above her.

"Now this he hasn't quite brought himself to sell. And after we've had a no-doubt horrible lunch, I expect he'll show you his water-colors. He's still got dozens of them, and they all add up."

Apart from the Ramsay, the other paintings in the drawing-room were unattractive; blackened portraits of ancestors, not one of the least intrinsic value. "That is Aunt Virtue," Polly said. "Isn't it a lovely name?"

"We'll call our first daughter after her, unless you think it would be too much of a strain. For her, I mean." Kit looked out onto a wilderness of garden, with an arm of the river at the far end. Crocuses and the beginnings of daffodils straggled in long grass and strange shrubs flowered in a tangle.

"It was lovely once," Polly said sadly, "when Mother was alive. She was a great gardener."

Wantage came to call them to the meal which was roughly laid in a panelled dining-room, a Georgian addition to the house, almost as cold as the hall.

"Not wine!" she exclaimed.

"Why not? I've still a bit left. Made Bareham go down to the cellar for it, which he loathes. He's afraid of spiders. Funny, that, for a countryman."

Luncheon was as bad as he had warned them it would be, though Kit didn't mind. He had brought the rest of his whiskey with him, and would not have drunk the wine, except as a cour-tesy. Here, however, Wantage was determined. "Know a decent bottle when you meet it? Don't suppose you do, the young don't drink wine any more. Don't sip it—here, take a good mouthful and swill it round your mouth. Now smell the *pourriture*. You can smell it, I hope? Though you smoke too much to have a nose."

Kit, stung by this, said his nose was quite acute: he had smelled burning only the other month when his friends hadn't.

"What was burning?" Wantage asked in his feeble voice. He was interested in most things.

"Clement left the iron on the board and burned his shirt. Luckily, he has more shirts than the rest of us."

"Electric iron? You've more luxuries than I have here."

Polly laughed at him. "Oh, Father, if you could only see Kit's luxuries! Mind you, I've made a difference. We're quite habitable now."

He said, "She told me you'd had bugs. Very hard to get rid of, I'm told. I've never seen one. What do they look like?"

"Like apple-pips," said Kit.

"We've had beetle in the wood. Damaging little blighters, and make a frightful row at night. They knock their heads on the sides of their lairs. That's the trouble with oak," Wantage continued, "they breed in it, and so do the spiders, though I don't mind them myself. Bareham says you have to live in sweet chestnut not to get spiders, but who ever had a house with chestnut beams? Do you know?"

"Now, dear," said Polly, "you mustn't expect Kit to know the most extraordinary things. It's not reasonable."

Kit thought how charming she was with him, almost a Dickensian daughter, though he adored her own kind of gentleness, which was without sentimentality. She was unhappy that her father would not come to the wedding, but she did not press him.

"It's not that I've anything against *you,*" Wantage said earnestly to Kit, "but I'd feel out of place with your friends, that's all. Anyway, I don't care to make the journey more than once a month. You'll have a better time without me."

When the meal was over, he gathered up the bread remaining on their plates. "Come and feed the swans. I always do, at this time."

They went down through the wild and straining garden, the dry sticks of the shrubs scraping about them like the legs of grasshoppers, and through a rusty iron gate on to the bank. The stream was narrow, and a few hundred yards away curved out of sight. Moorhens darted in the shadow of the banks, water-rats splashed in the reeds. "We have otters, too," said Wantage, "but we never see them. Only hear them at night—'Chee-chee! Chee-chee! Chee-chee!' They hunt them round here, but I tell them I'll raise Cain if they let their damned hounds on my land. I like otters, jolly little things."

"Where are the swans?" Kit asked.

"You wait and see." Wantage raised his head, and with the

most surprising volume shouted, "Swan! Swan! Swan!"—repeating this cry three times. "Now," he said, "they'll show up. They'll come from a quarter of a mile away."

They were quiet in the grey, whistling weather, Kit with his arm round Polly's waist and his cheek against her own, quiet for a long time. Then, far away, round the bend of the stream, the swans appeared, father, mother and two patchwork cygnets, coming with their slow, stately lurch towards the rotten landing-stage, growing larger and larger as they came.

"I had a boat there once," Polly said. "It was a rubber dinghy, wonderful, except when the sewage rose. It does, sometimes."

Wantage addressed the birds. "Now, you swan, stand right back: women and children first! Here"—to Kit—"you feed them, too. You can give it by hand to the cob, but be careful of the pen. She's a hissing beast, and she can turn ugly when she likes."

But the cob and pen sat back on the water till the cygnets had eaten their fill. Then the mother ate the food thrown to her, now and again flapping and hissing in a way that alarmed Kit very much. He thought of stories about the capacity of swans to break a man's arm, though it was his fingers he was chiefly considering. He had a disagreeable image of his hand chopped off at the knuckles. He was so reluctant to feed the father, when the bird presented itself, that Wantage took the bread from him and put it on his own palm from which it was gently taken. "You see? He's as tame as a canary. He's a fine fellow, that one. Not many of them will do that, though I've seen it at Stratford-on-Avon."

They watched while the swans streamed away out of sight, disappearing like ghosts beneath a black overhang of leaves and shadows.

Polly suggested they should go in, since it was getting cold. For a moment Kit did not want to follow. He was feeling at last the magic which had eluded him that day until now, a magic compounded of his love, the strangeness of the garden, the decaying house, the stately birds who had come a quarter of a mile at a cry. As they walked back towards the house, he tried to catch it all in a trawling net of words.

When they were indoors, and Bareham had brought in a scuttle of fresh coal, the old man (for Polly was the child of his middle age, conceived by an enormous effort of will and so a dream-like figure to him ever since) looked at them with a strange grudging-

92

ness. "Well, I suppose I shall have to think about a wedding present."

"That's not necessary, sir—" Kit began manfully.

"You can't call me sir forever, and I won't be called Father. You'd better follow the modern manner and call me George."

Kit suppressed an impulse to hilarity. Yes, he would eventually call the old boy George, but it would be difficult to make a beginning.

"Best thing I can do is to give you a picture."

Polly stood up and hugged him. "Thank you, dear. We'll take the Ramsay."

"No, you don't! I've got to keep something in case of need, and anyway, I like it myself."

She told him he was an old ass: of course she hadn't meant it.

"I never know when you mean things and when you don't." His voice was even weaker now, as if calling the swans had almost severed his vocal chords. "Besides, if I took it down, it would leave a beastly white patch on the wall."

"Don't be silly. You're going to leave it to me, anyway. You know I'd never take it from you now."

He rose, so tall as to stoop when he passed beneath a beam.

"You'd better come upstairs, both of you. Kit can see my water-colors, early English. Nice lot. Bought most of them for a song."

They followed him up the staircase, which would have taken a carriage and pair, and into the gallery, well-lit by a window, an addition of thirty years ago, which dropped the whole length of the house. Beyond it, the garden swayed, scraped and whistled in the rising wind. That night there would be a gale.

He had an excellent collection of more than a hundred drawings, though there were gaps here and there where he had made sales, and he had never bothered to realign the others. Kit, though he pretended a liking for pictures, had no knowledge of them and small visual sense. "That's a beauty!" he exclaimed at random, pointing to a dull romantic landscape of rocks and waterfalls under a leaden sky. He felt Polly nudge him, as if she would prefer him to keep quiet. She moved along ahead of him, peering at the drawings rather more like a valuer than a lover of art, and he saw Wantage smile a little beneath his grey moustache.

She stopped before a view of Rome, tan-colored and blue. "Two pictures?" she coaxed.

"Damn it, it depends which!"

She moved on again. "I'll have this one."

It was a Cotman, small, serene.

"Oh, all right, if that's what you want."

"And"—she moved back to the view of Rome—"this."

"Look here, Polly, that's my last Sandby!"

To Kit it seemed a boring picture. He found himself staring at another one, without seeing it.

"Oh no, my boy," said Wantage, "not the Birket Foster."

"I was just thinking of that myself," Polly murmured.

"No."

"Then the Sandby and the Cotman."

"You can't have both."

"One, then. The Birket Foster."

"Good God, girl, you haggle like a Jew!"

She came to hang on his arm. "You mustn't say that, darling. It is the heedless anti-Semitism of your generation. It's the last thing you can afford nowadays."

"You know perfectly well what I mean."

"So, the Foster?"

"No! The Sandby and the Cotman, if you really must."

"Done!"

With the bizarre formality of the Gryphon and the Mock Turtle, they joined hands. They might have been about to dance a quadrille.

Polly and Kit left after tea-time, though not after tea, as Wantage did not seem disposed to give them any.

"I'll run you to the station," he said, in the semi-questioning tone of someone who does not wish to do something. Polly said he need not. It was only a short walk. She had the pictures packed under her arm.

As they stood on the doorstep, he said, "When I see you again, you'll be married. Hope it works out for you. Good luck, anyway."

Then he said something else. "I know you're going to sell those two, Polly, and probably buy junk with the proceeds. I'd feel bad about it, except for that man Hitler. If we go to war with Germany again, those things are safer out of your hands, with

94

bombs and all that. Rather have the money than see them destroyed. I don't trust the man Chamberlain. Never mind about Baldwin, it's Chamberlain you need to watch."

"You see," said Polly, as they went down the rutted path past the Men's Club and the children's playground, past the wooded twin hills on which stood the remains of a Norman castle, "he is a very strange old man. He is a radical by instinct, yet he wouldn't believe it if you told him so. He is always quarrelling with other old peers about it. Sometimes I have a dreadful feeling that he has second sight."

Kit said it didn't seem like second sight to him to see what was happening to Europe.

"For us it wouldn't be. But for him?"

"I like him a lot. Do you suppose I shall ever manage to call him George?"

"I'm afraid I did some very hard bargaining. But we shall need some money, my darling, we really shall."

Kit wondered again whether he was a miser, and he voiced the thought.

"No," said Polly, "so if you're marrying me for expectations, you may get that idea out of your head."

They stood still for a moment, to stem the force of the wind.

Kit was a selfish man in many respects, who had been ready to sacrifice anything or anyone to his work. Yet he was entirely without greed, with no love for money, wanting it only for the bare necessities that made work and beer possible. His inner life, outside of that work, was a curiously unreflective one: everything that was there he devoted to the service of his writing. He had never loved wholly before, as he believed he loved now, and he was bemused by the richness of the new experience: therefore Polly's idle joke upset him a little.

They stood together on the little station, the flowerbeds just beginning to prick up into spring, two small people, rather more incongruous together than they knew. The porter stared at their backs, his gaze travelling down the neat one and the baggy one. Polly he had known from a child; her choice of companion puzzled him.

The train was signalled. It could be heard far along the branch line, coming from the next station: the wind drove the sound before it.

Kit said, "You didn't mean that, did you?"

She was bewildered. "Didn't mean what?"

"Marrying you for expectations."

She began to laugh helplessly. "My poor boy, you have spent an entire day amidst the tumbledown. He can't even give me a modest check for a wedding-dress, beyond the very modest ones I get at Christmas and birthdays. He is even hanging on by his toe-nails to pay Bareham, who merely purports to look after the garden, but has screwed him into paying the basic wages of an agricultural laborer, which go up and up and up. No, you'd better love me for myself alone."

The train came in and they found an empty carriage smelling of dust and mice.

"Only six days," said Kit.

Chapter Five

THE BACHELOR PARTY HAD BEGUN EARLY BECAUSE CLEMENT HAD A job to do in Scotland and would have to take the night train, Georgina meeting him later at King's Cross. He, Jo, Kit, Bobby Price, and two brothers, Geoffrey and Roy Beach, had already visited the Fitzroy and the Marquis of Granby and were back in Chelsea.

Kit was joyful. He felt as full with congratulations and admonitions as a cat with fish, Polly a dream to him, but a delightful one. He did not need her reality now, not in the last moment of his freedom. Not that he meant to be less free when they were married: she was docile, he would make her happy, she would allow him to be happy in his own way. Jo was joyful, too, if sensible to the fact that he had better take care: even though he was to spend the night with Kit, he wanted to be quite sure of getting there on reasonably steady feet. As it was, he saw the distance from the King's Road to Tedworth Square as a shining of infinite miles by moonlight, each yard of which must take ten minutes to traverse. It was nearly closing time: they were all to finish the party at the flat.

They had talked themselves out on the subject of weddings and had turned to literature.

"Tolstoy," said Clement, who always appeared to be sober even when he was not, "is the greatest of all."

"Pierre and his white hat on the field of Borodino!" Jo exclaimed, and did so with undue emphasis: in their society he could never quite rid himself of the need for over-stressing.

"You haven't had my family life," said Bobby Price tenderly, "in a back-to-back in a mining village. Now, the birth of Levin's child is for me—"

"Not, however, born in a back-to-back," said Clement.

"What does that matter?"

"Makes a difference, a certain difference," said Geoffrey Beach, who was rather stout and sexually attractive.

"I'm damned if I see the difference, boy. It's a universal experience."

"Not," said Roy Beach, thinner than his brother, more clever, a producer of radio plays, "if you consider the first thing a father would think about—a father in Levin's world, a father in Bobby's back-to-back. In the second case, he'd be thinking, How the hell are we going to keep him? None of your repulsion and responsibility stuff."

"Oh, shut up," said Bobby, "he'd have had enough time to think about that in the preceding nine months."

"I forget Levin," Kit mumbled, "who's he? I liked the man on the window-sill." He looked round him with a kind of fury which seemed to embrace the whole bar. "Man on the window-sill! *You* know, man on the window-sill!" Rage sent up his color. Why were they all so stupid? He could not, himself, remember the name of the man on the sill. But why the hell should they all pretend they didn't know what he was talking about? He suspected a conspiracy.

"Dolokhov," Clement said suddenly, as if he were indeed sober. His mind was on Georgina. They would make love on the train as it roared through the darkness. They both liked to make love in unusual places. He could imagine the rhythm of their bodies in time with the rhythm of the wheels.

Kit embraced him. "Yes! That's it. Dolokhov. You know. You understand. Sometimes I think, Clem, that you're the one who understands me most."

Jo was not at all jealous of this kind of thing.

Bobby, his nose more askew than ever, said in a high Welsh lilt: "He drank a whole bottle of brandy while sitting on the window-sill."

"Yes!" Kit cried. "And his name was Dolokhov. Everyone knows that. Not a living soul who doesn't know that."

Like many people in a state of drunkenness, he usually held to one name, or to one fact: in this case, a name. Dolokhov. Pride in memory, aural and visual, exalted him.

"A bear," he said mysteriously, "something about a bear. On a window-sill. Let's go back and try."

"I'm damned if you do," said Jo, "I've got to get you to the altar tomorrow, without a broken neck."

"Not an altar. 'A-a-way with all superstition. . . .'"

"You've got your references crossed, *bach,*" said Bobby. "That's not a wedding song. Please to save it for its proper purpose."

Geoffrey, who had a pretty tenor voice, now raised it and began, to a tune of his own making:

> "A bride, before her goodnights can be said,
> Should vanish from her clothes into her bed,
> As souls from bodies steal and are not spied. . . ."

He was a composer of film-music, modestly successful. The sounds he made were charming to him. He decided to set the whole poem and give it to Kit and Polly as a wedding present.

"Don't you talk dirty," said Kit, "not about me and Polly."

"Donne's not dirty."

"Dirty Donne, dirty Donne," Kit began to croon to himself, "dirty dung, dirty dung. You keep a decent tongue in your head! Let's go home now."

The lights were going out, the last orders had been called.

"I've got to get to King's Cross," said Clement. "I'm damned sorry I won't be with you tomorrow, Kit, but all good luck. Comport yourself manfully. I always did."

He left them on the pavement; he was glad to be gone. The prospect of Georgina was even more delectable now, and he hoped she would be in the right mood for him. He had been stimulated by this pre-Hymeneal evening, but now he had had enough of it. The other five linked arms, and sang their wavering way along the King's Road, between the lampposts of Radnor Street. Jo felt with relief that the night air was sobering him up, not making him worse. The sense of losing Kit, which had been with him most of the evening, no more than a hair's breadth of sorrow, but real enough, was giving way to an overriding sense of duty. Somehow Kit had got to be fit for the morning, and it would take him all his time to see that this was so.

They got up on the stairs somehow and into the flat that Polly had transformed. Even the narrow landing had been brought to a degree of elegance.

"Almost repulsively pretty, isn't it?" Kit demanded. "Don't any of you lot be sick on our nice new rug. There's always the sink."

"Speak for yourself," said Geoffrey. "Roy and I never are." He lurched, recovered himself, and demonstrated his stability by standing for a moment or so on one leg.

Jo was sorry Clement had gone. This wasn't, somehow, the right set. The Beach brothers were almost strangers. Bobby, however long they might know him, would always be one.

"And wipe your filthy boots before you come in here," said Kit, leading the way into the sitting-room, where Jo had earlier laid out beer and glasses.

It was a mild night. He opened the window onto the little balcony and the air poured sweetly in, ruffling the curtains which· had belonged to Alison's parents.

"A bear," he muttered, "we need a bear. Where the hell's the bear?" He shouted, "Where the hell's the bear?"

"I'll be the bear, boy," said Bobby, and with a rush and a growl made straight for him, heaving him back onto the divan. They were seized by a corporate silliness, all of them joining in the game. Kit, on his feet again, was a bear, too, chasing them round the room, which seemed to Jo not to contain five people but fifty.

At last, gasping and exhausted, Kit staggered away from them to the window and gave one last growl at the empty street.

"Now," he said, his eyes bulging, "what shall we do next? *I* know!"

Before they could stop him, he snatched up and uncorked a bottle of beer and swayed back onto the balcony.

100

Jo cried, "What the bloody hell are you doing?"

Kit had hoisted himself up onto the thin rail and was gripping the struts with his feet.

"Dolokhov! Dolokhov!" He began to drink, steadily, his body erect.

"For Christ's sake," said Geoffrey, moving forward, "someone's got to stop him!"

Jo held him back. "If you rush him, he'll fall."

Horror was suddenly upon them. It was like a scene in a nightmare, the small figure balanced on the rail, illuminated by the glare from the room, shaggy head tilted back, swallowing, swallowing. "For Christ's sake, Christ's sake. . . ." This was Bobby, as white as chalk.

"Don't speak," Jo muttered, "don't move, and don't follow me."

Dropping to his knees, he began to inch over the floor, slowly, noiselessly, out of Kit's range of vision should he, by this time, have any vision. He was conscious of the other men's breathing, which seemed to him as loud as the rush of the sea.

He was on the balcony now, crouching below Kit. It must not go wrong. Dear God in heaven, it must not go wrong. Rearing up, he grasped both of Kit's ankles and hung on with all his strength, shouting now for help.

Kit fell straight over backwards. The bottle flew out of his hand, smashing on the stones thirty feet below. Jo felt the strain of the dead and dangling weight, the agonizing pull upon his arms. Why didn't they help him? He couldn't hang on much longer.

Then they came out of stupor. Geoffrey had Kit's legs in his own grip, taking the burden from Jo. Roy and Bobby were leaning over the rail, groping for the arms, the shoulders.

"Heave!" Bobby yelled, and up Kit came, collapsing on them like a sack. Jo let go. He went out to the lavatory and was sick.

When he returned, Kit was holding court on the divan, seemingly sober and unshocked, merely reproachful that they had ruined his great feat. "Do you lot realize that you might have killed me, barging at me like that? God damn it, I might have been dead by now!"

Jo came to him. He was bitterly cold and shaking all over.

"You bloody fool," he said slowly, "if it hadn't been for us you would have been dead, with your brains splattered just where the rest of that beer is. And it would have served you right. You bloody fool, you silly, showing-off bugger!"

Kit blinked. "You're saying that to me?"

"Yes."

"*You* are?"

"Yes."

"*C'est Jo qui parle?*"

"If you weren't . . . if you weren't . . . so . . . I'd like to kill you."

Jo heard his own voice as from a long way off. His drunkenness had cleared away, but now he believed he was going to faint. Somebody was holding something to his lips.

"Go on, drink up."

It was Geoffrey, with a hip-flask. Jo tasted brandy and shuddered. He sat down beside Kit, who put an affectionate arm around his shoulder.

Kit coaxed: "A little drop for me, too."

"No. Jo's quite right: if he hadn't grabbed you, you'd be dead and the place would be crawling with ambulances."

"And since you're getting married tomorrow," said Roy, "the party's over. Come on, Bobby, all out."

Kit implored them not to go. Far from being over, the party had only just begun. He felt fine: he would be fine next day.

Jo, however, who had recovered himself, was firm. "Roy's right. We'll see you all tomorrow."

But this would not do for Kit at all. He would not let his friends depart like this. He was going to see them off, he would walk back with them to the King's Road. Though he did not look very drunk, he was rising to a manic state Jo knew only too well, for it was a state that would brook no denial of its own demands.

As they walked back up the street, it seemed to him that the walk down it, to the flat, had taken place hours and hours ago. He felt a longing for sleep so intense that it was strong as sexual desire or thirst in a desert.

Kit insisted on accompanying them as far as the corner of Oakley Street, where Geoffrey, Roy and Bobby caught their homeward buses.

" 'Tomorrow and tomorrow and tomorrow!' " he shouted after them.

"Bad luck," Roy called back, "get fined if you recite *Macbeth* in the dressing-room."

> "I'm going to be married today, today,
> I've been on the shelf for many a day,
> But I'm pleased to say
> That I've found a jay,
> So I'm going. . . ."

Kit chanted this at the top of his voice, remembering some ancient music-hall tune, later adopted as a regimental march, which had been sung to him by his mother.

Songs my mother taught me, Jo thought, and fell into the melancholy of weariness and of dread averted. All the same, he was comforted by the sight of his friend who, though walking carefully, was still managing to walk: and whose demeanor was more staid than the noises he was making.

"Let's go round by the Embankment," Kit said, "see the moon on the water. Looks round her with delight when the heavens are bare."

"No, you don't. I want to get you into bed."

"You haven't been *very nice* to me tonight," Kit remarked, in a strange spinsterly tone, slurring his words a little, "so I shall make you take a walk. Good for your health. Serve you right, too."

Jo, thinking it best to humor him, though with the longing for sleep beating in his head like a trapped bird in a thicket, began to walk with him down Oakley Street.

They had not gone far when they met a policeman on his beat. At once Kit made a rush for him, teeth bared, vigorously growling, and flung himself round his waist.

The policeman told him to let go. Kit embraced him more closely, pretending to slaver and bite.

"Look here, officer," Jo said, "I've got him under control."

"Then you'd better keep him under, sir, or there's going to be trouble."

The man was struggling to disengage himself. Jo tried to

103

help him. The growling had by now attracted a small crowd of onlookers.

Kit suddenly let go, fell to his knees and vomited over the policeman's boots.

"For Christ's sake," Jo said, "he couldn't help it! He's getting married tomorrow."

He had Kit in his arms, but fighting. He felt like Alice holding the pig, though more frightened. Kit was not a strong man, except in drink, but the quietude of his apparent recovery had lent him extra strength. He wrenched himself away, and with a flailing movement knocked off the policeman's helmet which rolled, blue and silver in the lamplight, into the scotch-broth of vomit.

"Now that," said the man, "will be quite enough."

They found themselves in the brisk, bright police station. Kit had slumped onto a bench and was sleeping. He looked very young and smelled appalling. Names and addresses had been taken.

"I can bail him out, can't I?" Jo asked.

After some dubiety, the sergeant agreed: and set a price of ten pounds on Kit's head.

"Can I use a telephone?"

This too was agreed: but when Jo was taken to it, he grew desperate. Ten pounds. From whom? He himself had ten shillings, Kit could have no more. Clement, the obvious person to ask, was on the night-train to Edinburgh. Bobby was not on the telephone; where the Beach brothers lived, he had no idea. Mildred? He dared not give himself away.

He did the only thing possible. He telephoned to Polly. Luckily, it was not late: even now, only twenty-five minutes past eleven.

He heard her voice, sleepy. "Oh, Jo, what is it? I was having an early night. Is anything wrong? If you want to bring Kit round, you simply can't."

Carefully, as moderately as he could, he explained the circumstances.

There was a long pause. Then she said, in a voice unfamiliar to him, "Ten pounds?"

"Yes."

"And I have to bring it to Chelsea?"

"I'm afraid so."

He heard her draw breath. Then her voice came, clear and silvery, "Will you tell the little sot from me, if he is in any condition to listen, that I have no intention of bailing him out? He may spend the night in the cells. It will do him good."

He had a vision of her, small, sweet-faced, the poppy-mouth set: perhaps in her dressing-gown—certainly so, and it would be a discreet brown one—her hair dangling upon her shoulders.

"Polly, you don't know what you're—"

"Yes, I do. And you are as much to blame as he is."

"Look, I don't want to scare you, but he was nearly killed tonight. It was a pure accident, but it did upset him."

"I'm sorry. Facts are facts."

"Look, you can't be serious! It was only a joke that turned out badly. You're getting married tomorrow."

This time the pause was longer. Then: "No. We are not."

"You can't mean that!"

"I can, and I do, mean it. I told you I would not have him arriving at the register office a staggering, green wreck. You must both learn to believe me when I am in earnest."

Were there perhaps tears in her eyes? Jo prayed that there might be, in order that she might be softened. But he was much afraid that there were not.

"Tell him," Polly continued, not sweetly, not icily, either, "that I will, in fact, marry him. But not tomorrow. He can spend his night in the cells and I shall come along and pay his fine, if you can get some information as to when the hearing is likely to be."

"Polly, let me tell you all about it. We were talking about *War and Peace,* and Kit played some damfool trick sitting on the balcony, and we had to haul him back. He damned nearly went over the rail. I was never so frightened in my life. I tell you, it was an awful jolt to him. Honestly, he isn't very drunk: it's delayed shock, that's all it is. Please help him, or he may never forget that you didn't—" He believed this was a cunning approach to her, but it failed of its purpose.

"Tell him I am beginning as I mean to go on. And, of course, give him my love."

Jo heard the click as she hung up, not a violent click which might have denoted anger, but a click that was business-like.

His heart hardened against her. What sort of girl was she, who wouldn't help a lover out of trouble, who would cancel her own wedding? She had been, he thought drearily, Kit's Little Nell: his gentle sweetheart. What had happened to her? He remembered the bright, oyster-colored eyes, the look of breeding he had so much admired, the look of gentleness. What the hell of a sort of girl was she?

Defeated, he returned to the desk. Kit was removed, smiling in his sleep, to the cell. A policeman lifted him with ease and appeared to be cradling him with the tenderness of the Virgin in a pietà. The smell trailed after them both.

"In a bad way," said the sergeant. "I wouldn't have his head tomorrow, not for a fortune, I wouldn't."

Jo was told to go home. His friend, he was informed, would appear before the Magistrates at ten-thirty.

He was so tired that he did not even bother to undress, but lay on the divan under an eiderdown. Ten-thirty. Wedding at noon. Well, there was still time. Of course, she had taken fright, but when she saw Kit next day she would relent. They loved each other. Nobody could doubt that.

The last thing he saw, before he fell into a graveyard sleep, was a vision of a curly black head dangling upside down over a vastness miles below, a vastness both grey and shining, stretching into nowhere, as vast as America by twilight, or as the great plain of Europe, under universal moonlight.

PART THREE

Alison Lost

Chapter One

JO WAS READING A LETTER FROM ALISON PETRIE. HE WAS SITTING
on the grass at the far end of the strip of back garden, his long
legs sticking up like a pair of callipers. Under the red hawthorn,
just outside the french windows, his mother sat in the bath-chair,
which was easy to trundle over the sill. The weather was very
warm. Cabbage butterflies flickered over Mildred's pansies, her
lobelias, her martial geraniums. It was Saturday morning.

May 26th, 1937.

Jo dear,

Yes, it's been a long time since I wrote, and I am ashamed
of myself. But I've felt for months that I was *walking under the
sea* and that the water is only now beginning to thin out and
get paler over my head. I'll be emerging soon, D.V., and we'll
meet.

How is your mother, and what sort of a time is Mildred
having? Above all things, how are you? I did think of you, even
in my ocean-bed condition. Duckford's like my book: it comes
out in September. They even "have hopes of it," which, com-

ing from them, is positively exciting. Here at home, I've been idling to a very bad extent, though I've given Father a hand with the interminable form-filling, visited the neighbors in my best Sunday-go-to-meeting frock, and ridden till my bottom's sore. Good for my health. I have also danced a good deal at grandiose local hops. We aren't County, but are just good enough to get invited. I have seen everything as through a wall of sea-water, which is vaguely unpleasant, yet in a way protective.

The day I thought Kit was getting married, I went to the cinema and saw the film round and round till The King. I couldn't tell you anything whatsoever about it, which, of course, would be absurd if you asked me to. I got an account of the reason for the delay from Georgina. It seemed incredible. But of course, when they did get married (I am still stunned by Polly's putting it all off for a fortnight!) I didn't know it, so I spent the day quite cheerfully polishing the book. One would suppose that I should somehow have *known* —just as one supposes a supernatural penny to drop if somebody you love dies a thousand miles away—but of course I didn't.

Damn me, I have just read back over all this and it looks as though I'm crying on your shoulder again. Don't worry, my eyes are almost dry, and the redness fading from my nose. Shall we go out next week and have a really expensive dinner? I am inviting *you*, as I have got my advance, so I don't want any stuffiness or hoity-toity in the matter.

I have been doing a lot of political work with the somewhat moribund local Party, though it makes Father furious. He and Mummy are good farming Conservatives, and will never be anything else. The bombing of Guernica was horrible. Jo, I am afraid we are going to lose that war. I go on hoping and hoping, trying to fight off despair. I shall be glad to be back in London. There is a dreadful sense of unreality about my part of the world. The cows moo, the sheep baa, the vicar calls, the skies are blue, Mother discovers a horrible plant called Stinking Crane's Bill in the coppice and is madly trying to uproot it. We might be living on a star. God help us all! I go on believing that He does, but it is time He began to show results.

Edna doesn't like the girl who took over my share of the flat and is ousting her, so I shall be moving back there probably next week. It will be a relief to touch earth again. Antaeus.

I've met one or two people you would like, including a man who is a regular in the army. He's thirty-three now and already a major, which is good going. Not stuffed at all, though not, as you may well guess, precisely *echt* Fitzroy. Also, there's a very nice girl called—poor dear—Fay, who has just come to live next door to us. Extremely pretty and great fun. She wants a flat in London as her parents madden her. They aren't Plymouth Brethren, but nearly. I might try to fit her in with Edna and myself.

So much for myself. Are you writing? If not, why not? Do you see much of Kit, or is the honeymoon still friend-excluding? God help me, I have hated poor Polly, but I don't think I'll do so forever.

By the by, I have a heart-sinking impression that Georgina is going off the rails again. Her last letter was full of somebody called Martin—very flippant allusions, but persistent. Poor Clem! He does live a knife-edge life, and she treats him abominably. Yet I like them both, though I don't think I should like her if she were attracted by anyone I wanted myself. She behaves with absolute ruthlessness. Then she wants everybody to love her just the same and is hurt when they don't.

Isn't the weather wonderful? I am writing this in the garden: I hope you're reading it in the garden, too. I have just heard a triumphant screech from Mummy, who must have hauled up another malodorous root, so I'd better stop. I'll ring you.

Love to you all,
Alison.

P.S. (1) Georgina says Polly got two pictures from her father as a wedding present, and put them up at Sotheby's. The two together fetched three hundred and fifty pounds, so it will be something to keep them off the breadline.

P.S. (2) I was awfully disappointed about K's book and know he must have been. It wasn't a bad reception, but it was shadowy. Of course he knew all the Fitzroy reviewers, but he *didn't* know Strauss, Gould or Spring, and since they didn't know him, he hadn't the advantage of a ready-made reputation. It is a wonderful book, I think, and I'm praying somebody picks it out later on. —"All right, Mummy, *I'm coming!*" A.

Bessie called out, "Jo, come quick! Such a pretty butterfly!"

It was a tiny blue one, like two adherent petals of a flax-flower, darting among white and yellow wings.

"Oh dear, it's gone away!" She spoke with real distress, as if she had lost a jewel out of a ring. "What a pity. Who was your letter from, dear?"

Long past resenting such queries, he told her.

"Has she got any news?"

He gave her as much of it as he wished to.

"Well, it will be nice to see her again. You must bring her over to tea. Where are you going?"

"Back to the other end. I don't like shade."

"Well, put your hat on, then. You might get sun-stroke."

This advice he ignored. Leaving her, he sat down to read Alison's letter again.

It was very like her: honest and generous, but with an undercurrent of violence. Some passages he read and re-read. He wondered, for a second, and with a prickle of anxiety, about the soldier, then forgot him. He knew a lack of generosity in his own being: he was glad she had been on the sea-bed, still submerged in her loss, not happy. If she had been happy in the country, he would have been afraid of those dances, those new friendships.

One sentence struck him painfully, and it was about Georgina. "I don't think I should like her if she were attracted by anyone I wanted myself." Now Alison knew perfectly well that Georgina had made some tentative attempts at flirting with himself and that she would have responded quickly enough had he reciprocated. Which meant that where he was concerned, Alison felt not the least jealousy. He supposed she never would, but did permit himself to day-dream, under the hot May sun, of how he might make her so. What about this girl, Fay? If, for instance, when they met, he paid marked attention to her, ignoring Alison in so far as politeness permitted? Sometimes these things worked. A triggering factor, maybe.

It was incredible now that she had ever let him make love to

112

her. Despite the memory of it, which both appeased and fed his hunger, he wished it had never happened. It had not begun something for them both, but had ended it.

The blue butterfly just touched the letter and sped away to poise upon a dandelion which had somehow escaped Mildred's attentions.

Mildred called from the house. Lunch was ready. Would he come and help her in with the bath-chair?

Jo had to bolt his meal and get to the Labour Party rooms as quickly as possible. There was to be a Spain demonstration on the cinder-path at half past two, and he had to finish painting a banner. He was there by half past one, breathless, feeling the gripe of indigestion: even so, he found Bobby and Sybil Rainey there before him. As he went in, they stopped talking. Both looked conspiratorial.

"Well," Bobby said, "we've got a fine day for it. Ought to have a good turn-out."

Sybil said she had got everything ready for Jo. The banner was stretched down with drawing-pins to the floor boards, paint and brush beside it.

"What is it?" he asked. "A 'Down with Franco?' "

"No. We've got plenty of those. It's 'Remember Guernica.' "

They sat and watched him as he worked, Sybil with the air of a prison officer.

"You're quite a hand at that," Bobby said, "professional, almost."

"It'll still be wet when we need it. We'll have to be careful getting it on the poles."

Sybil said she would see to that.

He painted in silence and he felt uneasy.

She said at last, "Look here, Jo, something's got to be done about Hatton, and well before the A.G.M. This is going to need organizing. The fact is, how many people can you get signed up before that? They'll only be wanted on the night, so none of them need feel we're going to work them to death."

"So you're going to pack the meeting." Jo kept his head down. Indigestion and disquiet were bothering him. "I can't say I like that."

"Look," said Bobby, squatting on his heels beside him, "you know and I know that things are too serious to have that brute mucking up even a small part of the organization. You're a soft-hearted chap. We're all aware of that, but—"

"This isn't the time for Jo's bleeding heart, or anyone else's," Sybil interrupted. "We've got to get a United Front, or there's no hope for anything. You know as well as I do that Hatton's only interested in keeping his nose clean with Transport House, in the hope they'll find him a constituency someday. Now then, who can you pull in? What about your mother and Mildred, for a start?"

"I can't do that!"

"Boy," Bobby said persuasively, "you must try, now! And what about the men in your works? Most of them think as we do. We want more of them in the Party, and not only the hard-shell unionists. Come on, you've got to try. Don't think I won't feel sorry for the man personally, but we've got to set our personal feelings aside. And you're with us, aren't you?"

"Of course I am," Jo said, and swore as he splashed some paint beyond the pencilled confines of a G. "You haven't got to ask. But as for my mother—"

"It's got to be anyone of voting age," said Sybil. "Anyone. The halt, maimed and blind, if necessary."

For the moment he detested her. Why did one so often detest people of one's own side? He looked up angrily, only to see her flush, and her face soften. Suddenly she looked almost handsome, and ten years older.

"I'm sorry. I didn't mean to put it like that."

He did not, for a moment, realize what she meant. Then he realized that the word "halt" could have been applied to his mother, though indeed she had not intended this.

"That's O.K. I didn't think anything."

But her softened mood persisted. She prowled round the room, pushing her hair into a peak above her high Flemish brow. "Oh, we've no time for the niceties, for the personal feelings. I don't fool myself about that. But there are times when I envy the people before us, the ones who could indulge themselves."

"Good God," said Bobby, "what's up with our Sybbo? You'll have me in tears in a moment. Jo, you've got to help."

Now, however, others came in, including Hatton, and there could be no further private conversation.

Almost before they had set up banners under the blossoming

114

trees, not far from the pond in which the little wooded island was alive with bathing children, a crowd assembled. The fine weather, certainly, had brought most of them out, for the sky was now a hot and solid blue and the water in the sun danced in formal golden scallops: but far more were graver, and more angry, than they would have been a year ago. The impression of "an outing" was less: the impression that genuine forces were gathering was far stronger, even on this one patch of meeting-ground, even in this single area.

Jo, in some ways timid, always dreaded the heavy heckling, the small Fascist contingents that would usually appear early on the scene. Today Hatton, who was a good and impassioned speaker, was heard almost without hostile interruption.

Several members of the local Communist Party and Left Book Club had joined the crowd. Jo saw Bobby grin to himself and he knew why: he was to speak next, and Hatton could not stop him.

Bobby, however, did not speak at once, but led them in "Riego's Hymn," which everyone seemed to know, and "Whirlwinds of Danger," which not so many did. There was the usual counterbawling of "United" and "Ye Workers," but the speech when it came, devoted entirely to the need for unity, was welcomed with something which, for an open meeting on the common, approached rapture. Was it, Jo wondered, going to be all right in the end? Were the forces they were symbolizing, on that beautiful day (once a day for punts on the river and dances by Japanese lanterns, a day for reading poetry to a girl under the trees, or driving down the Great West Road to the Ace of Spades) really coming into the ascendant? Would they be strong enough?

He thought of defeat, of loves that might never be fruited, of children unborn, of the darkening of the air by the huge black wings and the drumming of the earth underfoot.

He remembered the words of a poem just published, which had stirred him to the heart, and a generation to the heart.

"Tomorrow for the young the poets exploding like bombs,
  The walks by the lake, the weeks of perfect communion;
  Tomorrow the
  bicycle races
  Through the suburbs on summer evenings. . . ."

115

To bring that Tomorrow, was it so much to play just a small dirty trick on just one man? Such a small, insignificant dirty trick, in the face of the dirty trick of the whole world?

. . . *But today the struggle*—he noticed that some fool had folded the new-painted banner too closely and had smeared it. The fluff of flowers blew down from the chestnuts. He was not really a man for struggle. Yet he had to be.

He became aware again of Alison's letter, warm in his pocket. The bit about Kit's book. Was she really sorry? Was there a touch of malice in what she had written, a faint pleasure in something she might have thought of as divine retribution? He simply didn't know. She had been savagely hurt. It was credit enough to her that she was trying to wish Kit well.

The meeting came to an end with no more disturbance than a mild scuffle or so on the edges of the crowd. Nearer to his home than to the Party rooms, he asked Bobby whether he would mind taking the banner back. Bobby, good-natured, agreed. "Well, it's been a good meeting! Thumbs up for us."

Sybil, her color heightened by a degree of hope, touched Jo's arm. "You know I didn't mean that?"

"Mean what?" His mind was still on Alison.

"Oh, never mind." She turned away, as if she had been snubbed.

The sky was tinged now with violet, and the buttercups in the field before his house burned as if there were a spark of fire in every flower. The smell of the hawthorns was sweet, lead-heavy, faintly fish-like. He felt lonely and restless. He had been out rather too often that week to please Mildred: all the same, he felt he could not stay in that evening, listening to the wireless and to the run of his mother's voice, playing rummy. He wanted to walk by himself, to indulge in the dream-life so different from the "wild one." He would put her shadow at his side, making it, as he went, at first hallucinatory, then almost corporeal. He would talk to her as to a lover, they would quarrel (they never did, they were not close enough), and suddenly, under the trees dark against the sunset, she would fall into his arms. He would kiss her lips and she would give him the delicate tip of her tongue; it would quiver like a butterfly trapped in a web, beating not like a butterfly, but a heart.

116

It was always a shock, when such fantasies began to bud, to open the door of his own house and find reality hard and bare: in this case, Mildred squabbling with her mother. They squabbled infrequently, but when they did so it was with an upsurge of re-crimination for the old and the new, which never failed to horrify Jo nor to bring release and a kind of ghastly cheerfulness to both participants.

He heard them through the door of the sitting-room, which was slightly ajar.

"I don't in the least mind looking after you, Mother, if you wouldn't be so damned sweet about it. You're in pain half the time and I know it. Well, go on, yelp! But don't be patience on the monument, because I'm as much that myself as you are."

"I was not aware of smiling sweetly. And yes, I am in pain most of the time. Would it make you feel better if I did keep up a perpetual groaning? Do give me credit for a little personal cour-age, if you can't for anything else."

Jo, even in his distress at this kind of scene, retained some admiration for his mother's peculiar form of expression. It dated from the old days, when she and his father had been gracious hosts to people slightly, in the social heirarchy, more junior than themselves. There had been the musical evenings: friends brought their songs, secreted them on the hall-stand and hoped to be asked to perform. Two or three would have brought the same songs, but would not be deterred from performing by that fact. (He had once heard "Sing Joyous Bird!" sung four times between eight o'clock and eleven.) Jo, as a child, had shivered in pyjamas on the landing at the head of the stairs, listening entranced. There had been a man with a really fine voice, his name long for-gotten: "Ah, Moon of my Delight, that Knows no Wane!"

Then came the difference between a salary and a pension. No child ever cared much about a jolt down from one standard of living to another: yet few children failed to remember the day on which it came.

"Mother, you get so much credit, I wonder it doesn't choke you."

"Jo would never talk to me like that."

"Jo couldn't be bothered. He's full of his own life, whatever that may be."

117

"Do you suppose he drinks, dear?"

An earnest note, quite divorced from the tone of the quarrel.

"What's it to us if he does?"

"I shouldn't like to think——"

"He's like other young men. He enjoys a night out, and no more than that."

"You were saying, he couldn't be bothered. Do you mean he *would* speak to me as you do, if he wasn't?"

"Oh, for God's sake, Mother, you get me tangled up like a kitten in a ball of wool. Do stop it!"

"Did you say kitten?" Bessie inquired, silkily.

"What a filthy joke to make!"

"My dear girl, I assure you——"

Ashamed, Jo crept upstairs and sat before the foggy photograph of Alison for quite ten minutes before he noisily descended the stairs, whistling, throat-clearing, and so struck both women into bland silence. He had realized that for him there was to be no walk in the sweet-smelling sunset, no futile dreaming to end in a contrived, futile release.

Liver and bacon for supper, excellently cooked by Mildred, with fried bread and sausages. After the meal they played rummy, and Bessie won, hands down.

Chapter Two

ALISON, THE FOLLOWING WEEK, KEPT HER WORD: SHE ASKED HIM TO
dine at The Good Intent in the King's Road, but, she added, she
would be bringing two other people. Jo was desolate: this was not
as he had envisaged the meeting, not at all.

He said so to Kit, with whom he now had two nights out a
week, one in Polly's company, one not. This was a time when
they were alone. Since his marriage, a good deal of Kit's wildness
seemed to have dropped away: more often than not, he and Jo
went to obscure pubs where they could talk without interruption.

"Old Alison," Kit said, and shook his head. "Well, if I know
anything about her, the two other people are meant by her for
each other. So I shouldn't worry, if I were you."

His eyes wandered in the direction of a sailor leaning over
the bar, sleeves of his jersey rolled up to display an elaborate
scrolling of dragons and naked girls, blue and pink, with the word
MOTHER in Gothic script. "Look at that."

Jo expressed repulsion.

"No, you don't understand. Tattooing is the jewellery of the

119

poor," Kit said sentimentally, but loudly enough to attract the sailor's attention. He rose up from the bar and came to stand over them, a hulking man with a broken nose.

"Wouldn't think I was a pansy, would you?" he demanded, slightly teetering on the balls of his feet.

"And you wouldn't think I wasn't? Funny, isn't it?" Kit always had the courage of insolence.

"Come off it. Mind if I join in?"

"Yes, I do, rather. Buy yourself half a pint."

The sailor looked at him doubtfully, then went away.

"The jewellery of the poor."

"Oh, can it!"

"No, no, it's beautiful, really beautiful. I would like a butterfly on my wrist, but Polly wouldn't like that at all. Mine," Kit said dreamily, "would be pink and green."

About his book he was philosophical. Yes, he had expected more, and the thinness of his press had been a blow. "Also," he added, looking up lustrous-eyed and ruefully amused, "it was an effort for me to show my nose in the Fitzroy for a bit. I'd let them expect so much, damned fool that I am. I felt they were all sniggering at me, deep into their beers, sniggering up great belchy bubbles. Still, I shall survive."

It was two days before the meeting with Alison that Kit's survival was assured, and from the most surprising quarter.

In the United States there was a great non-academic critic, a man with the literary charging power of a rhinoceros. By sheer chance he had hit on Kit's book: and in *The New Yorker* had taken the opportunity to exalt it to the extent of two thousand words.

Alison, at the restaurant before her friends arrived, looked bright with pleasure: and all Jo's doubts as to her retributive instincts were settled at once. "If it had been me," she said, "I couldn't be more excited! He must have been having such a rotten time. You just look at this!"

Over a maidenly glass of sherry, which seemed to him appropriate for a more or less stately evening, he studied the review. It was heavyweight praise: it placed Kit with Beckford, with Peacock, with Firbank, on the stranger but long-enduring sidelines of literature. It was meant to make a writer, and Jo couldn't believe it would fail to do so.

120

"Does he know yet?"

"He will by now," said Alison, "these things get around."

"Will it mean money for him?"

"Not at once, I don't suppose. But it will mean an American publisher."

Jo recognized unworthy feelings in himself. Kit, failed, was still with him: Kit, a success, must go a thousand miles even further away than he had gone when he married.

Alison, he thought, was looking beautiful again: and he realized for the first time that during the worst days of her grief she had not really seemed so. She was wearing a little more make-up than usual, which suited her: a blue dress, with a darker blue string of beads, blue studs in her ears. Her hair, glossy, low curled now in her nape, tossed away the lamplight.

She was called to the telephone. When she came back, she said Piers would be a little late and had asked them not to wait for him. "Where's Fay, though?"

"I don't want Fay," said Jo, "I don't need her."

At that moment a tall girl came in. She had the face of a handsome bird, and much yellow hair caught in a ribbon and falling in a tail down her back. She waved to them from the door, gave her coat to a waiter, then rushed upstairs.

"She always does that," Alison said, amused. "She says she likes to be comfortable. Also, she tidies herself up with great elaboration."

The girl came down after nearly ten minutes and was introduced. Jo registered the fact that she was not quite a lady, as Alison was, and this put him more at ease. He had never thought about class when Kit was around: now, increasingly, he did. He could never seriously have expected Alison to marry anyone like himself, in a petty enough job, in a modest enough neighborhood —could he? Had he ever done so?

Fay Ellis had large grey eyes, brilliant enough to stare an eagle blind: she stared at Jo. "Nice to meet you." She raised her glass. "Cheers. What do you do? Alison told me, but it's slipped my memory."

He explained his job. She listened attentively, head a little on one side.

"But you want to write."

"I suppose I do. The urge gets feebler with lack of success."

121

"You stick to it," said Fay, with the air of one who knew everything about his past and future potential, "you'll be all right."

"What Fay hasn't told you," said Alison, "and I'm going to, is that she's had a great leg-up in her own job. They've just made her buyer for—" she mentioned a famous shop. "So that means Paris collections and all the fun of the fair."

"Let's go to Paris with her," Jo said, feeling serene and sounding silly.

"Like the end of Act II in a musical comedy."

"Thank you," said Fay, "but I don't want Alison stealing my thunder. This is my first chance to be Queen Bee." She spread her long hands across the table. "Yes, this is my chance." She gave a brief, brilliant smile. "But when I've established myself, we'll all go over together. Where's Piers? Do we eat? I'm famished."

They ordered the meal, Fay with great concentration. "I'm a hungry girl. I'm always hungry. And I never put on an ounce."

As they talked Jo learned that she was soon to move into Alison's flat, since Edna had found a better job in Manchester, which was her home town: that she and the missing Piers had had a mild love affair which was now fading away with no hard feelings on either side: that she was both ambitious and able.

She ate steadily, with open pleasure. She was, he thought, one of the most frank girls he had ever met, even franker than Alison, utterly devoid of Polly's prim elusiveness. Obviously, Alison liked and trusted her. But Jo hoped that the affair with Piers would revive itself.

It had begun to rain heavily: they could see the drops streaming like gold drops from a plum tree down the window-panes, hear people in the street running for shelter.

"He'll be drenched," said Alison.

"He won't," Fay answered. "He'll simply be later. I know him. He'll stand in a doorway for half an hour if he has to."

But in fact he came in at that moment, trench-coat glistening with water, raindrops on his hair which, Jo remarked, was prematurely grey. When the coat was disposed of, he came to greet them.

Piers Welford was on the short side, but beautifully proportioned. He had a dark, pleasant face, the mouth full and shapely beneath the slight moustache, the eyes rather light in color, steel-grey, heavy-lidded.

122

"I'm so sorry. I got caught up." To the waiter, "Nothing to start with, please. I'll have lamb chops."

His voice was clipped and clear. An army type, Jo thought, and was prepared to find him uncongenial.

"I don't mind you paying for the food," Piers said to Alison, "if I may buy the wine. Will that be all right?" To Fay—"Congratulations. Alison told me on the telephone. We'll drink to you tonight." He waved the wine list at Jo. "Any preferences? Suppose you choose."

"I don't know anything about it."

"Up to me, then. We'll have a bottle of No. 53."

"And how's the British Army?" Fay asked.

"A bit underpowered for the use we shall have to make of it."

"Shall we have to?" Jo asked.

The heavy lids fell, shot open again. "Of course. That's been obvious ever since we let Hitler have the Rhineland. Now we shan't be able to stop him, whatever my colonel may think."

They were all silent for a few minutes, depressed by these brisk certainties.

"Well," Fay said at last, "I hope they'll be able to stall him for a few years. I don't want him messing up my new job."

He gave her the paternal smile of old intimacy, which had left behind only a mild affection.

"I think you'll have time to establish yourself. What on earth are you eating now? Steak and kidney pudding? The girl's an ostrich."

"That," Fay said placidly, "goes uncomfortably near the bone."

"What's it like being a military man?" Jo asked, displaying a degree of bravado and once more sounding silly.

Piers considered this thoughtfully. He replied, "Not so bad, when you know it's going to be of some use. Drilling for drill's sake is a bore. I hated the army at first—I only went into it because my father wanted me to, and I didn't seem fitted for much else. But no, it's not a bad life."

"He looks quite harmless now," Alison said, "but you should see him at Aldershot."

Jo realized that she must have seen him there, and his fears flooded back.

"He becomes terrifying, all spit and polish, and when he

123

barks at the sergeant he startles the dogs and cats for miles around."

"S'truth," said Fay. "He manages to make an enormous amount of noise for a smallish chap."

He was now, he told Jo, on leave, staying with his father at East Grinstead.

"Just where you'd expect him to stay." Fay grinned, and tossed the tail of shining hair.

"She teases me. She wants to type-cast me, as they say in Hollywood. Alison, you are not to do the same thing. That joke goes a very long way."

He smiled at her, and she smiled in return. They held each other's gaze for a fraction of a second too long, and in that sickening moment Jo thought that he knew.

"Ah," she said, "I'm too subtle, too penetrating. I know your soul's really full of dark poetry, like Jo's."

"Of course it is. But I try to conceal the fact from my colonel."

"It can't be easy to hold radical views in your job," said Jo, who felt increasingly adrift. The evening had blackened: even the room seemed darker.

"Oh, but I don't, you know. I'm a Conservative, like my dad, but I'm not a Chamberlain one. We'll have to fight Hitler, and we've got to take such allies as we find lying around, the Russians included."

"What about Spain?"

"I don't want Franco controlling the Straits of Gibraltar."

"But you don't care about the Civil War itself?"

"Not much."

Jo glowered, and Alison laughed. "Do stop it! Piers is quite radical enough in his own way. A good many of his brother officers envisage some sort of deal, don't they?"

"I might," Piers said, "envisage one myself, if I thought there was a hope of this country being able to keep its nose clean. But that's not right-wing or left-wing politics: just bad politics."

Jo opened his mouth to protest: Fay, familiarly, smacked his hand. "Stop it. I am enjoying my food. I want a nice evening, not a political squabble. You let me tell you what women are going to wear next autumn. You in your small corner, Piers, I in mine."

124

He answered, his voice affectionate, but his eyes upon Alison, that he entirely agreed with her and was eager for the forecast.

To Jo, the evening seemed to drag on forever. At a quarter to eleven Piers rose: he had to catch his last train. He gave Fay a quick, brushing kiss, thanked Alison for her hospitality. He hoped to see all of them again, very soon.

When he had gone, Jo said, "You do seem to keep some odd company. Not that he's not a good chap. But politically—"

"I am out of Fitzrovia forever," Alison said, "so it doesn't matter to me what company I keep. I much prefer the product of Sandhurst to Bobby Price or Phil Christie. By the by, Jo, you can see Fay on her way. She lives out at Streatham."

He was bitterly disappointed, and when Fay went upstairs for one of her prolonged refreshing bouts, he said so.

"God damn it, am I never to talk to you again privately?"

"Of course you are. Don't be absurd. I'm coming to see your mother soon, anyway."

His temper rose. "Are you falling for that chap?"

"Who?"

"Don't say 'who?' It's hypocritical."

"Betrayingly so," said Alison, "or would be if what you suppose is true. But I don't think it is."

"I do think so."

"Dangerous of you. You might put the idea into my head."

"What would you have in common with a damned Sandhurst reactionary?" He had lost his head and he knew it.

Then he saw her smiling at him with a Gioconda smile, so knowing, so intimate, that he was silenced.

"My dear Jo," she said to him, "I love you dearly, but you are being a little obtuse, aren't you? Hasn't it occurred to you that Piers is almost certainly a Communist?"

Chapter Three

IT WAS ONLY ON THE LAST STEP OF THE HOMEWARD JOURNEY THAT he realized how surly he had been towards Fay. His thoughts had been too full to contain her at all; he had sat in silence at her side, on the top of the bus, all the way from Chelsea to Clapham Junction; now he was waiting for the bus that was to take her to Streatham.

And she was a nice girl, for whom he had felt an instant liking.

He said, "I'm sorry, Fay, I've been rotten company."

"Not rotten company. Just no company. But don't fret yourself, because I know what it's like."

He was defensive. "What what's like?"

"Well, you're carrying the torch for Alison."

"And now I may as well drop it?"

"I didn't say so. I don't think there will be anything between her and Piers. She may behave in a stuffy way when it pleases her, but actually she's not like that at all. She'd go dotty in Aldershot or Camberley."

The bus came along. Jo glanced at his watch. "Look here, I'll come with you as far as Tooting Bec. It's not much of a walk back for me."

She protested, but he was not to be budged. Once more they were jolting through the dark streets under the garish lamps and the flying rain.

"She isn't over that friend of yours," Fay said, "not yet. Don't you believe it. My, aren't we intimate after ten minutes? She isn't over him, though." She hesitated. "Look, I'm going to tell you what she told me, though I've no right to. A few days before she came back to London, she felt she couldn't bear life any more. So she got up and swallowed a handful of phenobarb."

Jo said nothing. He felt his stomach turn.

"Luckily, she then got scared stiff and put her fingers down her throat. So you see, she never really meant to do it at all. But she felt bad enough to convince herself that she did, and that's misery enough."

He said, rather angrily, "Perhaps you shouldn't have told me."

"Oh, I've got a reason. I know you're closer to her than anyone. That's why you ought to know these things. No one can really help her as you can."

She went on talking, but he did not hear her. He had a vision of Alison, in her bedroom in the country, the windows open to the dark and the scent of elderblossom, cramming the pills into her mouth and gagging as she swallowed. He shuddered.

"Yes, I can guess how you feel." Fay's voice broke in upon him again. "I'd feel like that, too. But the point is, *since* it happened she's been much better. It gave her a jolt, even to realize what she was capable of. Still, I don't believe she's ready for anyone else, even yet; not for you, not for Piers, not for anybody. And if your Kit"—her tone was scornful—"miraculously came running back, she'd throw *him* out with a flea in his ear. Here endeth the first lesson."

Jo protested that Kit was all right, that she didn't know him, she couldn't possibly understand what had happened.

"Maybe so. But anyone who can love as Alison can—they're rare animals. They deserve better than they get. I couldn't love in that way, or I don't think so."

He looked at her curiously, at the strong, avian profile, the geometric hair-line, dark-gold on the shining bone, a little darker where the roots emerged, so as to give the effect of a delicate pencil line, but then growing out natural and fair. "How do you know you couldn't?"

He saw the delicate rise of her lip. "Ah," she said, "you've just noticed my existence, have you?"

"Here's my stop," he said. "Will you be all right?"

"Of course. We'll be seeing each other again."

It was, despite what he had said, a long walk home. The rain had ceased, and the only sound in the world was the splash of a car through the wet or the patter from the dripping leaves. As he went, he charted his own moods. He might have been on a switch-back that evening, swooping up and down between light and dark at nightmare speed. Now he felt calmer, a little more hopeful because of what Fay had said to him. So long as Alison remained nobody's, she was not entirely lost to him. He began to think he had misjudged the long look she had exchanged with Piers: it was easy to misjudge such things. He felt an uprush of longing, almost a motherly one, to comfort her. If he had been with her that night in the country, if they had done no more than spend the evening talking together, she would never have made that absolute gesture of despair. Now he would have to keep it secret from her, how much he knew, and it was going to be hard. His mind, where Fay was concerned, fluctuated between anger and interest. He might use her to make Alison jealous . . . unless Alison had actually intended her for himself? But the old fantasy began to flare up: yes, it might be worth trying. Hadn't she always *used* him? Mixed with his passion for her, there had always been this touch of resentment. As he turned into the west side of the common, a prostitute spoke to him, quite a pretty girl, obviously not much more than an amateur.

"Want some happiness, dear?"

He stopped and looked at her, under a street lamp. She was very young.

"You ought to be home and in bed. By yourself. How did you get into this game?"

"You come and have a quiet chat with me and I'll tell you. It's what all the fellas want to know."

"How much?"

128

"Two quid. And I'm good value, dear. I know the way to heaven."

He gave her five shillings. "Run along."

"Come on, come on, I've got a little place not ten minutes away, ever so cozy and snug."

If she were not so young he might have been tempted. "And get caught for seducing a minor?"

She giggled. "A coal miner? What are you, a fairy?"

"Beat it. Buzz off."

She could not have been very hopeful, since she merely smiled at him and swayed off, her buttocks projecting, in the direction of the busy main road. He did not want her; yet he knew he would soon have to find a girl again. He was sexually hard-driven, far more so than Kit had ever been. For two months now he had not known even the release of solitary gratification, since this was inseparable from the image of Alison, and made him feel he had dirtied her. As he walked, he slashed at the laurels in the front gardens with his hand, sending up showers of spray to splash his own face.

He felt even more restless later in the month when he went for a meal with Kit and Polly at the flat. Their dove-like domesticity annoyed him: he found it hard even to believe that it was true. Polly, in pink lamplight, sat on a hassock at Kit's feet, her head against his knees. She believed, though she wasn't yet quite sure, that she was going to have a child.

"Me a father!" Kit cried. "I shall buy a waistcoat and a gold Hunter with a chain. And get a corporation to go with it."

He looked happy, in the exalted fashion of those who find themselves suddenly on a plateau where all is steadily sunny and there are no ravines.

"Furthermore," said Polly, "the news has stopped him from doing something very, very foolish." She added that he had been offered, for next to nothing, a converted barge on Chelsea Reach, and had thought how romantic it would be for them to live there. "But though rheumatism may be perfectly all right for me, it won't be for the baby."

"It was a beautiful barge," Kit said, "very glossy, blue and yellow, with a nice little lantern on the poop. Well, perhaps when he grows up a bit we can have one."

"Clement's on his own again," Polly said, "Georgina's gone off. Really, I do think she's a tiresome girl. I could never understand Alison liking her so much." She was the only one of them who could, and did, speak Alison's name with ease.

Kit stroked her hair, curled a strand of it round his finger. "Moral indignation."

"If more people were morally indignant with Georgina, she'd stop making her husband's life a misery."

"You'd never do that to me. Say you wouldn't."

"Not for such very frivolous reasons. Jo, you haven't seen the wedding photographs, have you?"

They were taken on the steps of the Chelsea register office, Kit rather sloppy, Polly very smart in a small hat worn over one eye. Jo stood behind them, looking like, she observed, the parson in *Jane Eyre*.

"St. John Rivers, I hope. He was coldly handsome." Jo pondered himself.

"Not a bit of it: Mr. Brocklehurst, the pillar of black marble."

"Oh, and of *course* there were bits about it in the papers."

The Hon. Paulina Reston, daughter of Lord Wantage, married today to the promising young novelist, Mr. Christopher Mallings. The ceremony private.

"Just think," Kit mused, "when the big boats went by, we'd have been rocked by the wash like babies in a cradle: we should have seen the green lights trail past us, at eye-level, and smelled the lovely mud and be moaned to sleep by the gulls."

"And coughed ourselves sick from morn to night." Polly got up. "Will Welsh rabbit be all right, Jo? I make it very well."

When she had gone into the kitchen, Kit told him that they would be going to Suffolk for the weekend. "Why don't you come, too?"

"Because Mother has a bloody old cousin called Dora at Haywards Heath whom she doesn't like at all, but she makes me visit her once a month on the grounds that she may die at any minute. This is my Sunday for the jaunt."

"Still, I suppose it gets you out of church?"

Not a bit of it, Jo replied; she made him go to Sussex in the afternoon.

"You are a damned masochist, you know."

130

Jo shrugged impatiently. Kit's total incomprehension of the life he led and why he had to lead it never failed to annoy him. What it must be like to be free, off the chain! There were even times when the idea of a war didn't seem displeasing. They would have to make do without him then, somehow. Kit's marriage had made him more aware than he had ever been of his own lot: recently, the peculiar smell of his house, which he had once accepted for its evocation of his childhood, had begun to seem to him distasteful, fuggy and stale.

The three of them had just sat down to supper when Clement, who still had his key, came pounding up the stairs and burst in upon them like an angry buffalo.

"Has that bitch been here?"

"Now listen," said Polly, "we don't know what you mean and nobody has been here at all."

"You know bleeding well what I mean! I mean, that bitch of a wife of mine. She left a note at the office saying that if I liked to pick her up at your place she might consider coming home. Why the hell should she be at your place, the damned randy cat?"

"Silence!" Polly said, "and pour yourself a drink. I don't suppose you feel like Welsh rabbit?"

He glared at her, his broad, handsome face suffused.

"I see that you don't." She gave him a mug of beer and made him sit down. "Now then, I do not know at all why she should want to meet you here. We have heard absolutely nothing about her."

"I'm not having her back this time! If she comes crawling in here, I'll drag her out again and give her the boot in the street."

"So long," Polly said steadily, realizing now that this could be serious, "as you do *not* make scenes with her in this flat."

"She can't have been gone more than three weeks," Jo said.

"Does that make it damned well any better? It makes a worse ass of me."

The bell rang. Clement banged down his beer, slopping it all over the carpet, and bolted for the door.

"You two go after him," Polly said to Kit and Jo, "this could just conceivably be dangerous." As they followed, she stationed herself on the balcony.

Georgina, carrying a suitcase, was on the top step, but at the sight of her husband she backed to the pavement and stood at bay. Jo had time to think how elegant she looked in the lamp-light, grey suit excellently cut, her hair swept up into a ring at the top of her head, before Clement grabbed her, seized case and bag, flung them into the gutter with both hands, and pulled her hair down over her shoulders.

"For God's sake, you lunatic—" she shouted.

He shook her violently back and forth till she gave a scream. She tried to pull herself free, but now he had upended her and was beating her as if she were a child.

"Don't stand there and do nothing," Polly called down in her clear little voice. People had come out on the balcony op-posite, curtains were withdrawn, casting rectangles of rose and yellow light over the stones, bystanders had gathered in knots at the corners of the square.

Kit and Jo pounced upon him, but he drove them off with his free arm. "Stow it, you fool," Jo cried, "you'll have the police here, next!"

Suddenly everything stopped. Clement released his wife and stepped back, breathing heavily. Straightening herself, she pre-tended to peer at him as if she were short-sighted. "Why, darling, you're drunk! How idiotic of you." Placidly she repinned her hair with what pins she could find and scooped up her bags. "Lucky neither of them's come open. I hate picking lipsticks out of the gutter. Let's go indoors now and talk it all over quietly."

Smiling, she went past him, past Kit and Jo, and into the house.

"Well," said Polly, coming to meet her, "that was quite a spectacle. Do hurry up, the rest of you. Is Clement still there, or has he retired from this earthly scene?"

He was shambling up in their wake, little expression on his face.

Polly, on the balcony, announced with clarity to the street that the performance was now at an end, and she swept the cur-tains across with a clatter of rings.

Georgina sat on the divan, accepted coffee from Kit, and ex-pressed annoyance that one of her stockings had laddered.

After storms, Jo thought, rooms seem very bright.

"Why did you come here?" Clement demanded. He was cer-tainly drunk, though they had not noticed this before.

132

"Because," she said patiently, "I left my key behind when I swept out of the flat. I couldn't get you at the office today, and since I didn't know when on earth you were likely to be back, I preferred to come to Kit's rather than shiver on my own doorstep."

"It's not your doorstep any longer," said Clement, "you haven't got a damned doorstep."

"I'm sure you'll think I have when you've got over your harsh feelings, darling."

"Where," he sneered, "is your fancy man? Does he need his teeth kicking in?"

She looked thoughtful. Jo knew she was afraid, and admired her for dissimulating with such skill, even though she was a little stagey about it.

"Well, honestly, perhaps he does: they're very ugly fouff teeth. That is, he needs it, though probably he doesn't want it."

Polly was now looking at her with open distaste. This ready denigration of a lover was not within her code of behavior. Kit sat silent and sparkling, enjoying himself.

"Stow that," said Clement.

"Look, I bear you no ill-will for making me look ridiculous in the street. In fact, I have never minded looking ridiculous. It's one of my strengths."

"You did look ridiculous. You looked the tart that you are." But there was now a very faint smile on his face, and Jo saw a flash of relief on hers.

She said: "I am going to tell you that I'm very sorry, and in front of *everyone,* which you will love. I made a silly mistake, and he was a silly man, and it is never, never going to happen again."

"If it does—" Clement began, and they all knew she had won.

Seizing her moment, she sprang up and put her arms around his neck. After a moment he kissed her, hanging onto her mouth like a fruit bat. Polly noisily stacked dishes.

They left almost at once. When they had gone, Kit said, "Well, that was a pretty scene!"

"It wasn't," Polly said sadly, "it wasn't even funny. And that false reconciliation was the worst of it."

He asked her what she meant, looking at her with the curios-

133

ity he reserved for her face alone, as if she were a book he found it difficult to read.

"They'll go back home and they'll make love," she replied, "just to forget how rotten it all is, and they'll talk about 'building up a new trust,' when they know they're going to trust each other as much as fighting crabs in a cage. I wish she'd go away and stay away. Clement would get over her if she'd allow him a decent time in which to do it."

"I don't like being acted at, either," Jo said, following an early thought.

She nodded and touched his shoulder in approval. "Nor do I. By the way, your supper's completely ruined. I'll have to open a tin."

Kit said urgently, "Darling? Love? Why do you always think people will get over things? I never would, over you."

She ran her hand through his hair. "Nor I over you. But we could conceivably be different from other people."

"Don't open tins," he said, "we don't want any food. Really we don't. We'll have some beer, and some bread and cheese. Is that O.K., Jo?"

But there was no more pleasure in the evening for any of them. He knew Kit and Polly were longing to obliterate, by real love, the love that had, must have, become synthetic for Clement and Georgina: all the same, he suspected that synthetic love is a powerful enough force for a lifetime, if two people are intent upon making it so. It could even be something more violent, more savagely sustained, than the reality, because more danger was inherent in it. He stayed for half an hour longer, out of the desire to make everyone feel that nothing had happened outside the region of farce, and then he went home.

"You're early tonight," Bessie called out to him as he passed her door.

Chapter Four

SUNDAY MORNING. A CHILLY GREY DAY IN JULY. THE SMALL PRO-
cession went across the common to the Congregational church,
Jo and Mildred in turns pushing the bath-chair in which Bessie
sat enthroned, wearing a new pink hat of her own unfortunate
choosing. Jo thought the three of them must by now provide a
familiar and rather silly sight. He himself was wearing a new suit
which had turned out to be too dark a grey: it made him look sal-
low and, as Mildred put it without kindness, like a churchwarden.

She was more tart than usual these days. It was months since
she had lost her auctioneer, and no other young man, as she derisively termed it, had come her way. Jo knew that, though she
was fond of him, she envied him his greater degree of freedom:
part of it, of course, he had shamelessly grabbed, on the grounds
that a man needed more than a woman, part of it was due to the
fact that he could always take a girl out when he felt like it. "It's
still the man who asks the woman to dance," Millie had said caus-
tically, "and it always will be. Don't talk to me about female
emancipation."

Bessie moaned a little as he jolted her over some rough

135

ground. "We really shall have to go round by the road next week."

"Nonsense," said Mildred, "it would take half an hour longer. You must grin and bear it."

"I may have to bear it, but I don't have to grin."

Despite this Sunday strain, which was never abandoned except in very wet weather, Jo had something to look forward to, since Fay and Alison were both coming to tea. He had not wanted both, but Alison had not cared (she said) to leave her friend to a solitary afternoon: anyway, two girls were better than no girls at all. In the past few weeks he had taken Fay out several times, which had not made Alison jealous, but had pleased her. She wanted him, he knew, to be happy: and indeed he usually had a good time with Fay, who was lively and good-humored and did not make him feel inferior. He was not in love with her.

They came to the church in Clapham Old Town which, presided over by a minister of exceptional imagination and oratorical power, had given Jo a misleading idea of the nature of most nonconformist chapels. The text of the sermon was as often from Shakespeare or Shaw as from the Bible: and there was a sophisticated literary and musical society which attracted people who would normally have sniffed at contact with the Free Churches. It was even smart enough to have allured a sprinkling of homosexuals. Jo hoped there would be the Vaughan Williams *Te Deum* that morning, which he enjoyed very much.

Mildred, as usual, was fretting about the Sunday joint, and praying that Mr. Cassell would not preach for too long. "It was burned almost to a cinder last week."

The organist was playing "Jesu Joy of Man's Desiring." A sidesman came to help Bessie out of her chair and stow it away in the porch. Pink hat bobbing like a lily on water, she made her slow way towards her pew, bowing with dignity to acquaintances left and right.

Jo was glad there was no Communion service that day: last time she had broken one of the tiny glasses borne round in objects like silver cakestands with holes in them, and the wine had stained her best coat. "I wish," Mildred had said at the time, "that I was C. of E. and could communicate at the altar rail. There's too much of a Nippy touch about all this." "Nippy" was the popular name for a Lyons' waitress.

136

Bessie, bowing her head, offered the preliminary prayer in her usual semi-audible fashion.

" 'And make Jo a good boy,' " Mildred muttered.

What Bessie had actually said was, "And bring Jo a good wife and Millie a good husband."

The *Te Deum* was not Jo's favorite one, but they did have a rousing setting of "For All the Saints." Nobody could have said this was not a cheerful church. That morning Mr. Cassell prayed for the writers, the artists, the composers—"for the creators wearing the flesh of man, who give us new worlds in which to take our joy." The text was from Spinoza, and the service concluded with the Sevenfold Amen.

"Thank heavens," said Millie, as they emerged into faint, sporadic sunshine, "that he cut it short today. The beef should be all right. We'd better look slippy, though, just the same."

They made good time across the big field, Bessie constantly protesting that they were throwing her around like a Guy on the Fifth of November—"which is just what I must look like, now I come to think of it."

Mildred told her she looked very nice.

"Our Kit," said Bessie, "seems to be an important person these days. Too grand to visit us now."

"Alison is still grander," Jo replied, rather huffily, "and she does. It's only because Kit's so busy and doesn't like leaving Polly much."

"Why? Is she having difficulties?"

"Not so far as I know. He just doesn't."

"Nose in the air," Bessie said firmly, "now those Americans are raving about him."

"They'll rave about Jo someday," said Mildred, speaking comfortably because they had arrived home and there was no disquieting odor from the kitchen.

"I hope I may live to see it."

There was the business of taking off Bessie's outdoor clothes, putting the pink hat back in its box, and escorting her safely to the lavatory. Then she had a small glass of sherry, her Sunday treat.

Tomorrow and tomorrow and tomorrow, Jo thought: he remembered Kit saying it. In the garden, beyond the windows, the roses looked tired and faded on their stems, and the grass dull.

The two cats (one had died), unsociable animals who refused to leave the kitchen, rushed up the trunk of a plum tree and bounced off it onto the wall.

His mother hoped Mildred had got a nice tea ready.

"I have not. These girls hardly ever want more than a cup, so they can keep their weight down. I've bought a Fuller's cake just for show, but they'll leave it, I warn you."

Fay had been to the house once before, and had affronted Bessie by eating only a scanty supper. "That skeleton," Bessie said, "could do with feeding up."

Like all people who receive few visitors, they were ready far too early, sitting in their appointed places on the edges of chairs, ears cocked for the sound of the bell. The Siva, which Jo had come to detest, was in its place above the mantelpiece and, having been given a good rub-up by Mildred, made itself far too conspicuous. A thin rain was metallic on the laurels.

"Do you think it might be a good idea to turn the fire on for a little?" Bessie suggested. "It's got much more chilly."

"Oh, Mother," said Mildred, "you know how stuffy we shall get if we do. Once there are five people in here, you can hardly breathe."

Jo, knowing Alison felt the cold abnormally, said it wouldn't be a bad idea to switch on just for ten minutes. This they did. The bars of the small electric fire turned grey, turned russet, sparked into red.

"Now," Mildred said fretfully, "we shall have to open a window."

The umbrellas of the young women, one black, one bright green, arrived punctually at the gate and were snapped down. Over the common, the lemon-colored sunlight pierced through the clouds, though the rain was still falling.

"Perhaps there will be a rainbow," said Bessie.

Jo let them in, and saw at once that both were cheerful. "Nice of you to come," he said, to Alison rather than to Fay, feeling that in some way it was nicer on her part, and at the same time resenting that it should be.

"Nice to be asked to tea," Fay said, "it's like Jane Austen or Compton-Burnett." Without his aid she hung up her emerald raincoat and hat. "I hope your mother hasn't strong ideas on etiquette, or leaving the spoon in the jam."

Bessie gave a little athletic bounce when she saw them, but as usual apologized for not rising.

"Mrs. Upjohn," said Alison, "you're looking better. Am I right in thinking so?"

Bessie clasped her hand for a long time. "Let's hope you are perfectly right. And how's our friend Fay?"

"She's just back from Paris," Alison said, "and full of herself."

"Skirts a bit longer," Fay rattled off, "hats smaller. Shoulders a bit more square. Colors, navy, white, yellow. A lot of stripes. So now you all know."

"Fat lot of use it will mean to me," said Mildred, but her face cleared. With Fay she was easy.

"Not a bit. Yellow should suit you and diagonal stripes are very slimming."

They talked of many things and in many moods: depressedly about Spain, where Bilbao and Santander had fallen to Franco: edgily about the Soviet purge of the generals, though on this subject only Jo and Alison were at all informed: in a gossiping spirit about the recent marriage of the Duke of Windsor.

"She's *chic*," said Fay, "but that wedding-dress was a mistake. Too like a caterpillar. She needs fullness from the waist." Despite her bold appearance, her lean hips, long legs, she was intensely feminine, more so, he felt, than either Polly or Alison.

He was unsure whether it was a trick of the light or not, for the sun was now pouring through the windows onto Alison's face: but it seemed to him that she was not merely in high spirits, but filled with an inner brilliance. Her eyes were glittering, her skin had a bloom on it like gold dust. He longed to have her to himself for a while.

This was not to happen yet. When Mildred rose to clear away the tea, Bessie told him he must show Fay round the garden. "It's looking nice now, and all Millie's hard work. Go on, Fay, it was far too wet last time you came. I want to talk to Alison for a little while, anyhow."

Alison's brows rose: she stared at Jo in puzzlement, then smiled. She said, "Yes, go and see the roses."

When they were outside, walking down the gravel path which sparkled with damp like the bed of a stream, Fay said to Jo: "What the hell was that in aid of?"

"I've no idea."

"Secrets?"

"I don't see how there could be."

"All very mysterious. Perhaps we're being thrown together?" She trilled the *r* dramatically.

"Perhaps, but I don't think so."

"Well, do as you're told. Show me the garden."

"On your right, lupins. On your left, more lupins. Those things in the middle bed are roses."

Fay laughed. "She does work hard, though."

"She slaves over it. All I do is mow the lawn. When's that book coming out?"

"Allie's? Beginning of September. I must say it seemed a bit involved to me, but it was fascinating. Have you done anything lately?"

"It's disappointing," Jo said. "No. I'm not going to make a success of my life that way. Perhaps in no way."

She flared up. "Oh, be quiet! I hate you to talk in that grave-yard voice. If you're not careful, you'll get stuck like it."

He asked her whether she supposed he wasn't stuck already.

"Kit's quite right about you. You've no fighting spirit."

He said quietly, "Don't be as imperceptive as he is. There are things you can't fight."

"There's nothing *I* couldn't."

They were near the house again, just outside the French windows which, since the room had become predictably hot, Mildred had left slightly ajar. Jo caught a glimpse of Alison through the gap, though he could hear none of the conversation. The brilliance had gone and she was wearing her poker-face. His heart sank. Bessie, animated, had laid a hand upon her arm.

"Something's going on," said Fay.

"Something's going to stop," said Jo, and he pushed the windows wide.

"Oh, *here* you are, dear!" cried Bessie, all smiles.

Fay murmured to Jo, "I'm going to give you your chance."

When the time came for them to leave, she said easily, "Allie, Jo can see you to the bus. I want to look in on the Thompsons before I desert these more or less foreign parts. Foreign to me these days, anyhow."

140

"Who on earth are they?"

"People I used to know in Streatham. They've just moved in round here."

"Oh, where?" Bessie asked, always interested in the least minutiae of local news.

"On the North Side," Fay replied without hesitation, "thirty or thirty-two. I'll have to find out."

When no one was looking, she winked at Jo.

"Oh, the *Thompsons*," said Alison, who had grasped the situation and was prepared to do whatever was wanted of her; but she looked unhappy.

They were no sooner outside the gate than Fay said, "God bless you, my children, take heart," and walked briskly away.

"Now, what the hell was up?" Jo demanded.

Alison did not reply, but walked in silence at his side.

The sunshine had deepened in tone and was sparkling for miles over leaves polished by rain. Cumulus clouds rode high above the trees against a sky cineraria with the promise of storm.

"I asked you, what was Mother up to?"

"Oh, nothing. Just nonsense."

"Look, we know each other well enough, don't we?"

"Of course. But it's slightly embarrassing and certainly not worth wasting time about."

Raising her arm, she snapped a guelder-rose from an overhanging bush, and the spray from it covered her shoulders. This seemed to refresh her, for her face brightened again. "Let me tell you something quite different. I was walking down Charing Cross Road yesterday, thinking of nothing in particular, when I had an extraordinary experience. Without any rhyme or reason it came to me suddenly that I didn't care about Kit any more. Not at all. *And that I never would.* For the first time since it all happened, I was absolutely free."

Jo dared not feel joy. Whoever she was free for, it could not be for him. Also, in his own experience, such mystic revelations never fell suddenly from heaven, entirely without cause. What had been the cause of this moment for her? Probably she did not know, or did not realize that she knew. All the same, he mistrusted her.

"It is quite wonderful, Jo. I could meet him anywhere, with Polly or without, and it would mean precisely nothing. I felt as if I'd been born again."

She let him take her arm as they crossed the road. "I'm happy."

"I'm glad. But now I want to know why you weren't happy when Mother was up to her tricks."

Then she admitted, slowly, even coloring a little as she did so, that Bessie believed she and Jo would like to marry, and had offered them room in the house.

"Oh, dear God," he said, and stopped.

"Don't take it like that. She's not young any more and she's romantic. She wants everything for her son. I should, in her place."

"To think that someone like you—"

"You mustn't say that. I'm not special."

"You'd love it, wouldn't you? Helping Mildred to polish all that ghastly brass, and pushing the bath-chair on Sundays. They might even let you write a bit if you didn't shout about it to the neighbors."

"I hate it when you sound savage. I'm fond of your mother, and I'm sorry for her."

"What kind of bloody fool does she think she's making of me?"

"In whose eyes?"

"Yours."

"You can't think that. It would be beastly of you if you did."

"You know damned well," said Jo, "that I'd sell my soul to the devil if I could marry you. And I know damned well that you don't love me."

"In a way, of course I do."

"It's a way that's no use to me. But even if you did, I couldn't—I couldn't—" He had a horrible feeling that he was going to cry. The common blurred before him, and all the sounds of traffic, of birds, of passing feet, were numbed.

"Jo, please!" he heard her cry, as from a long way off, and he steadied himself.

They were halfway down the long path and nobody was near except for some children kicking a football about.

She stood on tiptoe and kissed his cheek, then put her arm through his own. "There. Now forget it."

But as they waited for her bus at the top of the Rise he said, "Don't let us see each other for a week or two. After that, it will be all right again."

She made no protest. He did not look after her as she was carried away, but walked slowly home and shut himself in his room.

He had been there for about half an hour when Mildred knocked and came in.

"Yes? What do you want?"

"Mother's made a fool of herself. I got it all out of her. I don't want you to take it to heart."

He lay face down on the bed, not replying.

"Look here, it's not a five-act tragedy, and Alison's perfectly sensible. She must have made allowances."

He knew his sister wanted to comfort him, to jerk him back to a sense of reality (what had happened, anyway?), but he could not speak. He smelled her affection, never articulate, filling the room like some stuffy scent. It was part of Millie's smell, like the pink powder.

"I suppose," she said at last, "that you're going to behave like a child and lock yourself away. Can't you see it only makes things look important when they're not?"

He heard her padding restlessly about the floor.

"Well, if you won't talk, you won't. I only wanted to help you. Anyway, I've given her a lecture about minding her own business, and she's as chastened as she's ever going to be in this life. The Lord may be more successful than I am, in the next."

"Go away."

"I'm going. And I suggest you slip out to the pub. You can have a snack there. If there's just one thing I can't endure, it's meals in this house with everyone producing atmospheres."

"I thought you were going to the pictures with Eileen."

"Well, now I'm not. I don't want to. It's a rotten film, anyway."

He heard her move towards the door, heard the handle turn.

Then she said, clearly, even waspishly, "If you had a grain of sense in your thick head, you'd start to think about someone more our sort. Someone like Fay."

143

Chapter Five

"WHAT'S THE MOST SHAMEFUL THING YOU'VE EVER DONE?" KIT ASKED him.

They were at that low and broody hour, after an evening of drinking, which makes men believe they have sobered into coldness, and that they must either go to bed or drink themselves into cheerfulness again. This was a small beerhouse off Flood Street: they had visited all their usual haunts and had suddenly decided that they wanted to be left alone. It was one of the evenings when Polly should have been with them, but her doctor had discovered a rise in her blood-pressure and had ordered no alcohol, fewer cigarettes and fewer late nights.

Jo paid no attention. He was looking through the book reviews in an evening paper left behind on a bench by some departed customer. "Alison's struck it lucky."

The two weeks of separation after which he had hoped to see her again had stretched out into nearly two months. First, her mother had been ill and she had been obliged to go back to the country for nursing duties. Then the Upjohns, like everyone else, had taken their summer holiday: the usual gruelling one at Birchington, with Bessie's bath-chair in the luggage van: the slow

144

drool along the promenade, sniffing ozone with noses elevated at forty-five degrees.

"Bloody lucky," said Kit. "She's made now. *And* she makes money, which is more than I do."

"I don't see you've anything to complain about, not with being invited to go to America, all expenses paid."

"Well, I can't, not until Polly's had the child. That's what I'm looking forward to more than anything in my life. You wouldn't believe that, would you?"

"Yes, I would. I'd feel the same."

"Jo." Kit's beautiful eyes moistened. He still gave an impression of fragility beneath the great, thick-knit sweaters he affected: but he was filling out. Esteem, Jo thought, suited him, and was happy that he had worn it modestly, even in the pubs of Bloomsbury. Whether or not he was modest inside made no matter. Kit had an infinity of friends, and he never lost any. He demanded, and collected, love.

"Jo."

"What is it?"

"Let's swop secrets. We're young ladies in a dormitory, huddling under blankets with a pocket-torch. What's the most shameful thing you've ever done in your life?"

Jo was in the mood to consider this kind of game, which was one of Kit's favorites, very carefully. "I don't know. Let me think." For a moment he remembered the night when he had taken Alison, without her love: but that had not been shameful. He said at last, "I know."

It had happened only a fortnight ago, at the Annual General Meeting of the local Party. Sybil and Bobby had persuaded him to help them pack the meeting, so that Hatton might be forced out of the chair. Feeling the scurrying forces of the world too rapid for display of his finer personal instincts, Jo had somehow badgered his mother and Mildred, with two or three men from the works, to sign up as Party members, and had dragooned them along to vote. The room had been a sea of unfamiliar faces: the Trade Union faction had looked bewildered, Bobby and Sybil openly triumphant. They had brought in at least another half-dozen brand-new voters apiece.

It had been Jo's job to collect the ballot slips and take part, with Sybil, in the counting. Hatton was voted out, dismissed after fifteen years. Jo could not forget the sight of his face, all color gone from it, blue-white as a cod's, the mouth open, the eyes full of shock. "Mind you, he had been holding us back from doing anything useful. All the same. . . ."

Kit nodded. He saw the point, and he admired his friend's descriptive powers. "Blue-white, like a cod. Yes. Poor bastard."

"But that wasn't all," said Jo, "and I'm glad it wasn't, or I suppose I am. I'd got my vote, and Mother's and Millie's, in my left hand. As I got near that table I stuffed them into my pocket. Afterwards, I tore them up."

"So what are you ashamed of? Funking it in the end, or agreeing to it in the beginning?"

"Agreeing. Also funking. Because my destroying their votes did no good, and it hasn't been all that sop to my queasy conscience."

"It must have been a good scene, all the same," Kit said meditatively. His eyes hardened. "Yes, that's a fair stinker on your part, though I suppose not many people would think so. Out of interest, who replaced him?"

Jo smiled involuntarily. "One of the T.U. crowd, nearly as bad. Still sings 'Forward, Ye Workers.' "

"Look," said Kit, "all that's chicken-feed. I want to tell you what has made me feel the worst, because I have to get it off my chest. I'm not haunted by much, but by this I am."

He crossed his arms on the beer-smeared table. Over the flapping turtle-neck of the sweater his neck looked pale as a consumptive boy's.

"It was just after that awful business in the flat," he said. "The break with Alison. You remember."

Jo was silent.

"I didn't want her, and I did. Because I'd been hellish to her, I tried to blot out a major hellishness by a little one. To take my mind off things. Also, I wasn't really free from her: I wasn't sure what I wanted, to have her back or not."

One night he had, when he was pretty drunk, telephoned her, telling her that she must wait up for him, he needed to see her. "Which I did, really. Only it seemed to me, in a crazy sort of way, that if she wasn't sure that it was me 'phoning, I'd have a line of retreat if I wanted one. So I put a fold of handkerchief over the mouthpiece of the telephone and made myself sound a

146

little different, so I could deny it all afterwards. But I did mean to go to her, I truly did. I was in a crowd in a pub in Kentish Town. They were a scruffy lot, they made me sick, I wanted Alison to make me feel clean again. Then a girl came in, she knew them all and she took a fancy to me. Jo, she had eyes like a wild-cat's, and she was tart through and through. And I couldn't bring myself to leave her, though I thought of Alison waiting and waiting till I was too bloody drunk to think, and then I found myself at five a.m. in a bedroom with the tart somewhere near Paddington Station. That is the single, most shameful, thing I have ever done in the whole of my young life."

Jo stood up, feeling, but controlling, his unsteadiness. "Yes, it must be, just about."

"What's up with you?"

"Oh, I heard about it. She thought it was a joke by one of your pals. That swine Phil Christie was the one she picked."

"For Jesus's sake, Phil would never have done such a thing!"

"It's what she thought. I'm going."

Kit rose, too, far more steadily. "Now, what's the matter? I know you're mad on Alison, but she's never been for you."

"Damn your eyes," said Jo, frightfully, "she was for me once, which is more than ever she was for dear old Kit!"

The moment he had said it he was terrified. He prayed that his friend was too fuddled to have understood.

"You mean, *you* slept with Allie?" Kit demanded. He looked as wild as the girl he had described, in the pub at Kentish Town.

"Look here, boys," said the barmaid, with a clarion call, "if you're going to fight, you can do it outside. You'll find lots of lovely pavement there. This is, I may remind you, a decent house!"

Impelled by her mysterious authority they did, in fact, find themselves in the street. It must have been rough in the Thames estuary, for the gulls were wailing over the roof-tops, ghosts in the windy sky.

"I didn't mean that," said Jo, "of course I didn't."

"Of course you meant it! What else could you bloody well have meant?"

"You got me on the raw. I wanted to say something, just to shake you up."

"You know damned well you meant—how the hell did you manage it?"

"I didn't. I swear it. Can you imagine her letting me? I tell you, you got me on the raw."

"Anyway," said Kit, lapsing into the maudlin, "it wouldn't matter now, would it? There's no one but Polly for me. Polly for me."

They found themselves in step, softly carrying a song from a play of Sean O'Casey's which had enthralled them three years ago. Tenor and bass sounded sweetly in the night.

"Our mother the earth is a maiden again,
She's young and fair and a maiden again. . . ."

Jo soared upwards.

"Her thoughts are a dance as she seeks out her
    bridegroom the sun
  Through the lovely confusion
Of singing of birds, and of blossom and bud."

United, both of them. As they had ever been. No secrets fully attested, and so none given away. Nothing like a deliberate evocation of a shared past to muffle the divisions of the present. Tomorrow, Kit would not be sure what he had heard, whether he had ever heard it: even, if he had heard it, what it could possibly have meant.

Jo was conscious of the joy of being young, knowing that youth would not last forever. To hell, he thought, with silly scruples! He wanted as many lights as possible blazing in the darkening earth, Kit for his friend and Polly, too, Clement and Georgina, the obstinate hope of Alison. In a year or so, who knew what might happen? Living for today, he said to himself, living for today.

In the best of all possible worlds: which wasn't saying much.

Morning brought a letter from Alison which he read three times before he absorbed the shock at all.

September 29th, 1937.

Jo dear,

I want you to learn this from me before anyone else does. It is especially important for you to hear it, as you are the dear-

148

est of all my friends. You know that if I could have helped it, you would have been something more. But, dear, I couldn't.

I am going to marry Piers. (You remember meeting him at The Good Intent.)

Certainly Jo remembered.

He is a good deal older than I am—nearly ten years—and he will be offering me a strange sort of life. But I can adapt easily to strange sorts of life, and when I've settled down I hope you'll adapt to ours because I couldn't bear to lose you. I hope you would hate to lose me, even though I know I am hurting you.

This isn't something done on the rebound. However far I may have bounded, I've now bounded back to the proper place. I am very happy. Everything in the past seems like an ugly dream which, however it appears on the surface, is always a compound of the attractive and the sinister.

I want to have an engagement party at the Six Bells, with Kit and Polly, Clement and Georgina, Fay, and, yes of course, you. *I hope you'll come.* It will have an empty core if you don't, but if you don't I'll understand. Friday week, and we assemble at six.

Hell, nothing I can say is going to be right, and this letter's all wrong. But I had to tell you.

Love,

Alison.

His first impression was that he could feel nothing whatsoever. This was ink on paper, no more. Well, perhaps he had been preparing himself unconsciously precisely for this. Her brilliance on that Sunday afternoon: hadn't it made him suspicious? This could be borne, for the moment, even if pain came later. Numbed, he put it to the side of his plate.

Bessie said archly that she thought she had recognized the handwriting. Was there any news?

"Yes," said Jo, "she's getting married."

"Who to?" Mildred covered her toast carefully with marmalade, as if this were some work of precision nationally important. Her eyes were cast down.

He told them.

149

"Do you know," Bessie said in a small, surprised voice, "I always hoped it would be you?"

He felt he could not bear any longer their suffocating femininity, their dense, devoted coddling of his life. "I've got to be at work early this morning," he said.

The factory was a large and dingy one on the south bank of the river, with Chelsea presenting its rosy skyline across the dividing waters. That morning he was promoted to chief sales manager. At last he had money that he could call money.

"Cheer up, Upjohn," said the man behind the oversized desk, "you've gone up in the firm, not got the sack. Why the long face?"

Jo said, "Thank you, sir."

Tomorrow he would have an office of his own, with his name on the door: a typist all to himself. Prestige. Upjohn had risen in the world. Gone up. Upjo!

That night the pain began, the agony of loss.

It was several days before he could bring himself to reply to Alison, and when he did so he made it short.

Dear Alison,

Sincere good wishes for your happiness. Of course I wish it had been me. But if you are happy, I'll try to be, too. I'll come on the third, if I can manage it, but I've just got a boost to higher things, which will probably mean more overtime. Congratulations to you and Piers.

Love,

Jo.

It was to Mildred, when Bessie had gone to bed, that he was able to speak with honesty.

"The Lord does temper the wind to the shorn lamb," he said. "If I hadn't got promotion, I don't think I could have stood it as I have done."

"You've been very good," she answered unemotionally, "don't think I haven't noticed it. I don't miss much."

"It doesn't trouble me during the day. I enjoy my boost-up, my office, ordering Miss Finch around. And I lunch at the bosses' table in the canteen. I can hear myself using quite a different tone of voice. It's after work that I feel so deathly."

150

"Now, listen." Mildred lit a cigarette for them both and put one between his lips. "You know, with the sensible part of your mind, that you *will* get over it. You must, because no one can feel like that forever. You've always had a tendency to regard all your states as permanent, even when you only had a cold. A rotten invalid, you always were."

He protested, trying to smile at her.

"Oh yes, you were. But that isn't what I meant to say. I'm thinking long-term. Jo, it seems to me now most unlikely that I shall ever marry. If one day, when all this is behind you, you ever want to do so, then for God's sake *do,* and leave this place. Now that you're earning more, you can help me out with Mrs. Warren, so I shouldn't manage so badly."

He knew the extent of her unselfishness and was touched: but what she said seemed to have no meaning.

Mildred leaned back in her chair and puffed smoke at the ceiling. She was putting on weight. Already her face was beginning to have the same bow-fronted shape as her mother's. "Do you know, if ever I've longed for anything, what it was? For good looks. Fate wasn't particularly fair in giving what we have in the family—which isn't much—to you."

"You've got an interesting face, Millie. Some chaps are going to like it more than chocolate-box stuff."

"I wonder what I wanted just then?" she mused. "I suppose I wanted you to say that I *was* good-looking. Just how self-deceiving can one get?"

"Oh, don't be a fool. You are, in your own way."

"Dear, dear, dear, don't struggle quite so hard. I have no illusions. Jo, I want you to promise me that if you ever want to leave here you will do so without the slightest compunction. Crippled mothers are the responsibility of spinster daughters, everyone knows that. They have been from time immemorial."

"I shan't marry, so there's no use in discussing it. I know now it was crazy to set so much store by Alison. Even if she'd cared about me, she couldn't have married what I am. What we are."

Mildred said that whatever Alison's faults, she wasn't a snob.

"No, it's not snobbery. To be snobbish you have to think about who you are, and she never does that. But she would know instinctively that it wouldn't do. We're like a little jail here, with no prisoners except the warders. We're the warders. And she'd be far too wary to come in and occupy the first cell."

"Damn it, Jo, there are times when I loathe the sight of you! I do my best to make this a home, though I'm not good at arty touches, and I even enjoy polishing the brass."

"I know, I know. I didn't exactly mean that."

Bessie thumped on the wall. When Jo went to her, she said she thought she wouldn't be able to sleep unless she had some cocoa.

"Can't you hear the keys turning on us?" he said to Mildred when he had conveyed the request.

When she had again settled her mother for the night, she came briskly back into the living-room.

"Look here, I know what you're going through. But you've simply got to make a start on your own recovery."

"In a way I don't want to. When I'm miserable as hell, it means that something of her is still with me."

"Sheer self-indulgence. Now you go upstairs and take that photograph down. It does you no good. Tear it up if you can, or put it in a drawer if you can't."

He sat on the edge of his bed and looked at the misty face. Indulgently, he let himself cry. It was a luxury to cry, in his locked room, in the middle of the night. Putting out his tongue he licked up a tear and savored the saltiness. He stared at himself in the wardrobe glass, a tall, dark, wrecked, silly young man with a wet face, old enough to know better: the sight stiffened his resolution. He got up, took down Alison's picture and laid it right at the bottom of a drawer used for spare sheets and blankets.

Chapter Six

PIERS WELFORD, IN UNIFORM, STRUCK JO AS A STRIKINGLY HAND-some man: he had not realized this before.

Piers and Alison had come early, to corner a table that would take seven comfortably: Jo was the first guest to arrive. Alison was wearing a scarlet dress which threw color up into her cheeks. She looked nervous and happy. On her finger was a fine ruby, with a small diamond on each side of it.

"Now, dear," she said to Jo, "I am pretty well stuck with red for the rest of my life. I don't know what Fay will have to say about that."

"It was my mama's," said Piers, "and since I couldn't afford anything remotely so good on my army pay, I thought Alison had better have it. Let's have a pint before the others come, shall we?"

As he went to the bar, she looked at Jo. "Is it all right?"

"The ring? I'm dazzled." He felt calm, even debonair, even gay.

"I meant you."

"Oh, I'm fine. How's the book going?"

"I've sold nearly seven thousand," said Alison, "so I feel cock-a-hoop. But don't let Kit tell you it's a best-seller, because it isn't. That would be the worst slur he could think of, and believe me, he would think of it."

The words sounded a little spiteful, but the tone of them did not. She was speaking of Kit as if he were an ordinary friend, having meant nothing to her, someone whose foibles she knew and did not resent. She was enjoying her modest success very much indeed and did not pretend otherwise.

"I don't imagine I'll be popular when I have to live in officers' quarters," she went on. "I shall be suspected as a highbrow."

"Which you are."

"Yes, but I try to conceal it."

He marvelled at himself, at his own equilibrium. This was going to be quite easy, after all.

The pub was crowded only along the length of the bar where people were milling round the counter, reaching over shoulders for their drinks, trying to see whether the glass sandwich bells held anything attractive.

Kit and Polly came in, Kit excited, holding a handkerchief to his nose. "Clement warned me they'd get me! Thank God I dodged before they really had a chance. Hullo, Alison. Where's the military man?"

"He'll be with us in a moment. What happened? Polly, you look very pretty even with a dear little football under your dress."

"I don't look bad, do I? And I don't show at all from the back."

"I was just passing Whitelands Court," Kit said, removing the handkerchief to reveal the blood on it, "when some buggering Blackshirt darted out of his hole like a spider and poked me one on the nose. Polly kicked him. Polly kicked him where he sat, jumping from the chair she sat in."

"You didn't!" Jo exclaimed admiringly.

"Only his shins," Polly replied with her usual composure. "Then we ran away. It was lucky they didn't chase us, because at present I can't run very fast."

Piers came up and was introduced and heard the story. "I wish I'd been there."

"We could have done with the army," Kit said. "Anyway,

154

forget it. Congratulations to you both. Alison, you look like a poppy in July. It suits you."

The next arrival was Fay, flying in, golden tail wagging on her back. "Sorry I'm late. Well, ducks,"—to Alison—"this is quite an evening!"

Piers returned to the bar, brushing away offers to help, intentions to pay. "This is my party from first to last."

"Harrumph!" Kit said, when he had gone, "very smart, very abrupt. Will he let me stand easy, if I say yessir, no sir?"

"It is up to you," Polly said, "whether you will be able to stand at all in two hours' time."

"What's the matter with your nose?" Fay asked, and the story had to be told again.

"It wasn't so exciting as it sounds," Kit said, "and over in a moment almost before I realized what was happening. Dare we talk politics tonight, Allie, or will your young man have us all in the glasshouse?"

Jo thought he was being rather silly. Also, he remembered Alison's astonishing statement that Piers might be a Communist.

Certainly, returning laden from the bar, he did not look like one. He had the peculiar cut of the soldier of small stature, the compactness, the straight spine, the spring from the balls of the feet.

"You may talk politics," she said, "if you like, though he is quite good on other subjects."

Fay smiled at Jo. "Tell me about the new job."

"There's nothing much to tell. I like being a middling big frog in a pretty small pool."

"Can't toast anyone yet," said Kit, "not till we're all gathered together. Where's Clem?"

At that moment Clement and Georgina came in, faces sparkling with the fine rain that had begun to fall. He had his arm around his wife's waist, and Jo was relieved. He noticed, of course, Georgina's immediate interest in Piers: but since he fancied this would not be reciprocated, did not expect trouble that evening.

"I told you they'd be laying for you," Clement said to Kit. "You had your tip-off."

"They've taken a long time about it. Anyway, I'm not hurt."

155

When they were settled, Kit proposed a toast. "To the joyful mating of literature and His Majesty's Armed Forces. Love to you both."

"I hope to reign with your loves," Piers said. And they all, except Alison, regarded him with some surprise.

"Will you let him reign?" Clement asked.

Polly answered for Alison. "Naturally she will, as I let Kit."

Kit gave her a sidelong glance, and smiled secretly.

"When are you getting married?" Fay asked. "And where, and am I invited?"

"I don't know," Alison said, "that you will like it, but of course all of you are. We're being married in church."

"At the end of next month," Piers added, "just before Christmas. Furthermore, we've rented a house."

"In Betjeman country?" Kit inquired with a whoop.

"Precisely in Betjeman country," said Piers, "almost a bungalow. 'When sunset gilds the Surrey pines, the fam'ly usually dines.'" Alison gave him a look of pride, and threw Kit one of mischief.

"Piers," Clement drawled, easing his big body back in the chair, tossing the oatmeal-colored wave back from his forehead, "this is all your girl's fault. She gave us to understand that you were simply a Military Man—in fact, that's what we've been calling you. Could we have been guilty of a certain condescension?" Despite the ironic ring he had given to his words he had, in his own fashion, spoken handsomely.

"No, it's precisely what I am. But it doesn't preclude the reading of books. Why should it?"

"Anyway," said Clement, "the misunderstanding has rapidly been cleared up." He smacked his lips loudly, as if in appreciation of the beer.

"You are a narrow-minded lot, aren't you?" Fay said, beaming round at them. "You and your arty pubs, you don't think the world exists outside them."

"Peace, peace," said Kit. "But if Piers now tells me there is a world elsewhere, I shall crawl under the table and bay like a wounded hound."

"No, I don't know where that comes from," Piers said gravely.

156

He was older than any of them; Jo felt for the first time the distance those few extra years made. He was so impressed by Piers that even his jealousy for a moment lost its edge.

"As for the bungalow," Alison said, "Piers has got to settle me somewhere, because his outlook on the world is pretty dark. He doesn't know where any of us are going to be this time next year. He says Hitler's unstoppable."

"I refuse to believe that," Clement said. "If we can get together with France and Russia, we may be able to stop him. Anyway, each in our small way, we're going to try."

"Don't think I'm being defeatist." Piers frowned. "We shall all try. But don't hope for too much."

Georgina laid a seductive hand upon his arm. "You're honestly as grim as all that? Really and truly?"

Clement reached out and removed the arm. "You're my wife. Something for you to remember."

"Damn it, you—" she began.

"Oh no, no," said Polly, "no, you don't. In my delicate condition I must not be subject to upsets of any kind." Her eyes sparkled. "It is the atmosphere of *Cranford* that I most desire."

Alison laughed outright. "And it's my party, Clement, and I too desire the atmosphere of *Cranford*. Polly, when's it going to be?"

She replied, about the beginning of February. Yes, she was feeling wonderful, but had to be a little careful with herself. "You next, I hope."

"I fervently hope so," said Piers, "but—"

"He is going to say something about giving hostages to fortune," said Kit, who was still moved by an old resentment.

"Well," Jo said pacifically, "that's what one does. I think you and Polly are pretty courageous."

"So do I," said Clement. "Georgina and I haven't quite the guts for it."

Piers said, "But you imply that *I* am defeatist?"

Fay remarked that this was a score for him, and they agreed. Somehow, he had come to dominate them all, partly because he was older, partly because he was from an unfamiliar world: but partly, Jo thought, because, Polly excepted, he was the most serene of anyone in the party. Piers looked at Alison, now and

157

again, with possessive love: she, probably through delicacy towards Jo (or so Jo thought), seemed to treat him in precisely the same easy, affectionate way as she treated any of her friends.

Somehow, on this evening of celebration, Jo knew a calm that had not been his for months. It would not last: but for the moment he felt in his own secure, appointed place among others with appointed places. He was fond of everyone around the table: of Piers, in his uniform the color of golden fog, Alison in her scarlet dress, Georgina allowing the lashes to fall upon her desirous brown eyes, Polly with skirt stretched tight upon her stomach, Fay tossing her hair when she laughed, flashing her bird's profile from side to side, Clement, heavy with his not-displeasing cynicism, and most of all, Kit, proud father-to-be, still dabbing ostentatiously at a nose that had long since ceased to bleed.

"A toast from me," Jo said, "to Kit's and Alison's literary success, coupled with the name of Mr. Edmund Wilson and with the names of Gerard Gould, Ralph Straus, L. P. Hartley, old Uncle Howard Spring and all."

Piers renewed their glasses, and they drank.

"Give you one Wilson for six Strauses," Kit said to Alison.

"No. I'll take one for three, if you like."

"Bet I shall come out better than you do in the end."

"I'm quite sure you will."

"You know damned well I will!"

"I said, I'm sure of it."

"She's a popular girl," he brooded, "she's a best-seller."

She denied this. "A decent seller, that's all."

"You mean I'm not?"

"I sell more than you do, Kit, but I am not nearly such a lion. Doesn't that content you?"

"I want to have my lion and eat it."

Jo gave him a gentle nudge under the table.

Kit relaxed, and his blinding smile flashed up. He raised his tankard. "Just to Alison. Alison alone." Leaning over the table, he kissed her cheek. "Piers doesn't mind, does he?"

How was it, Jo wondered, that this evening which he had so much feared had settled down so well? Kit's sniping merely recalled the old, half-joking battles between him and Alison: if it had made a discordancy, it was one little more audible than the

158

most fragile note from a tuning-fork. There was no doubt that she, of them all, was the most completely content: it was this contentment, this love transferred from him, that had made Kit restless. Polly? She must have understood the root of the banter well enough: but she did not appear to mind it. Nor did Alison display for Polly anything more than affection. Had they all changed so much? Was it he alone who would wake next morning, undrugged, to the old wretchedness? At the moment he did not feel wretched at all, merely one among others having a good time.

He heard a tune running in his head, a tune invented by himself to old words. At first he did not recognize it, or attach words to notes. He went on drinking, talking with the others; and at a certain stage of the night, when the colors had blurred a little, faces grown less sharp, the lights around the bar more kaleidoscopic, he remembered.

> "I've lost Britain and I've lost Gaul,
> And I've lost Rome, but worst of all,
> I've lost Lalage."

He heard himself saying to her, in a voice loud even to his own ears, "I haven't, have I?"

Her face detached itself from other faces, sharp and planed, near his own.

"Haven't what, dear?"

"Never mind. Lucky man, Piers."

The soldier's face, also, sprang into focus. "I know I am."

"Isn't he a bloody lucky man?" Jo was shouting and he knew it; disturber of the peace.

"Of course he is," Kit said sharply, "but don't bellow. You'll have us all turned out."

"You're all sober but me. Why is that? Why is that, Fay?"

It was to her, and her alone, that it seemed right to appeal.

"Metabolism, I expect. Sit down, Jo, will you?"

Her hands were on his arms, resting him back in his chair. He was, he realized, very drunk, in no state to face the long journey home. With a wrench of will, he steadied his body, focussed his eyes. He asked Polly if he might come back with them for the night. Of course he could, she was going to suggest it.

Then time slipped from him till he found himself walking

down Radnor Street, supported by Clement and Piers. He heard himself asking where Kit was, where were the girls.

"Coming along behind," Piers said. "Take it easy, old boy. Careful, here's a curb."

Then Kit became visible, and Polly, and a light sprang up over a flight of stairs. He stumbled up them, Piers' arm about his waist. Jo was filled with love: he wanted to tell Piers what a good chap he was, suggest what a generous chap he was himself, but the damnable tune was so loud in his head that he did not believe he could hear his own voice even if he tried to speak.

After that there was nothing but darkness, till he woke in the spare room in the filtered light of a grey dawn, perfectly calm but with a pounding head. He got up very quietly, made himself coffee and took four aspirin tablets. Then he slept deeply till Polly woke him.

She looked very fresh in a pink dressing-gown, her hair held back with an alice band.

"What's the time?"

"Half past eleven. Can you eat some breakfast?"

He sprang out of bed. He was wearing Kit's pyjamas, which came halfway up his calves. "My God, I'll be late for work!"

"You won't, because it's Saturday. Come on, tea and toast for you, even if you can't manage anything else."

"I was bad last night, wasn't I?"

For him, she said, uncommonly: however, Kit had not been much better, and was refusing to get up at all. But, she added, she would wake him pretty soon even if it meant using a wet flannel.

As Jo tried to swallow a piece of bread, she watched him steadily, chin in her hands, her eyes bright. "Now look here," she said, "I know perfectly well that in another minute you are going to be remorseful and beat your breast. That gives me no pleasure, so don't do it. How are you feeling now?"

Muzzy, he said, but no worse than that.

"It was odd to see you quite so bowled over. Usually, it's Kit. Incidentally, Jo, I wish that boy would drink less. Try to make him, will you?"

This surprised him. Kit, he said, liked his night out but couldn't be described as an alcoholic.

"You don't see what I see. He used not to drink before six. Nowadays, he's perfectly capable of sneaking into the kitchen and taking a nip at half past four. Earlier and earlier. It's since he's been worried about my B.P., though the doctor says there's not the slightest need for alarm. Try to wean him, will you?"

Jo, revived a little by the coffee, asked her if that wouldn't be a case of the blind leading the blind.

"Then the one-eyed man has got to be king. Which is you. Hadn't you better ring up your sister, or are you really allowed out all night?"

He did telephone to Mildred, and when he returned to the table found Polly as he had left her, firm, pretty, unwinking. "I am very much in love with Kit," she said, "but if he starts drinking more than I think he should, I shall simply walk out till he pulls himself together. This I promise you. Baby or no baby. Could you eat an egg?"

He found that he was ravenously hungry. As he ate, he thought about her, and her curious marriage. There was, between her and Kit, a bond of remarkable strength: yet he knew she would stretch that bond a long way if she believed it necessary. There was something chilling about her sheer will, and it was all the more chilling because it was like an acid kernel within a nut of sweetness. Little, bright-eyed, crinkle-lipped, she had taken such strength from the world into which she had been born, a world that could never have been Kit's, and which, for his sake, she had deserted. Jo wondered what she was like in the very act of love, whether she melted then to Kit's dominance, or whether there was not, even in the explosion of joy, something within her that remained detached and cool.

"Can I borrow a razor?"

As he shaved he found himself humming "I've lost Lalage," and then he sang it outright, at the top of his voice. When he emerged, dressed, from the bedroom, Polly came and hugged him warmly. "I've just got that devil up. Won't you wait to see him?"

He thought, he said, that he had better be getting home. He might be keeping Mildred from something she wanted to do.

"You were very brave last night, Jo. Don't think nobody realized that."

PART FOUR

The Coming of Darkness

Chapter One

"HAS IT OCCURRED TO YOU," ALISON HAD SAID TO JO, WITH A GIO-
conda smile, "that Piers is almost certainly a Communist?"

He was not. Only in her innocence of him, knowing him so
little, had she begun to consider it even lightly. He was, as he had
said, a radical Conservative of the kind the young of the left
wing were only just beginning to understand: opposed to any
change in the manners and customs of what he regarded as a
decent and ordered society, by nature paternalistic, he was at the
same time intensely patriotic, and the tactics of the Chamberlain
government disgusted him as much as the tactics of those on the
left who demanded cuts in defense while clamoring for deep
shelters. He kept fairly quiet in the mess, where majority opinion ran hard against him, and was glad Alison had not let herself
be drawn into dispute with any of the other wives.

Their small house at the end of a sandy lane, not a bungalow, with pine-woods black behind it, was a source of comfort to
him. Here at least, into her sympathetic ear, he could pour the
political frustrations of the day. She could, she told him, have
been an actress: since their marriage she had been acting beauti-

fully, matching her behavior to the company in which she found herself. She had learned to trim her conduct to the niceties of rank, though she was aware that her reputation as a writer gave her certain subtle privileges of which she was careful to take no undue advantage. She spoke of her work only when urged to do so, and she entertained efficiently in a subdued kind of way. Certainly she was glad that Piers was a senior officer: one step down, and she would not find things so easy. For his part, he was not fool enough to suppose that some of the women did not hold her in a kind of dim suspicion: but certainly she gave them nothing they could take hold of.

Occasionally she would relieve herself by private outbursts. "Half your brother-officers would accept Hitler without turning a hair, if ever he overran this country!"

A cold January: they had no central heating. Piers stoked up the fire with logs and fresh coal.

"You're wrong there," he said, after some reflection. "If war comes, they will fight just as well as any of your old friends, and with as great a gusto. There you underestimate them."

"They'd fight with the same gusto against Russia."

"Certainly, against anyone who took a smack at us, or, come to that, anyone they were ordered to take a smack at. They are conditioned to take orders. But just as certainly, against Hitler. I only know one man in the mess who might be a potential menace, given half the chance."

"Who?"

"I shan't tell you. You may have to sit next to him at dinner, and your eyes might give you away."

Alison agreed that they might. There could be a limit to her good behavior.

She loved Piers deeply, though not with the passion she had felt for Kit: she was grateful that she could love him in peace. They could not have been happier sexually, and this happiness they hugged to themselves as something between a private miracle and a private joke. During a tedious party each would catch the other's eye across the dinner-table, remember, and anticipate.

Apart from the necessity for maintaining a public *persona* unlike her real one, she found herself enjoying army life. She liked to hear the bark of the drill-sergeant echoing through the

166

trees on a frosty morning, to walk by the parade ground and admire the rhythm and rattle of drill, to ride her bicycle down the
sandy yellow paths softened by pine-needles and to the village
where she did her shopping.

She had once heard from Kit, who was very funny about
mem-sahibs, and she guessed she had become something of a joke
in her old haunts. She did not care. Jo wrote to her regularly:
long, solemn letters containing news of friends who now seemed
to her remote. Reading between the lines, she gathered that he
was sleeping with Fay, and she hoped he might find himself in
love again. Georgina wrote to her flippantly: "I am still behaving
myself. Clement had to go to Paris for a fortnight, and he put me
on my honor. I am, rather precariously, still on it. It is a bit like
flagpole-sitting."

Yes, it was a happy but odd life for Alison, having all the
brilliant reality of certain dreams. She felt herself on a plane of
brightness, with darkness behind her and darkness, perhaps, to
come. This was the most of life she might have, and she intended
to enjoy it to the full.

Early in February they went up to London for a weekend,
and were caught in a dense demonstration in Parliament Square.
All good humor had deserted the crowds by now: there was
seething anger against the Government, and a seething private
fear. The police, frightened by this determination and by the
numbers milling around, lost their heads: Piers only just ex-
tracted Alison and himself from a baton charge, and when they
reached the sanctuary of Millbank she was white and shaken.
"This is what I'm out of," she said, "and this is what I should be
in."

"My dear girl," he replied, "you are going to be in far more
than you like, unless they can push Chamberlain out in time."

They walked along by the river, past the Tate Gallery.

"Suppose," she said, "there isn't a war."

"If not, we shall be sold down the river to Hitler."

"Suppose there is. And we win it. What next?"

"I shan't stay in the army all my life. You'll be glad, won't
you?"

"I'm not sure whether I will or not. What could you do?"

"Oh, come," he said, "I can teach. I have quite a decent degree in engineering. Or there may be other opportunities. I'm not inept."

She laughed, having recovered herself a little. "And we shall read Manley Hopkins to each other quite openly, and not behind drawn blinds, as if we were secret drinkers."

"If you propose that we shall start reading aloud, which I detest, then I shall stay in the army and end up a brigadier. Or even a general."

Privately, she doubted the latter. Though he was a good soldier, a part of him was as much a fish out of water as she was. His mother had been a passionate if eclectic reader, from her photographs something like a Burne-Jones girl, long-nosed, attractively phthisic, and those interests, which she had passed on to him, had stuck. It was at his father's wish that, to maintain the family tradition, he had gone to Sandhurst, where he had done well: but there were oddities about him apparent to others in the regiment, and she fancied that his promotion might not soar to any astronomic level.

"I wonder how Polly's doing?" she asked him.

Next morning she knew. She received a letter from Kit:

Alison dear,

Our child turned up nearly a fortnight early and was dead on arrival. I am writing to you because we can't bear to put things in the papers. Polly is physically well, but we are both so miserable that we can't see any life existing beyond today. I never knew I should care so much. It was a girl. I saw her, she was like a tiny soap-doll with black bootbrush hair. We are told encouragingly that we can have plenty more, as if *she* were no more than a pea in a pod, not a human being at all, not *our daughter*. I just sit writing to everyone, it's all I feel I want to do. Don't write to Polly, just to me. Love to you both.

It was the simplest letter Alison had ever known him write, only a touch of him here and there as in the bitter "dead on arrival," and the description of the dead baby. She was glad to find herself crying, to know she could feel grief for him: she had been afraid that, had all gone well, she might have felt an old and cruel jealousy. Now that he was deprived and punished—

168

"dear God," she prayed aloud, "don't let me think like that, in such words!"—she found in herself only sorrow. If she were not sorry, then why should she cry?

"Poor devil," said Piers, "let's pray it's all right with us." For she was beginning to suspect that she might be pregnant.

Jo wrote, "They have shut themselves up and see nobody. I never thought Kit, anyway, would be quite so hard hit. I did speak to him on the 'phone. He says they don't think they can bear to stay in the flat, and has wild schemes of getting a houseboat on the Reach. It is quite mad with things as they are, but it's all he will talk about, apart from the baby. Clement says if they go on like this, he's going to break into the flat and drag them out. The woman below does the shopping, Kit says, so presumably they do eat.

"Not much more news, except that Bobby Price has joined the International Brigade, and there are wild rumors that that beastly man Phil Christie is thinking of doing the same. I bet he won't. Mother and Mildred well, and send their love."

Piers and Alison walked through the pine-trees to the colonel's house. His wife was giving a cocktail party. They made their way by torchlight. He was troubled about her, for she had been uncommonly silent since she had heard of Kit's tragedy. "You're not thinking it might happen to you? All the statistics are against it."

When she replied, he heard the smile in her voice and was relieved. "Statistics! Just like you. No, not just like you, really."

"Let's not stay longer than decency demands. Let's get back early and go to bed."

"Yes," she said.

Raising the torch, he shone upon her face a ring of yellow light. "You look very beautiful, my girl. I'll teach you to look even more so later on." Putting his arm round her, letting the circle zigzag before them like a butterfly, he felt her shiver of promised pleasure, and was relieved.

He knew perfectly well that she was not entirely over Kit—he had accepted that when he proposed to her and when they married—but his confidence was so high that he believed he would possess her wholly in due time, if he were patient. Sometimes he felt as if he had raised her steadily, gently, out of a weedy river,

169

divesting her slowly of its green ribbons till there now clung to her no more than the faint satin stripe of a single weed. Soon, this too would uncoil, and drift away with the forgotten stream.

Brilliance poured out from the open doorway, the colonel's batman on reception duty.

"Major and Mrs. Welford, sir!"

Mrs. MacHaffie came to greet them, bracelets jangling on her bare plump arms. "Well, well! Piers, and our little celebrity! How are you, my dear? I've been reading your book. I'm going to tell you just what I think about it when I can get a quiet moment!"

"Ominous," Alison muttered as she went to throw her coat on the bed.

It was the usual regimental party, the women dressed to kill, the men flirting with other men's wives discreetly, within the confines of rank.

The colonel talked to Alison about Spain: he was opposed to a Nationalist victory, though not for ideological reasons. "Some of them here think I'm a bit loopy, but I say we don't want that fellow sitting on top of Gibraltar. He'll go in with Hitler and Mussolini, if it ever comes to that, and we'll be in a pickle in the Med. Not that I can stand the Reds, mind you, but we may be sorry for Non-Intervention one of these days."

"Oh come, MacHaffie," said the brigadier, "it's not up to us to stir the pot. If Hitler gets his damned Sudetens back he'll quieten down, you'll see. Be as quiet as a lamb."

"Nothing," said Piers, "is going to quieten him down. He should have been quietened in the Rhineland. Churchill's quite right."

"I don't trust Churchill further than I could kick him," the brigadier replied. "Wild chap, God knows what he could drag us into."

Alison said, for her indiscreetly, but in the voice of a Rosa Dartle who merely wants to know, "But aren't you all busy training for the day you do get dragged?"

He patted her shoulder. "That doesn't mean we want to be. We just keep in readiness, see?"

"Come along, Alison," said Mrs. MacHaffie, "I want you to tell me what you think of my teenies. My baby *vol-au-vents*. I made them all myself, with these fair hands."

170

Alison accompanied her, her smile glimmering. "Were you tactfully removing me?"

"Not at all, not at all! But you should be careful of teasing the brigadier. Poor man, he has no sense of humor at all. *I* say, shouldn't we all be the worse without it? Come, try a teeny. Is it good? If it's like cardboard you needn't be ashamed to say so."

Alison said it was excellent, which it was, and ate three more.

"Now," said Mrs. MacHaffie, "while we have got a moment to ourselves, let me tell you how much I loved your book. The only thing is, why had it got to be so sad at the end—why, my dear, you've got a sore eye!"

"I've had it for years: it's a broken vein. The ending is sad because that's what would have happened."

"One can only see it if one looks really closely—oh, I'm sure you're right. But I do feel life can be so sad itself, that when I read a novel I—oh, Joyce, here you are at last! I was beginning to wonder whether you were deserting us."

"Stuffing?" Piers asked quietly.

"Not much else to do," Alison answered, with her mouth full. "Anyway, we'd better make something of a meal, because just conceivably I shan't feel up to cooking later on."

"You will not feel in the least up to it, I can assure you, if I have my way." He smiled at her lubriciously. All at once, both of them were exceedingly happy.

For the rest of the party she was as good as gold, teasing nobody, for the most part avoiding the men, seeking out the women to talk of children, clothes, and the servant problems of civilian life. In military life, there were none. She allowed a timid subaltern to flirt with her in a timid way, and observed with pleasure that Piers had missed none of this.

My life, she thought, golden as a nice, fresh egg between the two slabs of black bread. She ate some more sandwiches.

Chapter Two

"PARIS IS ROTTEN, PARIS IS REEKING. THE FRENCH WON'T FIGHT."

Clement was visiting Jo, who could not leave the house because Mildred had been asked, by the brother of her auctioneer (now married), to a Masonic Ladies' Night.

"There's hardly a newspaper not in German pay, and all the bloody French do is to stuff their guts, drink like fishes and say how safe they all are behind the Maginot." Clement spoke in anger, fear and certainty. This was the week of the occupation of Austria: he had been in Paris for the third time that year. March winds howled in the garden, mashing the daffodils flat.

Jo looked anxiously at his mother and wished she would go to bed. But she did not seem perturbed.

"You really think so?" she asked Clement.

"I am damned sure."

"Oh dear, I can only hope you're wrong! I went to Paris once, the year before Jo was born. All the chestnuts were out, and the women looked so smart. It was really gay, just as people tell you. I drank champagne at a café in the open air, and I did feel such a dog! There were horse-drawn carriages then."

172

Clement said, "I am not wrong. And if war does break out, Mrs. Upjohn, Mildred ought to get you away from here."

"Leave my home?" She looked astounded. "I've lived here ever since Arthur and I were married. Nobody's going to shift me now, Hitler or no Hitler. Please help yourself."

She motioned with dignity towards the decanter and the siphon. Since Jo's rise in pay, there was sometimes whiskey in the house.

"Paris is gay now," said Clement, "that's the awful thing about it. They stand round the singers on the street corners and they sing to accordions, "Sur les Toits de Paris." Yes, and a new song about the whole world going *boum*. It never occurs to them that that's precisely what it may do."

"You say 'may,'" Bessie observed slyly, "which means you aren't *quite* sure."

"I am sure, but I go on hoping. Which means that I am of unsound mind."

"Oh, stop it," Jo said, "you're like a death-watch beetle. How's Georgina?"

"That lovely wife of yours," Bessie added, though she had never met her. She readily identified her interests with all Jo's friends, whether she knew them or not.

"She's all right," Clement said, without interest. He looked at Bessie and his face seemed to swell. "Yes, it's still gay, like La Belle Epoque."

"Belle what, dear?"

"The great dizzy days. Courtisans. The Opera. Offenbach. Can-can."

"I always wanted to see the can-can, but Arthur would never let me. Now you mustn't glare at me like that, Clement, or try to scare me out of my own house. Here I am and here I stay, no matter what happens."

Shortly afterwards, she did go to bed.

"I suppose one has to say she's pretty heroic," Jo said hopefully.

"One could say your ma's being blind as a bat. Get her out, the moment things become worse. Millie can go on with her teaching in the country."

"What will you do?"

"Be a war correspondent, of course, what else? Georgie will

173

want to show off in some spirited way, drive an ambulance, something of that sort. She's as brave as half a dozen lions, and of course, she'll meet such nice men."

"How are things now?"

"With her? O.K. Come Hitler, and I shall lose her again. Wars are made for the Georgies of this world. What about you? If it happens, I mean?"

"Oh, join up," said Jo, and suddenly glimpsed a better world. "Anti-Aircraft, if I can, something to keep me in this country, anyway. But look here, you must be exaggerating, Clem. We're pushing forward to a pact with Russia, surely we are?"

Clement said there was no "surely" about it. His visit to France had upset him badly, and he felt all the panic of Cassandra when no one would listen to a female crack-pot. He refilled his glass, without being asked.

Jo changed the subject. "What do you think about Kit and Polly?"

They had bought the converted barge, and were to move into it by the beginning of May.

"Mad as hatters, and Kit's been sousing ever since the baby died. They're both talking about starting another one, which isn't compatible with living on some damned damp houseboat on that stinking mud. But there's no sense to be got from either of them. I tell you what, old Wantage is furious, just for once. I gather he went and read the riot act, saying he wasn't going to have his girl put in mortal danger, but of course it got him nowhere. Meanwhile, Kit's off to the U.S.A. for four weeks, sea trips included, all expenses paid: Georgie thinks it will be a relief to Polly." Clement paused. "Does it seem to you sometimes that the lot of us, our lot, I mean, are being shaken up like Housey-Housey numbers in a bag? Life's disintegrating us." He made reference to a song of the day. "Was it 'Swell while it lasted?' "

It would last, Jo said steadfastly, but he said it without pleasure in the thought. He had come to the point when he needed to have forced upon him the changes he would never seek on his own.

"Did we really have good times? I often wonder."

"Yes. And we still can." Jo grinned. "Whenever I'm not on demos, or you're not, or whenever I'm not turning out cyclostyled agitprop in a basement. It's just about all I do nowadays."

174

"What about Fay?"

"Oh, she comes and helps in her spare time."

"No love-life?"

"There's been some."

"Fay's a good little bitch," said Clement, "better than all the other girls put together."

Bessie called out for something or other. Jo said humbly, "Excuse me. I won't be long."

Left to himself, Clement prowled the room, offered a drop of whiskey to the Siva, looked out into the blustering dark. It occurred to him that of all his friends of the "wild life," he liked Jo best, even while despising him: and saw that, for many people like Jo, the loyal ones who could, but would not, break away from their over-populated cells, war might have its advantages. For himself, he did, on the whole, look forward to it, even if it meant losing Georgina for short periods, long periods, even forever. He was the most politically minded of them all, and by far the most clear-headed. Life at the moment was a mess and Clement, orderly by nature, longed for any kind of straightening-out, even if it held the threat of death. Like many blustering men, noisy on the surface as the raging garden beyond the french windows, he had his inner horrors of worse things than war. He knew about the concentration camps, he knew what things had been done to others, could be done to him. He was secretly afraid, not of death, but of indignity to his living flesh.

He hummed softly to himself:

> *"Boum—*
> *Le monde entier fait boum*
> *Même le bon Dieu fait boum*
> *Dans son fauteuil de nuages*
> *Car mon amour*
> *Est plus vif que l'éclair. . . ."*

His voice trailed away. He was suffocated by the smell special to Jo's house, stuffy and sweet, with an undertone of clean but aging flesh. What a life! What hard luck! Poor old Jo, brimful of imagination that flashed like lightning and as swiftly died away, with no background, no taste except for words, stifled under a pink mattress of women. Not the best-quality down, either.

Clement realized how little his friends knew him: having had, on the surface, better luck than they, he had never told them much. The son of a successful barrister, educated at Winchester and New College, he could have lived a comfortable, cushioned life had he wished to. Even now, like Alison, he had comfort to which to return: his mother's house near Havant, where Georgina still slipped off for occasional basking, all the bath-towels pink, thick and giant-sized. Class-privileged, he had found those privileges a burden, both in the way of his friendships and his career. The "wild life," a social and sexual release for Jo, had been a social release for himself. If he had managed to keep his secrets, it had only been because of his seniority in years and income. But when war came, he was going to resume those privileges promptly wherever they were likely to come in handy. He gave the Siva another drink, and watched with satisfaction a golden drop form on the end of its nose.

Jo came back, smiling, a little sheepish. "She had actually put her foot through the sheet."

"Perhaps Millie made her an apple-pie bed."

"Stuff that! Anyway, I had to change it. Give yourself another."

"Thank you, I have already."

Jo hesitated. "Fay may look in."

"In which case, I shall take my departure."

"I didn't mean that."

"If you didn't, you should have."

Clement left: the time was ten-thirty. Within three minutes of his departure Fay, who had been lurking in the front garden of the house next door, put in an appearance.

Her hair was tousalled by the wind, she smelled of the wind and the night. They tiptoed past Bessie's closed door and upstairs to the bedroom.

"And what doom has Clement been forecasting?" she demanded, when she had pulled free of him. They were used to each other now, and her undressing was leisurely.

"The obvious."

"Do you think he's right?"

"He is persuasive," said Jo, stumbling a little as he pulled off his trousers.

She laughed at him. "You are so clumsy!"

"I am, aren't I?"

Later, as they sat up in bed drinking the last of the whiskey, not hurrying themselves since they knew Mildred, eyes open to

176

their pleasures, would never dream of interrupting them, she spoke to him seriously.

"Jo, I've been thinking. I imagine you don't want to marry me, and you know that isn't something I should ever clamor for. I shan't confront you with something in a shawl, or anything of that sort. But if you ever should, I would be prepared to live here and do what I could for your ma. That's all there is to it. Alison's gone now, and nice as the flat is, I don't care to go on sharing with random girls. I would take turn and turn about with Millie. Now say, 'Nothing doing.' "

He did not answer.

She said, her eyes bright and grave, meeting his own, "You have said it. Nothing doing."

"Look, Fay. God only knows what's going to happen in the next year or so. Nobody does. I can't tie you or anyone else down."

"O.K. You have said it."

He tried to protest against her fortitude, did not know what to say.

"We go on," Fay said, without heat, "as we are. That suits me. So long as I have you around, or you have me."

She slipped out of the bed like a lovely fish, long and bright, eeled into her clothes.

"Anything you want suits me."

Knowing she was a patient woman, he was scared: yet he knew he would go on desiring her. But he could not contemplate a settled future, not now. He did not love her. He did not think he ever would, and so he was the more ashamed.

But his mind was given, as he knew to his cost, to fluttering at random from point to point. His mother, under the chestnuts, drinking champagne. She had never before told him of her trip to Paris. Could it conceivably be that she had made the whole thing up?

Fay refused, as he knew she would, any offer on his part to see her to the tube station. She had just enough time to catch the last train.

When Mildred came in she offered him, as usual, something hot if he needed it.

She said, with a touch of sprightly malice, "What, all alone? I find it hard to believe."

He saw that she was flushed, more than commonly excited.

177

She had taken her coat off. Her solid shoulders shone like china above her dress of dark, discreet blue.

"I won't ask what you've been doing," she said, with the new, impudent touch he associated with her since he had begun his affair with Fay.

"I'd rather ask," he said, comfortable and neat in bed, "what you have. Do you know it's nearly half past twelve?"

"Mother would call me a night-owl. Well, I've got a new young man, or so I think. His name is Hansen, he's a solicitor, and his wife's in an asylum. Not a promising *parti*, exactly, but someone to take me out a bit. He's promised to 'phone me. What do you think of that?"

Jo asked how old he was, and was told, in his early fifties. "Rather old for me," said Mildred complacently, "but beggars can't be choosers. I must say I hope he does ring. I shall be keeping an ear painfully cocked."

"Any hope of his wife departing this mortal coil?" Jo selfishly hoped that there was not.

"I shouldn't think so for a moment. She's perfectly fit in herself, I gather. They've got two grown-up children. There was one late-comer who didn't survive. She went funny after that."

He asked her how she had enjoyed the dinner otherwise. All right, she replied, though the food was awful and half-cold, as it was at all public affairs. The highest number of people you could cater for and be sure of a happy result, said Mildred, herself an excellent plain cook, was eight.

Jo laughed. "Since when have you catered for more than five? We never ask more than two in for a meal."

"Just my judgment," she said, "just my sound judgment."

"Do you know what?"

"No, I don't. What?"

"You're looking quite handsome."

"It could be the flush of drink. I've had rather more than I'm used to."

"Or it could be love?"

She said she didn't think so. She was not one, as he well knew, to rush into things. "No raw girl," she added derisively, wishing that she were. "But I'd like just to go out with a man again. I envy you, you know."

She envied him his freedom. She had no sexual experience

herself, but was quite sure she would like it if she did. Only for her this must mean marriage, and she had small hope of that. Occasionally she had sought solitary gratification, but it always ended up in shame, and the sense that it was a lie and a cheat. She would have been horrified had she believed anyone suspected her of such practices.

"Well, good luck to Mr. Hansen. Has he got a first name?"

"Frank. One of my favorites." She yawned and stretched herself, arms high above her head. Jo noticed, in her armpits, a little dark fuzz and wished she would do something about it. But to suggest such a thing would have seemed to him the extreme of indelicacy, even though it was not always with delicacy that they talked to each other these days. He was relieved when she put her arms down again. "I shall call him that, never Francis."

In bed, in the dark, she re-lived the moments of the evening, which seemed in retrospect to have had a marvellous glitter, all the men handsome, all the women beautiful: but she knew that, apart from her meeting with Hansen, it had all been pretty ordinary. Most of the men either facetious or drab, most of the women middle-aged, and too noticeably "in their best." Tradesmen, she thought, as her mother would have thought. (Bessie's husband had been a Civil Servant, which put him several cuts above trade.) Yet, Mildred said to herself, what snobs we are! To get out of this kind of life, I'd settle for a well-spoken greengrocer.

Would he telephone her? Had he really meant it?

She was already beginning to forget the details of his face. He had been tall, had a small moustache. Blue eyes, rather tired-looking. Nose? Mouth? She couldn't remember.

Chapter Three

WHEN POLLY SAW KIT OFF ON THE BOAT-TRAIN TO SOUTHAMPTON, she was smiling and serene. "Have a wonderful time, darling, and do be careful how much you drink. I do wish I were coming with you!"

"Christ, I wish you were! But four weeks isn't such an awful time, and I'll write every day, I promise. Keep well for me, my love."

She stood watching the train until it was out of sight; then she let the tears fall, making little attempt to conceal them as she walked slowly back along the platform. Ever since the death of the child she had felt miserably weak: it was only weakness that had led her to accept Kit's ridiculous idea about the houseboat. Her spirit seemed to have deserted her. She had not even protested recently about his drinking, which had accelerated with his disappointment, nor found the heart to cheer him by emphasizing his growing success. She, like Alison, was basically a strong woman, her grip upon Kit hitherto so sure that she had been forced to play, sporadically, the part of a submissive wife. This had appeared to deceive him, or at least, he had wished to be deceived.

180

Now, bereft of him, she did not know how she was to endure the lonely weeks. Of course, such old friends as were still in London would come to see her, to "take her out of herself": she did not want them. The only person she would have wished to see was Alison, of whom she had once been fond, whom she felt she had betrayed: but Alison was in other circles now, and would not need her. The implicit reconciliation of the engagement party had since proved abortive.

The station, echoing hollow, full of crowds, full of noise, of the anxieties of arrival and departure, swelled her loneliness to panic. She could not make the journey home by underground. She would have to take the taxi that should not be afforded. The price of a meal? Two meals? She could not face the thought of eating, in any case.

On the doorstep, patiently awaiting her, was the last person she could have expected to see: her father. She stiffened immediately. She had never shown weakness before him, and she would not do so now.

"I thought you wouldn't be long," he said. "I've been doing a Sherlock Holmes performance, looking up the boat-train, guessing you'd see him off, and thinking I might possibly be of some use. I can give you lunch, anyway."

Then she did show weakness, and allowed him to hold her, rather awkwardly, while she wept.

"Feeling under the weather," he said, "perfectly natural. Worst time he could have chosen to go gallivanting."

The word steadied her, and she laughed. "It's going to be an exhausting trip for the poor dear. But come in. It was good of you to think you might be wanted. Actually, you are."

She told him there was no need to buy her lunch, at which he seemed relieved.

"I'll make us both an omelette."

He took from his pocket, with the munificent air of a Timon before his friends had let him down, a quarter-bottle of whiskey. "What you want is a mild stimulant."

"And it will be mild," she said, "by the look of it."

For the first time she noticed that he had brought something with him, a flat parcel roughly done up in newspaper and held together by several pieces of string knotted hairily together. "What on earth's that?"

181

"The Birket Foster. You'd better dispose of it as you did the other two. I can't have you starving."

It is surprising what a comfort an unexpected sum of money can be, even in the worst of emotional distress: it is sentimentality to suppose it could be otherwise. Polly's first thought was that the taxi had been paid for: her second, that the practical strains of life had for the moment been lifted. She gave him the most spontaneous kiss he had ever had from her since she was a child.

"I tell you," he said, "between the two of you, you'll ruin me. This means another dingy patch on the wall, or rather, a whiter patch on a dingy wall. But that Ramsay you don't get till I'm dead."

More people live histrionic lives, even if unrealized by themselves, than many people think. Wantage, in his selfish desire to be left alone amid a general crumbling which he felt to be both symbolic and pleasurable, had exaggerated in himself the genuine tendency to be a skinflint. He was not much fonder of Polly than a cat is fond of its kittens, once the weaning is over: but he did feel towards her a certain sense of responsibility. He had not opposed her marriage: this had seemed to him none of his business and in fact, since Kit's name had begun to creep into the news, felt it had not turned out so badly as might have been expected. He liked Kit well enough: what did worry him were the freaks that might affect Polly. She had had a bad enough time over the baby. He did not want her getting pneumonia on some damned silly barge. If she did, it would reflect on himself, and he did not want to be reflected upon by anyone; merely to be left alone. Should they really move to anywhere so crass, this would be bound to appear all over the papers. He hated the papers like poison.

"So now you'd needn't leave here."

She stared at him. "Why not?"

"I assume you're behind-hand with the rent."

"No, we're not."

"Then what are you doing such a tom-fool thing for?"

She told him Kit wanted it, and that it would be something that was at least their own.

He retorted angrily that they were asking for trouble. "If you get the war you and your friends are craving for, you

182

couldn't find yourselves in a worse position. I don't know much, as you'd be the first to admit, but I know about tactics. The bombers will go for railway junctions and bridges, and there will you be, right under a bridge, offering yourselves as sitting targets."

She was a little shaken. "You honestly think so?"

"I know it." He cleared his throat, as if to rid it of its chronic weakness. "My dear girl, I don't think, I *know*."

When he had eaten his omelette and taken himself off for a fleeting spell at the House of Lords, she unwrapped the parcel.

It was a vivid, clotted water-color, no more than five or six inches by seven, of a little girl in a white dress climbing over a stile in a woodland remarkably fertile with budding branches and wild roses, each rose a ruby, each leaf an emerald. It was thickly sentimental, but it was charming. For a moment she was almost inclined to keep it. Reproductions of Klee and Picasso could easily lose their initial excitement: but this was real, the painter's hand had touched it. If one kept it long enough one would find small birds in the thicket, ladybirds among the flowers.

But it could not be kept, as well she knew. Rather than linger all the afternoon in the desolate flat, she took the bus to Bond Street and put it up for auction at Sotheby's. The moment she had left there, she felt new tears rising, this time for the little girl she would not see again. She remembered that only one foot was visible, in a blue buttoned boot.

On the way back she played a game she and Kit had invented called Negative Shopping. This consisted in studying the windows of the richest shops, and deciding to what objects they would not give house-room if these were offered them free. She chose a golden teapot in the shape of a motor-car, a dress of red satin with elaborate ruchings, and a picture of two Puritans indulging in a secret carouse, being peeped at, through an open doorway, by a *louche*-looking maidservant. This kept her from crying again, it got her through the lonely day.

After she had received Kit's first letter from the ship—he had seen dolphins, he had won five pounds at Bingo, nobody on board had heard of him but they soon would, he adored her and he missed her—she began to pull herself together. The next thing she did was to get back her old job with Alison's publisher, which she would not have dared to do when Kit was home. She went to inspect the houseboat, put down a deposit, and arranged that it should be adequately heated by a coal-burning stove. Then she put in an appearance at the Six Bells, where she found none of her friends, but was accosted by Nigel Dobson.

"Mrs. Mallings, you remember me? It's been a long time, though. May I buy you a drink?"

"Tomato juice, please."

He hoped her marriage was very happy. In his experience, a somewhat vicarious experience, he admitted, it was always a risk.

"For me," Polly said, with some malice, "hevenriche blisse."

He blinked at her.

She added, "Piers Plowman."

"Oh, of course, I'd forgotten. Funny how one's memory weakens as one grows older. Where's Mallings?"

She told him, in the United States.

"A great country," he said, "a great country. But he mustn't be swept off his feet. He's still got a long way to go. Tell him from me to watch his step. The flash in the pan—that's something he won't want, don't you agree?"

Polly suggested that Kit's flashes were beginning to look like the aurora borealis.

"Still," Dobson said gloomily, "it doesn't do to reckon on the future. I may, of course, be wrong, but don't you think he still hasn't quite got his style under control?"

To change the subject, she asked him what he was doing these days. "Oh, marking time, marking time. If the world blows up I shall, of course, volunteer at once. That is, if they'll take me. My sight is a little defective." He had, he said, his car outside: might he run her home?

She did not wish to go home.

"You don't want too many late nights," he told her. "Forgive me for saying so, but you're looking a bit peaky. You need an iron tonic, or yeast. My mother swears by yeast, but you must get it fresh from the baker's."

She was glad when he excused himself. He had, he said, an important appointment with someone he need not name: and as she did not press him to do so, withdrew in something like disappointment.

Her next letter from Kit was not so reassuring. To begin with, it was only half a page long. He was, he said, so firmly on

184

the moving belt that he had hardly a second in which to write. He had given two lectures, both packed out. He was being looked after by a woman agent called Fran. "I love and adore you and think of you all the time, when I get any time to think. I go to Boston tomorrow."

She was worried not so much by the brevity of the letter, or by the news that his agent was a woman (an American beauty? she did not believe Kit would care), but by the shakiness of his handwriting. Normally large, fine and erect, neatly aligned, it now sprawled at a slight angle, sometimes sharply dipping as if the pen had skidded on the paper. Which probably meant that he was drinking too much.

She wrote a firm reply telling him what she suspected and begging him to take care. She also told him that, though she knew he wouldn't much like it, she had returned to work. "We have simply got to live a bit more easily than we do, and with you writing all day you can hardly notice whether I'm around or not. When you come back they will let me leave the office, as a prize concession, at half past four, so we shall have long evenings together. I'm working on the boat at weekends. It is beginning to look pretty, though I'm still anxious about getting it dried out properly."

To work again was a comfort, for it kept her mind from him for hours at a time. At the beginning of the fourth week, when she had started to count the days to his return, Alison walked into her office.

"Hullo, Polly! I heard you were back. How are you? Will you come out to lunch with me?"

Alison was dashingly smart, in one of the square-shouldered suits just beginning to be fashionable, and she looked happy. "Do come. I'm only up for the day, and I should so enjoy it."

They had once liked each other very much. In the small restaurant nearby, that liking began to return. When they had ordered a meal Alison said directly, "Let's push something out of the way. All the trouble's over and done with now, and none of it was your fault. I always knew that."

"I felt guilty, just the same."

"And I felt you damned well ought to, but that was unfair, and I'm sorry. Shall we forget all about it?"

"For God's sake, let's," Polly said, smiling.

"Good. We'll have some wine as a celebration, even if it does make us both sleepy for the rest of the afternoon. When does Kit come home?"

"Saturday," Polly replied, and flushed at the thought of it.

"He'll come back staggering under a weight of laurels, won't he?"

"So I gather. He hasn't time to write long letters, as he's always travelling. He will certainly be staggering under a weight of exhaustion. I hope not under anything else."

Alison hoped the return voyage would be a compulsory rest. She said, tentatively, how sorry she had been about the baby. (She had not wanted to mention it, but thought it would seem callous if she did not.)

"I'm getting over it now, I think," Polly replied. "I tell myself we can soon start again. It's Kit who can't even try to forget. Would you have suspected that?"

Alison said she didn't know, adding that she now thought she had never understood him very well.

"I pretend to myself that I do," Polly said, "of course, one must. But though he's the sun and moon and stars, there are things about him I don't understand at all, and I don't believe anyone ever will. Do you know, I'm suddenly extremely hungry? I haven't been, not for weeks."

"Good." With pleasure Alison watched her eat, noticing that she had grown much thinner. She was still neat, still pretty, her mouse-colored hair with a pewtery gloss upon it: but the hollows under her cheek-bones were deep enough to look greyish, even unwashed, and the cords in her neck stood out like those of an older woman's.

Polly looked up suddenly. "What about you?"

"About me?"

"I have a very strong suspicion. You needn't mind telling me."

"Yes, I am pregnant. I don't know how you knew."

"Mere guesswork. Something in your voice. I'm glad. You'll have good luck, I'm sure of it."

"So will you, next time."

"Yes," Polly said firmly, "I mean to."

Alison asked about their friends. Did they still make fun of her as a *mem-sahib*? Did they still think her marriage was an odd one?

Polly replied that Kit professed to find it so, and so did Georgina when the mood took her—"but then, she's rather jealous, you know. Randy she may be, but she'd really love it if Clement stopped being a bohemian, and she could be randy in a more stately way in grander circles."

Alison laughed. But what about Jo? How had he really felt about her and Piers?

"It's been good for him. You see, you always were something of a moon-goddess, miles above him, but now you're not even in the same universe. I think that helps a little. I wish he'd get serious about Fay, but even she makes him a bit diffident—you know, trips abroad, smart clothes, Paris collections. He is so maddeningly humble."

Here she was entirely wrong. Jo was not a humble man but a proud one, with a streak of vanity deeply concealed. It was true that he had come to feel ashamed about a background which, until two years ago, he had taken for granted: yet he was ashamed neither of his mother nor Mildred. He felt them good enough for anybody in the world, did not force himself to feel so, but felt it genuinely. He was not at all diffident about Fay. Had he loved her, he would have married her, would have managed it somehow, and would not have thought she had been entirely unlucky in him. But he would not have had her living among the Benares ware, pushing the bath-chair, listening night after night to Henry Hall.

"Yes, he is," Alison agreed. "If only he could have some luck with his writing! Even one story would help. Life hasn't given him much, has it?"

Polly finished her veal cutlet, and said she would like *canapés Diane*. "I am costing you an awful lot today."

"Not so much as all that, and it's in a very good cause. By the by, it is true that Clement once walloped Georgina in the street? Rumors did reach me."

"Certainly it's true. It was an extraordinary scene, and I had the front row of the dress circle."

"I wish I'd been there," said Alison enviously, forgetting the occasion upon which this had taken place: or perhaps she had never been told.

The two small, healthy young women were silent for a few minutes, eating with masculine appetites. It was extraordinary to both of them how easily strain had departed, leaving them in a simple amity of bodily hunger and a desire for gossip, for the picking up of lost threads.

Polly said, her face clouding, "But you know, those times are over, and for good. I try not to think of the world too much, but it's becoming far too black for people to roister in the pubs, or enjoy antics like that any more, except as a sort of fake. It always was a kind of play-acting, but now it would be a play within a play within a play, and the play on the very outside, if you know what I mean—something like the peel on a moldy orange—is a very nasty one. When I let myself think about it, I get more scared than I like to admit." She added, with compunction, "But of course, it will be worse for you. Piers would have to go at once, wouldn't he?"

"I suppose so. What about Kit?"

Polly shook her head. It was not, she said, that he was a coward: if bombs rained down on London he would stay there and, furthermore, stay there in a barge under a bridge, like the fool he was. Cowardice was something he had always pretended, to lend a sort of Barriesque charm to his pose of being smaller, more frail, than everybody else. In fact, if there was a fight of any sort, he would hurl himself into it against ridiculous odds, as he had done with Jo one day in the King's Road. "He went to Mosley's last rally and got thrown downstairs three times; one of them, to his everlasting disgrace, by some huge muscular girl with buck teeth. Clement had to hold him back physically to stop him charging in for the fourth time. But he says he will never kill. Or, more specifically, he says he will never kill anyone he doesn't know personally. I think that is a very nice distinction and shows his beautiful nature." She looked regretfully at her watch. She would have to be going. As she rose, she kissed Alison's cheek. "You can't think how glad I am about this."

"I am, too."

"I've never been able to talk to anyone as I talk to you. I've missed that."

"Then we'll always go on talking," said Alison, "whenever we can get together. Perhaps you and Kit could bring yourself to visit the quite agreeable zoo in which I live. It might remind you that you're something of a *mem-sahib* yourself."

They parted with promises.

188

Chapter Four

KIT WOKE IN THE PITCH-DARK TO GO TO THE LAVATORY. THE CUR-
tains were tightly drawn so that there was no gleam of light, and
the air was stifling. He got there somehow, but on returning to
the bedroom found himself totally disoriented. This was his last
night in New York. He was to sail next day.

He began to fumble around the walls, frantically feeling for
an identifiable surface, but all surfaces were the same to his
blunted finger-tips. He bumped into some article of furniture and
bruised himself. What was it? Something crashed down. Something off the dressing-table? Good. Then the bed must be somewhere about three feet behind him. That was where it was. He
launched out, his arms stretched like a sleep-walker's: and tripping
over an unexpected object, fell heavily to the floor. He lay there
for a while, the pile of the carpet comfortable to his cheek, and
tried to think. Then he rose gingerly on all fours, flailed around
for support, and finding none, nevertheless managed to jerk himself erect. Now he was completely lost, his memory also. Had
there been two beds or one? He blundered forward till he made
contact with the wall. Which wall? If he kept his head, and

inched around the room, never losing contact with solid objects, he was bound to find the bed. Suddenly his feet felt stone beneath them and he staggered hard against something that could only be the bath. How the hell had he got in there again? But the bath itself was a clue. If he could guide himself along the edge to the taps, the shower-curtains, he could find the door, be back in the bedroom. Yes, carpet underfoot. Well done. He stood very still, trying to be calm. Wait a few seconds and everything would be clear. The horror of darkness rose in him. He must not panic. If he could touch something soft it might be the blinds, he could open them, and the lights would break in. Outside the window was a red sign that blinked on and off; he had only to expose it, and he would be safe. You bloody fool, he said to himself, if you hadn't drunk so bloody much this wouldn't have happened. It has got to stop before you see Polly, because she will know. Ah! another flat surface. The chest of drawers? He fumbled again, and this time knocked over the glass of water from the bedside table, soaking the legs of his pyjamas. Never mind that. Here we are. One bed or two? Never mind. Feel first to the right, then to the left. He tried to do so, but his sense of distance was lost. Sleep-walking again, he struck out vigorously and this time found himself in space, in blackness soft as fur. His head was reeling. Half-crouched, he tried to will sensitivity into his fingers. Steady. He had only to reach the wall again, and all would be well. Important not to move more than an inch at a time. The blackness might have surrounded him for miles, for furry miles. It was as thick as a blindfold, like the fur of a black cat, suffocating, almost tactile. Play blind-man's-buff, he said to himself, that's safe. One always touches somebody in the end. *Somebody?* To touch the flesh of a cheek, to put a finger upon the socket of an eye? The thought terrified him so much that he took a long, incautious step, a step of escape, and his shin came in contact with iron. He fell for the second time and did not try to get up again.

It seemed to him, lying there, that however hot the room, a recumbent person should be covered. This was very important. He began to grope above his head, touched fabric, pulled it down above him. Then he slept.

He was awakened by a crashing at the door and an agitated voice shouting, "Kit! Kit! Let me in, will you?"

190

His eyes opened. There was just enough grey in the room, coming from a rim of light below the curtains, to make objects distinguishable. He was lying on the floor between the two single beds, draped with his own dressing-gown, every bone in his head and body aching.

"Kit, you've just one hour to get to the boat. *Will* you open up?"

When he had managed to do so, Fran Olson stared at him aghast. She was a tall, bony woman in early middle-age, with protuberant eyes and masses of gypsy hair. Striding past him, she flung back the curtains and the terrible light of morning poured in. He felt it like a blow in the face.

"For Christ's sake, what have you been doing to yourself?"

"I don't know. Let me look." He made his way to the bathroom mirror. His face seemed much as usual, unscarred, but very pale.

"You've got blood all over your left ankle. Will you get dressed as quickly as you can? Have you packed?"

Dumb, he shook his head.

"Well, I'll do it for you. Get your clothes on. The car's outside, and I've settled up at the desk. You can tell me all about it on the way."

Forced by her dreadful energy, he dressed somehow; not attempting to shave. Fran pushed him down on the side of the bed, tied his shoe-laces, combed his hair. "I told you what would happen!"

Still he could not speak.

"Well, you've rocked them all, my friend, your stock's a mile high, but you've rocked yourself as well."

She was feverishly opening drawers, stuffing everything she could find into his two suitcases.

"Polly," he managed to say. "I had something for Polly. A necklace, bright-blue one."

"I've found it and packed it. Come along now, and we may just make it."

Fortunately his hotel was downtown, near Washington Square, so the docks were not too far away.

They were in time for him to stumble up the gangplank just as the last call was being sounded for visitors to leave the ship.

"Fran," he began, "you've been wonderful, you've been the most wonderful thing—"

"O.K., take it as read." She kissed him hastily. "Hurry up, will you? Your bags are on board."

As the ship drew away over a pale-blue sea, so pale as to be almost white, not a ripple showing, he leaned over the rail blindly waving. He could not see her, but he knew she must be waving to him.

Somehow he found his stateroom, and he slept until half past four in the afternoon.

When he woke again, his head was clear. He had a shower, shaved, unpacked the tumbled clothes and changed his shirt. Pushed under the door he found an invitation to the purser's party: six-thirty p.m.

Yes, but he wanted a drink now.

Perhaps. But he wasn't going to have one.

He remembered, cursing, that he must have been too late to order, from the dining-room steward, a table to himself. This almost certainly meant that they would put him with two gabby married couples, and one spinster, equally gabby. Well, he would not bear it.

With some dignity, he went to the purser's office and asked whether, if it were not impossible by now, a change might be made in the table arrangements, and was comforted when told that this should be done. He walked through the sickly colored lounge, where people were still eating sandwiches and little cakes, and a three-piece band was playing "Smoke Gets in Your Eyes," till he came to the bar, where only a few hardened drinkers had yet begun the main business of the evening.

He pulled himself together as if he were reining in a plunging horse. No.

No.

No.

He forced himself to attend lifeboat drill, just to fill in time, then returned to the lounge where he ordered tea and, though it made him feel sick, he drank it. Afterwards he went out on deck, to watch the first smudged rosiness of the sunset streak the upper air. It was warm for early April and the sea was barely wrinkled, but leaning over the rail, he could see it being sucked down to the keel of the ship, a savage crystalline downpouring, pale as ginger-beer, with an occasional color-wash of the purest aqua-marine. He thought longingly of Polly, whom he would see so soon: how he wished she were with him now! He did not propose to let her stay in her job. We can get along, he said to himself, since I've earned a bit. I am an old-fashioned man. I do not wish my wife to work.

If he thought of her with longing, it was also with a touch of fear. He had always been chary of her resolution, and indeed, since she had used it so startlingly upon their first abortive wedding-day, had not cared to awaken it again. He must contrive to return home to her in a state she would find entirely satisfactory. I am not, after all, an alcoholic, nothing near it: I am merely a heavy drinker. But in this ship, I am not even going to drink heavily. I swear it. To himself in the glass: You have sworn it.

At the purser's party he discovered, to his astonishment, that he was not unknown. Even a fortnight of lecturing had caused several people to have heard of him. He knew he had been a success, but not quite how much. Before going to America he had never spoken in public before. When he tried it he found that, though sick with fright for hours before he walked onto a plat-form, he was not in the least frightened when he began, but could take immense stimulus from the sea of innocent, even not so in-nocent, young faces. He had chosen to speak on the English novel and the Irish drama. Lecturing one night upon the latter, with special reference to O'Casey, it had occurred to him to sing, unac-companied, those fragments from "Within the Gates" that he and Jo had once sung together: to sing in his fullest and finest bass, "Our Mother the Earth" and the mournful "Heavy Dragoon." This had been a riotous success: at all further lectures he had been required to sing, though he found this rather more difficult to fit into the context of the English novel. A freak success, per-haps? Conceivably. But, he thought grimly, enough to start him on his way, and none of his successes were going to be in the least freakish from now on.

Summoning his moral courage, he rejected Scotch and stood drinking sherry in minute droplets, clutching the stem of the glass as if it were a lifeline, switching his charming attention be-tween a Professor of Comparative Literature from Harvard, a simply dressed, almost conspicuously unobtrusive woman who turned out to be the heiress to one of the greatest fortunes in America, and a girl fresh from Vassar who knew his novel with disconcerting thoroughness. He was so exhilarated by all this that for the first time in more than three weeks he managed to go to bed quite sober.

Next day the sea was rough and Kit, sick as a dog, could not contemplate alcohol, even the champagne urged upon him as a prophylactic by a tender-hearted steward; so, for the next three days, it continued: till in the space of two hours the waters subsided as if awaiting a dove, and lay stretched out like grey satin under a thinness of mist. To celebrate the relief, he permitted himself to drink quite a lot, during the Bingo session, with an oddly assorted party, including the unobtrusive woman who, being the richest person on board, had naturally won the ship's auction. But after that evening, he did not backslide. It was with a grateful heart, feeling fresh as a daisy, not tired at all, money in his pocket, that he docked at Southampton.

And there she was, waving to him from the pier: he had not expected her to come all that way to meet him. Once through the customs, he ran to hug and kiss her, almost speechless with joy, and with his sense of purification.

"First class," he insisted, as she opened the door of a third-class carriage, "don't you realize those marvellous Yanks have paid for me every inch of the way?"

"Then you'll have to travel alone. My ticket's only a third."

"Do you suppose," he said loftily, "that I can't pay the miserable difference? Darling, we are going to drink Veuve Cliquot tonight."

"I hope," she said, as he stowed his cases on the rack, "that you've been drinking in moderation."

"Hardly at all," said Kit, looking injured. "Didn't I promise you?"

"But your writing was sometimes peculiar. When you did write."

"My dear darling, I told you, I had no time. I've been to—" He ticked the places off on his fingers—"Harvard, Yale, Cornell, Philadelphia, Columbia, and N.Y.U., and the Poetry Center, New York, all in fourteen days. And sober as a judge."

"I bet," said Polly. "Still, you look wonderful now." She found it hard to believe he was really there. He was the incarna-

194

tion of her long dream, fresh-faced, his eyes bright. She needed to touch him for reassurance, his hand, his cheek.

"So do you. Do you know the very first thing we're going to do when we get home?"

It seemed to him that he had never been so happy in his whole life.

Chapter Five

IT WAS IN THE MAY OF THAT HORRIBLE YEAR THAT HE AND POLLY moved into the houseboat. Jo had helped them in what spare time he had, which was less now than before, because Mildred was going out, rather defiantly, three times a week with her friend Mr. Hansen, about whom she had become secretive.

The boat, lying fifty yards or so beyond the bridge on the power-station side, was approached by a pier of stout planks, which could be treacherous on a dark night. It was painted in garish stripes and its name was *Halcyon Bird*. It had a large living-room with kitchen arrangements at one end, and a sleeping-cabin with four bunks in it. There was an Elsan closet emptied, Polly said, in slightly mysterious circumstances. A guardian of the shore dealt with it daily, tactfully insisting that it was better to do this when she and Kit were out. "We always imagined it being carried off miles away," she said, "but sometimes, when we've been in, the collection is followed within minutes by an ominous splash." They even had, and this was their pride, a tiny bathroom. "However," Kit explained, "it's better to have a bath at high tide, because if you have it at low tide, you find yourself shivering in three inches of water."

Their chief pride was the coal-fire, penned into an iron stove, powerful enough to pervade the entire boat; it was charming to come in to it from the chilly deck, or see it glimmering at dusk through the french windows astern.

"I have to say," said Kit, "that we're a bit malodorous at low tide, but when we're riding on the water—and believe me, strong men have been seasick—the air smells of the sea."

Jo insisted that it could not but be damp.

Polly insisted that it was not. She had not liked making this move at all, but had been unable to resist Kit's fervor for the unusual. She would soon, she said, get used to the noise of the gulls. Since she had resisted his attempts to make her give up working, and since he was beginning to earn quite a sizeable amount from writing for American magazines, a good deal of money was coming into the household. Out of it she had prettified the boat in a way that she herself held faintly in derision: it was a play-acting place in which to live, and she had made it look like one. Curtains and bedspreads from Heal's; tables and chairs bought in Portobello Road, stripped and painted white; reproductions on the walls of Lautrec theatre-programmes. "It is *twee*," she said to Jo, "don't you think so? That is the very word."

They had a housewarming—"The warmth is still needed, though we can easily become overheated," she remarked—to which all their friends came, including Piers and Alison. It began gaily enough, but gaiety, in those days, was usually sporadic, and before long they all found themselves talking politics. Piers listened quietly, and did not say much. Jo, Kit, Clement and most of their friends believed that the National Government's call for increased army expenditure was a fraud, a desire to put money in the hands of the arms manufacturers while driving the Germans into the war with Russia: they maintained that the Government did not want, and did not intend, to fight, but was prepared to make a deal with the Axis powers—and that if this happened, England would inevitably take on the coloring of a Fascist country. Of this they were all, especially Clement, who had recently been in Germany, and Jo, who had a black imagination, passionately afraid. But while they cried that Chamberlain was a scoundrel, Piers continued to think him a fool. Whatever the man's hopes were, they were stupid ones; Hitler was not

197

to be stopped by any device, though Piers had some vestigial hope of a pact with France and Russia that might put a little more strength into the country during the period of delay. He knew how weak its military resources were and found it hard to batten down his irritation when Jo inveighed against the idea of building them up. Alison, who had understood something of this also, and at first-hand, was now of Piers's way of thinking, though she remained far more radical than he.

The hero of the evening, in literal terms, was someone they all disliked. Phil Christie had been in Spain, had lost three fingers from his left hand in his first engagement, and had been sent home again. Still bandaged, he was cock-a-hoop and writing war poems. "Oh, it was all pretty much of a mess, but I somehow enjoyed it. You know me!"

"Were you scared?" Kit asked. "I should have been peeing my pants. To begin with, I hate loud noises."

"You're probably going to hear some pretty shortly," Clement said, in his light drawl, "so you'd better lay in a stock of cotton wool."

Phil squinted thoughtfully down his snub nose. His smallness of feature gave him an almost girlish prettiness; he had always tried to conceal his sexual ambivalence by clamorous flirtations with women safely beyond his reach, and he often wondered uneasily whether he did so with entire success. "I think one didn't have time to be. Besides, as I never had any clearly defined idea of what I was doing, I was too busy trying to work it all out to think about myself. No—honestly. I mean it."

Polly said to Alison softly, pulling the curtains back, "Look, isn't it pretty?"

It was a clear, starry night. The plumes of smoke from the four chimneys of the power-station were half-silver with the moon, half-russet with the perpetual London glow. A swan dived into the sparkling water, looking, upside-down, like a fancifully folded table napkin. A barge with a green light went by, trailing a string of smaller boats, and *Halcyon Bird* rocked gently on the wash.

Alison nodded, and touched her hand. For the past two days she had felt the child move. She looked at Piers, who smiled at her though the circling smoke-rings.

198

"You won't be scared, will you?" Kit asked him. "If it comes, I mean. Doesn't all that training help?"

"Come on," said Georgina, "speak up. We're dying to hear, and it isn't right for Phil to have all the glory." She shot him a glance of distaste. She had not liked him when he had all his fingers, and liked him no more because now he had fewer. Besides, she was the only one of them to be certain in her mind of his sexual proclivities: he had once been silly enough to try to flirt with her, and she had seen through his pretenses immediately.

"I think I shall be scared stiff," Piers replied slowly. "I have always been rather short on physical courage."

Phil gave an incredulous bray of laughter.

"Oh, I have. But I hope to conceal it when the time arrives. What else can anyone do?"

"Look," Jo said fervently, "that's defeatist talk. The time hasn't got to arrive!"

Piers said politely that he very much hoped it hadn't.

A voice came to them across the waters. It was Fay, late as usual, calling for someone to light her down the planks. Clement, who was nearest to the door, went to her aid.

She came in, tall, gaunt and dainty, kissed everybody and exclaimed with admiration. "Polly, it's marvellous! It's the *chic*est thing I ever saw." She must be escorted from stem to stern, she wished to miss nothing.

When this had been done, she came to sit by Jo.

"I've got something for you."

For several months past he had been using her office as an accommodation address for the stamped and addressed envelopes sent out with his manuscripts. He had hated Mildred to see how invariably they thudded back upon the mat: also, he had fancied that the change might even bring him luck.

"Let's keep our fingers crossed," Fay whispered, "this is from *The Adelphi*, and it isn't a thick envelope, it's a thin one."

He tore it open, and reddened up to his eyebrows. He could feel the hot flush rising, the dampening of his skin. He shouted, "They've taken it!"

Then everyone was excited, snatching the letter from hand to hand, blundering across the cramped space to congratulate him on this, his first, triumph.

199

"Bless you," said Fay proprietorially, "you deserve it!" She raised her beer mug. "To the first of many!"

He sat there dazed, scarcely able to believe his luck. *The Adelphi!* It could scarcely have been more imposing a start. For the first time he was one among them, not an outsider: he, too, could call himself a Writer. He looked at Alison, needing her to be proud of him.

"Jo," she said, "it's wonderful. Dear Jo."

Kit glanced up sharply. There was something in the tone of her voice which made him believe in the truth of something Jo had once let slip, then had denied. He could not repress a quite irrational pang of friendship betrayed.

Piers heard the note too, but he only smiled at her. She had told him everything before their marriage.

Jo rose suddenly. "Got to get a breath of air." He squeezed himself through the room and out onto the pier. Joy had made him feel sick, and he was afraid he might implement the feeling. However, he did not: so he stood for a few minutes alone on the planks, the light wind blowing his hair about, the gulls as high and buoyant as his own heart.

He thought, It's happened, it's happened at last, and to me it's a big thing, whatever it may seem to some of them. Alison, I shall love you forever, without hope, but that will be better than nothing. It is wonderful just to love. The world about him was beautiful, the plane trees emerald in the lamplight, the headlights of the cars tumbling like enormous jewels from an invisible treasure chest, the lace edging of the dirty river frilling out along the mud as boats went by in lace, frills, beery honeycombs of froth.

Fay came out to him. "Darling, are you all right?"

"Yes. I just felt suffocated. The grandeur went to my head."

She kissed him. "You know how happy I am?"

"Of course I do. You're worth six of me, Fay."

"In some respects," she replied briskly, "but not in very many. Do *not* let us have a masochistic display of any kind. I want you to go back in there and lord it over them. You lord it like hell."

"It's only one story, of course."

"Oh, shut up, and do stop the humility act. You're as proud as Punch, you silly old thing, so for God's sake *look* it!"

200

One day, he thought, he might perhaps marry Fay. It wasn't impossible.

Back in the cabin, he found the conversation had turned to writing in general.

"But you're an expert now," said Kit, "you tell us what you *want* to do."

Jo said, "I think I want to write the absolute truth, in so far as I know it."

Kit said, "I don't."

"Darling!" Even Polly looked surprised.

"I want to tell precisely what is not true, but what ought to be."

"Good God," said Phil, "Socialist Realism?" He tittered.

"No. I want to tell the truths that are sometimes there in dreams, but never here. Not here to touch, or analyze, or muck about with. When you see a dark woman in a dream, with her hands over her face and she won't go and you are terrified that she's going to take those hands away, then she is real. She is the sort of truth I care about. Not your kind, Jo, certainly not Clement's."

"If I adopted that kind of truth as my own," Clement said, "I should shortly be thrown off all my papers on my ear, which wouldn't suit Georgie."

"You could always write What the Stars Foretell, darling." She patted him on the head.

"I should have said," Kit went on, his eyes firing up with the heat of ideas that had only just occurred to him, but which he hoped to present as synthesis of others slowly and intellectually developed, "I want to tell what isn't true—what ought to be and what ought not to be."

Polly smiled inwardly. Quite unconscious of his motives, he was trying rapidly to re-establish among them the ascendancy he had lost for more than ten minutes through Jo's isolated moment of glory. This was part of Kit's strength, a part of the resolution that drove him on. He had never doubted his own powers: he was not going to have them doubted by others. Never.

Jo was puzzled and a little distressed, partly because he had ceased to be the center of attention, and partly because Kit seemed to him to be talking nonsense. He wanted to counter it, but did not know how.

Alison, however, said, "Kit, it won't do. A dream is a purely individual experience. It's hard enough to communicate, anyway. Why make it totally impossible, in any meaningful sense?"

"Yes, ma'am, yes, ma'am," said Kit, "hats off to our foremost lady novelist. All the same—"

"If you call me that again," she retorted, "I am going to throw a bottle at you. I would reply in kind, but a gentleman novelist you are not, and it's my variety of truth which stops me calling you one."

Clement cheered her. Kit pretended to duck a blow.

"If you tease Alison," said Polly, "we shall put you outside on the mud. Which is your rightful place."

"I will be a good boy. I am afraid of Piers."

"If truth's at the bottom of a well," Piers asked him, "from what well are you going to dredge her up? Simply from your own dream-life? It doesn't match with anything you've written yet," he added shrewdly.

"Hah!" Kit shouted, "I have readers in Camberley, readers in Aldershot. Officers' Messes resound with my name." Quietly he intoned a new song:

> "Readers in Camberley,
> Readers in Aldershot. . . ."

"Oh, some of us can read, you know. Some of us can even spell."

Kit saw Alison's swift grin of delight.

"Furthermore," Piers said with a touch of remorselessness, "I suppose there's always *Finnegan's Wake*. I've read the 'Work in Progress' parts. They're more interesting than crossword puzzles."

This, Kit felt, would not do at all. He explained to them patiently that none of them had understood him at all. Perhaps he had not made himself too clear: but his ideas were complex and still needed clarification even to himself.

"I understood perfectly," Phil said, looking somewhat portentous, "and I'm with Kit." He knew his star had long been in eclipse with them, and he wished to light it up again. Kit, Alison, even Clement, formed a pretty imposing circle these days, and one from which he did not mean to be excluded. "After all, what is truth but a metaphor?"

To this Polly nodded loyally. Jo thought: really, we are all

202

talking the most frightful rubbish. But, of course, he comforted himself, it was impossible to talk seriously about writing among a crowd of people without talking rubbish in the process. Out of the dust-heap, as it were, glittering things could be stirred up, and two or three fragments of nonsense, properly fitted together, might suddenly make surprising sense, like apparent nonsense-pieces in a jigsaw puzzle. Jo was as loyal to his friend as Polly to her husband. His moment having departed so far as the party was concerned, though still fiery in his head, he lapsed into silence, and considered Fay. He had never met a better girl: she became more physically attractive to him as the months went by, not less. If he were to establish himself as a writer, he would have more to offer her: that is, he would have a name, people would know about him. He could love Alison in one way, Fay in another. Like the Courts of Love. But a bloody awful way of loving, he said to himself, and probably a fraud in the first place.

"Stop looking as though your pet dog's died!" Kit exclaimed with sudden affection. "This is your night, and no one else's. Come on, we're going to drink to Jo properly. Jo!"

They managed to rise with some difficulty, catching the wash of some large ship as they did so. Alison tumbled back onto Piers, who caught her in his arms and held her there.

Jo, his pleasure restored, accepted homage. From then until the end of the party, Kit saw to it that nobody else should take the center of the stage; with his usual critical acumen, he felt it likely that there would not be, for Jo, many nights like this. He put an arm around the narrow shoulders and felt the run of affection returned beneath the cloth.

"He once told you," Phil whispered out of the side of his mouth to Alison, "that it was he Jo loved, not you. And you wouldn't believe him!"

She looked stonily ahead of her, pretending she had not heard. Piers did hear, but did not understand.

Phil felt himself jerked down onto a seat by Clement. "You say anything like that again, and someone else is going into the mud. There's a lot of it, too."

"Oh come, you know—"

"Yes, I do know you. So stow it, will you?"

Phil muttered something about people who couldn't take jokes.

As Piers and Alison walked back along the Embankment to the service flat where they often stayed on weekend leaves, he said to her, "What was that all about? Don't tell me if it's none of my business. But you petrified with rage in my arms. Darling, you turned to pumice-stone."

She considered this for some time. Then she replied, "Of course I would tell you, if I didn't think it would make you dislike Kit. It was a silly business, as I now know, but it seemed like a tragedy at the time. Only Jo and Clement came out of it really well."

"I think you'd better tell me. Otherwise, we'll have some tacky sort of secret between us, and that does no good."

She recounted, as drily as she could, the story of her first visit to the flat, and if she felt pain, did not show it in her voice.

But Piers, sensitive to her every mood, even to the hardening or softening of her bare arm when he put his fingers to it, understood.

"Christie is a nasty piece of work," he said at last. "I take it there was no serious suggestion that Jo was homosexual?"

"Oh, God no! But it drove Jo mad."

"Jo is all right. I like Jo."

"Of course, Kit was simply carried away by all the glamour, and he was pretty drunk as well."

"I'm glad I know, anyway. It seems to me that kidnapping you to the wilds of Surrey was precisely the right thing to do."

She laughed, and this time laughed easily.

"Feel better now?"

"Much."

"Still give a damn for any of them?"

"For Jo and Clement and Polly. For everyone but Phil, really."

She did not mention Kit's name, and Piers was pleased. He was going to own Alison, in time, completely: and when this happened he would not need to be quite so tender towards her. He would love her always, but perhaps not in the same cautious, semi-paternal fashion as now. He did reflect, in the honesty of his heart, that for her to have been so hurt by what he called, to himself, "that lot," was much to bear, since it was he who had the job of healing those wounds. It made him love her rather more, and think slightly the less of her. How had she ever been such a fool?

204

Chapter Six

IT WAS IN JULY THAT KIT MET, IN THE SAME WEEK, TWO PEOPLE who were to have a great deal of influence upon his career.

One was the woman to whom he never referred except as "Belphoebe."

The other was Porter Baynes.

Baynes was one of those mysterious critical forces which seem to spring out of nowhere, and get their teeth into literature like terriers into rats. Born in Leeds, the son of a Methodist parson, he had won a scholarship to Winchester and another to Cambridge. He had been two years at the university when he was sent down for brute idleness. (This may have been a shock sufficient to make him active in future.) Yet, having a nose both for promise and for danger, he had made valuable friends. It was one of these who had eventually offered him the editorship of a glossy magazine devoted to society, sport and the shires. Baynes had wisely left the débutantes and the Hunt Balls alone, but had introduced a literary page written by himself, which combined a certain gossip element with swingeing attacks upon people he did not like. Within a year he had acquired so great a reputation with his savaging tongue that his name was not only conspicuous in English literary circles but was being noted across the Atlantic. It had been a freakish career, and Baynes knew it: but had carefully calculated the value of his social contacts as well as his literary ones. He never attacked anyone in fashion, but could sniff out immediately those against whom the tide might be turning. When the heads tumbled into the basket, that basket would be held out by Baynes.

He was, however, by no means sure of his immediate judgments, and this uncertainty led him into mistakes which, if hailed at once as strokes of genius, wore badly with time: but it would take time to find him out, and meanwhile it was necessary for literary persons to approve him loudly in the hope of escaping him when their own turn came.

He had written a vituperative review of Kit's first novel, and it seemed implausible that, if ever they happened to find themselves in the same room, they would take to each other. Yet this had happened, and they had done so: or rather, as Polly suspected, Kit knew well enough where his bread was buttered to strike up the friendship. Somehow he managed to charm Baynes, as he had charmed so many people. "Talk about the attraction of opposites!" Clement remarked.

Baynes was thirty-four, a very thin, tall man with pale eyes, and a long, thin nose which came to a strange upturning of flesh at the tip. He was also club-footed, though whether more or less than Byron he never admitted. He soon found that, in their literary tastes, he and Kit had much in common. "But why," he inquired insolently, when they were in a crowd at the Fitzroy, "do you write such flubdub? Why don't you search for meanings before you sit down to scribble? Where's your moral stand? Have you got any? The talent's there, but you sling it around like a blind painter sloshing at a canvas in the hope he'll hit more canvas than wall. Ever tried thinking?"

He said this and many other things, all of which Kit bore with equanimity, not only because he was impressed by Baynes's rather unpleasant renown, but because, amid the torrent of abuse, there seemed to be a few drops of sense. Also, the physical disability, and to this Kit was always compassionate, made him feel that there might be at least that excuse for the slashing bitterness which had made the man hated, feared, and sought-after. As they grew

206

more intimate, he learned to give Baynes as good as he gave: it became a friendship based on mutual abuse, which had all the appearance of tenacity, although by Polly's rock-like refusal to have the man home, it was of necessity confined to the pubs. As time went on, mildly favorable references to Kit's potential began to appear in Baynes's columns.

Belphoebe was quite another matter. She was a spectacularly successful poet, then in her early fifties, famous not only for her work but for her antics and eccentricities. Her childhood had been miserable: when she grew up, she determined that she was not going to be miserable again if she had anything to do with it. To her sorrow, she had been born very plain: she fought to turn that very plainness to account, dressing in such a manner that before very long it was the fashion to call her beautiful. She had made herself into a figure of medieval splendor, and by demanding to be treated as a queen, succeeded in finding willing courtiers. Like Baynes, who despised her, she could use her tongue savagely: unlike him, she did so only under attack. She was generous in a wild, cornucopian way, not only with her hospitality but with her help for such young writers as took her fancy. Unlike Baynes, she could laugh secretly at herself, and sometimes, to her intimate friends, would laugh at herself openly. "Holding court today: two new literary duchesses. I wonder if I shall give either of them the right to the *taboret?*" People were usually frightened to meet her, but provided they did not put on airs, they found her warm and kind. She hated bad manners and pretense. She could smell pretense, as a cat smells mice in a wainscot.

She wrote to Kit, telling him she admired his book, and inviting him to luncheon. *"Luncheon!"* Kit said to Polly. "I have only eaten lunch before. Will she give me peacocks in honey?"

"Well, it sounds perfectly wonderful. Mind you smarten yourself up, because I shan't be here to do it for you."

When she had gone to work, Kit made himself as smart as he could, pressing his corduroy trousers, hesitating like Buridan's ass between two shirts, and finally deciding to wear a magenta one belonging to Polly, with his new saffron tie. He brushed his hair, polished his shoes.

In trepidation, he rang the bell of the poet's flat, and was shown rapidly into the presence of what seemed to him, at first, an altarpiece. She sat erect in a high gilded chair, a footstool at her feet. She wore a dress of peacock-blue velvet, girdled with gold, and flowing down over the footstool to the floor.

Kit greeted her and held out his hand. She looked at it but did not take it. "How do you do, Mr. Mallings. It is good of you to come and see me. If you go down the hall and open the third door to the left you will find a bathroom where you will be able to wash yourself."

It was only when he had fled there in shame, that he realized that washing himself was the only thing he had omitted to do that morning. He returned, clean, actually trembling. This time she shook hands heartily, smiled up at him, and told him to sit down. "And please smoke, because I do not mind it at all. I can see by the first and second fingers of your right hand that you are addicted to the habit."

Kit said, "I am very, very sorry I was dirty. I was so excited about meeting you that I forgot. All I thought about was choosing clothes you might like."

She laughed, and touched his knee. "I like them, and I like you. Mr. Eliot will be joining us soon. I hope you will like him."

A week later, an article by her appeared in one of the Sunday papers, pointing out how greatly Kit had been underrated, and how this must on no account happen in the future.

"Dear God," Kit said reverentially, holding the paper to his breast as if it were a baby, "dear God, please bless Belphoebe exceedingly and let her live forever."

Baynes was not kind. "You have some extraordinary friends, Kit, I must say. Can you possibly imagine this sort of thing doing you any good with people who count? Christ, that ghastly woman!"

"Damn it, Porter, you can't expect me to quarrel with her, even if you do! Anyway, I like her very much, and that's that."

"Of course you'd like her, if she fawns on you."

"Fawning," said Kit, remembering the incident of his unshaken hand, "was not quite what I'd call it."

For weeks he went round in such a daze of pleasure that he hardly noticed what was happening in the world, nor could Polly make him talk about anything but Belphoebe. Walter Runciman had visited Prague and had returned with cordial recommendation of the German claims in Czechoslovakia. The rallies in Trafalgar Square and before the Houses of Parliament thickened like black fog. There was turmoil in the streets, with running fights between demonstrators and police. On August 11th, Germany mobilized her army and navy, and Len Hutton scored three hundred and sixty-four runs against Australia at the Oval. At close of play Georgina, who had been to the match with a new young man enthusiastic about cricket, went to Chelsea Town Hall and enrolled herself as an air-raid warden. It was on that same night, also, that, rummaging for cigarettes in a pocket of Clement's coat, she discovered that he had a mistress.

She read the letter again and again, unable to believe what she saw. Was the writing just a little like his own? Could he have written it himself, and left it there just to pay her out for old scores and new? He was well aware that she hunted through his clothes for cigarettes when she happened to run out of them. She could not confront him with the thing, for he was in France again. She began to realize the truth, and when she did so, felt dazed, cold and terrified. She did not want to lose Clement. She loved him. He ought to know that if she had sometimes taken her pleasures elsewhere, it meant nothing at all. It was the way she was made. She started to cry, noisily, without control. What should she do? Weeping and snuffling, feeling the tumescence of her eyelids, she paced the flat, beating her arms to her sides. Ilse! The bitch's name was Ilse! How long had it been going on? She wanted to beat and bruise and kill. Frantically, she put through a toll-call to Alison, who listened in silence.

Alison said at last, "Well, try not to take it too hard. He'll be back, I'm sure of it. He's probably doing it because you've made him so miserable by doing precisely the same thing."

"Don't preach at me. That I can't bear."

"I'm not preaching, I'm stating facts, and they should comfort you. If this is a *quid pro quo,* then it simply can't last. Do give yourself a stiff drink, and have a bath and take a sleeping pill."

Georgina, by no means a heavy drinker, was drunk by the time she got to bed.

Clement would not be home for a week. Georgina went about in a nightmare, collecting her uniform of brown denim and steel helmet, having the suit altered to fit her, attending classes on poison-gas. Phosgene: smells like new-mown hay. Lewisite: like geraniums. How anyone was going to smell Phosgene at all in the stink of London's traffic fumes, she could not imagine. Sampling

209

the Lewisite in the gingerly fashion instructed, she wondered for a desperate moment whether she might take one quick sniff too many, and so put an end to herself.

But she was not, and she knew it, of a suicidal temperament. She was born by nature to face up to things, charge up to them in fact: she would charge up to Clement.

When her lover telephoned her, she told him sharply that she had nothing more to offer him. All that was over. There was no point in attempting to ring her again. Proud and virtuous, she went steadily round to the Six Bells where, by chance, she ran into Porter Baynes.

Kit had not introduced him to anyone of their circle, since he liked to keep his worlds separate: but Baynes and Clement had been at school together and knew each other slightly.

"Aren't you Georgina Maclaren? Baynes. It's a long time since we met. Have a drink. This is Ilse von Zurs who," he sneered, "is a real Baroness. She skipped out in 1934, like a sensible person."

It could not be true. The coincidence was too great. This must be somebody quite different, another Ilse.

A tall, slender, glittering girl, with brilliant blue eyes and hair like silver-gilt piled bounteously on the top of her head.

Georgina managed to say, "You were lucky to get away in time. Were you a political refugee?"

"Not really." The girl's accent was slight and pretty. "My mother was half-Jewish, yes. But we hated the Nazis. I am Austrian."

Georgina drank from the glass Baynes gave her without knowing what she was doing.

"Where's Clement?" he asked her, "Still pot-boiling in his own grand manner?"

She said casually, "Have you seen him recently?"

"Met him in Piccadilly a couple of months ago. We had a beer together."

The ice-maiden glittered on, unperturbed. Surely, if she had been *that* Ilse, she would have started at Clement's name? Georgina wanted to ask, "Have you ever met my husband?" Yet, if this were the wrong Ilse, the question would be ridiculous.

"I've got to go," she said, "I'm due at the post at eight, and I must change."

"Enjoying it? Must be like playing soldiers."

"It is the classless society," Georgina said, "the only one I've ever seen."

"I hope they will let me help," said Ilse, in that soft and pretty voice, "but I am afraid that if war breaks out I shall be interned. Always it happens so."

Georgina walked rapidly back to her flat, fighting her fears down. Of course it wasn't the same. It would have been impossible for the girl just to stand there and chat, without a quiver, if she had been Clement's mistress. Ilse was a common name and England was thick with Teutonic refugees. But wasn't it possible that she had been with Baynes that day in Piccadilly, and that he had introduced her?

On the night of her husband's return, she dressed very carefully and sprayed herself with Chanel's Gardenia, which he had always liked. It suited, he had said, suited her thick white skin, sweatyflowery. When he came in she kissed him with her usual affectionate briskness, and asked for his news. She had cooked him a special supper. No, she herself had eaten already; anyway it was past nine. In fact, she was suffering from nervous anorexia. All that day she had been unable to swallow a mouthful of food without gagging.

She washed up and returned to the living-room, where he was leafing through the pile of accumulated newspapers which he always liked kept for him while he was away.

She sat down, not at his side, but facing him. He gave her a look of mild amazement, his eyebrows hitched.

"Clem," she said, "are you sleeping with a woman called Ilse?"

He dropped the papers to the floor, then brought them together again into a neat pile.

"I'm sorry, Georgie, yes. How did you know?"

"There was a letter in your pocket."

He mumbled, "I suppose, unconsciously, I must have wanted you to know or I wouldn't have left it around."

The silence around them ticked like a clock. She twisted her wedding ring round and round her finger.

He added, "I'm sorry. But, you know, you aren't really in a position to talk, are you?"

She cried out, "That was a caddish thing to say!"

"How so?" He watched her narrowly. He had recovered from his first shock.

"Because it's different for you. You aren't like that. Oh, I know what you think of me, that I've been a cat on the tiles. But there's been no one but you for ages. There's never going to be again."

She did not even realize she had lied.

Slow, heavy, he got up and walked to the fireplace, where he tilted himself against the fender.

"This is only a passing thing, isn't it?" she said.

"No. No, I'm afraid it's not."

"You can't mean that!"

He said he did, repeated that he was sorry. She would admit that she had tried him enough.

"How long—"

"About a couple of months. Less."

"What's her name?"

"You know it."

"Her full name!"

"Ilse von Zurs."

Georgina wanted to scream, faint, fly at him, do something. But she felt as stuck in this horror as in the mud of a dream. "I suppose Porter Baynes introduced you."

"How did you know that?"

"Because I've met the darling girl. Oh, yes. In the Bells. She was with him. She heard my name, she knew who I was and she didn't turn a hair. She just kept on smiling her sweet, sneaky, filthy smile—"

"Watch out," said Clement.

"Like the cheap bitch she is—"

"I said, watch out. Please."

"The sweet little German cow, the fairy off the sodding Christmas tree—"

She did not know that she had been screaming, even that she had risen from her chair, until he slapped her face. She stumbled backwards, fell onto the sofa and sat staring at him, hand to her cheek.

"But you asked for it," said Clement, "and furthermore, the whole street must have heard you. I was simply dealing with hysterics in the only way I've been taught."

212

He came to sit by her. She was quiet now, falling into a strange dreariness where nothing seemed so terrible as it had done, and nothing would ever be right again. She told him that she loved him, she always had done. He couldn't blame her for what she was, especially since she had tried to change herself, yes, and had done so.

"I want a divorce," he said, "and I want it badly. Jesus only knows how long the world we're living in is going to last, but I want some kind of happiness before it blows up. Also, I want to make Ilse a British subject, if I can fit it in in the time remaining. I'll make you a decent settlement, and you'll get married again in indecent haste. Then we'll all meet in the pubs one day, and if you want a change you can always try to seduce me."

This was so brutal that she trembled with shock.

She could only say, "Don't."

He looked ashamed. "You've got to make allowances. This has been a blow to me. I've been travelling since dawn, too, and I'm dead tired. We'll talk some more tomorrow."

"Yes."

It was the end of one night and the beginning of another, the real night, lying apart from him.

She felt a sudden, horrible upsurgence of sexual desire. He saw it in her face, for he left her side at once. "No. No, Georgie, it won't do. Not ever again; not for us."

The desire fell away. "I'm very cold," she said, "it must have turned colder."

"It has, a bit."

"Pour me a Scotch, will you?"

He did so. "You aren't going to make trouble for me?"

"No," she said, in a dead voice, "not if you really mean it. Do I cite this woman or do you take a tart to an hotel?"

"Let's leave that for now."

They were parting at the bedroom door when he pulled her into his arms and she felt dampness on her cheek. He was crying. "Oh Georgie, Georgie, I've done it all wrong. It was a wretched way to do it. And I've behaved like a swine tonight. Oh God, I'm sorry, do believe that!"

Mechanically, she found herself comforting him, and when at last she had gone to lie alone she slept without dreaming.

Chapter Seven

ON THE EVENING OF MUNICH JO, WHO HAD NEARLY BEEN SICK
through joy when his first story was accepted, now vomited in
earnest, through sheer horror. Kneeling above the lavatory pan he
retched till the tears ran down his face and into the sour corners
of his mouth. He went to brush his teeth.

In the sitting-room Bessie, giving thanks to God for the peace
that would last her time, was listening to the wireless, from which
there poured a gay and swooping roundabout tune called "The
Umbrella Man," now closely associated in the public mind with
Neville Chamberlain. Mildred was torn between immediate relief
and fear for the future. She had thrust their gas-masks into the
cupboard under the stairs.

Clement Maclaren, sitting over coffee in Lyons' Corner
House, was so repelled by the rejoicing about him that he stood on
a chair and harangued the entire room at the top of his voice.
Willing hands dragged him down again, somebody kicked him in
the ribs, and he was thrown out into the street.

Sybil Rainey, doggedly addressing envelopes in the Party
Committee rooms, said, "War is now quite certain."

Polly and Kit both felt relief but, being ashamed to say so,

214

cursed the Government for a little while, then went to bed with headaches. For the past few days they had known a terrible awareness of the bridge over their heads.

Georgina took comfort in the warden's post, where there was a sharp division of opinion not dictated, in that "classless society," by class. She herself, an ex-printer called Les, Phil Christie (who, being in the same ward, had to her irritation joined them), an etiolated rich girl called Janet, and a one-armed sailor whom they knew as Bulldog, all felt angry, ashamed and fearful. Among the Chamberlain supporters were two other smart girls, a retired admiral, an electrician, and a garage-hand. Peace in our time! The old boy had brought it off.

Piers kept well away from the mess that night, since he could not bring himself to speak to anyone but Alison. If she felt gladness, it was because of the coming child.

Lord Wantage, the sole person in his village not to rejoice, and so regarded as of weak mentality, a holy idiot, deliberately went to the Blue Lion to express his opinions: had it not been for his social status, he would have been shouted down. As it was, sullen faces were lowered into beer mugs or looked quickly away. "This is England," he said, "and we've crawled to Hitler on our knees. This is the first time my country has ever made me feel sick to the stomach."

"Well," said Mrs. Harris, behind the bar, "I'm sure we've all got our own ideas. Be a funny world if we hadn't, wouldn't it?"

During the next uneasy weeks, when the hysteria of relief from fear had begun to subside, eyes were not meeting quite so easily, and Duff Cooper had resigned as First Lord of the Admiralty, Georgina sought refuge from her personal misery in the life of the post, dropping in every night even when she was off-duty. She was soothed by the peculiar comradeship which had grown up almost at once. At first, the working-men showed some nervous deference towards the smart girls: within a fortnight all that had been forgotten, except perhaps by the Admiral, though he did his best to conceal the fact. It was Georgie, Phil, Les, Janet, Bob, Ron, Betty, Tim, Doreen. The Bulldog, having been rebuked by the printer for using bad language in front of a lady, paid Georgina a treasured compliment, "Oh, our Georgie isn't a *lady!*" He meant she was one of them.

In the post, a basement ill shored up by wooden struts under a large private house, they drank dark-brown tea which had been stewing for hours and gave them all indigestion, studied manuals of first-aid, worked for their gas-tests, learned interminable lists of rendezvous points. Georgina won the gratitude of them all by inventing a series of graceless mnemonics, which made the learning easier:

> "One, King's Road and Lot's you see,
> Two, Junction of King's and Burnaby.
> Three is Edith Grove and King's,
> Four, Ashburnham, Latimer brings."

"It's all very fine and large, Georgie," said Les, "but if one's got to get to point twenty in a hurry, it's going to take some time to rattle through the whole poem. The war would be over by that time."

They went out on exercises, they learned to use stirrup-pumps and carry stretchers, they crawled through vans filled with tear-gas. There was much amusement when Georgina, riding round the rendezvous points on a bicycle, was challenged as to what vehicle she represented and replied, "I'm heavy rescue." She came top in the first gas-test and was awarded a chevron to wear on her sleeve. When they were not working, they usually played poker-dice.

Clement had moved out of the flat. Whether he was actually living with Ilse, Georgina did not know. She had at once started divorce proceedings, feeling that if she did not do so now, she would never let him go. She rarely left the post till the night-shift came on, and sometimes stayed talking with them till two or three in the morning. Then she slept late.

Phil was, as usual, pretending to be in love with her, and, getting no response, referred to his passion as "the desire of the moth for the star."

"That has always been a fraud," Polly said, when Georgina told her this. "It's a cover-up. What it really means is the desire of the moth for another moth."

At the end of November, Alison gave easy birth to a son, a beautiful child with eyes grave as Piers', and with her own wide brow. When Polly heard the news, she wept.

"Why can't I start again?" she cried to Kit. "What's wrong with me?"

216

She began to take wheat-germ capsules, and they copulated on certain favorable dates worked out for them by their doctor.

Belphoebe had become as fond of her as she was of Kit, approving her good manners, her demure prettiness, and her sense of fun.

"Polly, my dear," she said one day, when they were at her flat, "I know Kit has to tolerate that terrible man Baynes, but can you endure him? He takes little pot-shots at me every week, grapeshot, I admit."

"I cannot stand the sight of him, and I have asked Kit not to bring him home."

"Look, I do try to have it out with him," Kit said, "please believe that."

"Of course," Belphoebe said majestically, "he may be feeling more vituperative than usual, because I have been playing a series of little jokes on him. He doesn't know the source, naturally, but I don't suppose they sweeten his temper."

Polly asked what jokes.

"Every day I send him a little parcel. It gives Jeanie"—her secretary—"something to do." She clasped her beautiful Gothic hands, encrusted with jewels like devices of Fabergé.

"Do tell me what's in them," Kit pleaded.

"Why, anything that comes to hand! Nothing distasteful, that I need hardly tell you. Let me see, last week there was"—she ticked the items off on her fingers—"a piece of cabbage stalk, a couple of aspirin tablets, the top from a milk-bottle, a rather attractive pearl button, a few egg-shells, a thumbstall and a slice of stale cake. We pack them up for him very prettily."

"Oh, it can't be true!" Polly cried.

"My dear, it is perfectly true. Some of the parcels are quite large, and need a lot of tissue paper. It is quite unmalicious really: I simply like to think of him being puzzled."

"He's never said anything about it to me," said Kit.

"Of course not. He would feel that in some obscure way it was derogatory to his dignity."

But Baynes, through carelessness of Jeanie's, had found out the identity of the sender. On the back of an outer wrapping, half of Belphoebe's address had been just decipherable.

In the next fortnight there appeared an article by him, not in the glossy magazine but in a widely selling weekly review. It was a

217

massive attack upon her, upon her personality, her intellect, her poetry, her way of dressing and speech, so ugly in its violence that when Kit read it he changed color.

He said at once, "I've got to do something about this."

When Polly too had read it, she looked at him gravely. "This sounds a wretched thing to say, but I have to say it. If you defend her, you will make a lifelong enemy of Baynes."

"I know it."

"At this particular moment of time, and pray God it's a passing one, he is far more influential than she is."

"If I let this go, shall you think much of me?"

"Never mind what I should think. I'm seeing that your eyes are wide open to the dangers."

He hesitated. He was devoted to Belphoebe and he managed to get on with Baynes, and was grateful to him for making it clear that his, Kit's, was at least a mentionable name. Just about. He did shrink from the trouble ahead, but he said nevertheless, "Well, I am not going to let it go."

Polly said, "Good for you," and kissed him. Her smile was glorious.

Next day they saw Belphoebe. "I am going to answer this stuff, of course," Kit told her.

"My dear boy, don't. I am quite capable of springing to my own defense, and used to swatting blow-flies. I do not wish you to do yourself harm with Mr. Baynes. The man is a Zoilist, and there is nothing to be done about such creatures."

Polly asked what a Zoilist was.

"A carping and malicious critic, taking his name from a Greek called Zoilus, who made a preposterous attack on Homer. Not, Polly, that I rank myself with Homer. But yes, he is a Zoilist. Kit, please keep silence. You are on the way up, as they say, but I am as up as I am ever likely to be and far less vulnerable than you."

She had shaken him, and Polly saw this.

"I won't be seeing him any more, anyhow," he said, a little feebly.

"Excellent. Do not."

In the hall Kit spoke urgently to Jeanie. "Has she really been upset by this Porter Baynes thing? She doesn't seem so."

"Yes, she has, dreadfully. She doesn't show things, but I can always tell. I've never seen her quite so shaken."

218

"Good," Kit said, strength returning to his voice. "Then I know what to do."

Polly loved him for it.

First, he sent a short note to Baynes, telling him he could not let the attack on Belphoebe pass without reply, and felt it fair to warn him that he proposed to make one.

He then wrote a letter to the weekly, so excoriating and so witty, making such excellent play with the concept of Zoilism, that Polly said she could only believe it was written under divine dictation. "God's not so gifted as that," Kit said complacently.

No reply to the note had come from Baynes. "So watch out for squalls," Kit said, "we must steel ourselves, my darling."

"I think I am already steeled. At least, I hope I am."

The storm which broke when Kit's letter was published was of such proportions that it even caused comment in the popular papers. Like all such personalities, Baynes's had great appeal for a certain type of follower. He was quick to call up his cohorts, who abused Belphoebe and Kit also with all the fervor of those in possession of revealed truths. Belphoebe had her own cohorts, too, but fewer in number and, worse still, a good deal older than those of Baynes, who in any case usually expressed contempt for most established men of letters. In his own magazine, Baynes dealt with Kit alone, in a manner which gave the disquieting impression that he was actually frothing at the mouth.

"I am glad we live in a houseboat," Polly said, "even though damp does rise from the sheets every night, because here we are not actually attached to the earth. I am finding the earth very unpleasant."

Neither could open a newspaper for weeks without their stomachs churning, though they took some comfort from Belphoebe's expression to Kit of her gratitude and admiration. It was also a very funny letter. Polly said, "Well, at least she can laugh. I wish I could."

At the tail-end of the public correspondence came a workmanlike letter from Alison: "For two years past Mr. Baynes has degraded the language of literary debate."

His review soon carried a sneer, to the length of two thousand five hundred words, at Alison and her novels.

It might have been thought that this all-too-obvious process of tit-for-tat would have caused disquiet among the writing majority: but in fact they, like the general public, were enjoying themselves from the ringside seats. Human beings, most of whom have learnt not to take, or at least to express, delight in physical cruelty, enjoy the other kinds more than they like to admit, and Kit was, for a long while, seriously damaged. The correspondence had made its way across the Atlantic: and Porter Baynes, while careful to withhold permission for reprinting in the United States his initial attack on Belphoebe, who was greatly admired there, was happy to permit the one on Kit, which appeared in one of the more influential academic quarterlies.

Belphoebe sent Baynes a wreath of immortelles and an old Wellington boot. This time he wrote to her, threatening to prosecute her as a public nuisance.

"But I do not think, Kit," she said, "that he will try. He would look very foolish revealing the contents of his diurnal gifts in a witness-box."

Neither Kit nor Polly, during this period of strain, had taken much interest in the world beyond their own concerns.

The anti-Jewish pogroms in Germany, the now hopeless position of the Spanish Republic, had driven Jo to a state of such despair that after office hours he now saw no one but political friends. He tried to persuade himself that there was still time left in which Hitler could be checked: night after night he returned from the Committee rooms, white with exhaustion, smeared with ink from the inadequate duplicator.

Mildred, almost as worried as he, though Bessie seemed to have passed into some smiling Nirvana of her own, went with her friend to Astaire-Rogers films which, she said, were the only really comforting things she knew.

Then, one night after her mother had gone to bed, she came into the sitting-room and burst into laughter that had an hysterical undertone.

"Well, his wife's died at last! My God, Jo, he always let me think she was a gentle little soul, only mildly cracked, but it seems that she was much more like Mrs. Rochester. Did I ever tell you she had a lot of money of her own?"

She gave Jo a look of strange cunning. Something was to come.

"She killed herself. Do you know how she did it? She swallowed a teaspoon, and died before they could do anything about it."

220

Jo stared at her.

"One might say," said Mildred, on an upsurge of fresh mirth, "that she died with a silver spoon in her mouth."

"Don't! That's sickening."

She was silent. She sat with tears in her eyes.

"What's up?"

"Yes, it was sickening. I'm sorry. You know how one thinks of a ghastly joke and then simply has to make it, out of some sort of compulsion?"

"You never actually knew her. It's a beastly business, I know, but what are you so upset about? It can't be just that."

Taking out a pink pocket-comb, she ran it through her hair, which crackled with electricity. "I suppose I'd better tell you. Frank never said much about the future and us, but I more or less took it for granted that if anything happened to his wife. . . . The cream of the jest is that now it has, he's cooling off. I'm sure of it. He's been cooling off for weeks. I haven't much, Jo. I did think I had that."

He was full of pity for her, but did not know what to say.

She rambled on. "Yes, the nurses pounced on her at once, yelling for the doctors, and they stuck their fingers down her throat or whatever you do do, but she just suffocated. You'd think they couldn't kill themselves, wouldn't you, when they aren't even allowed knives and forks? He rang me this morning, got me hauled out of class. He was graphic. I can't get it out of my mind. He didn't say anything about seeing me."

Jo protested that, at such a moment, it was hardly reasonable to expect him to ask her out.

"I know, I know, I know. I'm just being silly. But I've been well aware for some time that he was going off me. God knows I'm nothing to look at, he could have any woman he wanted. But I did believe we were close. Poor sap, he even thought I was funny. He used to laugh at my jokes."

She dragged herself up, looking, for a moment, as old as her mother and as crippled. "Bed, I suppose. What is there but bed? Whenever I lie down it comforts me. I think, 'This is the only thing one *can* do, and one day it will be the last thing.' "

Christmas came, and January. In the middle of that month, Frank Hansen telephoned Mildred and asked her to marry him.

Chapter Eight

BY SOME LUCK IN THE DRAW, GEORGINA'S DIVORCE-SUIT CAME UP IN February, undefended. To her, it was a most curious experience, almost, as she later told herself, a mystical one. On her entry into the Law Courts, she had a feeling that she was accompanied by a large, hairy, consoling dog. She gave her evidence clearly, contradicting her own counsel when he made the suggestion that Clement had refused to speak to her for months. The judge congratulated her on the way that evidence was given. As she walked out, a free and desolate woman, into the bitter rainy daylight, she had a sense, as hallucinatory as the first one, that the dog had disappeared. One side of her was naked: where somebody or something had walked, she was alone. She felt the freezing of her left shoulder down to the finger-tips of her left hand.

She would have no reason to worry about the King's Proctor: since Clement left her, in fact, since the discovery of his infidelity, she had lived alone—chaste as a nun of the Poor Clares.

The winds blew and the streets were empty. Neither she nor Clement were famous enough to attract pressmen. She had had to cite somebody called Barbara, of whom she had never heard.

Nothing is more empty than Trafalgar Square, if one is walking in solitude. There are the thin week-day crowds feeding the pigeons: Nelson is, as usual, or would be if one could see so high, thick with lime-droppings. And fountains blowing sideways in a cold, wet place are the poorest of poor jokes.

She returned to the flat, where she switched on all the electric fires. Physical cold had stricken her. For the first time she knew what being absolutely alone meant. Solitude sharpened her vision, played tricks with it. Blue-and-white-banded mugs in the kitchen, formerly inert, took on a life of their own and spun like tops. The big double bed yawned—what a metaphor! The telephone looked, as it squatted on the desk, like a black and hopeless prisoner whose tongue had been torn out. Silence, silence everywhere. What the hell had happened to the great hairy ghost-dog, sprung from nothing? They had never had a dog.

Silence breathed like the wind through the boughs on a soft Irish day, breathed to her own rhythm.

When the telephone did ring, the shrillness made her jump. It was Clement.

"I only wanted to know how it went."

"Oh. As scheduled. What did you imagine?"

"What was it like? I've been thinking of you."

"In a subdued sort of way, horrible. I suppose it all took eight minutes at the outside."

He was quiet for a moment. Then he said, in a voice half-pleading, half-wheedling, "We did have some good times, didn't we?"

"A fat lot of use that is now," said Georgina.

"Anyway, I shan't forget. Nothing can spoil that."

"I shall forget as soon as humanly possible, because everything's spoiled. Totally. Well, I suppose I ought to wish you good luck: you've got what you wanted."

"Don't take it like that."

"And don't you be a bloody fool!" she cried, hanging up before she could burst into tears.

She was on the same shift, eight till midnight, with Les. All the evening he had been glancing at her in a puzzled way, and as they left together he said, "What's up, Georgie? You're not your old cheery self."

They were very friendly, though they had exchanged no

family secrets. He was a man self-educated to a very high degree, and widely read. If life had treated him differently, he might have become a scholar: he was interested in rare books, and collected them whenever he could get them on the cheap.

She knew he admired her, felt perhaps that he admired her rather too much for his own peace of mind. The society within the post was classless: she was not sure whether he felt it was quite so classless when they were off-duty.

"Walk along with me a little way."

He hesitated. "Yes, O.K. I don't suppose the Missus will worry if I'm not in bang on the dot."

She told him then what had happened to her that afternoon. Bullet-headed, a Saxon blond, his eyes round, brilliant, dark-blue, he gazed at her, sympathy mixed with curiosity. Divorces were not so common in his world.

He said, "Hard cheese! You very cut up?"

"Very."

Her shadow in the lamplight overtopped his.

"How any chap," he said slowly, "could do that to anyone like you beats me."

"I suppose there were faults on both sides."

He was gallant. "I don't believe you've got no faults. Got any faults," he corrected himself. "Anyway, we're all for you, down at the old post. If that's any comfort."

They were outside the block of flats where she lived. She said on impulse, "Come up and I'll give you a quick drink. You've never seen me in my natural habitat."

He shot her a quick, nervous, desirous look. "I'd like to, but it's getting late. Mrs. Armour"—this was how he often referred to his wife—"may be fretting."

"Ten minutes. Do. I don't like my own company much to-night."

So he went with her, and she poured him some whiskey. "Sit down."

He glanced round with interest. "Nice place. Haven't I seen that artist somewhere before?"

"It's a Dufy. It's the only really valuable thing we have. My husband was gracious enough to let me keep it."

"What, a real one?" He peered into it, delighted. "It's a naval regatta, isn't it? All those little boats, and people in carriages on the shore."

Soon he stood up to go. They were close together, and she saw his eyes open wide, his lips press tight.

"You can kiss me if you like," she said. She felt light-headed.

He said, "Now Georgie! Whatever do you take me for? Lady Chatterley's lover?"

"You could be."

It was a quick and frantic business. When he rose he looked leaden with shame. "I oughtn't to've."

"Forget it," Georgina said, lying face-downwards on the bed, "really forget it. It was all my fault. Anyway, you only dreamed it. Now go away."

She heard the clatter of his feet receding down the stairs.

Next time they met on duty, she gave no sign that anything had happened between them: but it was some time before he could regain his confidence. One night several of them went to a party in a neighboring pub and sang to the piano, "Any Old Iron," "Knees Up, Mother Brown," "Won't You Come Home, Bill Bailey?" Mrs. Armour was there, a pretty little woman, firm with her husband when she thought he had had enough beer. She and Georgie chatted together. Georgina liked her. Two days later she got herself transferred to the dépot.

In March she stood in the great crowd in Belgrave Square, mourning for the death of the Spanish Republic. It was a brilliant day, without cloud. The banners were out for the last time, the purple, crimson and gold. The beautiful flag slid down from the Embassy staff: the red and yellow arose, jerk by jerk, then streamed out with a mighty flapping against the sky. The band, the inevitable band which played without prejudice for Mosley or for the May Day rallies, broke into "Riego's Hymn": for the last time:

> "O joyous and fearless,
> Audacious, invincible!"

Men and women were weeping openly, tears pouring down their cheeks. For many, it was to be the most miserable defeat of a lifetime, the triumph of everything they hated and feared.

Leaving before it was all over, Georgina ran into Jo. He also had been crying.

"I can't bear any more of this," she said. "Let's find a tea-shop somewhere, for God's sake."

225

As they walked, he said how sorry he had been to hear of her parting from Clement.

"I suppose I got what I deserved. But now I simply cannot get over him. I've started playing around again, of course—I can't help it. But it's dust and ashes, the lot of it."

"I thought," Jo said, filled with his own distresses, "that he was as monogamous as a swan."

"So did I. But he wasn't. Kit's the last swan left in the world now. Naturally, I don't know enough about Alison's spouse." She smiled faintly. "I hope he isn't, I must say. I've always rather fancied him myself. What news of you?"

He told her Mildred was getting married. His face did not change.

Though Georgina had never met her, though Clement had once or twice done so, she knew the family history through Kit, and was astounded.

Well, Jo said, he supposed she had her own life to live. The man she was marrying was a dull dog, in his opinion, but steady enough and well-heeled. Thank God he was, because his mother would have to have a paid companion, and that was a heavy expense.

"How is she taking it?"

He shrugged, "She's always cared more for me than for Milly. All the same, she's taking it rather worse than I'd expected. Of course, you can see her point."

"What about you and Fay?"

Again he shrugged. They still, he said, saw each other quite a lot, but even if they had wanted to marry, it was impossible now. His mother would never endure losing both Millie and himself, and he could not bear the idea that Fay should come to live with them. "You know what her sort of life is like. And you can guess at mine." Fay, he added, was a born martyr, and his mother, without even realizing what she did, would have her battened down in less than no time. Pretty soon, he added grimly, there would be no need for any paid companion. Fay would give up her job, lose all the fun she was used to, and become nurse and skivvy in one. It was not what he would wish for any wife of his.

They found a shop and went in.

"Isn't it an odd thing," Georgina said meditatively, "that if

226

you loved Fay, you would sacrifice her without a thought? It's a very greedy thing, love."

He thought about this, and knew it was true. "Yes, I suppose I should."

She reached across the table for his hand and held it. "Jo dear, you can't have Alison. Not ever."

He shook her off. He said quietly, but for him violently, "What a foul world it is! All the good times have gone."

"The 'wild life,' " she said, teasing him a little.

"Yes. And some of us in our crowd—how we enjoyed ourselves!—are having their personal lives broken to bits, too. The only good thing I can think of is that Polly's started another baby. Did you know?"

Georgina said yes: Polly was one of the few people with whom she continued to keep in touch.

"That's why they weren't at the demo today. Kit thought it would upset her. Bobby Price was there, did you see him?"

She shook her head.

"He came through Spain without a scratch. I saw Phil, too."

"So did I, but I managed to dodge him."

The daffodils in a red window-box over the way shivered in the stiff bright breeze. A knot of demonstrators on their way home walked listlessly, with sad faces. A child who had been carrying a Republican flag let it trail behind him in the dust; his mother spoke to him sharply and he began to howl.

" 'Unarm, Eros,' " Jo said.

" 'The bright day is done and we are for the dark.' I know some Shakespeare, too. We 'did' *Antony* at school," she added.

"Sounds like a cliché, doesn't it? Yet it's only become really true, for me, anyhow, this afternoon."

"Come, come," she said gently, "we can't be mutual Job's comforters." Her long eyes searched his face, her gaze flitting like a butterfly to and fro, to rest upon his lips. "Cheer up, old boy. *I* shall try to. Can't I cheer you somehow? Isn't there a way?"

He knew what was in her mind and wondered why it should be that he had never desired her. She was so obviously accessible that most men did, sooner or later, though seldom for very long. He wasn't a prude, he had had many girls and would have others,

227

when Fay had grown tired of him. Yet Georgina did not stir his blood at all.

She smiled. "All right, so I can't. Poor Jo."

"The crossing-sweeper."

"Not quite that. Anyway, can we go to the pictures?"

He shook his head. He was waited for at home: as usual. And Fay was coming in.

It was not true: he was going to spend the evening with Polly and Kit, and did not want Georgina trailing him.

The houseboat, jolting gently on the tide, flew the Republican colors.

"You can haul those down," Jo said as he came across the planks, "it's over and done with. The bitter end."

"Was it dreadful?" Polly asked him.

"Worse than I can say."

"Come and tell us," said Kit, "and give yourself a drink. I'm going to have my first today. I've been virtuous since we struck it lucky again, or rather, Polly did."

The sunset that evening was beautiful, turning the river to blinding gold. There was a great band of sooty rose behind the four chimneys.

After they had discussed the demonstration, Kit turned the talk to other things. He had finished his new novel—"To be cut to pieces, of course, by Baynes and his poll-parrots. Oddly enough, it's far more the sort of thing he actually wanted me to write. Life's little ironies. You can look at the first two chapters, if you feel like it."

Jo was pleased, grateful for anything that might take his mind off the pressures of the world and of his own life. The opening of the book astonished him. The background was the first year of the Spanish Civil War, as seen through Kit's eyes alone, through an intellect basically apolitical, through emotions that were not. It was verbally elaborate still, to the point of being baroque: but beneath this was a solidity of structure Kit had not achieved before, and something Porter Baynes would have described as a "moral stance." The war itself was something only half-glimpsed, half-comprehended through the writer's dream, obliquely angled.

He remarked on this.

"Yes," Kit said, "that's what I meant. At this stage it isn't a real war at all. But towards the end of the book it becomes more

228

and more real, till even my beautiful verbiage begins to fall away like leaves from a tree, so you can see the shape of the branches at last. It ends as simply as anything in Tolstoy. Baynes will foam at his snaggle-toothed mouth."

"When did you finish it?"

"Today. It seemed to be the right day, somehow."

"Come outside," Polly said, "and see the afterglow."

The sky and the water were violet, and the moon was out: but the tall red houses along the Embankment seemed to be smoldering, as if they had captured the setting sun into the very honeycomb of the brick-work. The river smell was fresh and sweet. They watched the glow fade, the stars come out. One star fell, and the three of them "Ah-ed!" at it like children at a fireworks display.

"Let's go in now," Polly said.

Chapter Nine

TO JO, RAZORING HIS BLUE CHIN BEFORE THE BATHROOM GLASS, it occurred that hopes were inevitably dupes, and fears almost certainly not liars. Possibly he should have been thinking of other things, on the morning of Mildred's wedding: but he was not. All that had seemed over long before it began. The lines of the new life had been fixed, like stakes in cement.

He believed now what he was never to disbelieve for the rest of his life: that money talks, and that for the idealistic young, there is no practical hope of fighting it. No practical hope: but at least with profit to themselves, since it proved a life, a social purity, that might one day come to mean something, or to strengthen the lives of others. The rich men won, the poor went to the wall. Nowadays, anyhow. The Russian Revolution was a long time ago. He, a small, obscure man, had done all he could, as other obscure and small men had done their best all over England. If their children grew up to abuse them, it would not be because they had done nothing: but because they had not succeeded against odds those children would never be able to understand. Spain, the oriflamme of his generation, had sunk into the mud churned up by the big battalions. The little nations were going the same way. Alone among his friends, he suspected a secret world where the real decisions were taken, a world they could not imagine. What world? He did not know, he had no experience. But there was a They, infinitely powerful, to whom no echo of young and angry voices so much as penetrated. He was twenty-eight: old before his time, he suddenly knew these things.

Downstairs he found them ready and waiting for him, Mildred in a blue coat and dress with a flowery hat, already looking exhausted after the struggle to get Bessie into something mauve. She was now pinning to her mother's coat a bouquet of sweet-peas framed in asparagus-fern. The marriage would take place at their accepted church, but today there would be no pushing of the bath chair: they had hired a large car which, Mildred had directed, was on no account to have white ribbons on it.

"I can't believe it even now," Bessie was saying, with a tremulous smile, "I can't believe I'm really losing my little girl."

"I am not a little girl. I am thirty-three."

Bessie's smile faded, and her voice dropped down the register. She burst out, "Wimbledon is so far away!"

Mildred did not know whether to laugh, or to cry with exasperation.

"Mother, that doesn't sound like Marlowe's mighty line! Anyway, Frank and I will come and see you every weekend."

"So far away."

"For God's sake!" All Mildred wanted was to be left in peace to contemplate the miracle about to take place. She had believed Hansen was lost to her: yet he had come back as if there had been no cooling of their relations at all. She did not love him with a girl's passion: she knew that he wanted a wife as such more than he wanted her. He could not endure loneliness, and she had been the nearest person to hand. Better the devil he did know than the devil he didn't. But she was sure that she could make him content. Sexually, she was confident. And she was a good housewife. Above all, perhaps, she was filled with the joy of being saved, at this late hour, from leading apes in hell.

"How can you speak to me so roughly, on such a day?" Bessie's cheeks purpled over, not in a single flush but in veinous lines, cross-hatched.

"Mother, please—"

Jo said with relief, "The car's come."

It was not easy to get Bessie into it, less so to get her out, but somehow it was done, and she was making her snail's progress up the aisle on Jo's arm. Jo, of course, was to give Mildred away. There was a sprinkling of Hansen's relations, a few of Mildred's friends, neighbors, teachers from the school. The small reception would be held in a restaurant nearby. The honeymoon was to be in Juan-les-Pins.

Hansen himself was ready and waiting, a lean, composed, rather dusty-looking man with a good-humored face.

When Jo had settled Bessie in her pew, he went back to bring Mildred from the porch where she was waiting.

"You've got a fine day for it," he said to her fondly, "and you're looking very nice." He had got over the first wrench of knowing he must lose her, had accepted the difference it might make in his own life—perhaps a spoliation.

The organist, who had been contenting himself with some subdued ramblings of a pacific nature, burst into Lohengrin.

"Over the top," said Mildred.

Bessie wept in the conventional manner throughout the ceremony, mostly from rage: but when it was all over, and they had moved her into the vestry, she behaved in the bright, *grande-dame* manner she could summon at will.

"So I have another son," she said to the man not many years her junior. "Bless you, Frank, bless you, Millie. May you have many happy and fruitful years together."

When the couple had departed, Jo and his mother drove home together. Mrs. Warren would be waiting for them to help Bessie out of her finery; she was coming in during the daytime until the companion, who was not free for another week, arrived to take up residence.

"Well, dear," Bessie said, "you can't say I haven't been brave."

"You were crying non-stop from the sounds I heard, muffled as they were."

"It would be a poor mother who didn't cry at her own daughter's wedding. Didn't she make her responses beautifully? Of course he had to mutter his, men always do. It always seems to me a bit insulting. She looked quite pretty, didn't you think?" She put

232

her arm through Jo's. "Well, dear, you're all I've got from now on."

She was not sure whether she really minded having him all to herself. She would not be selfish enough to keep him tied to her apron-strings: when the companion came—

"Is it Miss Pease, or Miss Rees?"

"Who?" His thoughts were far away.

"The companion, of course."

"Miss Pease."

—he could go out every night if he liked and she would be tolerant if sometimes he came home a little the worse for wear. After all, he was twenty-eight and men had to enjoy themselves in their own fashion. Her thoughts had become peaceful. It had been such a nice little wedding, nothing flashy, or in any way unsuited to Mildred's age: not so nice as her own, though. She had worn white, with a veil like a cloud of steam, and had carried pink roses, forget-me-nots, and asparagus-fern. She hoped the honeymoon would be as good as hers, too, though she doubted it. She smiled in succulent memory. How right it had all gone from the very beginning! She had been one of the lucky ones.

For, though Jo and Mildred had never suspected such a thing, she had once been as highly sexed as they. Nobody would ever know how she had suffered from bodily deprivation after her husband's death. It had taken a good deal of conquering. All that was long past. It was quite ten years since those urges had tormented her in the night, when she had lain wakeful, her teeth clenched, longing for sleep. It was to this aspect of herself that she had half-consciously alluded when begging Jo to remember that she felt young, young, inside her thickening flesh. He had been irritated by such talk, fancying that she referred to skittishness at dances, romps with young men, giggles with her girl-friends. She had tried not to allude to this imprisoned youth, yet the longing to do so all too often overcame her. By doing so, she could make something of that sensual past revive in her memory. Like many women, she had known the ugly urge to confide in her children in a way that was not right: not because of any perversion of the mind, but out of the desire to slash down the gap between the generations, to cry out—You and I, we are not different animals!

"Yes, quite a nice little wedding," she repeated, hearing in her own voice a note of denigration which she at once regretted. Mrs. Warren had got her into night-dress and gown, so that she need not come in again at bedtime. Jo and Bessie were sitting over a late tea. "Does it strike you, dear, that he is just a bit like a hen?"

He was startled: then he laughed. "I know what you mean, but I don't really understand why he does."

"The beginning of wattles. He pokes his neck out, too. But I am sure he is a very kind man."

Frank Hansen did look like a hen, and he was also kind. The honeymoon, if not so exacting as Bessie's had been, was perfectly satisfactory in all respects. Mildred suited him well. He was surprised to remember how he had nearly run away from her. What a mistake that would have been! He liked both her competence and her sharp tongue. She was able to make him laugh. Besides, she had become a very promising bridge-player.

But one thing Mildred had never suspected was that her rather dry and elderly solicitor was a man of advanced visual tastes, although he seemed to know nothing of books and music: he absorbed everything through his eyes. On the first occasion when she had seen his house at Wimbledon, on the edge of the common, she had thought the furnishings bleak and queer, and had at once made up her mind that she would soon be having everything looking cozier and more to her liking. She did not admire the functional Swedish chairs, the bright hook-rugs—these she found garish—or the prints of silly birds walking upside down, which he told her were by Paul Klee. She inferred as much: but he was unexpectedly stony. He did not want anything touched—but she might, of course, do anything she liked with her own bedroom. She asked him if all this had been his wife's idea. He gave a glimmer of a smile. "No, my love. She never liked it at all. It is just something that pleases me."

Never one to pick quarrels about matters of no real significance to herself, Mildred resisted further protest and after a while she began to wonder whether her new surroundings were not, in fact, rather smart. She would quite like to be that. She was content to allow him to choose some of her clothes, and was surprised at the result.

Each Sunday they spent with Bessie and Jo, who were to visit

234

them shortly. Wouldn't their eyes pop out on stalks! Mildred's heart warmed to this thought.

She soon found, however, that living in Hansen's comparative splendor was making her see her old home as through the wrong end of the opera-glasses. It all seemed so poky, so far away and, yes, dark. There were too many shadowed corners. And was there a fusty, jujube-like smell in the air? She had noticed for the first time what Jo had noticed years ago. But she gave no hint of this new feeling, and was proud enough not to hint to him that Frank did not enjoy plodding through those very large teas now bought, on Bessie's detailed orders, by her somewhat aggressive companion, Miss Pease. If I've started to "look down on them" (God help me, she thought), I'm damned if I'll ever have Frank doing so. Even to feel that he might brought to her an upsurge of defensive affection for her family, especially for Jo.

He, on his part, was well aware that she was drifting away from him on a current unexpectedly swift. He was glad she was happy, but he could not control a sting of resentment. He missed her far more than Bessie did. Bessie was lucky in Miss Pease, on whom she could sharpen her tongue as a parrot sharpens its beak on cuttle-fish. Miss Pease was tough enough, and already felt herself indispensable enough, to be a worthy adversary. Although, paradoxically, he was tied more to his mother than ever before, she appeared to need him less. He had resumed his relationship with Fay, and spent the usual time on what she called his "agitprop." He did not in his heart believe any amount of political agitation was going to do any good by this time, but still he labored on.

It was now July, and Winston Churchill was urging a military alliance with the U.S.S.R. Approaches had been made, but in a way that inflamed Jo and his friends; a Foreign Office clerk had gone to Russia on a slow boat. Slow boat! With the world racing to war!

Their fury was exacerbated by a degree of incomprehension. All of them imagined a Foreign Office clerk to be some withered and lowly Dickensian personage who sat all day on a tall stool copying letters in purple ink and duplicating them on jelly. Clement, now married to Ilse, thought the misconception the funniest he had ever heard, but he could not get Jo to laugh at it.

They were together in a bar when the news of the German-Soviet pact came through, and Jo blanched with horror.

"Didn't you expect it?" Clement asked. "How simple you chaps are! It's been obvious ever since your namesake said he wasn't going to pull other people's chestnuts out of the fire."

"I can't believe it. I simply can't believe it."

"It might have helped if we'd sent your Tim Cratchit on a fast boat, of course, or even on an aeroplane; but I doubt it. You'd better shift your ma to some rural spot."

"I can't believe it."

"My only fear is that Ilse's still going to have an awful time, British citizen or not—do stop sitting there looking like a cod on a slab, and pay attention to what I'm saying. Get your ma away."

"She wouldn't go."

"You must make her."

But Jo was right in supposing that his mother would refuse to budge. "I'm not afraid," she said. "You think I will be, if it happens. Well, I shan't, that I promise you."

He did not urge her further. Secretly, he was expecting another Munich; the old conjurer with the bootblack moustache coming up with yet another repellent dove—he feared this far more than the coming of war.

What, he asked, did Kit mean to do?

Kit said, "I was going to tell you about that." They were sitting on Jo's lawn, in the twilight of a summer's day. The grass, new-cut, smelled juicily sweet. In rustic Clapham the birds twittered before bedtime.

Jo heard a note in his voice, something between satisfaction and fear. "What's up?"

"You know I said I damned well wasn't going to kill anyone I didn't know? I stand by that. On the other hand, I felt I couldn't face going off and registering as a C.O. I should only make myself offensive at a tribunal, and they would clap me into uniform out of pure dudgeon. So I slipped off to the doctor, when Polly was looking the other way, and made him take a look at me in the hope of finding something that might exempt me in any case. He found it." Kit paused. Jo was frightened.

"He says it's nothing. People can live with it forever, but that the army won't want me around. I've got a congenital heart disease."

"Christ!"

"That's how I felt, at first, but he's an honest chap and I trusted him. I badgered him to tell me whether I was really in any danger, and he said, no, I wasn't. So I have to go on his say-so. I'm not, however, telling Polly till after the baby's come."

Kit looked serenely up at the branches of a tree, arms bony round his knees. The leaves gave the intersections of sky a greenish tone. Outside the tree the sky was lavender-blue; within it, turquoise.

Jo was terribly afraid. Could one have a congenital heart disease and not be in danger? He felt he could not bear to live in a world without Kit, however infrequently they saw each other.

One wretched morning at the end of August, when the hordes of labelled children were being marshalled at the railway stations to be carried off God knew where, when mothers were crying, when frantic teachers were attempting to keep everyone's courage up by initiating choruses of "Little Brown Jug" or "Clementine," Lord Wantage appeared on Chelsea Embankment in a large hired car and told the driver to wait. After a brief conversation with a policeman he strode down the planks, the cardboard gas-mask container bumping against his shoulder-blades, identified his daughter's boat and boarded it.

"Father!" Polly was so startled that she dropped the frying pan, and half-scrambled eggs slopped all over the floor. "Damn, damn, damn, look what you've done, making me jump like that!" Reaching for a damp cloth, she began to clean up the mess.

Kit appeared: he had been reading in the sunshine at the stern of the boat. "What on earth are you doing here, George?" He had learned by now how to address his father-in-law informally.

"I've come," said the voice, weakly but firm, "to get you to pack your things at once. You're coming down with me to Suffolk."

"Of course we're not, Father! You must be mad."

"I'm not the one who's mad. Do you realize, you silly girl" —he eyed with distaste the shape of his grandchild-to-be—"that you could have that baby at any time, today or tomorrow?"

"It's not due till the ninth of next month."

"What makes you think it's acquainted with the calendar? Ignore that revolting stuff and do as I tell you."

"We'll do no such thing," said Kit, "we're staying put."

"You needn't worry about making arrangements. Just get your clothes. I've told the peeler over there that the boat will be empty. He says you must lock everything up and he'll keep an eye on it."

"Father," Polly said, "this is our own life and we shall do as we please with it. Anyhow, as well you know, I greatly dislike being rushed about anything."

"If you two imagine I particularly want you in the house, upsetting Bareham and making everything untidy, I do not. But I have a duty to my daughter, of a sort, and I refuse to leave her in this idiot place, probably to be killed within the first few days."

Kit wavered. Polly, seeing this, wondered whether it was on his own account or hers. But she had never had reason to doubt his physical courage, whatever modest disclaimers he might have made. Suddenly the whole life of the houseboat seemed a fantasy life, something they could never have sustained. Already, it seemed to be falling away from her. Kit slithered on the cooling scrambled egg, clutched at the sink and swore.

Polly felt the child's acrobatics, the heaving up at one side of her belly, the whale-like subsidence. She saw by her father's fascinated gaze that the movement was perfectly visible. "All right, we'll do it. But if nothing's happened within a fortnight at the outside, we're coming back here." She had forgotten that the baby was likely to be born by then and she herself incapacitated for some time to come.

"We'll see about that. Pack up sharp, now."

As they threw their clothes into the cases Kit said, "It's no good pretending I'm not glad, in a way. But I wouldn't do this if it weren't for Polly."

"You foolish chap, that is the whole object of the exercise."

Both, as they followed Wantage up the gangplank, felt like children who had disgraced themselves and had been taken in charge by the headmaster. Polly looked back once at the painted houseboat rocking so gently, so prettily, on the wash. Her throat contracted.

Their bags were thrown hastily into the boot and the driver ushered them into the back of the car. Wantage liked to sit in front.

They held hands as they were driven away through the sunlight of the fear-constricted streets. Another part of their lives had come to an end.

238

Chapter Ten

GEORGINA WAS LYING IN HER BATH, AMID THE SCENTS OF DUSTING-powder and of rose geranium bath-oil, listening to the Prime Minister's elegiac and huffy declaration of war. The sun was pouring through the frosted windows and sliding agreeably up and down the walls like the shadow of a golden animal trying to scrub a persistent flea from its flanks. Nothing the voice was saying seemed real.

The moment it had finished, the sirens sounded, howling over London.

She sprang out onto the mat, towelled herself feverishly, put on her uniform over her naked body, and snatched up the paraphernalia of torch, whistle and gas-mask. Tearing off her bath-cap she bundled up her hair under the steel helmet. She knew her instructions and was too intent upon them to experience fright.

In those days, however, instruction as to what a warden's duty must be should the sirens sound was considerably more vague than instruction on the subject of phosgene gas. Too far away from the depot to risk a dash there, Georgina felt that the only thing she could do was to get out into the street and hold up the traffic.

The wail had subsided, with a final moan that was like the

expression of unsporting defeat. The trees shone in the sun. People were standing in knots, looking up at the unblemished sky, with something more like curiosity than fear. Georgina realized that she had come out in her bedroom slippers, but decided that nobody was likely to notice. There was a fair flow of cars flashing past her. Suppose she did stop the drivers. Where on earth was she to put them? She saw no other warden in sight, no policeman. She looked around her. There was a covered stone passageway leading from the pavement to the courtyard of her block of flats. It looked safer than most places. She wondered whether she should put on her mask, but decided not to: it might create panic, make people believe there was a gas attack. Also she did not find it especially becoming, and believed that if she were to have sufficient *mana* to halt drivers in their tracks, she had better look as comely as possible.

A lorry full of potatoes was approaching. Boldly she stepped into the roadway, blew a blast on her whistle and held up her hand.

"Please draw into the curb and get yourself quickly and quietly into shelter."

She was astonished when the man obeyed, and other vehicles behind him followed suit. Power! All because of a boiler-suit and a tin hat. She knew a curious exhilaration.

The driver of the lorry came over to her and laughed. "You're the niftiest cop I've ever seen! Where do we go to, darling? All in it together now."

She marshalled him and other drivers into the passage, unnecessarily telling them to keep calm. The shock of the siren seemed to have induced a corporate euphoria, rather than anything else.

Another driver observed, "There seems to be a war on. Has one been declared?"

She told them it had, and returned to her post, parking and evacuating six more vehicles. She had packed together in the dubious shelter more than thirty people: by now, cars and vans were immobilized on both sides of the street, and drivers beyond her range were finding their own places of refuge.

Time went by. Nothing happened.

"Aw, come on, Hitler," one of the men exclaimed, "I haven't got all day, even if you have!"

240

The euphoria was beginning to wear thin, restlessness taking its place. One woman was afraid, and crying.

"Look here," Georgina said to her, "do try not to worry. It's probably a false alarm."

"If that's the case," said the man she had first evicted from his van, "I'm getting a move on. I'm not staying here, not for J.C. himself."

"Sorry, it's orders."

"You move out of the way, beautiful. I've got work to do." When he pushed past her, he was followed by a tide she could not stem. He jumped into the lorry and drove away. Soon, her whole triumphantly halted convoy was on the move again. The last man to go to his car slapped her bottom genially as he dodged by her. She was left with the crying woman on her hands, considering what she could possibly do next, when the All Clear sounded.

It was only now that she felt herself trembling with relief. "What did I tell you?" she asked the woman, almost angrily. "All right, you can go home."

She went down to the dêpot, where she found an inquest going on as to the usefulness of the warden's service on this particular occasion: it was fierce and recriminatory. The District Warden hectored them, denouncing his chiefs. "I don't know what time we've got left, but there's got to be a crash-training programme, and I'm going to see we get one. I've made representations to the Town Hall, but they're in such a ferment there that nothing makes sense to them. Pray God we don't have any more siren larks till we're a bit better organized."

As usual, they settled down to cigarettes, and cups of dark, stewed tea.

"What was your contribution to the war effort, Georgie?" someone asked her.

She replied sadly, "Well, I held up all the traffic in Flood Street—rather fun, actually—and stowed the drivers under cover, but they all got away before long. I don't think I have much natural authority."

When the sirens sounded, Polly and Kit were rambling depressedly round the garden, trying to shake off the immediate effects of Chamberlain's broadcast.

The sound was terrifying, since the siren mast was only a

241

hundred yards behind the house. Polly gasped and stumbled. Kit held her tightly. "Not wasting much time," she managed to say, her voice thick. Wantage came out to them. "Quick off the mark! But we ought to be all right here, unless he means to plaster the whole of England."

They stood in the unmown grass, staring up, like millions of others, at the bright sky, their ears attentive for the first swarm-like drumming of an air armada. Kit was aware of the extraordinary beauty about him, a beauty intensified to the point of hallucination by his fear. Michaelmas daisies, marigolds, burned in the borders, pink climbing roses hung in bulky swags on the walls of the garden shed. The copper beech was sheened over by the joyful sun. Holding her against his side he could feel the racing pulse of Polly's heart.

"Better get inside, I suppose," Wantage said. "Perhaps we ought to be in that blasted cellar."

Bareham came out, agitated, gas-masks in his hand.

"This is a fine old to-do, sir. Didn't lose any time, did he?"

Polly pushed away the mask he was thrusting at her. She was feeling unwell. She could not bear to move.

"I'm not going in. Not yet. Please let me alone."

Kit told her she must. "Come and lie down, anyway. You're as white as a ghost."

"Well, it was a shock. But I'm not scared, you must believe that." She was not: she was feeling too ill to be.

"Do as you're told," her father said sharply. "Bareham, get the cellar-trap open in case we all have to go down there."

"Not me, sir. I'd rather have Hitler than them old spiders. I'll only come if I'm driven."

Kit led Polly from the garden. This time she did not resist. She lay down on the sofa, and he covered her with a rug.

Feeling a hot dampness between her legs, she cried out, "I think my water's broken! Or if it's not that—" But she was right. "Kit, this means the baby's coming. Get Dr. Stephens."

He was not in, but the other doctor from the far end of the village came at once. He told them to call an ambulance.

Kit was telephoning for one when they heard the All Clear.

"Thank God for that!" Polly said, relaxing, her eyes fast shut.

"False alarm," said her father, "I knew it was."

242

"Because it wouldn't have made for what they call optimum conditions," she managed to add.

He grinned at her. There were times when he felt she was really his girl, of his loins, but better than he.

A phlegmatic man as a rule, he was as filled with anxiety as she and Kit. He stood helplessly by when he realized what was happening until the doctor, who wanted to make an examination, turned him out of the room.

"Where were you meaning to have it? Addenbrooke's?"

She nodded, and gasped. She had felt the first pains.

"Well, this may be a pretty quick business. All the same, you'll have plenty of time to get to Cambridge. I'll ring them now."

When Kit returned to tell her the ambulance was on its way, he dropped to his knees beside the sofa and she held his head between her hands, fumbling through his curly hair. She had the illusion that he was the coming child, as helpless, as vulnerable, as tenderly and as un-sexually desired.

"Someone will have to pack a few things," the doctor said.

Kit got up. "I will, I know what she needs."

It seemed to him that this nightmare through which he was passing had been heralded by his unnaturally heightened vision of the garden's beauty. At that moment, the world had taken on another dimension, and by the sinister device of that beauty had issued a warning.

Polly drank a little brandy, and it composed her.

"You're not to worry, Father. This is going to be perfectly all right. All will go well."

Wantage was dreading another air-raid warning, the mad assault upon the ears that had sent all the birds wheeling in panic over the chimneys. "I'll come to Cambridge with you."

"No, dear. Just Kit. That is, if you don't mind. I don't suppose ambulances are particularly roomy."

Kit brought her suitcase downstairs.

"Put some cigarettes in," she said, "it will probably be the first thing I shall want when it's all over. Very shocking. I can see the nurse's face. Pure quince."

He looked at her. "Is it hurting?"

"Hardly at all, as yet."

The doctor asked her to time the contractions.

243

"Don't worry, Mrs. Mallings, you won't give birth on the way. That I promise you."

The ambulance came.

She had been in the hospital for just over an hour when she did give birth, quite easily, to a living daughter.

Alison was alone with her son when the sirens sounded. Piers had left her a fortnight ago for one of the transit camps on the south coast. After the first shock, she found she was not at all afraid. She picked up the child, who had been swivelling on his stomach in the play-pen, and took him to the garden shelter, five feet deep below a mound of concrete. She heard the telephone ringing from the house, but paid no attention to it. She knew it could only be one of her neighbors, offering comfort. She was filled with a kind of acceptance for herself and the little boy: it was only for Piers's safety that she was anxious. Since the birth she had begun, as he joyfully realized, to love him fully: and with the pain of parting from him fear for herself had departed also. The kitten raced down into the shelter and skipped joyously around making pounces at imaginary mice. She took it onto her lap beside the child. It nestled at once, its purrs reverberating round the confined space. She considered her new passivity, did not understand it, but was grateful for its mysterious descent. She did not really believe what might be about to happen. Her thoughts were multi-colored, dream-like, not without an element of delight. Child and kitten comforted her.

Bessie, Jo, Fay and Miss Pease had listened to the Prime Minister's broadcast. Fay shrugged and smiled. Bessie said, "Poor Mr. Chamberlain, he sounds heart-broken! I always knew Hitler would let him down."

"Everybody knew it," said Miss Pease, in a tone of extreme exacerbation, "except him." She was a short, stunted woman with fine fanatical grey eyes and much untidy grey hair held in a bun by tortoise-shell pins. She had a nose like a tapir's.

"He did his best," Bessie retorted, "so it's no use being wise after the event."

"Wise after the event, Mrs. Upjohn! I'm sure I told you often enough what would happen."

The sirens rose. Fay leapt to her feet. "What, already?"

244

Jo was frozen by an immediate, shameful terror. He stared at the windows, criss-crossed with sticky paper, and focussed his eyes on one cross only, silently praying.

"So that's it, is it?" said Miss Pease, in a governessy voice. "Come along, everyone, into the passage. It's the safest part of the house."

Bessie said steadily, "I'm not going into any silly passage. You go. I'm going to finish the Sunday papers."

"Of course you must," Fay cried out. "Jo, come and help her!"

The moment of fright had passed from him; he obeyed.

"I'll put a chair for her out there," Miss Pease said, "and find a more comfy one later, if necessary."

Still indignant, Bessie allowed herself to be persuaded. They sat in the porridge-colored hall, their backs against the panelling. Fay squatted on her heels and lit a cigarette.

"Ridiculous," Bessie said, "we must all look like a lot of stuffed dummies."

The sunshine, pouring through the strips of stained glass, threw brilliant jellyfied blobs of pink and green over the lino- leum.

"It doesn't matter in the least what we look like, Mrs. Up- john, if we're in a place of safety."

"There isn't any safety. Don't be silly."

They waited. "Are you petrified?" Fay whispered to Jo, "I can't think why I'm not. I ought to be. I suppose I just can't be- lieve it."

Bessie began to worry audibly about Mildred.

"She's better off than we are," Jo said. "They have a damned expensive shelter in their garden, and that's where they will be, snug as bugs in a rug."

They listened to the silence which, in their imaginations, was visible, gold and blue, every leaf turned to sculpted stone.

"They're coming!" Miss Pease exclaimed: but she had heard only the heavy purring of an oncoming car.

"Nonsense," said Bessie. "They'll be brought down by the barrage-balloons. Jo, I wish you'd get me a chocolate biscuit, I feel I've got to have something sweet. And you might put the ket- tle on. We shall need a nice cup of tea when this is all over."

Fay said she would do it, but Jo refused to let her. "Mother can manage without a biscuit till we see what's happening. At least we're protected here from flying glass."

"On a Sunday morning, too," Miss Pease said, severely. "Lucky we weren't all in church."

They had stayed home for once to hear the broadcast.

"That's the All Clear," said Fay, springing up from her ankles.

"I told you," said Bessie, "that we'd never let them get through. Who do they think we are?"

They were glad to get back to the sitting-room and drink their tea. Bessie observed, glancing round her with satisfaction, that if every family had behaved as well as they had done, the Nazis would have something to reckon with.

"It will all be over by Christmas," she added confidently, "you'll see."

After the joint and Yorkshire pudding, for which only Bessie displayed a hearty appetite, Fay told Jo she must be going. He saw her to the gate, and they gazed across the golden common, where few people were walking that day.

"Well, duck," she said, "that puts paid to the Paris collections, and pretty well paid to my job. I'm going to join the A.T.S. I shall be a very good female soldier, and they'll give me a commission in no time. What will you do?"

"Wait for my call-up. I shall have to stick by Mother till the last moment. I do want to get her away if I can, and it will be an awful business moving her."

She stared into his face, longing for him, but his mind was miles away. She thought of a song, "It Was Fun While It Lasted," but it brought her no increase of stoicism. She was in love with him, she had hoped he might one day love her. Now there was nothing for her to do but get over it.

"Jo," she cried out, "it is like the end of the world, isn't it?" But she was thinking of other endings.

Ilse, the sugar-plum fairy of Georgina's hate, was crying hopelessly and Clement, now a military correspondent but still not assigned to a theatre of war, stood over her, not knowing what to do. The sirens had just wailed into clotted silence.

"No, no, no, don't touch me."

"I bet my bottom-dollar this is a fake. Some sort of Chamber-

246

lain swiz to get us all into the appropriate mood. There's not the least need to be frightened."

"I'm not frightened, not of bombs. But I am frightened that *he* will win and they will come for me. I would rather die than that."

Like many people who thought they might be on a blacklist, he had prepared for this eventuality with the right kind of pills to take, should there ever be no hope left. There had been nothing dramatic about it at all: it had seemed a mere exercise in common sense.

"Balls," he said. "They aren't going to win. The worse thing that can happen to you, if this damned government gets in a panic, is to be sent to the Isle of Man after all, where, I may say, you will be a bloody sight safer than the rest of us."

He slid his hand down the nape of her delicate sugar-stick neck, from which the gilded hair curled so prettily away. "If you don't stop crying like that," he added, "you'll make yourself hideous, and you wouldn't like that, would you? Neither would I."

He was in love with her, even though he had to admit that she was somewhat lacking in fiber. He thought fleetingly about Georgina, and wondered what she was doing at that moment.

Ilse cried on, in a luxurious passion of tears that he could not help envying. He hauled her up from the cushions on which she was lying and shook her soundly. Though this made her hiccup, it did at last bring her to a state of reasonable calm. He knew a heightened awareness of her beauty, of the very grain and flaking of her flesh: of the lovely coloring, delicate as that of a Meissen shepherdess. He could not help but think of her as an *objet de vertu*, come to life, but to a life infinitely distressful.

"A stiff Scotch," he said, "is a cure for most evils. You powder that swollen-looking blob of a nose, and then drink up. You've got to keep steady, because there may be worse than this to come."

The All Clear.

"I said it was a swizzle! Now you listen to me. The Nazis are not going to get you, even if you don't watch out. I don't believe they can ever invade us, not with our fleet and our air cover. But if it should ever happen, if you're in real danger and I'm not there, you'd better swallow one of these. I'm told it's very quick."

She looked at the box he had drawn from his pocket, and her blue eyes widened between the wet, ferny lashes.

"You won't get these till I'm sent abroad for what is likely to be a fair stretch, and don't you think it. But if you ever take one out of sheer funk, when there's not the faintest need, Christ have mercy on your soul."

She took a tablet in her hand, holding death.

"This is true? It is really true?"

"It is quite true," he said, "but you are not going to have it, certainly not yet. And, almost certainly, never." He took it back again.

PART FIVE

Changing Relationships

Chapter One

IN EARLY MAY JO WAS DISCOVERED TO HAVE, TO HIS PARTIAL
relief and his mother's dismay, a slight shadow on a lung; unsuspected, but now, it seemed, arrested. However, the army was not
enthusiastic about him, so he joined the wardens' service and began watching for the fires that had not yet descended from a cloudless, magnificent heaven.

"For Jesus' sake, we are a pair of crocks!" he exclaimed to Kit,
who was now working in the Ministry of Information. Polly had
insisted on leaving the country to be with him, and they were settled in a block of flats in Chelsea Manor Street, not far from Georgina.

"Usefully, don't you think? Anyway, there's obviously nothing much wrong with you, and according to a chap in Harley
Street, whom Polly forced me to consult, I can live with my groggy
heart for ever and ever, amen."

He would have liked the M.O.I. better, he said, if all his worst
enemies had not ensconced themselves therein, their horrible
names on pieces of cardboard along the corridor. "Baynes is at
the far end," he told Jo. "I always have to creep out of my room

251

and look right, look left, look right again before going out of it, in case he scuttles out of his own room like a black house-spider, and pounces on me."

He had reasons for being cheerful and for not being. On the credit side, his daughter, whom they had christened Ruth, was healthy, beautiful and good as gold. On the debit side, his novel, which had just appeared, had sold little, since no books were selling, and had been systematically torn in shreds by Baynes and his friends. Elsewhere it had been praised, and was having respectful treatment in such American periodicals as were unaffected by the long shadow of Baynes's influence.

"Oh, what other name do you suppose has just cropped up again? Nigel Dobson."

"You saw him?"

"No, I met a chap in a pub who knew his parents. Apparently he joined up at once; the army took him, goggles or no goggles, and buzzed him off to France. Extraordinary. Would you have thought he was the type?"

Jo said he didn't know what anyone's type was, even his own.

He was relieved that he need not abandon his mother, yet sorry not to have a chance of heroism, too. He had never minded the thought of fighting. Perhaps, in the army, he could have made something of himself. He had sold no more stories, and was dispirited; he did not expect to write again. There seemed little cheer in the waiting world, under this glowing, golden and ominous spring, with the skies starch-blue day after day, and with the hawthorns and chestnut-trees on the common bending under their weight of blossom, when every morning brought worse news. Fay was a first lieutenant in the A.T.S., stationed somewhere in Surrey. He had seen her only once during the past few months. Walking beside her over the grass, she dazzlingly smart in uniform, he in his churchwarden's serge, he had felt humiliated yet happy, a Betjeman hero strolling with his euphoric Amazon. The disciplined life suited her perfectly: she shone with it. She enjoyed command, she told him, and the girls seemed to like her, even the difficult ones, the tarts and the lesbians. "I give them buckets of sympathy, but they know I won't take lip and I won't take disobedience. Some of them are rather like kids from rotten homes who have never been given an order in their lives, and enjoy it when they do get a few. It makes them feel secure. By the by, I think I've got promotion coming up soon, so keep your fingers crossed for me."

The first personal tragedy happened towards the end of June, when the invasion scare was at its height, when the country had been warned that the church bells, now silent, would ring out all over England if an attempt at a landing were to be made.

Ilse had not wanted to be very far from London, since Clement's comings and goings were still frequent, and she did not choose to be far from him: but she had allowed him to rent a cottage for her not far from Runnymede. It was down a remote lane, with only two other houses nearby. On one of the beautiful, endless afternoons, when the meadow-sweet was thick in the ditches and dogroses sprinkled the hedges, she was returning on her bicycle from the small cluster of shops where she collected her rations. Clement was in Portugal. He expected to be there only for a few days, and she was looking forward to his return. It was very hot and the road, unmade, was bumpy. Dismounting, she began to wheel the bicycle.

All at once the church bells began to ring: first from one spire and then another, till the whole countryside resounded with the clangor.

A neighbor, who had come to his gate to stare apprehensively at the sky, had seen her stand stock-still, gripping the handlebars, for a long while. He had called out to her, but she had shaken her head and made a gesture with her arm, as if to keep him from approaching her. Then she had wheeled the machine to her own gate, and propped it carefully against the palings. She had gone indoors.

There she took from her handbag the pill Clement had refused her, but which she had stolen from him before he went to France. She went into the bathroom, where she drew a glass of water and, sitting on the lavatory seat, swallowed the cyanide. Death, the coroner said, had come very quickly.

"It would have been less ghastly," said Polly, "if there really had been an invasion attempt. But it was all due to one stupid parson with the wrong information getting the wind up. What hell it must be for Clement!"

Jo had gone to their flat for supper. The little girl, eight months old, who had Kit's eyes and Polly's mouth, was crawling about the carpet, making strenuous attempts to haul herself upright by grasping at chair-legs. Polly picked her up and fondled her, as if for comfort.

"I only met her once," Kit said, "she was extremely pretty, almost in the film-star class. But she hadn't much personality, and she dreaded Clem leaving her. She was scared silly."

"Georgina—" Polly began, then stopped.

"Yes, I know," said Kit, "it seems callous to say it, yet awhile. But this will make her hope again."

Both of them saw a good deal of her these days.

Polly said, "I never met Ilse at all, but I feel I want to cry. It makes it worse, somehow, when somebody dies who is beautiful. Though I know that is thinking quite wrongly. Oh God, I wish this weather would break! It ought to match all the anxiety, all the misery!"

Kit took his daughter from Polly and jigged her on his knee. He ran his fingers through her hair, still fair; but it would darken. Sensuously he smelled her cheek as if it were an apple. "Did we tell you what happened to our houseboat?" Polly smiled. "They commandeered it and turned it into a landing-craft. It went to Dunkirk. We're very, very proud of it," she added. "We hope it was the one that brought Piers back, but when I asked him he said he was in no state at that time to identify individual transport. It would have been nice, though, wouldn't it?"

"Have you seen him?" Jo asked, his mind on Alison, whose letters had been few and far between.

"No, but he telephoned. Now he's just cooling his heels like the rest of us. When is something going to happen?"

"Poor old Bobby Price," Jo said. "They wouldn't have him in the army because he'd been in Spain. Isn't it crazy? He thinks Hitler will go for Russia in the end."

"His books are terrible," said Kit, "only the Russians love them."

Polly rose to put the child to bed. "Supper's cold, so we'll have it the moment I've tucked her down."

"Call me to say goodnight to her." Kit went to the window. The inevitable, unnerving sunset stretched away behind the chimneys to a greening sky. "You know, Jo, whenever we're together now, I feel it is for the last time. We are living with last times, don't you feel that?"

254

Jo did not know how he felt: he could not quite catch Kit's elegiac mood. Despite his own disappointments, he could not escape from personal hope. Hope of what? He didn't know that, either, but he could not believe in finalities any more than Kit, who found poetic beauty in the idea of them, really could.

"Do you remember Dolokhov?" Kit did not turn round.

"Do I not! It would have served you right if you'd broken your neck."

"Polly served me right on that occasion. She's done so twice since, when I was drinking hard. She just walked off and left me till I'd stopped. Once was when we were in the flat, and once on the houseboat. She is a very severe girl. I wish you'd get married, old boy. It's a blessed state, even if one does pick a tartar. But," Kit added, "a tartar swaddled in swansdown." She called out to them from the bedroom. He turned now, his face brilliant. "And *this* is worth all the world! I can sit and watch Ruth for hours, just the movements of her miraculous hands."

Jo went home to find a letter from Alison waiting for him.

Piers had a week's leave. They would love to see Jo again after so long a time. Could he come down on his next off-duty day? There was a good train from Waterloo, the ten twenty-seven arriving at eleven thirty-eight. She would meet him with the car. "Do come. It will be a wonderful but in some ways a daunting prospect. We've all got so much to tell one another that I'm beginning to have a sore throat before we even start.

"Georgina spent a day with us last week, very bright, very brittle, very guarded. She didn't mention poor Ilse. She still doesn't quite understand why she can't share Piers with me—luckily he isn't that way inclined, though he's quite fond of her. Isn't it odd that she can be so racketty, and still pine for Clement? I have no idea what her chances are now."

She wanted Jo, Alison continued, to see her son, who was now eighteen months old and, everyone said, very tall for his age. "Heaven knows why he should be, neither Piers nor I are giants. But I hope he keeps it up."

She had not mentioned the child to him, since she had replied to his formal letter of congratulation, nor had he to her. Even now, he wondered if he could easily bear to see him. He despised himself for his long hankering—four years, now!—after someone he could never have, and wrote her a letter of refusal: but the dragging, destructive love, lessened a little by time but still tenacious, made him tear it up. He could not lose her friendship, even if it meant facing the son he wished he could have given her.

She was standing on the platform waving to him. She wore a flowered cotton dress and was hatless. When he jumped out of the train she ran to him, kissing him either with the reality, or the pretense, of complete unselfconsciousness.

"You're looking fine," he said, and held her from him for inspection, "and as pretty as ever."

She was twenty-seven: she could have been five years younger. Still the broken vein in the intense blueness. She now wore her hair below her shoulders, and her skin was brown with the sun.

"And you," she said, "are looking just as handsome and just as solemn, but we'd better hurry up because I've left James in the car."

He was strapped into a carrier, slung between the front seats, a very handsome, composed child with a bright broad smile. "How do you do," he enunciated distinctly, when Jo had gingerly shaken his hand.

"Get in," said Alison, "plenty of room for three of us."

"How do you do," James said again, "how do you do!"

"I don't know how to talk to children," Jo said shyly, as they drove out of the station yard, "I feel this one may be too clever for me."

"Oh, I expect he'll talk to you, though. His vocabulary isn't very wide as yet, but he displays it to maximum effect." She spoke with the false casualness of the mother more than normally proud of her son, who hopes her pride will not be too apparent. "Roll the window down, and you can smell the pines."

When they reached the house she released the little boy, who at once went off to play in a sand-pit.

Piers came out, in white shirt and flannel trousers. "Hullo! I didn't hear the car. How are you, Jo?" He said to Alison, "Did you remember my slacks?"

"Oh God, the cleaner's! No. I was so excited by seeing Jo that I forgot."

"I can understand that, my love, but don't forget again."

It was a perfectly commonplace exchange, yet Jo, whose antennae were always acute, and on this occasion made more so by joy, strain and the old jealousy, understood in a flash that relations

256

between them had not only changed but deepened. Piers had spoken good-naturedly, but not quite in his old paternal way: either he had become firm with her, or it was their mutual pleasure that he should pretend to be. Their eyes met; they gazed at each other for a fraction too long to conceal one of the code messages of a rich marriage.

"I'm a bad girl," she said, "I'll run in and fetch them immediately after lunch."

"You won't, because the shop will be shut. Jo, shall we have our drinks in the garden? Scotch for you?"

They sat in deck chairs beneath the trees, watching the little boy dig steadily away, fetch water in a tin cup from a bucket, and pour it into the holes he had made. Ice clinked in the glasses. Jo flicked a wasp from his tumbler with a blade of grass. Piers leaned back, arms locked behind his head, and Alison sat on the grass at his feet. It was another day in that summer of conclusions, a day full of bees, butterflies and slatted sunlight.

"How nice this is!" Jo said.

Alison wished it could last forever.

"We have to enjoy every oasis to the full," said Piers, "before we have to march off again with the bloody camels. Tell us your news, Jo."

They exchanged gossip at first, while the wife of Piers's batman brought them food on a tray: chicken mousse, salad, apple-charlotte. She took James away with her, to eat his dinner indoors, then have his nap. Jo exclaimed at the munificence. "It's not black market," Alison explained, rather apologetically, "except for what might conceivably be described as a regimental hen. Things are still easier around here than most places, and we get plenty of eggs."

Jo asked Piers, with all the diffidence of the civilian who has as yet seen nothing of war to the man who has fought, what Dunkirk had been like.

"I often ask myself that. It was such a muddle, you know, that one didn't have much time to think. I was sorriest for the private soldier. Even to be a lance corporal was better than nothing, because you had responsibility for other people. I know I was glad I had."

"You didn't think of me and James at all," said Alison positively, but her eyes inquired.

257

"No. Not at all. All I had in mind was getting to the landing-craft, and seeing that the men kept together and kept down. They went on dive-bombing us and shooting up the beaches, so the hullabaloo was terrific. I lost all sense of time. I haven't really a clear picture of anything except the half-hour when I was wading out in water up to my armpits shouting sweet nothings. Oh, and of being sick as a dog all the way back. The navy would never have suited me."

She took his hand and held it, which made Jo feel lonely.

"Well, it was a pretty wonderful victory for us," Jo said.

"No," Piers replied, reaching for a cigarette, "it was a damned awful defeat. But I don't doubt that the right psychological line was taken with the public at that particular moment."

"What do you think is—" Jo began, then stopped. He was afraid of seeming to pry into military secrets.

"Going to happen next?" Piers spoke easily. "I don't know. No inside information. But I suspect the Germans will switch over to night-bombing before very long, and when that happens I shall be glad Alison and Jim are out of London."

"We often call him Jim between ourselves," she murmured, "we use the stern James to show off to our guests. What he is called eventually will be his own choice."

Jo asked whether their own surroundings would be so safe. Piers replied that he thought bombs would not be wasted so lightly in Surrey, even where there were military establishments. If the Germans had any sense, which he thought, on recent showing, that they had, they would go for docks, factories, marshalling yards, bridges and the like. Releasing Alison's hand, he said, "How's Fay? She seldom writes to us now."

Jo remembered that they had once had a brief love-affair. "Or to me, much. But I gather she's had a step-up in rank."

"She'll make an excellent soldier." Piers looked amused. "I'd far rather have her than my colonel."

"I should have done well, too," said Alison, "if I'd had the chance."

He laughed at her. "Too small. And too forgetful."

"Damn your slacks! He bears grudges," she added to Jo. "I should have been wonderful *theoretically*. I should have read Clausewitz and stuck pins in maps."

Piers teased her, wound her hair round his fingers, let her go again. Now, perhaps feeling compunction, she came to sit by Jo. "I shall hold your hand for a change. Piers won't mind." She looked anxiously up at him. "Listen, dear, I do worry about you. Is your mama still unbudgeable?"

"Entirely. And so is Miss Pease. They both behave as though they're heroines, and damn it, I believe they will be when it comes to the test. They don't in the least mind the bangs even now. But that makes it worse. If only either of them would show a tremor of fright, I'd have them out tomorrow, though God knows where they'd go."

Alison said she knew of an empty bungalow not half a mile away; she was sure she could get hold of it, if she went about it firmly enough. "Tell them that. You will, won't you?"

The enchanted afternoon came to an end. She kissed him good-bye at the gate. Piers drove him to the station.

"Give my love to Fay," Piers said, as the muffled headlights swerved around the black hedges. "It was never very serious between us, but I am fond of her. By the by, I did think it might have been you. I know how she felt about that."

"I couldn't have given her anything."

"Only what she wanted. But it's not my business."

"I'm glad about James. He's a fine little boy."

"We think so."

Piers said nothing further till they drew up in the yard. Then he said, "Jo, always remember that if things get bad in London, and you want to get out of it for a few days, we're here: or if I'm not, Alison will be. We're both fond of you. And I know—"

Jo waited.

"These things can't be said." The voice in the darkness was troubled.

Jo said, "But thanks for trying."

In the following week, the bombing by day was intensified: and at the end of August, there began the bombing by night.

Chapter Two

THE BOMB SQUEALED THROUGH THE AIR, CRASHED TWO STREETS away. The whole building shuddered even to the basement, where they had taken up their accustomed cover for the night.

Kit looked up, pen poised. "How do you spell 'heterogeneous?' "

Polly clenched her teeth. Because he had only the late hours in which to write, he was writing furiously, oblivious to anything going on around him. She felt, in a bewildered way, that he was not even being brave: simply, his work so absorbed him that nothing else impinged on his consciousness. Rolled in blankets on her own mattress, Ruth in a carry-cot at her side, she was terrified.

This she had never expected to be: she had always assumed that she would be calm in any circumstances, as her father always seemed to be, and that in emergency she would have to support and comfort Kit. She was so ashamed of her fear that she fought bitterly against showing it. She could, she believed, succeed in this if only he would show the faintest tremor himself: but he had taken to bringing down with him an old bed-table which served him very well as a desk. While she read, or tried to read, praying that Ruth would not wake, he wrote steadily late into the night, the damp-looking cigarette drooping from the side of his mouth. His cigarettes were invariably wet, the nicotine staining the paper.

There was room for about thirty couples in the basement, which had now been reinforced by steel and concrete. Some people from the block, the young and childless, sometimes the very old, did not use it. There were five or six carry-cots, like Polly's, holding babies who slept like death or cried in meaningless spasms for hours on end. The older children seemed for the most part to find the shelter-life good fun; some of them made a nuisance of themselves, playing touch around the mattresses or jumping over those who were trying to snatch some sleep. It was pretty noisy there till about midnight, when the All Clear usually went, to be followed by a second warning signal a few hours later.

" 'Heterogeneous,' " Kit repeated, "do help."

She spelled it for him. His eyes opened in surprise. "What's up?"

"What should be?" she managed to say, forcing irony. "That last one nearly hit us. Of course nothing is up."

"Cheer up, darling, it's the one you don't hear that catches you. The more bangs the better." He returned to his work. During the day he was laboring on a propaganda film, designed to encourage steel production. It was a relief to write his novel in the evenings. Sometimes, using a small-voltage lamp that clapped onto the desk, he would go on writing long after everyone else was asleep.

Noise was muffled to some extent in the basement, but the anti-aircraft guns near the river crashed that barrier, and the throb of approaching bombers made the boards tremble underfoot.

"That one was close," Polly's neighbor whispered, a young woman, who was knitting and smoking furiously, a baby of three weeks at her side. "He was early tonight, too. It looks as though he's going to have a regular party, doesn't it?"

Again the whining squeal. Polly put her fingers in her ears. She felt, rather than heard, the impact.

"Kit!"

"Noisy bastards," he muttered, his hand not pausing in its rhythmic progress across the paper.

She lay down and brought the blankets to her chin. She was

trembling so much that she feared he might sense the vibration of her body despite the few inches between their mattresses.

A young man squatting on the far side of the shelter stood up. "Anyone want a cup of char if I make one?"

"What's the time?" asked Polly's neighbor, who was called Lisa.

"Ten to ten."

"Wouldn't like to fix his bottle for me, would you, Steve? I don't want to slope out of here myself while Jerry's so active, but if you're going to be a hero—"

"Give it over. What do I do?"

"Just heat it in boiling water. Five minutes will be enough."

Thank God, Polly thought, Ruth was old enough to sleep the night through, and usually did.

Somebody switched on a radio. Dance music, like syrup on buttered bread, slowly spread into the room. This always made Polly want to scream: she had to hear what was coming and the music might obliterate a warning.

She thought: I cannot bear much more of this, I shall have to go back to Suffolk. But leave Kit? How could she do that? Even if she could bear the parting, she would endanger him, for without her he would never go down to the shelter, but sit scribbling through the most violent raid, in their third-floor flat. She pretended to sleep. Then Ruth stirred and flung wide her satiny arms. Polly sat up, covered her, cooed to her. She must not wake, not now.

The music pumped on and on, "Moonlight Serenade."

Steve came back with the bottle wrapped in a flannel duster. "Here you are, Lisa. Better give it to her now, or it will get cold again."

Since it was just ten, the baby was wakened by its internal alarm-clock and began to cry. "Come on, poppet, drink first, change later."

A girl rose up to help Steve bring in the tea-things: they laughed together as they left the shelter.

And I, and I, Polly thought, am too petrified to stir a muscle.

"Cup that cheers," said an elderly Civil Servant, "bottoms up. We'll get the All Clear any minute now."

Listening for new sounds, she had not realized that there had been quite a long silence.

The Civil Servant was proved right.

"There, love," said Kit, "that wasn't much to write home about!"

Gratefully she drank her tea, thinking of the extraordinary pleasure relief from fear could bring, even a temporary relief. One day, if I come through, when it is all over, it is a pleasure I am going to miss, one I shall find myself longing for.

Steve went out to look at the weather, and when he returned announced cheerfully that there was something of a mist getting up. "With any luck, that'll be the last of him for tonight. Keep your fingers crossed."

"If it really gets thick," Kit murmured, "we might risk going upstairs. I rather want to make love to you."

She knew she must let him, even if, all the time, her ears would be straining. Their love-making had recently been confined to rushed embraces between his return in the evening and the getting of supper.

"Give it an hour," he added, "and I'll be just about through."

At last he put down his pen.

"Marvellous! Precisely eleven twenty-three. An early night for once. You stay there while I reconnoiter."

He returned to report thickening fog. "Come on, my heart, get up them stairs."

"I'm staying down," said Lisa, "I'm perfectly comfy and if I disturb baby again it will be absolute murder."

Steve, another young man and a middle-aged couple, had already taken the risk and had gone.

As they climbed the basement stairs to the lift, carrying the cot between them and using their free arms for other impedimenta, Polly found herself shivering.

"What on earth's the matter?" Kit asked her, concernedly.

"I'm frozen stiff."

"But it's stifling in the shelter and God knows the building's warm enough! You shall have some brandy when we get back."

They opened the front door of their flat, went into the living-room and could see that the black-out curtains were fast drawn, since no ray of light, however feeble, penetrated them. They turned on the lights. The curtains were billowing gently in soft pregnant heaves.

"What a damned nuisance," Kit exclaimed, "we don't seem to have any glass left!"

It had been a freak of blast. When he made an inspection, he found that the middle window only had been smashed, leaving the other two intact. Nothing in the flat was broken except a Lalique vase, a wedding present from Clement and Georgina, which had toppled from the mantelpiece and fragmented on the tiles below.

He said irritably that the room would be unliveable for days. All they could do was to fix up cardboard to keep the draughts out, until it was their turn for the glazier.

Polly stonily picked up the cot and deposited it in the room next to their own, as usual leaving the door open in case the baby cried. Then she went into the kitchen, where Kit found her in a rage of tears.

"Darling! It's only a bit of broken glass. What's upsetting you so much?"

She said, "I am frightened. I can't help it, I didn't mean you to know. I am miserably ashamed."

He sat down facing her.

"My love, I know it's noisy. But ours is probably one of the best damned shelters in Chelsea. Practically nothing but a direct hit—"

She screamed at him, "I don't want a direct hit!"

Then she looked up and saw, through the kaleidoscope of tears, that there was a glint in his eye. Somehow, he was pleased. The seesaw on which she had held their relationship had for the first time tipped his way. This rallied her spirits.

"Yes, I'm cowardly! Now you know. But I'd be less so if *you* showed some decent, human sign of fear, however slight, and didn't just sit there writing away like a madman, and asking me to spell things for you just when a bomb's dropped!"

He was smiling. "Polly, my love, my only love, it was nothing much tonight. And I don't believe you're a coward, any more than I'm a hero. I shall shiver like a leaf, the moment I feel I ought to shiver. I have great faith in steel and concrete." He reached out to

264

hold her hand. "You must go back to George if you want to. But, darling—unless you can't help it, please don't."

Speechless, she shook her head. She had a terrible sense of self-betrayal. He was the last person to whom she should have discovered her terror.

"You know," he wheedled, "that I wouldn't stop you, even for Ruth's sake, if I didn't think we were pretty well O.K. here. And it would be awful to get back from the grind every day to an empty flat."

"All right," she said, sucking up the brandy he had given her gingerly, as through a straw, "I shall pull myself together. I shan't go. Don't worry, I shan't go."

Though there was only one heavy raid over Chelsea that night, the incidents, as they were melopoeically called, had been bad ones: in the first, Phil Christie won the George Cross. Georgina, with her ambulance crew of a nurse and two stretcher-bearers, pleasant homosexuals of cool temperament whose courage even she admired and envied, stood above the wrecked house. Phil was under the rubble, fighting to free an elderly woman from a beam that had fallen across her chest. There was a reek of gas from a broken main. They could hear the woman first screaming, then wailing, but there was no room for the doctor to get to her. At any time the remaining wall might collapse.

Phil was shouting encouragement in a way that sounded peculiarly jocose, but they could not hear his words. The wardens had ringed the area with lights, through which the mist was coiling more thickly every minute. "Good grief," Georgina said, "they're both going to be killed!" The Heavy Rescue squad had arrived and were debating whether anything more could be done, but the residual fabric was too dangerous even to be touched.

In half an hour Phil had removed the beam. He came wriggling to the surface covered in dirt. "She's O.K.: just listen to the row she's making! You can shore it up above her now, because the bloody beam's holding back part of the wall and there's room for the doc to maneuver. We can get her out quite easily."

"Well, well," said Georgina, "that was quite a thing."

"Oh, you're there, are you?"

"In fact, it was a marvel."

265

They were round him, congratulating him. The District Warden said he would put in a report.

Phil looked smiling at his feet. "I just didn't stop to think about it. I never do think. You know me."

Bessie and Miss Pease had their mattresses permanently in the passage, and, since they both wore wax ear-plugs against the noise from the bombs and the guns on the common, usually managed to get a surprising amount of sleep. Jo, on duty at the post, never knew when he would get back to find them dead in the wreckage of his home. Their lack of fear seemed to him not sublime but ridiculous. Neither of them seemed to realize that their obstinate presence in London was an additional strain upon himself. He was as scared as most people, but at least he had action to anaesthetize and at times to exhilarate him. He could not imagine how the two elderly women, with nothing whatsoever to do but wait, could remain so placid. They had refused to go to the comparative safety of the garden shelter. No, said Bessie, not with her arthritis: even if she could manage to clamber down there, she wouldn't do it. It was reeking with damp, she insisted, and had a nasty moldy smell. Miss Pease observed, not too realistically, that she had only one fear and that was of being trapped. They had brought a spirit-stove into the passage so that she would not have to go to the kitchen to make tea while a raid was in progress. She and Bessie appeared to believe that creature-comfort could go no further.

Alison, alone with her son since Piers had been sent to the Middle East, heard the bombers passing over nightly. Once she saw a plane falling down the sky like a great chandelier of scarlet lusters. Several times she had been to the well-constructed dug-out at the end of the garden, but this had upset James, who was just old enough to fear the unusual: she soon abandoned the practice, but put up his cot in the knee-hole of a heavy Victorian sideboard, which would hold up under a fallen roof. Piers had fitted shutters to the windows before leaving her.

She thought about her friends in London, and was far more afraid for them than for herself. In a way, she envied them, and wished she were with them. Piers's going had been a wrench that she had accepted, at first, less than philosophically. (She had cried through the nights as she had once cried—she could scarcely believe this now—for Kit.) Since the alteration in their relationship, she had known a new wonder. To lose all this, when he was suddenly quite new to her! It was as though no other love had ever existed.

She did voluntary work with other lonely wives, making "comforts for the troops," and during the long afternoons of sewing and gossip found herself seeking for the slightest opportunity to say his name. She dragged it, as well she knew, into the most surprising contexts.

Chapter Three

WHEN GEORGINA FOUND SHE WAS PREGNANT SHE BURST INTO A FIT of helpless laughter.

What a crazy joke, for this to happen to her, of all people! A fine fool she was going to look. She knew who the father was, of course; a flight-lieutenant with whom she had had a dreary and trivial adventure just before Christmas and who had now been posted abroad. Not a married man: she believed he would marry her cheerfully, if he knew what had happened. But she was not going to tell him. She did not fancy him at all. A dull dog.

This was during the bombing lull in the latter part of February 1941. Alone in her flat, she went on laughing until she began to cry. Knowing that wouldn't do, she got up, mixed herself a stiff drink and sat down to think things over.

She would have the child, of course. She was far too fastidious to consider some back-street abortion and, moreover, she had a very strong respect for life. This creature, already forming in miniature, was to have its chance. It meant, of course, leaving the dêpot pretty soon, since nobody would desire a pregnant ambulance driver. Well, she felt she had done her bit already, and at least she

268

could retire with honor. Or dishonor, in a sense, since they all knew she was a divorced woman. But they were not important to her, the gossipings, the jokes that would take place behind her back. She patted her stomach, still perfectly flat. "You and me, chum," she said to the foetus, "we'll get on all right. The trouble is, what's your surname going to be?"

She still, of course, called herself Mrs. Maclaren: but felt that to register the child under Clement's name would be indecent. Anyway, it would be a long time before he heard anything about it. She would, she supposed, have to revert to her maiden name, which was Hartopp. "Master Hartopp," she said, "let me introduce you to your mother."

She had no intention of returning to her own mother, who had never liked her in any case, and now lived with a third husband in Redruth. The best thing would be to move out of London and find a good nursing home, where, if questions were asked, nobody would be particularly shocked if they got the answers. If they were shocked, be damned to them.

Clement had made no move to see her or to write to her. So far as she knew, he was still in the Middle East: none of her friends had had news of him.

Luckily, she had money of her own. The important thing was for her to find a small house, in Kent, perhaps, or Sussex, where she could settle down. Not too near a town, even if there was fun to be had there. "Master Hartopp, you are going to let me in for a tedious life."

The most frank of women, she was not prepared to be secretive about her condition, which she certainly did not admit as a plight. Yet she did mean to keep it from Clement, partly because she believed she must make a fool of him as well as herself, and partly because he was the only person whose derision she would fear. Derision? Wasn't she letting him down in her mind by supposing he might laugh? He was a violent man, certainly, but not a moral lout. She forced to the back of her mind the ugly thought that if she had lived till now on the hope that he might return to her, that hope had now been knocked on the head.

Next day she went to the District Warden, a cool man, not unlike Piers to look at, though a good deal taller. She said she must leave the service and explained why.

"Congratulations, Mrs. Maclaren," he said blandly.

"Come off it. You know and I know. But to be honest—human nature being what it is—I am really rather thrilled."

When she had to hand in her kit, she felt sad and somehow degraded, rather like Dreyfus. She retained only the chevron she had won for proficiency in the gas-tests, and locked it away in a drawer with her pieces of jewellery.

Then she went to call on Polly and Kit. She was pleased to see Polly looking composed, and prayed for her sake that the air raids would not soon be resumed. Georgina was one of the few people who had known of her terror, and she had been angry with Kit because he had never seemed to realize it. It was true that Georgina did not much like women; but, like many of her kind, she often found herself fighting, for some obscure, almost chivalric reason, on their side. Certainly she would fight for Alison, if this were ever needed, which seemed improbable.

She told them the truth, baldly.

"You can't go through with it," Kit said at once, "there must be ways and means."

"Of course there are, but I'm not interested. This is my pidgin, and it isn't one I find hard to bear. It even coos to me."

Polly said, "Clement ought to know."

"Why? It's no affair of his."

"I still think he ought."

Georgina said that if they seriously thought she was going to crawl to Clement on her knees to beg him to give her son a name—

"Son?" Kit interrupted.

Certainly, she replied—if so, they could think again. Master Paul Hartopp had a name; in fact, two names.

Alison, when consulted by telephone, was more practical. The bungalow into which she had hoped to move Jo's mother would be free again soon.

"Done," Georgina said briskly. She asked if there was a local maternity hospital not strictly dedicated to the military.

"I can find out. Shall I go ahead?"

"Yes, my effective friend, you go ahead."

Within two days, Alison wrote to say that she had arranged all things, but that the bungalow would not be vacant till the middle of April. Georgina began to plan the move. The air raids on London had started again, and for the first time she was really scared.

270

It had been so different, when there was no one but herself to worry about and nothing much to look forward to. Like Jo, she had been buoyed up by the excitement of action: now she hated to be alone when the sirens went. She took to using Polly's shelter, no more than a hundred yards from where she lived.

"It's a comfort to have you here," Polly said, when Kit had gone out to coax cigarettes from under a friendly counter, "because I get more and more pusillanimous every day. I can't tell you how much I loathe admitting it."

"My poor Polly Perkins, everybody does."

"Yes, but not as I do. It is very odd, really."

One night of heavy cloud, when a raid seemed unlikely and Georgina had stayed at home, she heard the bell ring with such prolonged shrillness that she was startled out of her wits. When she did not answer it at once, it shrilled again: this time someone was keeping a finger on the buzzer.

She opened the door. Clement pushed past her and walked in. She could do nothing but stare at him.

He was in uniform sloppily worn, and he had lost a good deal of weight.

"Are we going to stand in the hall all night?" he demanded. Taking her arm, he drew her after him into the sitting-room, where he stood in his familiar posture, heels propped on the fender.

"And what," she said, trying to sound airy, though she heard her voice crack, "are you doing in this country at all?"

"Spot of leave. They'll be sending me somewhere else soon, Greece, I expect. Now you tell me something. What's that kid's name going to be?"

"Who the hell told you?"

"Polly. I ran into her this afternoon. When I asked about you she colored up like a beetroot and was so damned evasive I knew something was up. So I hammered at her till I dragged it out."

"What bloody right has she to meddle in my affairs?"

"Never mind that. Have you got any Scotch?"

"Of course not. Who do you think we civilians are?"

"I thought you wouldn't have. Gin?"

"There's some rum."

"Filthy. But go and get it. We've got some hard talking to do."

He sat down, and did not speak again till they both had glasses of rum and lime-juice.

"Now then. Do you know who the father is?"

"Of course," she answered indignantly.

"No need to put on airs. Does he know?"

"He doesn't and he's never going to."

"Was he important?"

"No. It was a silly little affair. It didn't last a week."

Clement was brooding, and she did not dare to speak.

He said at last, "You didn't answer my first question. What name are you going to give it?"

"Mine. Hartopp."

"You're not. It's going to be called Maclaren. Oh, not that I've all that much use for you, but I don't like any poor brat getting the rotten start you're planning for it."

She asked whether he thought she would have done anything so low as to register the child in his name.

"I appreciate the moral rectitude, so far as I'm concerned. But I'm thinking of him. You wouldn't, or couldn't give me one—"

"Couldn't."

"Let that go. But I'm prepared to take on this infant and try to forget it isn't mine. We'll have to be married again, like it or not."

She lost control, crying out that he need not make a martyr of himself. All their friends would know the truth anyway.

"Well, the kid won't, and as for all our friends, they can go boil themselves an egg. Since we weren't married at the time you conceived, I'm not even technically a cuckold."

"If you cared for me . . . " she began.

"If you mean, am I in love with you, no. But I know you back, side and foremost, and I can put up with you. I've been used to it. I haven't got over Ilse, and I don't suppose I ever shall, but that doesn't mean that you're going to mark that child down as a bastard."

Georgina tried to steady herself. He did not know what he was saying, he was acting on an impulse he would regret. She couldn't let him do any such thing.

"More heroics. They don't suit you. You know perfectly well

that whenever I say a thing I mean it. Where's it going to be born?"

She told him that, and about the bungalow.

"Good idea. What did Alison tell the hospital? What name did she give for you?"

"I suppose," Georgina said, "Maclaren. Oddly enough I didn't think to tell her otherwise."

"Well, that's one thing out of the way. I'll get a special license, and we'll be married again as quickly as possible. I don't expect to be here more than a fortnight, and after that God knows when I shall see you again."

"Clem, I'm sorry!" She had begun to cry.

"One thing I won't stand for, is you behaving like a fallen woman. We've got to get along as best we can, and any Magdalene stuff would drive me mad. I'm not going to rub your sin into you, or anything of that sort. I never expected you to be living a life of chastity and accidents will happen. Get it into your head, I'm not doing this for you at all."

He picked up the bottle, which was nearly empty. "I'll bring you Scotch tomorrow. I can usually wangle some."

He rose. "Well, that's all for now."

She was dazed. This simply could not be happening. "Don't go just for a minute."

"I've got someone to see, and I'm late already."

"I only want to start believing that this is real."

"Oh, it's real enough. Good-bye." He gave her a casual, brushing kiss on the cheek. "I'll be round about ten a.m. We have practical arrangements to make."

He was gone. The sirens sounded, but she hardly noticed them. She said aloud, "People can't be so *mad!*" Slow joy rose in her. He did not love her: she could see that. Nevertheless, behind the almost insensate generosity, there must have lurked something not quite so selfless. He was lonely. They had, in the good times, liked each other. Perhaps he could not be bothered to shop around for a new wife. Anyhow, Georgina thought, at least I love him. That will probably do for us both.

She had, in fact, not erred in thinking his magnanimity a little suspect. A man of impetuous nature with a tendency towards dramatic decisions, he had been spurred by Polly's com-

273

munication to act in character: certainly he meant well by the child that was not his own, and it was good to play out nobly a gesture real enough in itself. But, though he would never admit it, he had been more in love with Ilse's beauty and docility than with her inner essence. The shock of her death had left him miserable and empty, but—this he tried not to think about—he had made rather too swift a recovery. Their marriage had been so brief and so dream-like that it might never have happened at all.

For some time past he had found himself hankering again after Georgina. He felt ashamed that this was even possible, for basically he was, as Alison had once said, "a kind man." He had put off getting in touch with her, day after day, week after week. But he had gone to Chelsea hoping to get news of her, so that he might telephone when the time was ripe.

Well, he thought, as he went to bed at his club, there had been news, no doubt about that. Would he ever fall in love with her again? He did not know. Things were too sudden, confused, histrionic, and he could not yet think them out. But he was sure that he desired her, and hoped he had concealed from her, that night, every trace of it.

She was not, of course, for his instant taking. He would move into the flat after the marriage, but not touch her till after the child was born. They would not have many days together, in any case, before he was shipped off again somewhere. He grinned in the dark. He could control his desires whenever he wanted to. But could she? She would have to.

Like Georgina, he had barely noticed the sirens: like her, was fast asleep before the All Clear.

Chapter Four

"IT'S NICE TO HAVE YOU FOR A LONG EVENING AGAIN," BESSIE SAID TO her daughter, "and not have you scuttling away straight after tea."

"It wasn't fun to be caught in the open when the raids were on," Mildred retorted. "Not all of us have your sangfroid."

It had been quiet over England since the invasion of Russia, and social life was warming up again. Jo frequently spent his night off with Kit in the pubs of Chelsea and Bloomsbury, no longer so afraid to be far from his mother. She and Miss Pease had deserted the passage and returned to their beds.

"I must say, Frank," Bessie went on, "you've smartened my little girl up. We hardly know her these days."

He smiled, the quiet man, at her and at his handiwork. Nothing could have made Millie handsome, but she had come to look almost distinguished, her hair well-dressed, her clothes chosen to conceal her dumpiness. "She looks very well in green," he said.

"I always thought blue was her color—"

"You two can stop talking about me as if I weren't there."

"Surely," said Bessie, "we're talking about you because you're so very much there?"

275

Jo, bored by the familiar, half-affectionate, half-hostile snacking, told Miss Pease that he would make the coffee, and went out to smoke a cigarette in the kitchen. In a few moments, Mildred followed him.

"You're looking down-in-the-mouth," she said. "What's the matter?"

"I don't know. I suppose I'm a bit under the weather. What with the damned war going on and on, and this house—I wish you wouldn't let mother take a rise out of you all the time. It's bad for her."

"She doesn't really. I respond with some vivacity just to please her. She has to play her funny little games, you know: she hasn't so much left."

"She plays the same ones with Miss Pease, and they both seem to enjoy it. I only wish I did."

"You make me feel guilty. I suppose I am."

"Oh, nonsense. No one expected you to give up Frank."

"She did."

"Well, I didn't, and if I don't feel badly about it, there's no reason for you to."

She slipped her arm for a moment through his.

"Cut and run, why don't you?"

"No temptation strong enough." He put the percolator on a tray, poured hot milk into a fussy jug with a design of rosebuds.

"Have you heard from Fay?"

"Not a line."

"Well, I have."

Miss Pease came out into the kitchen.

"Mrs. Upjohn asked me to go and see what had happened to the coffee," she said, with an air of complete dissociation from her errand.

"Do you mind taking it in?" said Mildred, "we'll be along in a minute."

When they were alone again, Jo said: "When?"

"I met her in the tube. She's on leave. I thought you might like to know."

He thanked her.

"Will you get in touch?"

"She doesn't seem to want me to, or she'd have written."

Mildred told him not to be a fool.

"Oh well," he said, "I'll think about it. Come on, back to the gay festivities, the halls of dazzling light."

They played rummy, then listened to the nine o'clock news, which was bad: the Germans had taken Smolensk.

"I don't think the Russians can lose in the end," Frank Hansen said. "Anyway, we must pray."

Jo thought of the endless plains, the endless battle. Last week he had had his thirtieth birthday.

When Frank and Mildred had gone home, he dialled Fay's number: she was out.

The following night he met Kit in the Six Bells.

Kit looked at him. "What's up with you? Why the funeral face?"

"I don't know. I seem to get fagged so easily these days."

"Let's make a night of it, then. It'll buck you up."

Kit himself looked well, and in high spirits. He was beginning to put on weight. In the room crowded with people in utility clothes, he stood out like a parrakeet: orange jersey, turtle-necked; trousers of fawn corduroy, none too clean; black hair curling up above his forehead as if he had just plunged his fingers into it.

"Where did you get that rig?" Jo asked him.

"Sweater and pants from Fran Olson. She sends Polly and me clothes parcels, which we much prefer to food."

Jo inquired after Ruth, and received an ecstatic answer. "Now the raids have stopped, I'm glad Polly didn't take her out of London. The flats are as safe as you can find anywhere. She always pretended to be scared, though. I never really believed it, not of Polly."

People came up and talked to them: Jo thought how slowly it had taken him to realize that his friend was, if not yet famous, extremely well-known and much admired. This was not now merely a coterie admiration. He remarked on it.

"If you'd get off your arse, or rather, get on it, and write some more, the same would happen to you."

"I can't, not any longer." Jo grinned sourly. "I shall go to my grave with that one story to my credit. As it is, I carry it around in my breast pocket, like some aged actor with a couple of faded clippings."

"Let's see it again."

Breaking free of friends, they went into a secluded corner.

"Now keep quiet for ten minutes," Kit said. He spread the story in front of him, propped his head on his hands and read it through with absorption, his lips moving silently now and then as if to test the flow of a sentence. He looked up. "It is really extremely good, I hadn't realized quite how much. If I were you, I'd cut out that last line, though. It's a bit like the curtain dropping with a thud. Look at it yourself. Do you see what I mean?" He had the excitable air which took him whenever he was criticizing a piece of writing, no matter how good or how poor it might be.

Jo said that he saw, perfectly, but it was too late now.

"Bosh. You'll write a dozen more and then you can collect them in book form."

Despite himself, Jo felt a vestigial degree of hope returning to him, as Kit had meant that he should. Then a figure caught his eye. "Oh no, it can't be! Not Dobson!"

The bulky figure in uniform, two pips on the shoulder, came bearing down on them. The light flashed off his glasses, as if they were windows at sunset.

"Mallings! Fancy running into you. And Upjohn, too. Mind if I sit down?"

Kit said no, not at all, but that they had to be going in ten minutes.

Dobson observed that much water had flown under the bridges. He was, he said to them, on furlough. What were they doing these days? When told, he pursed his lips. "Rough luck. You're both missing something."

"What have we missed?"

"The show at Dunkirk," Dobson said quietly. He added, with what seemed genuine regret, that he had been transferred afterwards to an anti-aircraft battery on the South Coast. "Eyes not so good as they thought. What kept you two out of things?"

"Just piffle," Kit said shortly, "but enough for the authorities. And I don't feel wistful at all, Nigel, so don't look at me in that sorrowing fashion."

"I say, I wasn't! I know you're doing your bit. Still managing to write? I saw that story of yours, Upjohn. Ages ago. Quite promising. A country needs its writers," he added, "even in these days."

"You always bring us comfort," Kit said gently.

278

"Well, I say we're all in it together, whatever part we play as individuals."

"At any moment," said Jo, "you are going to hand us white feathers."

Dobson's eyes were plangent.

"Damn it, Upjohn! I was only saying that no chap need feel guilty nowadays, even if he isn't in the front line." He asked Kit how his beautiful wife was faring. "Please give her my greetings."

Kit inquired, with kindness, what Dunkirk had been like, and received from Dobson the usual description.

It was only then that they noticed he was wearing the ribbon of the Distinguished Service Order.

"Good God! What did you get that for?" Jo exclaimed.

Dobson lowered his head and paddled around with his finger in a drop of spilled beer. "Nothing much. Just what most people were doing, only someone happened to be looking my way."

"You," said Kit, "are the very first war hero we've met. Congratulations."

"Oh, I say, not a hero! Only doing my duty in a perfectly ordinary way."

Hero or not, they were glad when he rose to go, removing the necessity for them to seek another pub yet awhile. "Meeting my young woman." He looked at Jo. "You ought to get married, Upjohn. Nothing like it. Of course, you may be by this time, for all I know."

"I'm not. And last time we heard you on that subject, you were advising Kit not to."

Dobson heaved a great sigh. "One of these days, perhaps you'll stop pulling my leg. Well, so long."

They looked after him as he fought his way to the doors.

"In this life, one may expect anything," Kit said.

"I can't help envying him."

"Oh, I can, easily. But Dobson! *Dobson!*"

They talked of friends, picking up threads. Clement was in the Middle East, Georgina living near Alison in Surrey, expecting her child at any moment.

"With luck," Jo said, "it may quieten her down."

"Did you ever enjoy Georgie's favors? She always had an eye for you, though she never liked me much."

"No, I didn't. I wasn't going to be half-murdered by Clement. He is an extraordinary chap!"

"Play-acting. He can't resist it."

"Nor resist Georgina, when it comes to the pinch," said Jo. He added that Alison wanted him to come down and see her again, and that Piers did not object. "I'm getting over it," he said, "or I think I am. But I still funk going."

Kit said dreamily, "Oh, I don't see why you shouldn't. She's not likely to betray the serving soldier, anyhow. She's a dear good girl, and she would have hated to be married to me, did she but know it. Really, I did her a good turn, when you come to think of it." He looked at Jo and his eyes widened. "What, you still feel like that?"

Jo said restlessly that they might as well move on somewhere else.

"Let's go up west to the Salisbury."

"Oh God," said Kit, "it's full of pansies or exempted actors, or both together. Let's try the Marquess of Granby."

As the evening wore on, Jo thought how little, these days, drink seemed to affect him: how little now, in contrast with "the wild life," Kit drank. He had hoped to recapture that night something of the vanished years, but they remained elusive. Though he realized the slight blurring of his speech, he knew he was inwardly sober: coldly, drearily, so.

At closing time they looked at each other.

"What next?" Kit asked. "We could get a last one at the Pheasantry." This was a Chelsea club of which he was a member.

"No. I'm tired. I must be getting back."

Kit said curiously, "I didn't upset you, did I, being facetious about Alison? You know how fond I am of her really. But she does linger round the edges of a bad conscience, and that makes me want to take it out on her a bit. It's one of my more unpleasant traits."

"It wasn't that. It's just that I can't get wound up to the party spirit, as I used to."

"Come back with me and see Polly."

Jo shook his head.

Next day he went to the doctor, who merely said he was a little run-down, and gave him a tonic. The bottle of medicine was a comforting sight, a beautiful clear green. It made Jo feel that somebody, at last, was trying to help him. Emboldened by this, he telephoned to Fay again. This time she was in.

She had only two nights left before her leave was up. Yes, she would love to see him. Where? He suggested a restaurant in Soho. He thought he could switch his duty with any luck: if he couldn't do so, he would ring her again.

She was not in uniform, but wearing a silk dress much the color of his tonic. She had cut off her long golden hair.

"I had to," she said. "It was too much of a business pinning it up so it was above my collar. How are you, dear?"

Jo said he was fine. "And you look wonderful."

She did: her cheeks pink and fresh, her splendid eyes full of light. He felt awkward with her, and wished he had not asked her to come.

"What's eating you? Something. Mother driving you potty?"

No, he replied, it wasn't that. In fact, he didn't know what it was, unless it was the general drag and weariness of war.

"Better resist that," said Fay, "because it's going to go on for a long, long time, or so Piers says. I had a letter from him last week."

Jo looked surprised.

"Oh, he's never quite lost touch. But don't get any wrong ideas. Most of it was about how awfully he missed Alison." She blew a perfect smoke-ring.

"What repulsive food this is," said Jo.

"It's the same everywhere. You know, Piers and I were keen on each other only for about a couple of months, and neither of us was serious, but somehow it was great fun. I don't think he'll ever forget that part of it, and I know I won't. That's why he writes: because it helps him to remember when things were happy-go-lucky, tra-la-la!—and no bruised hearts involved."

He was suddenly aware that she had something important to tell him, and he wondered whether he would mind it when she did.

She chatted idly till coffee was on the table. Then: "Jo, darling. You know how I've felt about you all these ages. I don't mind you knowing it: one can't help these things, and I'm not much of a one for false pride."

He stretched out his hand and laid it upon hers.

"I thought I wouldn't get over you, and I'm not sure that I

have quite. But time's going on for me, or I feel it is, and I can't carry a torch forever. I want to settle down as soon as I can, and put me misspent youth behind me." She smiled at her own false Cockney. "Dear, I've met a nice man whom I like a lot, and we're going to be married. Do you care?"

He said slowly, "Of course I care. Everything's going to be emptier without you, one more person gone. But I can't be the dog-in-the-manger. I've given you nothing."

Her eyes filled. "That's not true. You've given me wonderful things."

"Who is he?"

"Oh dear," she said, with a gulp and a smile, "there's a funny side to that. His name's Charles Nesbitt and he's a sergeant. What on earth will it sound like when we have to be announced anywhere? Sergeant and Captain Nesbitt!"

Then she could not stop laughing. Jo laughed, too.

"Mind you," she said, "there's a second funny side, as well. He's miles out of my social class. His father's quite rich and he went to Harrow, only for some reason best-known to himself he won't even try for a commission. He likes being a N.C.O., says it's peaceful just doing more or less as you're told, not having the top responsibilities."

Jo said, feeling the shock of her news would strike him later on, that it didn't sound a very promising preparation for civilian life.

"Don't worry, there's a good job waiting for him in papa's business when he gets his discharge. If he ever does. Sometimes I feel that none of us will."

She showed him the photograph of a stocky young man, pug-nosed, with eager eyes. "The odd thing is," she mused, "that he's a marvellous sergeant. Most of the men think he's mad not to want a cheese-cutter and a swagger-stick."

Jo called the waiter whom he knew slightly. "We want to celebrate. Have you anything decent left to drink? Any brandy?"

"Do my best, sir. Congratulations to you and your lady."

"Yes," said Fay, "of course he'd think it was us."

They sipped South African brandy, astronomically priced.

She leaned over and kissed his cheek. "That's partly because I'll always be fond of you, and partly to please the waiter. Jo—you haven't minded much, have you? In a way, there's no reason why you should, but I don't think it's easy to let anyone go quite, even if one doesn't care for them; not in that way. I know Kit was dog-in-the-manger about Alison for quite a while, even though it was he who threw her over. Polly always realized that, but then, she was secure enough not to worry."

He said resolutely, "I do mind and I don't, and I hope you're going to be tremendously happy."

"We shall rub along. He makes me laugh, and that's very important, don't you think?"

Joe tried to smile. "I was never a great repository of humor, was I?"

"Don't be silly. Of course you were, in your own fashion."

He was anxious to leave her now, for he had felt a violent and ridiculous urge to ask her to marry him. He looked at his watch. "I've got to take midnight shift," he said, "I must go."

She walked with him to the Piccadilly underground station. At the top of the stairs, she hugged and kissed him. "You'll like Charles, I know, and we'll go on seeing each other. So you haven't lost anything, have you?"

He kissed her in return, but did not speak.

His mother called out to him as he went into the house. "You're early! That's nice. Come in for a moment, dear."

She was in bed reading, the inevitable cocoa cooling at her side.

"Well, and how was our Fay? Any news?"

He told her.

"Well, well, well! And I always thought it would be you. You ought to be lucky at cards, oughtn't you?"

Relief had brought to her a malicious sparkle.

"Spare me that."

"Now what have I done? You were never half so fond of her as she was of you."

"I was probably wrong not to be."

"Well, well, well. Our Fay. Come on, let's have the details."

Patiently, he gave them. He would rather stand there in the bright, cluttered, biscuit-smelling, cachou-smelling room being teased by his mother than go upstairs to solitude.

"Quite a catch for her. Because you know, dear, though she's a very nice girl, she's just a little bit common."

"Fay's one of the most uncommon people I know."

"I didn't mean that." Her little nose tilted.

"Mother, who the hell are we to look down on anybody? We're lower-middle-class, no more than that—"

"How can you! Your father—"

"Then what would you call us?"

"Upper-middle," she replied, stately.

"What rubbish!"

"Well, middle-middle. But not lower." She peered at him. "I really do believe you're upset about her! If you wouldn't ask her yourself, whose fault is it?"

"I'm going to bed."

"Yes, sulking." Her voice was complacent. The last danger had been removed.

He said, "God damn," and banged the door.

Chapter Five

GEORGINA WAS BASKING IN THE JOY OF HER SON. SHE HAD ENDURED a long labor, but it had all been worth-while. Now, as she suckled him, she found a new sensual pleasure, more delightful than any she had known. He was a small baby but a very hungry one, seizing on her nipple vigorously, as blissful as she. If he were like anybody at this stage, she thought he was like herself: one blessing. She could not trace on his features any sign of his almost-forgotten father.

"You're a lucky one, you know," the nurse said. "Sometimes one has an awful tussle over feeding."

Georgina replied that God had made her an excellent cow.

It was cozily warm in the private room, the more pleasant because of the November day beyond her windows: the naked boughs, lying against the mist, looked like trees in a Japanese print. All her friends had sent flowers, had embowered her in chrysanthemums. Propped up against the reading-lamp was a telegram from Clement:

"GLAD ABOUT YOU AND OUR SON WRITING LOVE."

The baby slid off her breast and fell asleep at once.

"I'll take him away," the nurse said, "and you can have your nap. By the by, Mrs. Maclaren—ten cigarettes a day only, and that's ten too much."

"You know it's all I smoke," Georgina said reproachfully, opening her narrow eyes as wide as she could.

"I know you nip extra ones and hide the butts in an empty matchbox."

"You shame me. Yes, upon occasions I do slip up. But don't you think you're rather dreadful, trying to catch me out? —Oh, do leave him with me, just for ten more minutes."

Alone, she held the little body close to her, savoring the smell of staling milk and talcum powder. The baby hiccuped twice, stretched his eyes and began to cry. She hitched him competently over her shoulder, patting him to bring up the wind. He belched noisily, regurgitated food trickling from the side of his mouth like liquid cotton-wool. "Greedy-guts, aren't you?" She cleaned him up with a tissue, kissed him, talked to him seriously. "I wonder what you'll be like when you grow up? Elegant, I hope. I should like an elegant son. And I hope you'll have brains, though I'm not sure where they're going to come from. Still, if you're moderately witty it will do. Do you think you'll be witty?" The baby gave a huge, mature yawn. "Do stop me if I'm boring you, Paul."

After Georgina had rested, Alison came in, bringing four new-laid eggs and a copy of *The Last Tycoon*. She was looking tired and rather thin.

"Oh, bless you! I'm completely out of reading matter. How's Jim? Any news from Piers?"

Alison said she had had a letter from him that morning. He was more hopeful about the war in the desert, more hopeful about Russia, since the failure of the offensive against Moscow.

"If only the Americans would stop dithering and come in," said Georgina, "we might get the whole business over earlier than we think."

Alison replied despondently that it would need wild horses to drag them.

"Then, dear Lord, do send them a few wild horses. You look rather down."

"I'm restless. Furthermore, I'm sex-starved."

Georgina giggled. "That, from you! I expect you could do something about it if you wanted to."

286

"I could, of course. But I won't. I'm dead tired because I sit up reading half the night. It may be a phase, but it's a damned long one."

There was something, Georgina thought, that was not being told her. She said tentatively, "Specific temptation?"

"Not really."

"Some nice young man pursuing you?"

Alison smiled then. "The son of our colonel, no less. Tim MacHaffie."

Georgina was indignant. "Why isn't he in the forces, instead of trying to seduce a soldier's wife?"

"Do you know what you looked like, just then? The perfect British matron."

"That's what I'm turning into, praise be to God."

"He was in the RAF as a rear-gunner, but he had a crash. He's invalided out. He has a beautiful figure and a very small head, and a small, comic face. He has absolutely no moral sense at all. He asks me what harm would it do either of us, if we were only having a little passing fun?"

Georgina looked more like a matron than ever. "Do you mean to say you've let him get to the point where he can make a proposition like that?"

"I haven't let him get anywhere. I haven't even let him kiss me. But he drops in uninvited, and he makes me laugh, and he says precisely what he chooses."

"You must tell him to stay away, then. That is, unless—" Georgina looked sly.

The brief light passed from Alison's face. "Yes, I know I should. But he is fun, and so few things are. Damn it, I'm not a cheerful visitor, am I?"

"But I don't like the cheerful ones much. They're so uninteresting. In a place like this you'll have to be careful of scandal, no matter how spotless you may be."

"Oh, he's discreet. He slips very gently in at the back door when there's no one around. We only talk and drink, and he tries to wheedle me into bed, quite without success. I don't really think he's expecting any. But I'm ashamed of it, all the same."

Georgina said curiously, "You're not falling in love with this man?"

"No. There's only Piers. But—" Alison's mouth trembled. She forced it into a hard line.

"Poor old girl. I know what it's like, or rather, I knew. Life's hard for us as well as for the men, isn't it?"

"I never suspected it would be so hard for me."

The nurse brought tea for them both, tiny sandwiches, synthetic sponge-cake with soya-flour marzipan.

"You must cut that cable," Georgina said firmly, after a while. "Believe me, Mother knows."

Walking back from the hospital, Alison heard footsteps behind her. She turned. Tim MacHaffie came up to her with his light, limping run. "Let me see you home. There are wolves in the woods."

"You are one of them. Yes, if you like, but you can't come in."

"Why can't I?"

"Because I'm not going to let you make love to me any more, even in play."

"Then I won't, I promise. Come on, Alison, don't be stuffy! We'll talk strictly about angels on the point of a pin. I have the most fascinating theories on the subject."

He stopped in front of her, looking down from his great height, smiling freshly as a boy.

"Tim," she said, exasperated, "you know perfectly well that Piers would be angry."

"But I'm not doing anything! Don't we have nice times together?"

"Caesar's wife." She tried not to smile back at him, but could not restrain herself.

"That's better. Come on, the fog's getting thick." He accompanied her to her gate, springily, with confidence, and put his hand to the latch.

"No. I've told you."

He looked at her thoughtfully. "Another time, then. Bless you, my beautiful." He kissed her before she could stop him and went whistling away up the road, hands in his pockets.

She felt disturbed and miserable. She would in any case, even without Georgina's warning, probably have refused to let him visit her that evening, with Mrs. Baldock still in the house, though he had been there openly several times. Yet she felt her hand had been forced, when she had not wished it to be.

The woman, a daily help who had been with her for a month

or so, came downstairs to greet her. "Our Jimmy's sleeping like a top, and I've put some potatoes to bake for you in the oven. There's still some of the cheese pie left." She was a pink, beaming, motherly woman with only one apparent fault; she stole things. Alison knew this perfectly well, but competent help was so scarce that she had overlooked the disappearance of spoons, napkins, towels, even trinkets. "Is there anything else I can do for you, mum? I'm in no hurry."

"Are you sure? I wonder, then, if you'd mind washing out a couple of Jim's shirts? I feel so tired tonight."

"Do them in a jiffy."

Alison went upstairs to look at the little boy, then into her room, where at once she saw that something was missing. Piers had bought her, just before he went away, a set of six china kittens, painted with valentine hearts. Now there were five.

Suddenly, that seemed the last straw. Filled with a violent irritation not far from rage, she burst into the kitchen.

"Mrs. Baldock! I can't find one of my china cats, the ones on the bedroom mantelpiece. Has it got smashed by any chance?"

The woman slowly withdrew her soapy arms from the basin, and dried them on the towel. The motherly look deserted her.

"Mrs. Welford, you know I'm not a smasher. I've never broken one single thing, not since I've been with you."

"Then where's that cat?"

"How should I know?" She paused. "The window-cleaner came yesterday."

"It was there this morning."

"You're not saying it was me who took it? What should I want with a silly thing like that?"

"My husband gave it me. If you do know where it is . . ." She paused. "Anyway, will you have a hunt for it tomorrow? It might have fallen down," she added lamely.

The woman put her hands back in the basin, rinsed the shirts, and hung them up to dry. Her eyes were cold. "Yes, mum, I'll have a hunt round tomorrow. I'll be saying goodnight now."

When she had gone, Alison, whose anger was spent, was dismayed. What had she done? For the sake of an ornament, she had lost the kind of woman who might prove irreplaceable. She did not expect to see her next day.

But Mrs. Baldock came as usual, and at eleven o'clock announced that the kitten had been found just under the edge of a carpet.

"How wonderful of you!" Alison exclaimed in relief.

"I never did think you meant it was me, mum."

"Of course I didn't."

"Because you'd think twice before doing that, wouldn't you?"

Nothing more was said, and Mrs. Baldock resumed her old motherly manner. Nothing more was stolen, either.

The winter crawled on, misty and damp. Georgina returned to her bungalow with the baby. Both were extremely well, and she seemed able to take housework and child in her stride. The cable—"our son"—was now folded away with the chevron in her jewel-case. She met and liked Tim MacHaffie, whom Alison still allowed, weakly, to call on her once a week, though she had forbidden further attempts, however light-hearted, to coax her into going to bed with him.

"But," Georgina said, "that one is an awful menace, believe you me, and I think it will be safer if I join some of those cozy evenings, even as the gooseberry."

She made a point of this, bringing her contented baby with her in the carry-cot. Tim did not seem to mind this arrangement in the least, and Alison breathed freely again.

On December 7th they heard the news of the bombing of Pearl Harbor.

"Now they'll bloody well have to come in!" Georgina cried triumphantly. "Three cheers for the Japs. But were they quite mad?"

The only explanation, Tim said, was that the Japanese believed they could cripple America permanently: which, he added, they couldn't. The U.S.A. would build up to naval strength again in less than no time.

"It's wonderful not to be alone any more," said Alison. "It beats me now how confident we felt of victory when it was hardly reasonable to suppose we had a dog's chance."

"It was a God-given euphoria," Tim replied, "and I'm damned if I know how we should have stuck things out if the Lord hadn't obliged."

They rehearsed, almost as if the war were already won, the days of siege; Union Jacks waving over the rubble of homes in ruin, signs chalked on blasted shop-fronts: "Business as Usual," the stoical shelterers in the tube stations entertained by concert parties.

One more National Anthem was added to the long list played before the nine o'clock news.

After Rommel's first retreat, Piers wrote hopefully to Alison, hinting at the possibility that his regiment might be withdrawn to other fields of battle. "But if it is, I shall hope to get home for a while first. Keep your fingers crossed, my darling, and please think of me as often as you can. *Do have any fun that's going,* even if it's only a village hop. It must be very dull for you day after day, even with Jim's company. You know how absolutely I love and trust you."

She was a little puzzled by this last sentence: he had never found it necessary before to speak of "trusting." She wondered whether even he was finding fidelity a little hard, whether he had spoken of his trust in her in order to strengthen the resolve he had made for himself. Now that the upsurge of sexual stress had weakened, she found herself aching less for his body than for his companionship, for the total sharing of life.

She did go dancing several times, usually in a party with Georgina, Tim and a friend of his. It bewildered her now that she could even fleetingly have thought of betraying her husband, merely for a passing gratification. She must have been, she thought, as mad as the Japanese.

Chapter Six

ONE EVENING IN FEBRUARY, WHEN GEORGINA WAS BATHING PAUL, Clement walked in.

"You're damned lucky I didn't drop him!" she cried out.

He stood looking down at the child. "He's just like you, thank God. And I expect, through sheer propinquity, he will pretty soon get to look like me. That'll puzzle people, won't it?"

Determined to be calm, she took up the baby and spread him on a large towel across her knees. "I do think you might have telephoned. What were you trying to do, catch me out?"

He put a hand to the nape of her neck, gathered her hair together and gently pulled it. "What a vulgar girl you are! You should be ashamed of such thoughts."

She asked him when he had returned, when he was likely to go away again.

"I got back this morning, had lunch with my editor and came straight on here. Nothing's sure yet, but I think they'll be sending me to Burma."

She dabbed the creases dry in the baby's groin and under the weaving arms. She was aware of looking maternal and efficient.

Clement seemed to be interested. "Now do you powder him?"

"Certainly not. Old-fashioned. It's quite unnecessary if you dry them properly."

Clement took one of the small hands in his own. "Hullo, old man. Liking it here? Tolerable?"

She put Paul into his night-gown and took him up. "Make yourself at home while I get him into bed. He was fed early tonight so I haven't that to do."

She fussed around the nursery for longer than was necessary, hoping to still the storm Clement had aroused in her before she faced him again. It was just like him to startle her in such a fashion, typically dramatic, typically mischievous. Taking off her apron she sat down to comb her hair, still damp with the bathroom steam. She thought defiantly: Anyway, I'm still a damned pretty girl.

When she went into the sitting-room he took her at once in his arms and put his tongue between her lips. The kiss ran through her like the electricity of suckling.

"Nice?" he inquired.

She rubbed her cheek against his, moved her mouth round again till it met his own.

"When will you be for me again? Ready yet?"

"Yes, ready. Ready now."

"Sure?"

"Oh God, yes!"

When he took her, she experienced absolute satisfaction for the first time in her life.

"What on earth are you crying for?" he asked her after a while.

"Bliss, sheer bliss. And shock, I suppose."

"Was it so good?"

"It was wonderful. Never before like that, never."

Rising on his elbow he looked down at her, at her flushed face, her spread and tangled hair, darkened with sweat. She whispered something he did not quite catch.

"What?"

"Are you sure it's all right? About Paul?"

"For the very last time, yes. He's mine now and that's that. I accept full responsibility, and I'm not going to mull it all over

again. If you ever give me one of my own, it will make no difference. Now shut up."

She lay quietly in his arms, trying to hold the moment which
was all of beauty. The only real beauty she had ever known. She
said, "Do you love me?"

"What are words? I want you again, and I mean right now."

"Yes, yes. Quick. I want you, too."

Once more the miracle happened. Afterwards she said,
"Anyway, I love you."

"Good," said Clement, "you go on that way."

She thought how delightful were the pleasures that followed
love-making, the slow and drowsy rising from the bed, the leisurely dressing and neatening, the pretense of coolness and poise
above the beating sense of triumph; the cigarette, the drink, the
talk of other things. "Are you hungry?" she asked him.

"Not particularly. Say in an hour. Show me the establishment first." They went through the small house, his arms hooked
casually about her shoulders. "Not bad. You've made it quite
nice, in fact."

"Oh, I was never too bad a home-maker. The curtains are a
sort of sacking, all I could get, but I dyed them myself."

They returned to the living-room, where she busied herself
laying the table. "You've chosen a lucky day. There's the remains
of one of Alison's fowls."

"Oh yes! That reminds me. I saw Piers when we recaptured
Bardia and had a chat with him. You'd better not tell Alison yet,
in case she's disappointed, but I shouldn't be surprised if he got
back, too, before long."

Georgina was joyful. "I do hope so! She really had been going through hell without him."

"He thought his regiment might be withdrawn, but now it
looks as if only he is. They may want him to train troops in India,
for the Burma Front. If that happens, he's pretty sure to get
home leave first."

Georgina asked if she might not even drop a hint, but he
shook his head. "If she's in the state you say she is and she gets let
down, it will only be the worse for her." He paused. "Surely she,
of all people, hasn't been playing fast and loose?"

"No, but I fancy she was very near it at one time."

He whistled. "What restrained her?"

"Me, partly—no, don't laugh! It's true. Me, and, of course, the old Alisonian morality."

"What times we live in," he mused, "and what changes we see. That's what makes life worth living, never having the faintest idea what's round the corner. Even if something ghastly's on the way, I should always have to know just what it was. I remember how, one night in the desert, when I was up in the front lines and things were sticky, I thought, Don't let me get killed because I have got to know who wins the war."

She laughed, and touched his hand.

"And you didn't get killed and you won't."

"Not if I can help it, believe you me."

"Not knowing who won," said Georgina, "would be exactly like seeing *Othello* for the first time and being taken out before one knew whether she got strangled or not."

Shortly after their meal he said, "I'm dead tired. Let's go to bed, and I mean to sleep. What about you?"

"Just wait while I give Paul his ten o'clock feed and I'm with you."

"I'll watch."

He did so, smiling as if he were both pleased and amused. "He stuffs away, doesn't he?"

"He's a pig. He sleeps like one, too, blessedly."

When they were lying in the dark, she said tentatively, "Clem?"

"Yes?"

"You're not asleep?"

"Not quite."

"I want to say something. It's easier just now."

"Go ahead."

"You do realize something quite different happened to me tonight?"

"I rather fancied you had a good time."

"I think I'm going to be all right from now on. No more running around. I don't believe I shall ever want to again."

She heard the smile in his voice as he answered her. "Curious chances bring us to curious things, don't they?"

"Clem, your cable, when he was born. You don't know how much that meant, and I somehow felt it was tactless to tell you. It was the one word."

"Carefully chosen, I assure you. But on the whole, I think, the right one. Now stop talking, because I am floating off into the bottomless pit and I don't want to be called back."

She woke in the middle of the night, in a panic lest it had all been a dream. Then, putting out her hand she touched him: and when she had done so realized his familiar body smell, sweet, rather strong.

The marine-like smell of his seed, still fresh.

Piers and Alison were walking in the pinewoods on a mild evening early in April.

She was only yet recovering from the initial daze of his return, and they had talked for the past two days of little but themselves. The time of joy must be so brief that she wanted to hold fast to it, never thinking of the hour beyond the present one, or wishing to let the outer world intrude. Now, however, she began to speak of Georgina.

Georgina, never reticent with any woman she happened by chance to like, had been dithyrambic about the night of her husband's return, and very explicit. Alison told the story, in slightly primmer fashion, to Piers.

"Well," he said, "it does seem rather too good to be true, don't you think? Too much like the proverbial happy ending. Can the leopard change its spots?"

He was over forty now, and quite grey, but his body was as trim and youthful as ever.

Alison explained, with the delicacy she found necessary when talking to Piers, that feeding a baby not infrequently reinforced the sexual urge: that was something few people realized. "If she's really satisfied with Clement, she may settle down. She was horribly lonely."

"And you?"

"You know."

He tightened his arm around her. "You saw people, didn't you?"

"Not many recently," she replied, ashamed that this was in part a lie.

"Not Jo? I hoped he might be down now and then. You didn't mention him in your letters."

She replied, a little sadly, that though she had written to Jo several times he had always made excuses to stay away. He had, she thought, been frightened to see her alone. Perhaps he was right. "But oh, dear, this damned war does make for a drifting! I feel he's out of my life, that a whole part of it has gone with him. I know I couldn't give him anything, but I was fond of him, all the same. Jo is a great dear."

Piers observed that it was not only the war that made for such dispersal. It was a part of growing up, inevitable, painful. To some extent it was a social drifting. Kit was bound to separate himself increasingly from some of his friends, partly because of his growing fame and partly, since Polly's father died, because of an increasing standard of living. (Lord Wantage, though not, as Kit had hoped, a miser, had left Polly the house, his pictures, and some six thousand pounds.) "And you," Piers went on, "you get on in the world through your own efforts, and I've been forced to lug you into a new avatar, even if it's an odd one for you. How do you think Jo feels, stuck where he is, still in the same house with that old mother, the only one of you all who hasn't moved on?"

"That's what I'm afraid of, that he thinks we'd care, that he feels we've grown beyond him. I should hate him to feel that. God knows I've been assiduous enough!"

"Tell me about the past year. Who did you see mostly?"

"Georgina, of course, Polly sometimes. And the people round here. What's the matter, darling?"

He was looking at her strangely. They stopped in the middle of the path. The sky was still an egg-shell blue behind the blackness of the pines, though the sun was falling. The carpet of pine-needles rustled suddenly, as if some small animal had scampered through.

"I want to show you something rather disagreeable. I didn't mean to, because I don't believe a word of it: but, as you know, I don't like to have secrets from you."

He drew from his tunic a sheet of paper, many times folded, and he opened it. It was printed in grubby, uneven capitals, tending to a backwards slant.

"DEAR MAJOR YOU OUGT TO KNOW THAT MRS. W. IS SEE-ING A LOT OF MR. MACAFY HE IS ALWAYS HERE. IT IS A SHAME ON A SERVING SOLDIER. A WELL-WISHER."

"Well-wisher!" Alison said lightly, after a pause, "Hardly an original mind." She could not control the rising flush. She knew the author, or thought she did. "You can't believe there's the slightest truth in this?"

"That you've been cheating me? Of course not. But have you seen much of Tim?"

"A bit. He called round sometimes."

"Now listen," said Piers, gripping her arms, "I very much want to know who sent this object, which reached me about three weeks ago, and I also need to know why you didn't mention Tim among your callers."

"Then you're not so certain—" she began, as contemptuously as she dared.

"Don't stall. For the ninth time, I'm well aware you've done nothing wrong. But I do want to know why Tim's name never came into tonight's conversation."

She told him. She had at first enjoyed Tim's company, and had then realized that it was unwise to go on seeing him. Yes, he had tried to make love to her, but only verbally: she had never really believed that he meant what he was saying. It had been an amusement for him, and for a while it had amused her. "When I told him it must stop, he took it with perfect equanimity; after that, I only let him come when Georgina was here."

He looked at her, his eyes grave. "Let's root up the mandrake, and hear it scream. Then it goes on the rubbish heap. Did the idea ever attract you, even for a moment?"

She took some time to reply, and when she did so, was steadfast. "For a moment, and no more than that. I could never have cared for Tim, not in that way. But I was feeling the physical separation at the time, more than I ever thought I should. Was it always so easy for you?"

"By the dispensation of providence, I've been too busy fighting and being scared stiff of Rommel. I told you I was a coward. There has been no one else for me at all." Then he was silent, as if he had reined himself in.

"Fine," said Alison bitterly. "I did indulge, for no more than a fortnight, in a very mild verbal flirtation rather on the lines of a Restoration comedy. Well?"

"Here's a nice log to sit on, so let's sit." He kissed her. "It doesn't sound at all terrible, and I never thought you were a Georgina. Satisfied? Do you want to say you're sorry?"

"Not much. It was so very little to be sorry for."

298

"Infidelity of the heart?"

"Certainly not. Just a brief temptation of quite another kind, and it was never real."

"Don't let it happen again." He was smiling now, and she knew that such fears as he had, despite himself, entertained, had disappeared.

"I thought there was something odd about a letter you wrote me, about trusting me. You never thought that needed saying before," she said.

"And of course it never did. Equally, I should never have written it. But this sort of anonymous rubbish, however absurd, is always upsetting. Who wrote it? Do you know?"

"I'm pretty sure. Mrs. Baldock."

He was astounded. "I thought she was the perfect treasure! The *Gea Tellus* of Aldershot."

"So did I. Now she'll have to go, and God knows where another damned treasure will come from."

"Why did she do it?"

Alison told him about the incident of the china kitten, of the unwise accusation.

"I see. I think you'd better keep her for a bit, though. There's no reason why she should get any instant gratification out of her beastly hand-work. Has she reverted to normal?"

"Oh entirely, on the surface. But I hate to think of a woman with the capacity to do such a thing having any charge of Jim whatsoever. People who write anonymous letters are so ugly inside."

He said she might well be right. After some thought, he suggested that Mrs. Baldock should be retained during his leave, and then sent packing. "I will do the packing myself, so there's no need for you to worry. I shall just show her this"—distastefully he refolded the paper and put it away—"and tell her we know she wrote it. In the meantime, you can be quietly looking around for someone else. You are quite certain she's the culprit?"

"Of course I am. It's exactly like the notes she puts out for the milkman, all bending backwards."

"So that's that. All over. I love you very much, and I don't even forbid you to see Tim, so long as he restricts his wooing. He's a nice chap."

Feeling as if he had opened the door of a cellar in which she

299

had been confined and had let her out, she loved him even more for the firmness of which his generosity was an essential part.

It was typical of Piers, that when he ran into Tim in the village one Sunday morning, he asked him to have a beer at the pub, and showed him the letter. "I know there's nothing in this: people on active service get this sort of thing more often than one imagines. Still, it's fair for you to know about it."

Tim's small face reddened.

"No, there is nothing in it." He added honestly, "I do find Alison extremely attractive, and I did try to flirt with her, more to relieve the boredom than anything else. I think I never meant it seriously: I hope I didn't. But in any case, I apologize."

Piers said he did not propose to tell Alison he had spoken, and wished Tim to say nothing either.

"Of course I shan't."

"I haven't forbidden you the house," Piers said, smiling. "In fact, come and have a drink with us tomorrow, round about six."

"It is time," Tim said, with genuine compunction, "that I grew up. You've been fine about it all."

"No. I just know Alison."

When Piers, three days before he left for the Far East, showed the paper to Mrs. Baldock, he was horrified to see the change in her personality. The real face seemed to emerge from beneath the motherly mask, the color draining even from her eyes. She did not say a word. She collected her outdoor clothes, her apron, her working-slippers, and took the wages he handed to her. "That's a month's notice," he said.

She walked out of the house.

"Easy," said Piers to Alison, who had emerged trembling from the sitting-room, where she had kept her ear to the door. "No denials, no fuss. And Hughes's wife will be coming in to-morrow."

They learned from a neighbor, who had also employed Mrs. Baldock for an hour or so, twice a week, that the woman had gone to live with her sister in London.

Chapter Seven

JO WAS WRITING A NOVEL. THE SKIES WERE QUIET, AND HE HAD more peace in the warden's post than at home, where his mother and Miss Pease had developed a pleasing relationship based on a series of pitched battles, and Bessie, when not engaged in warfare, complained constantly in tones of jocular querulousness about the disappearance of white bread, the miserliness of the tea-ration (though Mildred, who liked coffee better, sent her an extra packet a week), and the overwhelming tedium of life in general.

In this novel, a story of early childhood, lay all his hopes. It was going well, he thought, and was eager for Kit to read it, for he believed that he was free at last from his influence. Since her marriage he had not seen Fay nor had he wanted to. He was having a casual but consoling love-affair with one of the girls at the post, an easy girl who would go to bed with anybody, and was pleased to do so with him. They met in her house one evening a week when they were sure her parents would be at a whist-drive. What with this bodily assuagement and his absorption in his writing, he was more nearly happy than he had been for a long time past.

The book was, of course, about himself, Mildred and his mother, when he was ten years of age and the days of mild prosperity had not yet departed. It was delicate and sensitive in tone (those qualities being, at the time, much admired) and flowed freely. His only trouble lay in his struggles to disguise Bessie and Mildred as far as possible, so he might give offense to neither: but he was apprehensive lest they might see through such simple devices as giving the former big black eyes and the latter long yellow hair. However much he tried to invent a new structure upon the basis of reality, they persisted in coming through it as the outline of an old painting will slowly but certainly make its ghostly appearance through a new painting superimposed upon it. Still, he comforted himself, he could always make necessary alterations when the book was finished.

Meanwhile his political activities had slackened off, and he had even been idle in making propaganda for a Second Front in Europe. The local Party was not as it had been: after the invasion of Russia, Bobby had been accepted into an Anti-Aircraft battalion stationed in Kent, Sybil Rainey had gone to live with her invalid mother in Ireland (being now in much the same position as Jo) and the Party had been more or less handed back to the older Trade Unionists. Hatton, ironically enough, had regained the chairmanship, a fact that both irritated Jo and soothed his still-uncomfortable conscience.

He sent the first half of the book to Kit, who had asked to read it. Kit was, as he knew, a rapid reader, and when no word came from him for a fortnight Jo began to worry. It arrived at last. Would he come to supper on his first free night, and they would talk about it? Kit added, "I must say, it's most interesting. It's like you, but not at all like what you've written before."

Hardly knowing whether or not to take this for encouragement, Jo went to Manor Street with some trepidation.

There he found not only Kit and Polly but Kit's parents, mild, rather silent people, who could scarcely keep their eyes from their brilliant child, as though they found it impossible to imagine that it was from their loins he had sprung.

"We've heard so much about you," Mrs. Mallings said timidly. Jo, too, could have been a god of some sort, if perhaps a lesser one. "So much that we thought it would be nice just to stay and meet you."

302

Mr. Mallings explained that they hardly ever came up from the country these days, what with the trains so crowded, one often had to stand in the corridor.

"And so dreadfully dirty," his wife added.

Jo was called in to admire Ruth, now over three years old, a beautiful child, high-spirited and advanced for her age.

"I will read to you," she said to Jo, drawing towards her a spelling-book, "not the words with pictures because I'd know, but the plain ones. Ox, cat, hen, hat, cow."

He admired her.

"It's perfectly genuine," Polly said, "it's not mere memory. You try her with a word of your own."

Jo wrote "top" on an envelope, and the little girl read it at once.

"She hasn't seen that one before."

"I'd like a top," Ruth observed, on a note of inquiry.

Jo said he would give her one.

"Don't let her cadge. She's a demon for that."

They returned to the sitting-room, where supper was set out.

"After the war," said Polly, "if there's any real food ever again, this is going to be called dinner, and Kit will have to put on a jacket for it. I'm so tired of all this squalor that I propose to revert to type."

The Mallings parents smiled nervously: they had always been a little in awe of her background.

When they had gone, and Polly had cleared the meal away, Kit brought out Jo's manuscript, dumped it down with a business-like air on the table before him. "Now then. Let's get down to it."

"Is it any good?"

"Hell, I can't answer that one! Yes and no. You'll sell it, I'm pretty sure."

"One thing to look forward to, anyway." Jo felt his upper lip stiffen, as with novocaine. He wanted to be somewhere else, back at the post, in bed with Kathleen, even at home playing rummy.

Kit twisted himself in the outsize sweater. "Mind you, I'm not God. I may be wrong. It may be far, far better than I think, or the other way around. It's not like *me* any more," he added rather naïvely.

"Another blessing."

"The people are good, especially your ma."

"It's not meant to be her."

Kit said Jo could tell that to the Marines: it was pure Bessie, and if she didn't like it, that was to be endured. "But I am waiting for something to happen."

"They do happen! John's gone to school for the first time and had a fight, and his father's fallen ill, and Felicity's had a disappointment over her birthday party—"

"Not precisely high drama," Kit said, "on the scale of *The Revenger's Tragedy*."

"God damn it, nothing much happens in your books!"

"Oh yes it does, only you can't see it all that clearly because I don't over-emphasize. Physical events are running like an underground river non-stop under my complicated verbiage. You need a good hard structure."

Jo felt chilled and miserable.

"Don't look like that," Kit said, "it's going to be quite easy to straighten it out. Why don't we map something out together?"

"You think it's terrible. Just say so and I'll tear the whole thing up."

Polly, who had just come into the room, said sharply that he would do no such thing. "I liked it, I can tell you. You know Kit can't criticize anything without being rough, but that anything he says is useful."

Kit said earnestly that he did not mean to be rough, and went hastily into a list of all the things he had genuinely admired. Jo was a little mollified by the extreme care with which his manuscript had been read, though he was still depressed. "So you see, Jo, it's thoroughly worth-while. Look here, what's going to happen in the second part?"

"Well, the father dies, Felicity has her first love-affair and thinks her heart is broken."

"Racier. And John?" Kit's tone held a light but fatal undertone of amusement.

"Oh, John," Jo said, "he drivels away into the nonentity he is." He rose abruptly, swept up the book, and threw it onto the sofa.

It was Polly who stormed at him first. "Really, you are behaving in a very *wet* way, and very defeatist. We both hate you when you're in one of your masochistic moods!" To counter the effect of her words, she put her arm round his waist, which felt to her like the stony waist of a statue.

Kit said, "If you're going to talk like that you can bugger off! The bloody book's going to be all right, if you work on it, and so are you. Now, suppose I try to jot down something of a coherent story-line, which it needs—"

"Thanks, but I don't want to talk about it any more. I'm grateful for all the trouble—"

"God, you sound like a vicar congratulating a helper at the jumble-sale!"

"—for all the trouble you've taken."

"Jo," Polly said, in her small, firm voice, "sit down at once." She made him do so. "Now then. This is Kit. Understand? And this is me. We both love you, and we know you're going to make it in the end. But if you become hysterical, and destroy what you've written, or simply don't go on with it, we are neither of us going to see you again."

"Not," Kit said, bright-eyed, "ever. Come on, come on, snap out of it! Let's go to the pub."

"Thanks, but no."

Polly asked, "Have you got another copy of that at home?"

"Yes."

"Good. We'll hang on to this one." Before he could stop her, she had snatched up the manuscript and retired with it. They heard a bang, and the scrape of a key.

She returned, pink and defiant. "It's in the chest and there it is going to stay."

Jo stared at her in anger: then subsided. "Do as you like. I don't care." He really believed that he did not. He had absorbed the shock of disappointment. What had he expected Kit to do? Prostrate himself with a cry of *"Hommages littéraires?"* Kit had not, and only a wish-fulfilling vision could have suggested that he might have done so. This was something to be put up with, along with so many other things.

Kit suggested they should, after all, go to the pub, if only to the beerhouse down the street. After some argument they went, feeling something of the tension relax as they left the flat. Luckily they met no one whom they knew, for Jo's spirits were at a low ebb. It was only at closing time that he said, "I don't know what's the matter with me. Usually I can take criticism."

"No," Kit replied, "it's that I put things badly. A book's not like a short story, it's too sustained an effort for the writer just to go and throw it away if it doesn't seem to be working out. But yours is going to work out, I'm sure of that. Look, when I've got a few ideas for under-pinning I'll write to you. How about that?"

Jo thanked him.

In fact, though Polly and Kit were both afraid they had damaged his self-confidence to a dangerous extent and had been upset by his outburst, he had never been more determined to continue with anything in the whole of his life. He found himself suspecting Kit of jealousy. Was that altogether absurd? Kit was often jealous of other writers, as he had been of Alison. Though why the hell he should grudge me a miserable bit of success, Jo thought, the evening still rankling with him, God knows. He's got enough of his own.

When he came in his mother called out to him as usual, but there was a peculiar note in her voice. She was sitting up in bed, the carbon copy of his book on her knees.

"Who said you could look at that?"

She opened her eyes very wide, half-mocking, half in real surprise. "You left it lying around, so there couldn't have been anything secret about it. You know how interested I am in all you do. What other interests in life have I?"

"It isn't finished. It's only a draft. I don't want anyone to see it before it's complete."

"I am not surprised," Bessie said silkily, "that perhaps you didn't want *me* to. Or Millie."

"Why not?"

"Well, you've set us both up as figures of fun, haven't you? A couple of Aunt Sallies?"

"It's not about either of you! It's all invented!"

"Come, dear, come, I wasn't born yesterday. The mother is quite obviously meant for me. I do hope you're going to alter her, or I shall never be able to face anybody again."

He saw that she was on the edge of tears, those suspect tears she could summon up at will, but which, all the same, never failed to distress him. She was like one of those film stars who have the gift of requiring no glycerine. This time he did not propose to yield to her peculiar talent.

"Look here, of course there's something of you in it, but the rest is imaginary. That's the way writers work, put several people into one person."

306

She asked him if he were going to print it, and when he replied that he thought it unlikely a publisher would take it, sighed ostentatiously in relief. This easy dismissal of any hopes he might have angered him.

"Mother. Suppose, by writing *King Lear,* Shakespeare had hurt the feelings of one living old man? Do you think he ought to have torn it up?"

Bessie's jaws clenched. "If *King Lear* hadn't been written at all nobody would have missed it, would they?"

"No. But would you have wanted him to destroy it?"

"I think perhaps Shakespeare might have been a *kinder* man than my son," she replied absurdly.

Jo walked up and down the room, pausing to finger the lace runner upon the bureau, to examine the saucer in which the pot of African violets stood: it was dry. He took some water in a toothglass and poured it round the flowers. He caught sight of his mother's face in the mirror: it was watchful.

He came to sit on the end of the bed.

"Mother, when my book is finished I will show it to you and Millie, and if there are any details you object to, I'll try my best to alter them. But I am not going to let you interfere with my work as a whole."

" 'A little dumpy woman in a blue silk frock with daisies on it.' Fancy you remembering that dress, I wore it twenty years ago. 'A little dumpy woman.' I don't know how you can!"

He said wearily. "I will make her six feet tall and as gaunt as a ladder. But that will have to do, and in any case it will send the character all wrong."

She remarked, not everyone could be a real writer like his friends Kit and Alison. It had been very exciting to see his story in print, but he oughtn't to put too much store on writing a book. It was simply that she did not want him to be disappointed: he always came first with her, she had an older and wiser head than his upon her shoulders.

He kissed her goodnight, and took the typescript away with him.

"Dear me," said Miss Pease, as he passed the kitchen door, "Mrs. Upjohn's all of a dither tonight. She thinks you've put her in a book."

He shrugged impatiently.

"It's not for me to say," she added, "but if I were you I

wouldn't pay too much attention. She'll get over it, as she does over everything."

"She'll have to," he said sharply. "Some part of my life has got to be my own." He wondered how it happened that Miss Pease had become so intimately a part of it.

"You go right ahead, Jo, go right ahead and let nothing stop you. She always shows her best side when you're not around, so you needn't worry about her as you do. As for Mrs. Hansen—"

"What about her?"

"She could do a bit more than she does." Miss Pease had never liked Mildred. Jo defended his sister as best he might: she was always busy, she lived a good way away, her husband did not like her to go about much without him.

"Much more, in fact," said Miss Pease.

Chapter Eight

ALL THROUGH THE BLACK SUMMER OF DEFEATS, THE EIGHTH ARMY in retreat to Alamein, the Germans overrunning the northern Caucasus and already at the approaches to Stalingrad, Jo worked doggedly at his novel. Though he no longer believed the war would be lost, he could see no end to it: his writing gave him escape into another and more amiable world.

Mildred, who had been staying for a week to help nurse Bessie through a gastric attack, had gone back to Wimbledon. Without her competent stridency, which was increasing with the years, the house seemed very quiet.

One morning, two days after her return, she telephoned in a state of such distress that Jo could not at first hear what she was saying.

"You've got to stop crying," he said, "I'm not catching one word of it."

He heard a snuffle, a gasp, the violent eruption of a blown nose. "It's Frank, he's been arrested."

"Good God, what on earth for?"

"Some wretched little girl says he exposed himself to her on

309

the common, the night before I came back. Oh, Jo, can you get over here? It's awful! He's got bail, of course, but he won't speak, he won't say anything, he does nothing but cry."

Jo said he would come immediately. He told Bessie he was going to spend the day with Kit.

"But Mrs. Hurst is coming for supper!"

"I can't help that."

"Well, you might have let me know before. She was so looking forward to seeing you, she only remembers you as a little boy—is something wrong?"

"Kit's not well," he lied, "Polly wanted me to come."

"Not anything serious?"

"It looks like the same thing you had."

"Well, that's not a matter of life and death!"

He said he was sorry.

He found Mildred sitting like stone in her smart Swedish drawing-room, her face swollen, her eyes hardly visible between the folds of reddened flesh.

"What are people going to say? We have such nice friends around here."

"That's not the first consideration," Jo said. "Where's Frank?"

"Upstairs, lying down."

"Have you taken anything for your nerves?"

"Phenobarb. I had the doctor in—of course he had to be told."

Jo lit a cigarette and put it between her lips.

"I suppose," he said, "that it's all nonsense? though even if it is, it may be hard to prove. How old is the girl?"

"Fourteen, the dirty little . . ." Mildred gulped. "She waited till next day to tell the police, and then they came round here. She said she knew him by sight."

"But hell, her unsupported word against a man like Frank—"

"He did it once before. He told me. We needn't fool ourselves."

Jo went cold. "When?"

"More than seven years ago. He got off with a fine then, and he's lived it down. God knows he has."

"It looks as though he hasn't."

"Don't be a brute!" Her eyes flared.

Jo tried to believe what she was telling him, but found it hard. What was the state of mind of a man who, even if the urge to such a thing was strong, would take a risk as appalling as this?

"I didn't mean to be, but we have to look at the facts. What's going to happen next?"

"He comes up before the magistrates on Wednesday. They can—they might—send him to prison."

She started up as her husband came in. He had been crying for a long time, but now he looked calm, dehydrated.

"Hullo, Jo. I have to apologize to you, as well as to Mildred."

Jo felt as if he were in the presence of some monster separated from him by a sheet of plate glass: he knew he must not betray this, that understanding must not totally fail him if he were to be of any use to Millie at all. He simply said, keeping his voice steady, "What are you going to plead?"

"Guilty, I suppose."

"You mustn't!" she cried out.

"That will make the child out to be a liar." Colorless, tall, thin, a model of propriety, Hansen seated himself, his hands clasped upon his knees.

"I bet she did something to ask for it! What does it matter if she does look a liar? That won't brand her for life. But you—"

"She did nothing to ask for it," Hansen said. "You were away—it was an impulse."

"But the doctor will speak for you—"

"I know it. He will do what he can." The pale eyes, like tarnished silver, searched Jo's face. "You can't help what you are thinking of me."

"It's a psychological thing," Jo said, hearing his own voice very loud, over-confident. What he was saying sounded, even to himself, ridiculous: false as a comedian's patter. "They can't make it very bad for you, even though once before . . ."

He saw Hansen's color rise like a dye from his corded throat to the sharp line of his cheekbones, and stop there. All at once he was filled with a dreadful suspicion.

He said, "Millie, go and get us some tea. I want to talk to Frank alone."

As she passed him, he thought he heard her mutter, from between clenched teeth, "Obscene."

311

Hansen, when the door had closed, looked at him steadily. Even to Jo, who had prided himself on his tolerance, he was obscenity made flesh, the more terrible because he looked so ordinary, so grave, so respectable: and now, so naked.

"Frank. Were there other convictions?"

"Three, over a period of fifteen years. I can't tell her that."

"You'll have to. What happened before, what did they do to you?"

"Probation. A psychiatrist. Then fines, and more psychiatry. This time I shall be sent to prison, I'm sure of it."

"How was it kept so quiet?"

"After the third time, I changed my name. It used to be Svensen. That was such a long time ago, I thought it would never happen to me again." He held out his hand, palm upward. "Jo, will you touch me?"

Jo felt his stomach turn. "What do you mean?"

"Just my hand. I shall feel less alone. I shall feel I am still of the human race."

The begging palm, surprisingly rosy and cushioned, trembled on the air. Jo stared. Then he laid two fingers across it.

Hansen withdrew the hand, and closed his eyes. "Thank you."

The physical contact had shaken Jo back into a sense of their common humanity. "Obviously," he said, "you couldn't help what you did, I realize that."

"I wonder what you can possibly realize? The desire is never with me until it springs, and when it does I am quite helpless. I can't help it any more than you can help reaching for a cigarette. What's wrong with people like me?"

"They'll be lenient."

"I don't think so. This is not so much the ruin of my life but of Millie's. I shall be able to bear it, but she will not. She will lock herself up as if she were a prisoner, too. She was so proud of this house, so proud of her friends."

"If they're decent friends, they won't let her down."

"Don't you think they will? Perhaps."

She came in with the tea and served them in silence.

He said, "I think I'll take my cup to my own room. Thank you, Jo."

312

When he had gone Mildred whispered, "What has he been saying to you?"

He told her then that she had got to face the worst. In confessing to a single conviction, Hansen had been brave, but only partially so: uselessly so. There was every reason for fear. She took the shock with a stiffening of her whole body. Jo put his arm round her but she threw it off.

"Can you manage," he said, "to be kind to him?"

"Did you manage it?" This was a scream subdued.

"I think so. I tried. Can you still be fond of him?"

"Christ!"

"You've got to pity him."

"I don't know him. He's a total stranger."

"It sounds absurd," Jo said slowly, "but I think it would help if you could bring yourself to touch him, even to pat him on the shoulder. Will you try?"

"I can't. I should be sick."

"Hasn't he made you happy?"

"What a poor fool I must have seemed to him all this while!"

"No. You know how he feels about you. This thing is only a rare impulse that he *cannot* control. If you don't stick by him I think he'll kill himself."

"You think that?"

"He's desperate."

She was silent for a while, and he could see the inner struggle. "Can it be kept from Mother? That, at least."

"God knows I'll try. *The News of the World* just won't arrive one Sunday morning, and when I go to the shops for it, they'll have sold out. She'll grumble, but she'll forget quickly enough. I think I ought to warn Miss Pease, though."

"Have you got to?" Mildred's throat moved.

"Keeping things quiet from Mother is going to take some doing. I shall need all the help I can get."

"All right." She rose. "I'll do what I can. I'm going to lie down now, and I'll try to look in at Frank on the way."

The following Wednesday, Hansen was remanded for psychiatric examination: it was not until a fortnight later that he was sentenced to a month's imprisonment, the magistrate observing

313

that society was in grievous need of protection from such as he. Hansen stood with head bowed, a well-dressed, harmless-looking man, only his eyes moving as if in prayer, turning upwards.

Jo and Mildred were in court, and Mildred's head was high. When she said good-bye to her husband, she steeled herself to kiss his cheek. "It won't be so very long," she said.

"No." But he was shaking with terror. "Not very long."

On the following Sunday night, Jo and Miss Pease were sitting with Bessie, who had been successfully blindfolded, when a neighbor came in, a woman Jo particularly disliked. Before he could stop her, she had flung herself on his mother, kissing and patting her.

"You poor dear, we're all so sorry for you and for poor Millie!"

"What—" she began.

Jo jumped up.

Miss Pease, however, was quicker. She said in a high, clear voice, "We didn't mean you to know. Millie was in a car-crash, but she's quite all right now. Only a couple of broken ribs."

The neighbor stared. Jo gently kicked her ankle.

"Oh I see. I thought Mrs. Upjohn knew."

Bessie was indignant. "Fancy you daring to think I shouldn't be told about my own daughter! Is she in hospital?"

"She was, for a couple of days," Jo extemporized, "but it was so slight that they strapped her up and let her convalesce at home."

"But why should I have worried all that much about a couple of broken ribs? Even if it is Millie."

"Well," said Miss Pease, "we did think the damage might be worse, in the beginning, and then when it wasn't, we saw no point in mentioning it."

After some rather uneasy chat of a rambling nature, the neighbor rose to go. She whispered to Jo in the hall, "Oh dear, what you must think of me! But I was sure she couldn't help knowing."

"She isn't going to, not if we can help it."

"Is Millie terribly cut up?"

He said shortly that of course she was: but she fully understood that her husband was a sick man.

The rest of the evening was taken up with Bessie's tirades

314

against what she chose to call treachery. "To think I didn't even get the chance to write to her, or send her some nice flowers! I'll write before I go to bed, and one of you can run to the post with it. Miss Pease, I'll thank you not to hide things from me in future, I'm not half-witted."

"I did what Jo told me."

"I employ you, not Jo. Remember that."

"Well, I was put in a false position." Miss Pease was quite enjoying the conspiracy.

"If there are any false positions to put you in, I'm the one to do it."

All the same, Jo thought, they would be lucky if they could hoodwink her forever.

As Hansen had predicted, Mildred locked herself up, not wishing to see even Jo. It was something of a relief to him, since the constant surreptitious visits to Wimbledon had been something of a strain. He returned with relief to his book, spending most of his free evenings at home, which was gratifying to his mother.

Kit wrote to him sympathetically. "Give our love to Mildred, and tell her this isn't the end of the world. One thing about the damned war, it obliterates everything else: we can hardly have two-day wonders these days, let alone nine. Who is going to care about poor Hansen and wretched school-girls on the common? They ought to train the little beasts better, tell them what to expect if they go rambling about all by themselves in their tempting black stockings and gym-bloomers. I can never look at one myself without a lubricious eye, though I shouldn't be driven to extremes. Come to us when you can—I want to see more of the book."

It might be all very well for others to forget, Jo thought, but Hansen would live in a mud-bath of shame and self-hatred for the rest of his days and this shame Mildred would share. It would be better for them if they moved from their neighborhood, to a place where people "would not know." He supposed they might do that. He could by now forget easily enough, reproaching himself only for the moment when compassion had seemed impossible, when he had cringed from the contact of his flesh with his brother-in-law's. For most people, living was like the slow and painful scramble over rocks at low tide: the slither on weed into water, the emergence with twisted ankle, the renewed and aching progression from danger to danger with the smooth, dry sands so far out of sight. Cut and bleeding, still we go on: the wounds heal, but fresh ones are made. Do I feel that because of my class? Are people like me always unable to ride life easily? He thought of himself as an aristocrat, graceful, airy, with high-pitched voice: "Did you hear about poor Frank? Quite absurd, wasn't it? So tiresome for Mildred." Yes, we are the respectable ones: we have only respectability to lose.

A letter, unshocked, came from Alison. "Make them come down to me for a weekend. Nobody here will have the slightest idea of the trouble, and Mildred should be given a chance to feel like a normal person again, both of them should. 'There but by the grace of God'—naturally."

Yes, for her too it was easy, and for Kit and Polly. He looked resentfully round his bedroom, still the result of Millie's indifferent tastes: pale-brown paper with a dado of pink and blue flowers, fawn carpet, threadbare in places, dressing chest of fumed oak with green handles, green curtains of a material called "slub": three tepid water-colors, *Highland Heather, Corfe Castle*, and, yes, *Rocks at Low Tide*.

When the war was over, there was going to be a change, in himself, in all this, and in all that it stood for. He thought he felt the freshness of the sea at his back, could see, almost within a stone's throw, the first firm scalloped parallels of the sand.

Chapter Nine

THERE ARE TIMES IN LIFE WHEN, TO ANY GROUP OF FRIENDS dispersed, nothing seems to happen.

They meet again. "Well, what's the news?"

"I don't know that there is any."

So it was with them all, throughout 1943.

In the January of the following year, Bessie celebrated her sixty-fifth birthday, with what Jo called a flourish of trumpets. The neighbors were there, and Alison came to London for the day. Mildred was there, and Frank, more silent than ever, not wanting to catch anyone's eye. The Hansens had been living, since his release from prison, near Haywards Heath, where nobody knew them nor was given the slightest chance to do so. Bessie could never understand why they had deserted the smart house in Wimbledon.

"Oh, because of the bombing," Mildred said, "we got tired of it."

"But there wasn't any bombing to speak of, then!"

"Well, there may be more to come. One never knows."

317

Bessie chewed the cud of her thoughts, which were only vaguely suspicious ones. She did not know what to be suspicious about.

Clement came and went, in and out of England: Georgina, so Alison said, seemed satisfied to stay quietly at home with her son, now two and a half, handsome and placid. Alison's own son had just gone to nursery school. "He isn't as good-looking as Paul, but, thank God, he's clever. He can read quite fluently."

"But ought he to?" Bessie demanded. "Aren't you scared to strain his eyesight?"

Alison replied that he was unstoppable, and she refused to eat more than a square inch of birthday cake. "If I do I shall get fat, like Georgina."

"Fat?" Jo exclaimed.

"Perhaps I exaggerate. But yes, she will be, if she isn't careful."

Kit and Polly arrived at the party unexpectedly, with their daughter, who was now nearly six. Bessie cooed and clucked at her in a fashion that made Ruth frown: she was old enough to resent being treated as a baby. She had grown into a withdrawn, wary child, and Polly told Jo that this worried her. "She likes to play all by herself at school. She's extremely anti-social. If I ask her friends to tea she is meticulously polite, but she glowers at them. I don't understand it at all."

"Shut up," said Kit, "she'll hear you. Anyway, she's perfect as she is, and I wouldn't have her otherwise."

The little girl was in a corner, looking at a picture-book they had brought with them. The lamplight threw the shadows of her lashes to fence the apricot softness of her cheeks. Her hair was quite long, the curliness bound into a plait with an orange bow upon it.

"Wouldn't you like to run in the garden, pet?" Bessie asked her, forgetting the time of year.

"No, thank you," said the child, "I hate fresh air."

"I'm with you," Miss Pease said, "so do I. And I have to do all the shopping."

Ruth's mouth quivered; then she broke into a blinding smile. "You could order by telephone."

"If you do that," said Bessie, "they only send you things that are nasty and stale."

318

"I wouldn't mind, if I didn't have to go out in the snow. I don't care however stale things are."

"What, don't you like to play snowballs?"

"No. I don't like playing anything."

Bessie clucked disapproval.

"Oh, she gets plenty of exercise," said Polly, "whether she's reluctant or not. I see to that."

"Yes, you brute," said Kit, "you do. I don't believe freezing round Battersea Park does a ha'porth of good to anyone. I'm on Ruth's side."

Are we all getting middle-aged? Jo wondered. No, not yet. But I think we are preparing for it. I know that if we did all the things now that we were doing eight years ago, we'd look pretty silly. Every age prepares for the next: that's how we eat time away. We should never prepare ourselves for anything, not even for death.

Alison asked him quietly about his book.

"Oh, that. It's been the rounds. I don't think I shall send it out again."

"May I read it?"

"If you like," he said indifferently. "Kit thinks it's a stinker."

She was startled. "Of course he doesn't! He can't."

"He said so. In so many words."

She glanced indignantly across the room, to where Kit was charming Miss Pease.

"How foul of him!"

"No. It was my fault. I kept on badgering him about it, making him read all the re-writings, and he hedged and hedged till I couldn't stand it. I said so, and he told me that if I wanted the truth I could have it. He was quite right."

"Kit isn't God!"

"No, but he's a good critic. I daresay God would be no better. Certainly He'd be no more experienced."

He could look at Alison now without desire, though still with love. His sexual urges, always strong, were satisfied these days by a typist in his office, a stocky young widow who could buck like a broncho and had no intention of marrying again. She had found her way to a good time, and Jo was not her only lover.

"Kit!" Alison called imperiously.

He came over to her. "Hullo, proud beauty. What's the matter? Why that beetling brow?"

"Did you tell Jo his book was no good?"

He said reasonably, "Well, it isn't, and he knows it. He'll write another, and that one will be."

"Always so sure you're right!"

"Read it, and you'll think the same. Won't she, Jo?"

"Yes, she will think exactly the same."

Kit crouched on his haunches, staring earnestly into Jo's face. He said with compunction, "No, that wasn't fair. Alison may think differently. Give her the chance. I could be wrong, you know."

Jo felt suddenly weary, and wished the party would end. Here he was, with three of his closest friends: and they did not belong there, not at all. Not to him, only to themselves and their own lives.

The brief but sharp resumption of the bombing in February made Polly determined to leave London. Though she had ceased to show her own terror, which Kit had, in any case, never really credited, she pointed out to him that Ruth was old enough to be frightened. This the child was, though she did not speak of it: she lay wide-eyed and pale on her mattress in the shelter, staring up at the ceiling, flinching and trembling as the guns fractured the sky and the bombs fell. In the daytime she would hardly eat, nor would she play at all, but sat listlessly turning the pages of a book, not seeing them.

Here Belphoebe came to the rescue. Her secretary, she said, owned a cottage on the river not far from Staines, which was standing empty. They had better all move into it, and Kit could travel daily by train to London. He was not enthusiastic about the arrangement: still, he saw the force of it, and he thanked her.

"My dear boy," Belphoebe said, enthroned in her high-backed chair, as calm as always, "you must forgive an aging woman if she scolds you a little, because that is what she is going to do."

They were alone together: even Jeanie was out.

"I think you are one of those strange people for whom physical fear does not exist. That is not to your credit: it merely means that an element of the normal composition is missing from your own."

"Oh, I'm scared stiff, like everyone else," he answered lightly, for the moment believing what he said.

"No, my dear, you are not. I am not entirely out of sympathy with you, since we are not altogether unalike. To make a confession that I would make to no one else, I fear Baynes more than I fear bombs. Dear me, what pleasure that thought would give the brute! Every time I publish a poem, or worse, a volume of poems, I am sick with fright. And of course, in the air raids, I much dislike the noise, though I am not as yet afraid of death. But Polly is different. She is brave, as you are not, because she is frightened, as you are not, and she has made a gallant attempt at concealment. For you to keep her in London for another week, and that poor beautiful child as well, would be the height of callousness. The cottage is furnished: I expect all three of you to move at once."

She folded her long parchment hands in her parchment lap, and the great rings flashed lightning from her fingers.

"So that's my scolding," said Kit.

"Yes. And your marching orders."

"They shall be obeyed."

"Naturally. It is extremely rare for me to give orders of any kind, marching or otherwise, but when I do so I expect obedience. By the way—"

He smiled at her. Something was coming.

"An admirer sent me a gift the other week, a brace of pheasants. But alas, they were delayed by rail. They arrived in an odor far beyond that of sanctity, with blood all over their tailfeathers. I got Jeanie to keep them—on the bathroom window-sill —for a few days longer, then she parcelled them up in a great deal of brown paper and sent them to Mr. Baynes. It is to be hoped that he was hungry."

Polly was so glad to be out of London, and Ruth looked so much happier, that even Kit felt he ought not to regret Manor Street. It was true that the trains were few and slow, and that he had to get up much earlier in the mornings: but he was pleased to see Ruth's color return, and with it her appetite.

The cottage was small and rather ugly, but it was comfortable enough, and there was a little orchard with a field beyond. Ruth, who had never before had the chance to pick flowers, brought in great handfuls of primroses, woodspurge and dandelions. Spring was early that year.

Every afternoon Polly took her down to the river to feed the waterfowl, or to walk on the island beyond Penton Hook lock where the willows were mealing over pale as honey for Easter.

"Pussy-willow," Ruth said, "little grey mice."

Now that the raids had ceased again, Kit came home only at weekends, or perhaps once during the intervening period. People were waiting for the invasion of France, and when it came, drew a sigh of fearful relief, believing the end must be near.

To Polly, though she listened anxiously to the news bulletins, these were charmed days. One Saturday Jo came down to see her, and they walked over to the island to sit beneath the trees, while Ruth, her dress tucked into her knickers, paddled in the sandy margin of the river and trailed a jam-jar for tiddlers.

He had been reading Virginia Woolf's last novel, and was haunted by it. "'Dispersed are we,'" he quoted. "That goes round and round in my head. 'Dispersed are we.'"

"Not so very. Of the old crowd, only Piers and Clement are out of England. I think we've been pretty lucky. Don't be so mournful!"

"It's the cut of my face," he said, "I can't help it." He laughed. "I'll tell you who has drifted back, though. I met her in Regent Street last weekend. She is Mrs. Nesbitt, pregnant, and very odd."

"How odd?"

"You see," said Jo, "though a non-com, he is grander than the rest of us, always barring you, and Fay has become grand—nicely grand—with him. She is stately and doesn't say 'Cheers, dears,' or call one Ducks. It's very sensible of her, I think. She's got her discharge, of course: she says the army isn't pleased with her at all."

"So many babies," Polly said, following Ruth with her eyes as the child made a collection of pebbles and swans' feathers; "the life-force is very strong. Do get married, Jo, it's high time you did."

"People are always on at me about it, like Shakespeare at Southampton. I've often thought those sonnets must have been damned irritating at times."

"I wasn't irritating, was I?"

She looked shining and fresh again, her old sparkling primness returned to her.

322

"I didn't mean that. Oh, I'd marry, I suppose, if I wanted to. I dare say Mother could manage, after all."

"You know perfectly well she could, and would, after an initial rumpus."

"I never wanted to marry anyone but Alison."

"There will be someone else."

"Maybe." But he had a haunted look.

"Why wasn't it Fay? Tell me if it's none of my business."

He gave her a curious side glance. "You won't like it if I tell you. You won't like me."

"You don't know what I shall or shan't like."

"Well, chiefly, I think, because I was a snob."

"You were what?" Polly laughed aloud.

He said, with a shade of resentment in his voice, "It's all very well for you. But when we were boys, Kit and I had to haul ourselves up by our bootstraps. You don't imagine I always had a nice BBC accent, did you? He did—it came naturally. But I spoke good old Clapham sub-cockney. It was quite a sweat getting rid of that."

She refused to believe him.

"Do as you please. Of course, I still live as I did when I was a boy: I don't seem able to get out of it. But I wanted to be one of the arty gang in those days, and I had to sound like them. Fay would have been . . . pulling me back. How's that for a perfectly revolting confession? As if I had anything to be pulled back from!"

"So the irony is—" she began.

"Precisely. Now she's gone beyond me."

"None of that would have mattered if you'd been in love with her."

"I suppose not. I don't know, because I never was. But now, I'm suffering from just a touch of dog-in-the-manger."

Polly laughed and sprang to her feet. "Time for tea. Ruth!"

She dried the child's legs, put on her socks and sandals. "Such lovely feathers! You've chosen all the best."

"Here's a stone like an emerald. Do you think it's an emerald?"

"I think it's as lovely as one."

"What is it?"

"A little piece of bottle-glass. The water washes it smooth."

"I think it must be an emerald. I wish I could have it in a ring."

"That wouldn't be impossible. We'll see what we can do. I make no promises."

They returned to the cottage. While Polly went into the kitchen, Jo picked up the book she had been reading, a long novel by the Soviet writer Tikhon Mamònov, which was enjoying enormous wartime success. He opened it. Red and White Armies clashed on the illimitable plains, thatches were burned, Cossacks on their wild strong horses shouted and bawled as they charged. He turned to the last page, where a man stood weeping over a woman's grave.

She came in with the tray, settled her daughter comfortably and tied the bib around her neck.

"Is this good?"

"We think so. Kit says he's one of the few great living writers, though he's getting on now. He must be over fifty."

"I wish," said Jo, "my name was on that cover. Or on any cover, come to that. I'd settle for a cookery book."

"It will be, one of these days. Did Alison read your manuscript?"

Smiling, he said yes. She had been angry with Kit for condemning it, yet, with her usual awful honesty, had felt she must condemn it herself—in a kindlier fashion and less categorically, but the writing between her lines had been sharp as the shadows of grass-blades at midday.

"You would think I was crazy, wouldn't you," Polly said slowly, "if I said I was glad? You see, though Kit is a darling and helps all kinds of lame dogs who think they can write, he would always be just a little jealous of anyone in our circle who wrote really well. And I think you do write well. Sometimes I am almost sure it would have been Alison for him rather than me, if she'd simply been someone's secretary."

Jo denied this, and looked uneasy.

"You think I'm unkind to him? No. I love him dearly, but I know his weaknesses. I was almost afraid that book of yours might be very good, and he couldn't bring himself to say so."

"Really," Jo exclaimed, "you can be a monster of selfishness, when you really try!"

"I know how that sounded. But I couldn't bear it if ever

324

envy got on top of him. I was sacrificing you to him, and I admit it was bad."

When he left her, she came to kiss him at the gate. "We will give the neighbors something to talk about. Jo, when you do find that splendid girl, who is even now coming to you from the future, promise I shall be the first to know?"

"The very first."

One night, there came the long Alert. Ruth slept through it, but Polly lay with pounding heart. She heard an occasional drumming in the skies, then a long silence: but the All Clear did not sound. Despite her fear, she fell asleep: when she woke at six o'clock, it was piercing the dawn. Had the raid lasted all night? Had there been several warnings, several All Clears, and she had not heard them?

Kit came home next day. Yes, the Germans were using a new weapon, un-manned missiles. Some had fallen on London. There had been comedy on the roof of one of the Ministry buildings where the staff had rushed to see, as they thought, bomber after German bomber shot down in flames, and had cheered the sight lustily.

That night, they came again. Kit, holding Polly in his arms, consoled her as the skies filled with throbbing. "It seems to me pretty evident that we're out of the direct path here. All we do is to hear them go over. Anyway, so long as we do hear them, it doesn't matter. It's when they cut out that one starts to worry."

The raids went on and on, and what Kit said appeared to be true. Since there were no heavy guns in the neighborhood, Ruth continued to sleep peacefully: Polly was even emboldened enough to go once with Kit into the garden, and follow the fiery course of the bombs through the skies until they met the distant barrage, no more than the rumbling of trains through the night.

All day, all night. They began to get used to it and, during the daytime raids, to soothe Ruth by explanations about "practicing." Polly was only frightened during the hours of daylight, frightened for Kit in London. For herself, she felt very little fear. Her neighbors were more apprehensive. "I know it's awful of me," one of them said, wild-eyed in a village shop, "but when I hear one bumbling across, I find myself praying, 'God give it strength!'"

One evening Kit telephoned apologetically to say that he could not get home, he had to finish a film-script, and the last train would have gone before he had done so.

"Will you be all right, my darling?"

"Yes. But I wish you were coming back, all the same."

"Sweetheart, the Ministry's got a wonderful shelter and I promise both to work and sleep there. Will that satisfy you?"

"It will have to, I suppose."

"But I'll be home by lunchtime tomorrow, with a bit of luck and a chicken from Belphoebe, bless her lavish soul. Good-bye for now, and I love you."

Heavy-hearted, she left Ruth with the daily woman and rode on her bicycle to the shops.

"Well, it looks as if we're off their road," the grocer said, "though they say Croydon's getting it something awful." He smiled at Polly, whom he liked: he thought her gentle and sweet, and a lady. He was sorry for ladies, who, he believed, must find the stringent rationing far worse than people like himself did. He gave her just a little more butter than was her due.

It was a chilly June, a month of low and heavy cloud. The island was drained of color, even the masses of loosestrife reflected in the stream were deadened from purple to grey. Ruth was fretful that afternoon. As the siren howled for the fourth time she said, "Mummy, I wish they would make it stop. It hurts my ears. I don't know why they have to make noises just for practicing."

"I expect they have their reasons," Polly said lightly. "If they told us everything the enemy might get to know about it, and that would never do, would it?"

At midnight, when the skies were filled with the loaded pulsing of machines, Ruth awoke and began to cry. Far off, there was an explosion. "May I come into your bed?"

"Of course you may, pet. And now, try to go to sleep again."

"Mummy, I don't like it. It's like animals coming nearer."

Her fear began to infect Polly. "They're miles away," she said. She felt the hot, damp cheek against her shoulder. "I'll tell you what. If by any chance you're not asleep within ten minutes, I'll bring us both some milk and biscuits, and we'll have a real picnic with crumbs all over the bed. Wouldn't that be fun?"

"I want them to stop."

"They will, soon. Just as soon as you're asleep."

Another explosion, nearer. Polly went cold.

"Mummy, what was that?"

"Darling, they do all sorts of mysterious things we aren't told about. In a war, you see, people have to practice, even if it is a nuisance for the rest of us."

Ruth gave a single tearful scream.

"Listen." Polly sat up and gripped the child by the shoulders. *"There is nothing to worry about.* Now, very soon, we'll have our picnic, and then we'll feel lovely and drowsy, and before we know it, it will be daylight—"

"I want Daddy! Where's Daddy?"

In the light from the low-powered lamp, which was always kept lit, Polly saw the huge round eyes, brown and lustrous as seaweed, the stained cheeks, the lips parted in hysteria, so that the row of upper teeth flashed and glittered.

"I told you, he had to stay in London for his work. You'll see him tomorrow."

"Daddy!"

A bomb came lurching through the dark, so heavy, seemingly so low, that Polly fancied it slicing through the gable of the house. Woman and child listened, straining. The noise droned off, and at last fell silent. "You see?" Polly demanded, with idiotic triumph.

Dear Lord Jesus, look after us. Dear Lord Jesus.

Another was coming. She cried out, to drown the noise— "We'll have our picnic now! There's some of the jam-sponge left, you can have that, if you like—"

Ruth hurled herself into her arms, crying, trembling.

Dear Lord Jesus, *don't let her be frightened. . . .*

The engine cut out.

Polly threw the child upon her back, herself crouched over the body.

PART SIX

Light on the Common

Chapter One

AS SOON AS THE WAR IN EUROPE WAS OVER, KIT WENT TO AMERICA on a protracted lecture tour. It seemed to all his friends the best thing for him: since the death of his wife and daughter, he had done little but write and drink, refusing all comfort, seldom setting foot outside the flat. Grief and a wholly sedentary life had fattened him: he filled out the big sweaters now, and his features were blurred by flesh, only the eyes wonderful.

Jo saw him off on the boat-train. "You'll be seeing the place from coast to coast, meeting new people. It will help."

"Maybe," Kit said, without interest.

"And you'll be a lion. Do you remember when you always wanted to be?"

"I don't care what sort of animal I am. Just give me a hoop, and I'll jump through it. That's what they're paying me for." He settled down in the carriage and opened a newspaper. "Don't wait."

"Of course I will."

"I hate good-byes. Look after yourself and don't worry about me."

He would say no more. Jo, despairing, left the compartment.

Dispersed are we.

Not that he was free from his own troubles. Two months ago, Hansen had taken enough sleeping-pills to kill himself, and Mildred, widowed, shattered to find that he had left her little more than the house and some debts, had returned stony-faced to her mother, summarily dismissing Miss Pease.

It had been impossible to conceal the suicide verdict from Bessie, who had badgered Millie so urgently for the cause of it that in the end, brutally, she was told. Her response, after the initial shock, was characteristic. "Well, you're lucky to be rid of that one."

Jo, who a few years ago would have given anything for his sister's return, now found that he resented it. In the old days, she had had her own acid verve: this had deserted her. She went about the place silently, briskly, efficiently, talking as little as she needed to. He found he was missing the lively bickerings of Bessie and Miss Pease: they had irritated him once, but now he saw that they had served a useful purpose in keeping his mother alert, in giving her an interest in life. It had been an amusement for her, sitting so long in her chair, to think up some striking verbal probe with which she would pierce her companion the moment she came in from shopping, well-knowing that this would be met by an adequate and sportsman-like riposte.

"Say what you like about Pease," she said to Mildred, "she kept me going. She and I were used to each other."

"There's no room for the two of us, Mother," Mildred retorted, "and she cost too much. You're better off with your own in any case, with Jo out so much."

He was. The end of the war had brought to him, as to most people, an enormous sense of release: for six years he had been tied to Clapham by war work or by his own job, and he was sick of it. He proposed to be thoroughly selfish, to try to recapture, if he could, some ghost of the "wild life." Georgina and Clement were back in London, Alison and her boy also: Piers, still in Burma, was a full colonel now. He did not think, he wrote, that the war with the Japanese would last long.

So Jo went out and stayed out, sometimes pretending, for decency's sake, that he was kept late at the factory but more often volunteering no explanations at all. He simply could not stand too much of Mildred, in her present state, although he was quite well aware that his mother hungered for his company.

He saw more of Clement than of anyone else. Georgina was tied to the house a good deal with the child, and did not seem to mind being left out of the life of the pubs. Like Kit, she had put on weight, though not so much. At thirty-one she was, though still good-looking, showing a touch of incipient matronliness: she knew this, and, in some mysterious fashion, it diverted her.

Clement, out of uniform, twice mentioned in despatches, had found a new and better job in Fleet Street as parliamentary correspondent to one of the more influential papers.

He sat, bland, unbuttoned, rather drunk, one night with Jo in El Vino's, both of them cocooned about by smoke and liquor fumes. "Good old Georgie," he said, "she does try. To give me one of my own. I mean, not that I feel Paul isn't. I don't feel that at all. But no luck. If it weren't for one thing, I'd be scared about my own fertility."

"That bloody Buchenwald film," a man was saying behind them, "I can't get it out of my system. I've been droning the *Dies Irae* all day. Christ help us all."

"What thing?" Jo asked.

"*Solvet saeculum in favilla.*"

Clement turned his head. "Stuff it, Charlie. We've all seen it, and we want to forget for a bit."

"What did your audience do? Some of mine giggled."

"Shock. Takes some people that way. Mine were like mice."

The drone continued behind them, a drunken bourdon. "*Teste David cum Sibylla.*"

"Let's find a quieter corner." Clement said, gathering up his beer and Jo's. They moved away.

"Oh, that! Well, you all thought I was such a hero, getting Georgie out of her fallen plight. She thought so, too: which is how I keep a grip on her. You won't tell?"

Jo shook his head vigorously, so that the room swam round him. He steadied it on a neck of iron, eyes front.

"There was a nice little bint in Tunisia, whom I got in the family way. Luckily she lost it in good time, and no harm was done. So you see? Nothing wrong with me at all. Fit as a fiddle and ready for love."

Jo did not quite know why he should feel so shocked but he did.

"God," said Clement, "was I scared at the time! Not that it didn't happen to a lot of chaps, but of course, they all ran hell for leather when the army moved on."

"Well"—Jo sounded belligerent—"isn't that what you'd have done?"

"I don't know. I suppose so. She wasn't quite a tart, though, and she had a terrible dirty old dad and ghastly relations, hordes of them."

"So?"

"I tell you, I don't know. I like kids, though that one wouldn't have been a practical possibility. I suppose I'd have tried to pay the tribe off."

Jo realized muzzily that he was not so much shocked by Clement's desert adventures as by the discovery that the *preux chevalier* side of him had inevitably become a little tarnished. "Christ, I'm a prig."

"Are you? What about?"

"Oh, I don't know. Don't know why I said it."

"Pretty Polly Perkins of Paddington Green. That was the bloodiest thing."

Jo agreed.

The man who had seen the film moved past them to the bar, still bumbling between his teeth.

"Salva me, fons pietatis."

"Come on," said Clement, "let us seek brighter lights. More cheerful company. All these types have been to public schools. So have I, but I've managed to forget."

"What I need is coffee."

"Not a bad idea." He hailed a taxi.

"Where are we going?"

"Dorchester. Always drink coffee in perfect comfort. Can't bear slop on bars and flailing dish-cloths."

They walked into the hotel steadily enough and sat under a potted palm.

"Better," Jo said after a while.

Music was playing some way off, soothing in the golden light, an old tune:

334

"So I smile and say,
When a lovely flame dies,
Smoke gets in your eyes."

Clement droned, *"Dies irae, dies illa, solvet saeculum—"*

"Don't you start that, for crying out loud!"

"Sorry, sorry. That bloody man. Thinks he's the only bleeding-heart in Fleet Street." ·

Some one in a shining evening dress was shining down upon them: Mrs. Nesbitt, and Sergeant Nesbitt, too. The sergeant still in uniform.

"Dears, imagine seeing you here!"

They sprang up, tottering a little as they did so.

"Charles, you know Jo. This is Clement Maclaren, another old friend. Clement, this is Charles. May we sit down?"

A different Fay: perhaps not profoundly different, but no, not the same.

"Perhaps we're butting in on a private conversation," Nesbitt said, with a smile of possessive, tender rebuke.

"No, no, no," Clement protested, "we're delighted. What are you drinking?"

"You must let us," she said, "please!"

He replied promptly that he would have a pink gin.

"I will have another cup of coffee," Jo enunciated carefully, "because I am not altogether sober."

She said she was very happy indeed to see him on the town again, and asked for his news: which he did not give her.

"We're celebrating," Nesbitt said, "for the first time in months."

"Oh, but they don't know!" Fay cried, in the new, careful voice. "We all lose touch so terribly, don't we? I am a proud mama!"

"A daughter," said Nesbitt.

They congratulated her. "What's her name?" Jo asked, for something to say; he was feeling, as he had felt with Alison's child, that somehow the child should have been his. He found it hard to imagine, in this smart, poised, pretty woman, the girl who had so often been happy with him in his dismal room, on his rather lumpy bed, joyfully eeling between the sheets.

"Lucy Victoria."

"Proper names in more senses than one," Clement drawled. Nesbitt shot him a swift glance, either of puzzlement, or of resentment that the least joke should be made about any baby of his.

She said, "Charles's choice, but I like it. I'm afraid I began to think in far more *ornate* terms—"

Odd word for her, Jo thought.

"Amanda, or Jacqueline. But no. And now I'm so glad I was restrained from my wilder flights of fancy."

Oh, not Fay, not Fay at all!

Yet Jo realized her cleverness. She was not going to make a fool of herself by pretending she was on precisely the same social footing as her husband—until she had firmly established herself there. Then she would do so.

"Someday I'll find you, moonlight behind you . . ." Clement hummed, spurred by a name.

"Oh, those were the days!" Fay exclaimed. "Coward and Cochrane—all gone now."

All gone, thought Jo, when the bombs wrecked the bowling green of the Six Bells, and the little weeping fountain: that was the real end.

They fell to talking of the plays, the films they had enjoyed in the nineteen thirties. Jo covertly examined Nesbitt. He was stocky, bullet-headed, snub-nosed: and, indefinably, well-bred in an easy, not unpleasingly arrogant fashion which made Jo envious. He would have liked to be born as this man had been. Not, of course, that it was going to matter any more. He firmly believed in the coming of a richer world for all and in the classless society, in which people like Nesbitt would have to take their turns in the queue with everybody else. He felt suddenly strong and vengeful.

The conversation had changed. Fay was saying in a spurt of laughter, "We put it down for Eton before it was born, but the sex was wrong. How terrible to call her 'it!' "

Jo saw her with sharpened eyes, erect in the ice-green dress, spine like a ramrod, hair, now long again, gathered on the top of the bird-like head. He said, "Excuse me," and blundered off.

He sat on the lavatory seat, having no need but solitude, and for a moment to put his head between his knees. That had been Fay, his girl, now a million light-years from him. Nesbitt? What

336

had he done to disquiet? A cubic man in the uniform of a sergeant, by choice a non-com, who had said almost nothing.

It was with some composure, steady on his feet, that he returned to them.

"Jo," she said, "I must find you a perfectly marvellous girl. Unless, of course, there is one?"

Fay, playing Lady Bountiful.

He said there was nobody in particular.

"Charles, do you think he would like Una?"

"Darling, you really must not expect me to know what other people might like. Don't be presumptuous."

"My sister-in-law," she explained to Jo.

He thought: Then not for me.

"She's lots of fun. She is, Charles, isn't she?"

"She has great verve," he replied good-humoredly, "and certainly she makes an awful lot of noise."

Clement yawned strikingly, without covering his mouth. Stretching his arms above his head, he rose up as if hoisting himself by invisible ropes. "Come on, Jo. Bedtime."

"Let's not lose touch again!" Fay pleaded. "Here, I've got a card."

"Do come and see us," Nesbitt said, "we should like it."

Promises were made.

Jo and Clement walked down Park Lane towards the tube station.

"Well, well," Clement said, "that is our own Fay. Your Fay, rather. Nice, isn't she?"

"I thought he was a bit of a stick."

"Pleasant enough stick."

"Trying quite hard to put me off his sister," Jo said, with a broad grin that was not very sincere. "Fay's an idiot."

"He may well be saving you from his sister for all you know. What's up with you? More chips on the shoulder?"

Jo did not reply.

He was elated by the victory of the Labour Party in July, and astounded. Though he had done a great deal of house-to-house canvassing, which he detested, he had always returned in a state of puzzlement, his lists marked heavily with D.K.s, "don't knows." People had been unwilling to talk, except for those who, worshipping Winston Churchill, had driven him away with imprecations. He had not believed Piers, who had warned Alison in a letter what would happen. The English, unlike the Americans (he said), did not elect warlords any longer: they had learned their lesson with the Duke of Wellington. The serving soldier, grateful for Churchill's lead in battle, still associated him and the Tory Party with the hunger and unemployment of the thirties: they would vote against him.

Jo had not believed this at all. Yet his own candidate had won the seat for the first time: there was a celebration dance at the Town Hall. Together in serpentine swathes, arms linked, they danced "The Palais Glide" and "Horsey, Horsey, Don't You Stop." It was here that he first spoke to the daughter of the new Member, a tall, dark girl whose plainness made all the more remarkable her great glittering eyes, green as his own, but flecked like moss with spots of gold. Her name was Davina Hoyt; she was twenty-two, and in her third year at the London School of Economics.

Jo felt shy about asking her out, since her father had been translated to such greatness: like Trollope, he had an ineradicable feeling that "to sit in the British Parliament should be the highest object of ambition to every educated Englishman," though he himself would rather have seen his name upon the cover of a book. However, that dream was over.

He did ask Davina to dance, and finding her direct and easygoing, suggested another meeting. She seemed quite pleased. He hoped she would not think him too old for her.

He was happy till the news came of the dropping of the first atom bomb on Hiroshima. While his mother and Mildred found it hard to conceal their approbation, he felt that by this horrible action England had lost all vestige of the moral initiative which had been hugged so closely to her soul.

"Nobody wants all those people to be killed, of course," Bessie said, "but it's bound to make the Japanese surrender. Then Alison will have Piers home again!"

"There was no need for it," Jo raged, "the Japs were making peace overtures any old how. Was nobody humane enough to try and stop it?"

"Well," Mildred said, "*we* didn't do it. It was the Americans."

"Do you suppose we didn't know? That we didn't agree?"

"Oh, do sit down, dear," Bessie said. "You're making me giddy, walking up and down like a caged lion. What's done can't be undone."

"One does, of course, feel awful," added Mildred, cautiously.

All the same, there was rejoicing in many public houses that night.

But when the second bomb was dropped three days later, both Mildred and her mother fell silent.

Jo sought out Davina, who was as miserable as he. She said, "It was done in our name."

"To show the Russians what we've got coming to them, if they give us any trouble."

"Father won't admit that. But I think he feels disgraced. I know I do."

Next, he sought out Alison, who said steadfastly, "Of course I want Piers back. But not at such a cost. Nothing at such a cost."

Salva me, fons pietatis.

In September, the Japanese surrendered. At the end of that month, Piers came home.

Chapter Two

MEANWHILE KIT, SWIMMING IN A HAZE OF ALCOHOL AND AN ADULA-
tion he had never before experienced, was being led by Fran
Olson from state to state through America. It was so exhausting
that there were times when he had not the slightest idea which
state he was in.

He had two lectures, one upon his own novels, the other on
English poetry. He had abandoned the trick of singing to his
audiences, which had at first attracted so much attention, but in
the drinking sessions afterwards, spurred by undergraduate admiration, he would sometimes spontaneously invent tunes for any
poems they might care to name, and sing these till it was obvious
that he must be reverentially taken up and put to bed.

He did not find so much reverence in people to whom the
influence of Porter Baynes had extended, but he learned how to
deal with them. They would inevitably expose their interests by
attacking, not himself, but Belphoebe. To this he would listen,
for a while, in a deceptively humble manner, head bowed on his
chest. Then he would rear up, flash the rays from his eyes like a
searchlight upon them, and counter-attack in terms of vivid
abuse. He was better at this than they were and succeeded in

340

turning diatribe into such a work of art that it was not infrequent for people who did not give a damn for Baynes or his opinions to goad him into such displays.

Not that he would be goaded if he did not wish it, or think the moment inopportune. His grief for Polly and the child was so deep that it seemed to have wrenched away one of the cores of his nature to leave a cell of emptiness, into which he could retreat in coldness and caution whatever his condition. Here he could be watchful, could bide his time.

He found some comfort in the admiration of the young women, any of whom seemed ready to sleep with him. Fran warned him against this, but the warnings were, at that stage of his misery, quite unnecessary. He wanted no woman. Still, his ego was much stimulated by their maneuvers, their snugglings at his feet, their naïve, pure eyes upturned to his own.

"Their mothers," Fran said, in a way not at all American, "should have spanked them long and often at an age when there was still hope. On their little asses."

She watched his drinking in so far as she could, and for her sake he tried to control it before giving a lecture. Afterwards, he did as he pleased.

"The trouble," he said to her plaintively, "is that there is no decent beer in this place. God, it's pee! I don't want the hard stuff, but what else am I going to do?"

"You will take one highball this evening," she said, "and make it last an hour."

"No hour ever invented has been the right length of time for a highball."

"It's got to be."

Many girls, jealous of her apparent dominance, thought she was his mistress, and privately they derided his poor taste. This she found entertaining. She was, in fact, a lesbian, with a perfectly stable, discreet relationship in New York which she expected would last her lifetime: but she never told Kit this, and he did not appear to have guessed.

One evening he said to her nervously, "Fran, I don't know where I am or what I'm supposed to be doing."

She stared at him. "Of course you do!"

"I don't. I'm dead tired, and my memory seems to have gone."

"You're dead drunk."

"Drunk, not dead drunk. But for Jesus's sake, tell me where I am, because I swear to you, I honestly do not know!"

He had just returned from drinking with new friends in one of the colleges.

She helped him up and took him to the window. Sunset was rosy behind cupolas of blue and green and red and white: from the campanile, sweet bells sounded.

"You are at Harvard. You're going to have dinner alone with me, whatever you may have planned, and then you are going to lecture, in a perfectly sober manner, on your own novels."

"Christ, where? Here?"

"In the Sanders Theatre. This is the high point of your trip, son."

"Oh, Fran, I can't do it."

To her horror, he began to cry.

She nerved herself to deal with him. "What does you good? I know, Worcester sauce and oil of cloves. I'll get the damned mess for you if I can. Meanwhile, you stay here and rest, and when I come back I'll have some sandwiches sent up. You have got to eat."

"No, I shall be sick."

"And a good thing for you if you were."

She took no chances: she locked him in the room and took the key with her while she visited grocer and chemist.

When she returned, he was in a deep sleep. She ordered sandwiches and a pint of milk, and sat over him anxiously, hearing the clock strike the hour. She knew that she would have to wake him soon, and dreaded what condition he might be in. But suddenly he woke of his own accord, rubbed his eyes, then smiled at her sweetly.

"Better now. Fran, I believe I'm hungry."

"Here's your witch's brew, if you still want it."

"I don't, though it was kind of you. How long have I slept?"

"An hour and twenty minutes."

"How much time have we got?"

"Three-quarters of an hour precisely."

He ate wolfishly, pushing aside the dill pickles. She had ordered egg sandwiches, knowing they would not upset his stomach. In these states he became prone to anorexia, unable to swallow anything that was not soft. Even chicken sandwiches often defeated him.

"Well," he said at last, "ready to go. Am I decent?"

Like a nannie she washed him, combed his hair. "Now you are. Go out and slay them."

She sat in the front row of the crowded hall, her hands tight-locked between her knees. She was praying.

He was introduced at some length by the Professor of Poetry, then he stepped on the stage to the tumultuous ovation he had come to expect. He felt quite well, and perfectly calm. He let his gaze travel up to the gallery, play round it, then slowly descend to the body of the hall.

"Ladies and gentlemen," he began. "I am going to talk about me. It may be painful for you to listen to so much egocentricity, but you have brought it upon yourselves. Needless to say, I would rather talk about me than about anything else, but . . ."

He had lost the thread. Panic-stricken, he stood silent, staring around him. If he could see Fran's good horse-face it would be all right, but he didn't know where she was sitting. He could hear the breathing of the silence and it terrified him. For how long he stood there, at the rostrum, the green-shaded light shining upon his half-sheet of notes, he could not tell.

The Professor was muttering something to him, but he could not hear what it was. The glowing faces, hanging wreathed above the galleries, seemed to him disembodied, like cherubim.

He caught sight of Fran, half-risen in her seat, and he knew what to do.

"Ladies and gentlemen," he said, enunciating with more than common clarity, "I'm afraid I am not well. Forgive me."

He walked off the stage.

Fran, ignoring the susurration of pity and protest, ran after him.

He was lying on a couch, sipping water. He said, "They must fetch me a Scotch. Don't let them go home." He caught the Professor's sleeve. "Tell them *not* to go home, please! I only need ten minutes."

"Better do as he says," Fran whispered. She turned to a graduate student, who seemed to have some sort of official standing, "And get him that Scotch. It is the only thing to do."

Fifteen minutes later, Kit walked out again onto the stage, and without further preamble or apology, gave the best lecture of his tour.

Afterwards he walked back to Lowell House, where he was to be entertained, in the midst of a crowd of adorers. "If they'd got a carriage," Fran whispered, "they'd take the horse out of the shafts and draw you themselves."

She was sick with relief; even when he started to sing, when he finally drank himself into sleep.

Next morning, when she went to his room, she found him clear-eyed and alert. He had even had a shower. "Now where?"

"You nearly killed me with fright last night."

"But it was O.K. in the end."

"In the end. One night it won't be. Kit, you've got to pull yourself together."

He made her sit beside him and held both her hands. "Dear Fran, kind Fran, who is so patient with me and to whom I am so bloody. That is what I'm going to do. I promise you. Please, where do we go next?"

"To New Haven, and that will be the end."

"Thank God."

"Breakfast is ready."

With an effort of will which he was still able to exercise, he did not break that promise. Though he would never for the world have let Fran know it, the experience of the previous night had terrified him.

Lecturing in Yale, he was duller than had been expected, and some people were a little disappointed: but his charisma did not fail him.

He spent the next night in New York, then flew back to England, sleeping nearly all the way. "Something attempted, something done," he assured a startled real-estate man, who was in the next seat, "really does earn a night's repose. Do try it some-time."

He was met at the airport, to his sleepy pleasure, by Jo. Jo, he thought. There's no one else now whom I care about so much in this world.

Jo in a dark business suit, shirt very white, tie a political red. Shoes well shone.

"Oughtn't you to be at work?" These were Kit's first words.

344

"It's Saturday."

"One forgets."

"How did it go?"

"Roses, roses, all the way. But a lot of myrtle, mixed in my path like mad. I have some money stored in the Chase Manhattan Bank. Next time, I ought to be able to take you with me."

"Have you had breakfast?"

"No, I couldn't wake up enough. But I wouldn't mind some now."

To Jo, nothing could have been more encouraging. In the airport lounge, he watched with motherly approval as his friend ate sausages and bacon.

"It's odd," said Kit, "but I couldn't help expecting a brass band out for me here. There, it was all brass bands, or the equivalent. When we go together"—Jo glowed, and knew he was glowing—"we shan't visit the Bible Belt. One gets the stuff all right, but it is so surreptitious. Every time I had a drink, I felt like a secret masturbator."

"What are you going to do now?"

"Oh, go home. To such home as there is."

"I wondered," Jo said tentatively, "if you'd like to come to us for a few days. You could hole up. Millie will feed you, and you needn't see mother. The spare room is quite decent."

Kit considered this. Then he said, to Jo's surprise, "Thanks. Yes, I might as well. I won't be expected to chat?"

"You can remain completely incommunicado, if you like. But there are things you ought to know." He told him about Hansen's suicide.

"Well, I was surprised when I heard Millie was back with you. Odd that he should have taken so long about it."

Jo tried to explain Hansen as well as he could. A man who married for refuge: and failing the refuge Mildred had brought him, had been unable to go on. But only after thought, after much thought. In fact, a thoughtful man, considering his own condition, probably knowing it could never be rectified. People like Hansen were never reckless: and by their careful calculations, probably caused more misery than people who were.

"Did it hit Mildred hard?"

Jo contemplated this. The lights in the restaurant were very harsh, making worse the eternal harshness of arrival and departure. "I don't know. She forgave him formally, I suppose. But it could never have been the same."

He asked what arrangements Kit himself had made for his return. Was there anything to be done, were there messages to be conveyed?

Kit replied that the charwoman would have had things organized. Perhaps he had better telephone to her, saying he would not be returning for a day or so. "She won't be pleased. I bet she's cooked me bacon-cakes." He added, "But I shall be glad to go to your place." Then he looked into Jo's face. "All O.K. with you? You look peaked."

"I get tired so damned easily."

"Better see a doctor."

Jo shrugged this aside. "It's nothing."

Kit went to telephone the daily woman, Jo to ring Mildred. Her voice was sharp. "What will he want immediately? Food?"

"He's had that. Bed and a hot water bottle, by the look of him. Expect us in about an hour and a half."

But it was less than that. Kit, newly rich, had hired a car. They rolled through the stiff suburban roads, the houses trim and anonymous as maidservants. Nothing of interest, nothing to like or to dislike.

London shuddered in upon them. The yawning of Hammersmith, the funnel of the Cromwell Road. At last, over the river and up the hill onto the familiar common.

"I slept for hours on the plane," Kit said, "you'd never think it, though."

He slumped into sleep again, his head on Jo's shoulder. Only when they stopped at the gate did he awaken: instantly, and alert. "He's been paid, or he will be. Give him ten bob." He put the note into Jo's hand.

Mildred came out to greet them. "See the conquering hero comes. Did you conquer?"

"Tolerably. No, I did conquer."

"Get in quickly before Mother spots you. Your bed's ready. Jo will bring the bags."

Kit felt immersed in care and kindness, undeterred by the bleakness of her face, which in any case he could not see clearly.

346

He was put in Miss Pease's old room, where he dropped his clothes onto the floor, and slept at once.

When he awoke, it was dusk. Mildred had come soft-footed into the room with a tray, and had turned on only the shaded bedside lamp so as not to disturb him too sharply.

He turned up at her his great, tired eyes. "Would you mind if I stayed here for a bit?"

After all, these were the surroundings into which he was born, his old school only a mile away, with the great soft common in between, and the sunset sweep of the Rise. Here he had been a boy, and as a boy, comforted by parents who, in those days, had been the people closest to him.

"Up to you," said Mildred, "no trouble to me."

He stayed for more than three weeks.

In the mornings he lay working or reading in bed, his breakfast brought to him by a rather silent Mildred: with her he could make little contact. With Bessie, however, it was different. For an hour every afternoon he sat and talked to her, teasing her in the way she liked, drawing out from her the family and local gossip that he stored away in the back of his mind in case it should ever come in useful. Privately, he thought she was an octopus of a woman, half-shrewd, half-naïve: yet she made him feel like a son, gathered in, comforted and irritated at once, as his own mother had comforted and irritated him.

He had made no attempt to see his parents since Polly died. They had moved again, this time to Somerset. They did not like making the journey to London, and he could not be bothered to visit them: there might have been the ocean between them.

Sitting with Bessie before the fire, the wintry garden beyond, they talked about ages.

"Do you know how old I am, Kit? Nearly sixty-seven. Not bad for an old 'un, eh?"

"And do you know how old I am? Twenty-six."

"That you're not! You're thirty-two. I know, because you're almost exactly two years younger than Jo."

"No. None of us, of my generation, is ever going to be as much as it says on our birth certificates. We shall all subtract six years, for the war. It was such a waste of our lives: we shall simply refuse to accept the years it put upon us."

"I must say that sounds pretty fanciful!"

"Not really. I simply tell you, we are all going to feel younger than we are, for the rest of our lives."

"I never concealed my age," Bessie said proudly, "I've no use for women who do. What's the point? Sheer vanity."

"Oh, I don't mean that I'm concealing mine. I simply don't believe it's as much as it is."

Bessie said she could not credit that Jo thought of himself as a raw boy.

"I'm not sure he ever thought he was a boy at all."

She was indignant. "I'm quite sure he did! He may be a bit of a sobersides, but he's quite ordinary."

"No, he's not ordinary." Kit was silent. Then he said, "Would you mind very much if he came to live with me for a while?"

Her mouth opened. "Whatever for?"

"Comfort to me. Might be a change for him. You could spare him, couldn't you, Bessie"—she had come to like this informality—"with Mildred home all the time?"

She said, "If he got married I'd have to spare him. But I don't see why he should want to leave a comfortable home. Besides, he'd be farther away from his work."

"His work is just about equidistant between your place and mine."

"Too much would devolve on Millie."

Kit told her, affectionately, that this was bosh and she knew it—didn't she? Jo was out nearly every night in any case.

Her lips trembled. "I like to hear him come in, though. Oh, you think I'm selfish, I know that, but there's not much time left to me."

"Years and years."

"You know I had a stroke."

"You'll live to bury us all. Bessie, I need him rather more than you do at present."

She said how sorry she was for all he had suffered.

"Not asking for sympathy. Asking for Jo." He added, "You love me, Bessie, don't you?"

She was affronted by his acting, which she recognized, but in the depths of her nature was hopelessly, helplessly, stirred by

348

that strand of it which was not acting at all, which could have spoken to her if she had been different, and if he had.

Color filled her plump cheeks, seeming to swell them. "Go on, ask him, then! I don't mind. Do what you want, both of you. I won't have it said that I ever stood in his way."

Now she wanted nothing more than to be rid of him, to have him out of the house.

He took her hand in his. "That's a darling. You can be, if you like, can't you? Nice Bessie."

Thinking he had won a triumph, he could scarcely wait till Jo came in, to break the news. To his astonishment, Jo refused.

"Why on earth not?"

"I don't know. Mother, I suppose. She's been complaining of her heart again. What can one do?"

"She didn't complain to me."

"Anyway, I can't make a move, not just yet. I haven't the energy. I've been feeling dog-tired lately."

"Then go and see a doctor," Kit snapped. He was filled with disappointment. Their evening in the pub was not a cheerful one. Kit badgered, Jo was unbudging.

"Damn it, this may be your last chance to cut loose!"

"No, it won't. But not now."

In fact, Jo did not want to move so far from Davina, with whom he believed he was falling in love. But he did not say so.

Chapter Three

HE WOULD NEVER HAVE SUSPECTED, MEETING HER AT THE LABOUR Party dance, that she was very lively and more than commonly talkative. At one time, this might have irritated him: now he felt that she supplied much of the energy increasingly lacking in himself. Her step was light and quick for so tall a girl, her eyes invariably sparkling. She had pretty dark hair, curling naturally, but a rather coarse skin, with a Charles's Wain of tiny moles on one cheek. A hair grew out of one of them: one of these days, when he knew her better, Jo was going to ask why on earth she didn't cut it off.

She had taken him to the House of Commons to hear her father's maiden speech, and afterwards to tea on the terrace. They went out together once or twice a week, but he had not brought her home. This girl, he well knew, was not one of those who would go to bed with him, or with any man, before marriage, and she was young enough to deter him from attempting the role of seducer.

Her mother had been dead for some years, and she had been accustomed to keeping house for her father in the intervals of

350

her studies. At housekeeping she was not, Jo discovered with some relief, particularly competent, always forgetting something she should have done, something she should have brought back with her from the shops. Fortunately there was a daily woman of remarkable alertness, who seemed perfectly willing to do most of the work and let Davina, of whom she was fond, have all the credit.

"You're twelve years younger than I am," Jo brooded, one soft afternoon in the spring of 1946, when they were returning from a small black-market restaurant they had discovered in Vauxhall Bridge Road, where they could dine by candle-light and eat disguised horsemeat. "Does that seem an awful lot?"

"Oh, you're young for your age," she replied confidently, her arm in his. "I always imagine you just as you must have been in those terrific pre-war days you're always telling me about. I do wish I'd been there! I'd adore to be wild and not too respectable. Those girls you knew don't seem to have been."

"One of them was."

"Only one! Which?"

But of Alison he had told her nothing.

"Susan something. I forget." This was pure invention. He went on: "Perhaps you might knock six years off my actual age, as Kit says we're all going to do."

"You've never let me meet your Kit. Is he too precious? You needn't be jealous, you know. I'm sure he'd terrify me."

Yes, Kit was precious, even more so since the recent disappointment Jo had dealt him, and was ashamed of. He wanted to keep him to himself, a part of the days before the war, not intruded upon by young women of another generation. But it wasn't only that; he was afraid Kit might not like Davina, think she was plain, resent her easy flow of chatter, never profound, but never unintelligent.

As it happened, the matter was taken out of his hands. They had just left the pub across the common one night, when they met Kit.

Jo asked what on earth he was doing there.

"I got restless, and looked in to see you. Nobody seemed to know where you were, so I thought I'd try here. Let's go back inside, shall we? I'm thirsty, if you're not."

His eyes were steady on Davina's face. Jo introduced them,

and they returned to the mullioned bar. The back part had been bombed, but the windows, the manager's pride, were still intact.

"I've wanted to meet you," Davina said, "but Jo has been extremely cagey and I was too wise to press him. You're very like your photographs. Do you have one taken every two years or so? I hate seeing a writer look quite different on the backs of his books from what he actually is. It's cheating, somehow."

"Ever since I began to get fat," Kit replied, "I have been scrupulous in that respect. I could show you beautiful Shelley-like photographs taken no more than four or five years ago."

"I hate my own photographs, they're worse than I am. Please—" As he began to protest, she held up her hand. "I'm not being mock-modest. I am no beauty. That is *why* I can't risk candid-camera stuff. I was always being taken at Daddy's side during the election, looking monstrous. God knows why the voters didn't reject him."

Kit said, "You are not beautiful, but you have the most wonderful eyes I have ever seen in any face in my life, except, perhaps, in my daughter's. Let that content you, and beshrew conceit."

"Am I conceited?" She looked astonished, but not at all abashed.

"Certainly you are, and all the better for it."

Jo went to the bar for drinks.

"You know about me," Kit asked, "I mean, about my wife and little girl?"

"Yes. There's nothing for me to say, is there?"

"Not really. I only wondered if he'd told you. Do you like him?"

"Jo? Of course I do."

"Very much?"

"Yes."

"Then go on liking him as hard and deep as you can, because he needs it."

"Don't you need someone?"

Knowing he had attracted her, he meant to counter this effect as quickly as he could.

"Not you, anyway."

"Well, damn *you!*" Davina exclaimed, quite cheerfully. "I didn't mean that at all."

352

"I'm not going to need any girl again, or not seriously."

"But—"

"I know that. I'm quite sure."

Jo came back to the table, mugs clutched to his chest.

"Getting on nicely?"

"Very," said Davina, "though I'm inclined to think the conceit isn't all on my side."

Kit grinned. "Not bad, my young economist. Do you know, all my life I have dreaded meeting an economist, as I might have dreaded meeting a hippogriff? Now I see they are not altogether without light."

It was a comfortable evening, the most relaxed Jo had spent in a very long time.

They both saw her home. She lived not far away in Clapham Old Town, in the top flat of a handsome Georgian house. "Is this suitable for a Labour member?" Kit inquired. "Surely it would look better to his constituents if he lived in a back-to-back."

"I have to be considered," said Davina, "and I can be very selfish."

The men walked over the dark fields.

"She is extremely attractive," Kit said, "and I mean that. Few people are going to realize just how attractive she is, till it hits them below the belt. Do you want to marry her?"

Jo said yes, he believed he did: but she was much younger than he, and he had no idea whether she took him seriously.

"I think she might. You've never told me much about her, have you? Is she the reason why you wouldn't come to me?"

"Partly."

"And partly Bessie—still?"

"I'm not sure. I think if I could have Davina, I shouldn't let her count any more."

"Davina wouldn't come to live under your roof."

"I know that."

Kit turned his face up to the hawthorns, which were just coming into bud. "If there's one scent that takes me back through the years, it's that one. I feel I've still got my school cap on, that it's Sunday evening at twilight, and I'm ogling little girls in gym-slips."

"Me, too."

"You didn't ogle half as much. I used to catch them in my

net, and throw you all the nice ones I didn't want myself." He added in disgust, "Look at the damn place now! A mess of allotments and bloody gun emplacements. Can you ever imagine them clearing it up? They won't even try."

The moon was full and brilliant in a windless sky.

Both felt the tug of the past, painful and alluring, and were swept by their affection for each other. What they had shared together would never be lost, but held in a world of its own into which no new faces could ever penetrate.

How right women were, Jo thought, to be jealous of the friends of their husbands' youth! They could never know what those young faces had been like, what secrets had lain glittering behind the young eyes that were no longer apparent in the middle-aged ones, veiled and veined with the cautions of time. Did men feel the same about their wives? He did not believe it, nor believe in theories carelessly tossed around by Clement of the vast conspiracy of women. His was the conspiratorial sex and always would be, for his was the sex for the deep and dark friendships, some untouched entirely by sexuality, some with a single gold thread of love not entirely free from it. Friendships strengthened by that thread, the existence of which could never be spoken of without love's destruction.

Standing muddled under the may-trees, he confused that love for Kit, which was stranded from an entire lifetime, with growing love for Davina. If he had to choose, could he give up one for the other? He could have given up Kit for Alison, he supposed . . . could he? Quite?

It was through Davina that he saw Alison again, with whom he had entirely lost touch.

He had gone with her one evening to the London School of Economics, to hear a lecture, and afterwards to have coffee and sandwiches in the canteen. He was busy collecting their food on a tray when he heard her address someone behind him.

"Hullo, Colonel! Since when have you taken to extramural activities?"

"I haven't," said a well-known voice, "I was working late and I suddenly felt hungry."

It was Piers.

"Good God," he said to Jo, "of all people to meet! Do you

354

know you've hopelessly deserted us, and that Alison is sulking? Miss Hoyt, this is Mr. Upjohn."

"I know Davina," Jo replied, "in fact, I'm her guest. But it's even odder to find you here."

Piers said, not a bit of it. He had resigned his commission immediately the war was over, and had been lucky enough to find the bursarship vacant at the L.S.E. "Did you really not know? Haven't you seen the Maclarens?"

"I've seen nobody for three or four months."

Davina was glancing from one face to another, obviously suspicious: who was Alison, and why should she sulk? But she said, brightly enough, that Colonel Welford had been very kind to her, disentangling some difficulties about her grant.

They sat down at a table together. "Alison's having another child," Piers told Jo, "we're immensely pleased about it. Won't you come and dine with us one night soon, and bring Davina?"

Since she was Jo's friend, Piers gave her, easily, her Christian name.

Jo congratulated him and accepted for them both.

When they left the building, she asked whom Alison was. "Piers's wife."

"So I gathered. Aren't you stating the obvious?"

"Sorry. They've been friends of mine for ages."

"Why is she the one girl you've never mentioned to me? Because she was special?"

"It was a long time ago."

"I hate things being concealed from me!" she burst out. "I hate it even if they're no business of mine. You were in love with her, weren't you?"

Jo felt the anger that springs from guilt. He did not reply.

"So much so, that you wouldn't even speak of her to me?"

He said, "She was Kit's girl, not mine. He let her down and it was my shoulder she wept on. Does that satisfy you?"

"No, it doesn't! You've been so confidential, you've told me everything but that one thing, while I've really told you everything. So you're still in love with her, isn't that it?"

"Don't be silly."

He was too angry with her to take pleasure in this surprising upspurt of jealousy, though he believed he might do so later on.

"Because if you are, there's no point in us going on seeing each other. I know plenty of other men," she added childishly, and he was touched.

"Of course you do. I never knew why you spent so much time with me, anyway."

"I'm *not* going to dinner with the Welfords. And you needn't see me home, I'm all right by myself."

She ran a few paces ahead of him, and marched along the lamplit pavement at high speed. She was only twenty-two.

Jo felt old, far too old for tantrums. He had begun to quicken his own step: now he slowed down, and soon lost sight of her.

But as it happened, the tube train was delayed, so he found himself on the platform at her side. He gripped her elbow.

"Now listen, I'm sorry I haven't mentioned Alison. I promise you it's all over now, but it did leave a sore spot."

"It's a question of trusting."

"It's also a question," he said wearily, "of wanting to know everything about someone." He thought of Browning: "Where the apple reddens, never pry." Was he about to lose this rather tentative Eden? "It's impossible, as you'll find out later on. We've all got little cells with shutters on them, which are far better left to moth and rust. You wouldn't really want me probing into your every thought, and you know it."

"So I'm probing, is that it?"

The train came in. They sat together in the brutal light.

"I didn't say so."

"You meant it. I can't bear being with you any longer, if you're going to pretend that I probe. I can't bear to be despised, by you or anyone else."

"Next time you take to your heels and run," said Jo, humor returning, "you should make a point of catching some unfamiliar vehicle. That would put me off the scent."

"There will be no next time."

"Yes, there will, when we have dinner with the Welfords."

She gave an unexpected giggle. He took her hand and squeezed it.

Before he had even considered what he should say next, the words came. "Are we going to get married, sometime?"

She turned to him, her eyes filled with tears. There was nobody else near them, so he kissed her.

356

She said, "I don't know. Are we?"

Bonnet over the windmill, Bessie forgotten.

"I'd like it. I don't know whether you would."

"Jo, I—"

"Yes?"

"I'm damned if I'll say it first."

He told her he loved her: had she ever doubted it? (The very faint doubt was left for himself. Yet he felt happy, invigorated.)

"I love you," she said, savoring the words as if they were the first trimph in a foreign tongue.

"When shall it be?"

But now, she told him she would have to finish her course: they would have to wait for another year.

"I suppose it will take me about that time to"—he sought for a phrase, found a magniloquent one—"settle my affairs."

So it was arranged, in the tube train rattling under the earth, in the brutal light, in the stale smells of twenty-four hours, of smoke, of human exhalation, human sweat. It began to seem to Jo paradisal.

Chapter Four

KIT WAS TRYING TO CLEAR UP. THE DUST AND MUDDLE OF THE FLAT, which the daily woman had tried in vain to keep under control, was made more squalid by the dashing Allan Ramsay which occupied half a wall: the only painting Polly had kept after her father's death. She had sold all the rest. Though they had, for a long time, been quite well-off, and his own earnings steadily increasing, she had never been able to escape the fear of a reversion to penury. Anxious Polly: he knew that now. It was the last thing he had ever expected her to be. He had married her for those qualities that had made him love her: not only her Kate Greenaway prettiness, but her devotion, her comforting sternness when the need for it arose, her imperturbability. He had not wanted anxious people about him, so had never admitted, in her, the anxiety she kept so little below the surface.

Jo's engagement, for some reason Kit could not comprehend, had stimulated him to do what should have been done long ago: to clear the cupboards of Polly's clothes, to go through her desk and throw out whatever he did not want to keep. It was a horrible task, and as he went about it, he tried to keep his thoughts

358

neutral. He wished for a moment that he had asked Alison to help him.

She and Piers were living now in a flat on Cheyne Walk below Beaufort Street, precisely overlooking where the houseboat had been. He was not surprised that they had not asked him there: he had seen them once or twice, but always, on some excuse, they had taken him out to dinner.

He envisaged the newly habited boats rocking on the tide, that must now be filled with the sapphires, the sequined gold, of the evening. The eternal river would be serene.

He thought he could bear to look down upon it now.

Lips tightly shut, he went about his business, stopping now and then for a drink: not too much of it, though. He needed a clear head. He never allowed to the forefront of his mind the thought that Polly's death had in one sense, though one only, been a relief: now he could not only drink what he pleased, but had a good reason for doing so. Not since she died had any of his friends made the slightest attempt to restrain him, though he had seen respectful nervousness, more than once, upon their faces.

Underclothes clean and neatly folded, stockings in separate plastic bags, one bag for odd ones. Shoes on a rack; dresses, skirts, jumpers, on hangers. What to do with them all? Give the daily some, find out from Alison where to send the rest. In the desk, a file of receipted bills, a few letters, none important. Then, sticking up from the back of a drawer, a sheet of paper, roughly scribbled.

"I am so scared, I am terrified, I am sick with fright. Why can't he see it? Does he do it purposely? I never knew Father frightened in his whole life, so why should I be? The shame, shame, shame. If I write it down, it may go away. I AM SCARED, I, POLLY, AM SCARED. I am a disgrace to myself and to everyone. What's wrong with me? I hate my face in the glass. I, POLLY, AM YELLOW. Now isn't that better? No, no, no, no, no, it's not, not yet—" There was nothing else in the drawer but a box of matches, half-open. Had she been interrupted in an attempt to exorcise her fears by burning, as once she had exorcised Ruth's nightmares? He remembered her sitting by the little girl's bed, patiently eliciting details of the dream. She had then taken a small piece of paper and made a précis of it, reading the child what she had written. With a show of ritual, she

359

produced ashtray and matches, and, while Ruth watched wide-eyed, burned the paper to ashes. "Now," she said confidently, *"you will never have that dream again."* Invariably, this had worked.

Kit tore the writing up, put the scraps in an ashtray and set fire to them. If he read it again, he would remember. But even so, he sat for a long time at the little desk trying to make his mind a blank, but crying just the same.

Chapter Five

BESSIE RECEIVED HER PROSPECTIVE DAUGHTER-IN-LAW WITH AN AW-
ful stateliness which, Jo knew, boded no good.

She could be lofty when she pleased, but this blend of lofti-
ness and embattled welcome was something he had not seen before. Nor had Mildred, who went about grinning with face half-
averted.

"Well, my dear," said Bessie, having made Davina pull a
chair so close that their knees almost touched, and breathing
cachous at her, "if you are going to be Jo's wife, you will want to
know his little foibles."

"I've grasped some of them, I think," Davina murmured,
making Mildred grin again. "It would be better if I knew yours,
so I didn't drop bricks or make you dislike me. I—"

"Dislike you?" Bessie's small eyes widened, and her submerged nose quivered at the tip. "I'm sure I'd never dislike any
choice made by a son of mine. And I think he will tell you that I
am a very foibleless old woman, all said and done."

Jo, embarrassed, made play with strengthening the splayed
leg of a tindery coffee table.

361

"Well, I think I'm easy-going," Davina said, "so I hope we shall get on."

She was pleasant to Bessie and respectful: but not overly so, as even Alison would once have been. Girls, thought Jo, were changing.

"Of course, you're a very young thing and you may find him set in his ways. He's very much a man for his family and I hope he always will be."

"With a bit of luck, I hope to give him one of his own."

"One what, dear?" The note was one of bewilderment.

"Family."

"Oh, come, come, what early days for that!"

Jo could not repress the run of hot pleasure which travelled into his loins. He would like to be a father, had always wished to be. But he somehow felt that Davina was not being exactly delicate.

Meanwhile, she shone her splendid eyes at Bessie, gaze unwavering. "I don't know. I like the idea of growing up with my children."

"I wish I didn't feel it was all so strange," Bessie said, "talking about families. Call me a silly old fool if you like, but even Jo still seems a baby to me."

"Well, he's not," said Mildred, setting the gross, inevitable tea upon the table, "and what's more, Mother, the idea has only this moment occurred to you."

"You are *both* babies to me."

"Funny sort of baby I am, God help us."

"It's only the way mothers do feel."

"I don't think I'd want mine to go on being babies after they weren't any longer," Davina mused.

Bessie said she must forgive her for saying it, but experience taught one quite a lot of things. She added quizzically, "All those years of study wasted!"

"Oh, but they won't be. Anyway, I can always go back to my work later on."

"So you say, so you say. But the ties get stronger. Stronger, you know, not weaker. Time passes, and then suddenly one's too old to think of anything but one's Own."

"Mother, don't be a death's-head at the feast, Davina can't even conceive old age, nobody can, at twenty-three."

Bessie spread helpless hands, and the quizzicality became even more pronounced. "That's the way they treat me! Big brutes! Well, Davina, I can see I shall have to count on you to defend me."

It seemed half a century ago since Alison had been badgered into consuming the kind of meal Davina was being badgered about now.

"Don't be silly about your figure. Have some of this nice sultana bread."

Mildred gave a sigh of exasperation. "Mother, none of them eat these days. Didn't you know? They're a new breed of female."

"Well, I think we were all far happier when we didn't talk about slimming all the time but ate sensible meals."

Afterwards, Bessie sent them off for the traditional walk in the garden.

"I'm much afraid," said Davina, "that your mother can't stand me. Still, I tell myself it would be the same with anyone you brought home."

Jo replied, without much conviction, that Bessie had obviously taken to her at first sight. "It's just that you don't know her idiom." They were out of sight of the windows, so he kissed her. "I love you very much. You're far too good for me."

"We shall be good for each other."

"Do you think this house is awfully ugly?"

She said quickly, no: why did he ask her that? He told her how Kit had once, abruptly, made the fact plain.

"Very rude of him. All the houses are alike, anyway, miles of them, right along the edge of the common."

"Not your house, though."

"No." Then she said there might be another flat vacant in hers, in the New Year: it was on the ground floor, and darker than her father's, but the rooms were big. "Would you like me to speak to the owners about it?"

"Speaking could do no harm, I suppose."

She upbraided him for sounding so doubtful. They would have to live somewhere, wouldn't they? And some of the flats had long tail-ends of leases attached, so that the rents could not be raised. "Besides, you'll be near your mother. She'll like that. It will comfort her for the wrench of parting from you."

Jo said recklessly that he didn't give a damn for the wrench. His mother had had him to herself for thirty-four long years.

"Still, she's not young any more."

"Nor am I."

She looked at him intently. "Don't say that. Don't you dare."

"I've got six grey hairs, I'm always getting fagged out, and I've done nothing with my life. Kit and Alison really went away from me long ago, though they don't know it. They've been successful."

She stroked his cheek. "You're being silly. Anyway, I don't mind her going away from you."

"That old thing?"

They had dined at the Welfords. Alison and Davina had seemed to get on well together, though the former, heavy with pregnancy, had been in no lively mood. She had harked back to Churchill's Fulton speech, which had frightened her: was it all to begin again, with a new enemy?

"Yes, that old thing. Don't you like me to be jealous of you?"

He smiled. "I find it so hard to credit that anyone could be. Yes, I do like it, rather."

Mildred came out to them. "Come and have some sherry. Mother's in a celebrant mood now."

" 'What can't be cured—?' " Davina suggested.

"Nonsense. You're completely gathered in, ere the winter storms begin. You and I are going to get on all right." Indeed, she was looking at the girl with more than common approval, and her eyes, as she turned to Jo, were conspiratorial.

Bessie celebrant was rather worse than Bessie stately. She was all too obviously putting a good face on things.

"Well, dear, we've all got to come to terms with changes, haven't we? I've quite braced myself, now I've met you. And I daresay you'll spare my boy to me now and again, won't you? I've had my little weep, and now I'm cheerful again. Besides, I've still got my baby girl."

Mildred begged her not to be idiotic. Small, square, without light, she refilled the glasses. Since Hansen's death, the fleeting comeliness, or near-comeliness, had deserted her. She was a middle-aged woman, set in her ways: ways that she did not love.

364

"You see?" Bessie cried. "That's all the respect I get from them!"

As Jo walked back with Davina to her flat, he was surprised to hear her speak frankly.

"I shall get on with Mildred, but I don't think I can bear it if your mother doesn't stop that possessive stuff. It wouldn't be so bad if it was real, but it isn't—quite. It's a sort of game she plays with you because she knows she can get you on the raw. She's delighted that we can't marry before I'm through my finals: she's buying time. Anything might happen between now and then, mightn't it? Well, it won't. I'm going to marry you if it's the last thing I do."

They had come to the summer pond, to the sugar-loaf island, its gilded leaves rattling on the light wind.

"Before your time," Jo said, his hand on her shoulder, "they used to let the children splash about naked. It was an idyllic sight in its own way. Now they have to wear drawers."

"You didn't answer what I said."

"You didn't ask a question."

"No, I made a statement. Jo, this afternoon has worried me a bit. You won't let them fence you in?"

"Certainly not."

"Promise me."

"I do promise." He thought with longing of the two of them, in a house of their own, interested in nothing but each other. His thoughts consumed the months, as a lawn-mower consumes the long grass. The months sprayed up like chopped chives, bright and green.

"I'm damned if I can imagine," Clement said to his wife, "what that girl really wants with Jo. Time is gumming him up, and he looks like it. She's an attractive piece, too."

"Older-man syndrome," Georgina replied, "if that's the word. And Jo is still something, God knows why. I always thought so, in my less regenerate days."

"Her father's going to do nicely for himself, so I'm told by those in the know. Minor ministry at the end of this government, with any luck. And she's marrying into that terrible family, Oedipal ma, tragic sister, Niobe, all tears. Though to be honest,

I've never seen Mildred when her eyes weren't as dry as two bits of tailor's chalk."

He threw a ball to the little boy, who caught it felicitously. "What do you think of that? We'll be seeing him at Lords one day!"

Georgina was smiling inwardly over something Clement would never be told. That afternoon, taking Paul to buy clothes at Daniel Neal's in Kensington High Street, she had run straight into his father. He had greeted her floridly, had given only a brief glance to the son he would never know about. A silly man, as she had always thought. She felt no emotional or visceral stir, only a secret amusement.

In the January of the following year Davina, who had chosen Georgina, out of all Jo's friends, to be her own, broke in upon her, wild, and in tears.

"He says he can't marry me. He says he's ill, but he refuses to tell me what's wrong."

"Wait till I get Paul to bed, and then we'll sort it all out." Georgina was firm. She settled Davina with a drink and cigarettes, and told her to pull herself together: but when she returned Davina was still crying, her eyes and nose swollen, a sodden handkerchief gripped in her hand.

"I refuse to talk to you till you've quietened down. There is probably something very silly behind all this, but we've got to root it out. You don't suppose there's anyone else?"

Davina gave her nose a great blow. No, she didn't suppose that: it would be too unlike him. But he had been getting more and more morose, less inclined to take her out in the evenings, and had at last, under her pressure, gone to see a doctor. "Oh Christ, what is it? He's got to tell me!"

"Certainly he has," Georgina said astringently, "or you'll only think it's syphilis."

"I have thought that!"

"Nonsense. Not Jo. You go and tell him you expect it's leprosy and propose to buy him a bell."

"How you can laugh—"

"Someone, it seems to me, has got to. Look here, this must be a passing thing. Can't you just sit it out?"

On a blurt of tears: "I'd taken the flat!"

"And you'll both be in it, snug as bugs in a rug."

Georgina, still with her old glow but plump enough now to be described by the malicious as stout, sat relaxed on the sofa.

"Is Clement in?"

"No, he's in Ireland. So you can talk on, or cry on, as you please, without fear of interruption."

"You two are so happy. It makes things worse."

"Well, we weren't, once upon a time, far from it. So cheer up."

Davina said, more calmly now, that if Jo would not marry her she did not know how she was to go on. She would go on, of course: but how? Her father had never cared for the match, though he had loyally concealed this, making Jo feel welcome as a son-in-law. But she herself could think of no other man, not now, not ever. "Yet," she said, in a burst of anger, "what is there to him? A dull job, a dull future, a bloody family."

"Oh, he has something," Georgina answered, "though I've never found out quite what. I never felt my urges extending to Kit—and believe me, that's something—but in the dark ages, when I was not the respectable girl you see before you now, a roll in the hay with Jo would have suited my book. So you're by no means unique."

She paused.

"Now, listen. He has got to tell you what he *thinks* is wrong with him. If you can't get it out of him, then I shall set Alison on to the job."

"I don't want Alison interfering."

"Do stop being a jealous half-wit! She never gave a damn for Jo in that way: if she had, he'd have been settled in life by now and you wouldn't have had a look-in. He's no longer carrying a torch for her—my thirties' phrases, you must forgive them—and he never will again: but he does listen to her."

"The repository of human wisdom," Davina said bitterly, for the moment forgetting her terrors about Jo in resentment of Alison.

"That isn't much to be, if you're nothing else. What she and Piers have become is just plain smug. So you've no need to worry. Damn it, she's only just had Christian!"

Alison's second son had been born the previous autumn.

Davina wrung her hands. "Georgina, he isn't going to marry me, I know it. He's as hard as nails about that."

"Maybe so, but you're going to want to know why, and mind you get it out of him. We really can't have whispers and half-sighs, not in this day and age. You try a frontal attack."

"I have tried."

"Then try again, damn it! It's no good you sitting there like Alice in the pool of tears. Jo has got some bee in his bonnet, and we've got to de-sting it."

Paul, in pyjamas, came amiably in. "Mummy, you forgot to give me my glass of water." He stared at Davina. "You look funny."

"I've got a bad cold."

"Oh, damn your water! Go back to bed at once, and I'll bring it you."

"You want the orange aspirin," Paul said concernedly, "the child's aspirin. It's very good."

He went out again, Georgina following.

Davina thought, there will be no children for Jo and me.

She met him next night and found him obdurate. "It's just that I don't appear to be a very good life. I shall never marry anyone, it wouldn't be fair."

"For Christ's sake tell me what's the matter, or I shall think—"

"It's not venereal," said Jo, with the nearest thing to a sneer that she had ever seen upon his face. "Furthermore, I expect to live quite a long time. But I can't marry."

"You don't love me."

"I do. That's what makes it so hard. You go away and find someone else. I'm too old for you anyway and far too tired."

"Let's live together," she said desperately, "just do that!"

"This from you?" His voice was tender, remote.

"From me."

"No. That would be no use."

She sank to the floor, looked up at him once, then laid her head on his knees.

He would never see such eyes again. Yet was she a very marriageable girl? He wondered, even in that moment, whether this had begun to count for her.

"We'll see each other still," she said.

So it went on, through the bitter winter, with fuel restrictions and the fires burning to a glimmer, snow like the tracks of

368

giant snails over the iron common, and into the doubtful spring.

It was not until the spring that he broke the news to Bessie and Mildred, both of them naturally suspicious, since they had seen so little of Davina, that they were not to be married.

The real cry of horror came from Bessie. "Why not? What are you talking about?"

She had, with immense difficulty, adjusted to the situation. Re-adjustment, however much to her advantage, would be hard and painful.

"It just wouldn't work for us."

"Well," said Mildred, "is that happy news for you both, or for Davy, or for you? Good God, you had an escape-hatch and you seem to have slammed it shut. Serve you right."

"Don't question me," Jo said, and watched his razor profile on the wall as he had watched it one night long ago. He felt the strain in his swivelling eyes. "Things have gone wrong. That's all I need to tell you."

He was in bed that night, falling into sleep, when Mildred came to him. He pushed at her with his hand, as if feeling repulsion.

"No, you don't," she said. "You've got to tell me what all this is about. I swear I'll keep it from Mother."

"There's nothing to tell. I just don't want to get married."

She talked to him gently. She realized, she said, that she had been poor company for him or for anyone else since her return home, and that he and she had drifted away from each other. She was going to try to mend that. They had once got on together, hadn't they? Confidence had always been a relief for them both. She knew he was unhappy and she wanted to help him.

"I'm not unhappy. Leave me in peace."

"It's only a few weeks since you were over the moon about Davina."

"Well, now I'm not. I can't face the idea of marrying, and that's that!"

He jumped out of bed, his face so angry that she retreated, as if in fear that he would hit her.

"Isn't there one room in this bloody house where I can be private? Get out of here, Millie, because I won't stand it!"

Courage returned to her. She stood four-square, her back

against the wall. "Don't you glare at me like that. I'll have the truth about you if I have to stay all night."

With a sudden movement he seized her, turned her about, opened the door and thrust her into the passage. Since the door had no key, he wedged his chest-of-drawers against it. He listened. Frightened that her mother would awaken, she did not cry out, though he could hear her heavy breathing.

After a while she turned, and went away.

They ceased to question him. He saw nothing of Davina, would not open her letters. Soon, it was as though she had never existed, nothing left of her for him but a long ache, a nightmare sadness.

PART SEVEN

The Children

Chapter One

ALISON'S LUCK: IN MAY, A DAY AS WARM AS MIGHT HAVE BEEN EX-
pected in midsummer: the chestnut candles waxy in rose and
white against a sky of postcard-blue, leaf-shadows spattering gold,
dry turf, springy, hot to the hand.

She had gathered them together in Richmond Park for a
picnic to celebrate James's brilliant closed scholarship to Oxford: he was over seventeen now, had been for nearly five years a
scholar at Winchester.

A clever boy, James, taller than his parents, mysteriously wil-
lowy: not so handsome as they had supposed he would be, but attractive and graceful; brilliant eyes, Piers's eyes, seeing all things.
Very courteous, too: the manners of the heart. She did not think
she had taught them to him. Her second son, Christian, ten and a
half, knees drawn up as he lay on his back, eyes closed against the
dazzle of leaves, would be more beautiful, not so clever. But a
contemplative child, with ideas of his own.

They sat round the white cloth, spread with plates of chick-
en, ham, pâtés, bottles of champagne (frozen strawberries and
Coca-Cola for the children) ; nearly all her old friends, like her-

self, middle-aged. Only Kit and Davina were missing. Even after all these years, she had not cared to ask them.

Strewn like flowers, she thought, middle-aged flowers: but we are that.

She looked first at the other children, Lucy Victoria Nesbitt, aged twelve, in white dress with scarlet polka dots, hitching herself onto a paling to gaze over it at the red deer: Paul Maclaren, nearly sixteen, square-rigged, overly mature, sending a glance of appraisal at Lucy. Then she looked at the women of her own generation.

Only she had kept her figure. Georgina was definitely stout, but buoyant with it, spreading pink skirts over the carriage-rug, a glaze of content (so far as one could see) overlying pink cheeks. Fay, though she had thickened round the waist, still wore the girlish pony-tail of golden hair, and it suited her. The lines around her eyes and mouth, and at the corners of her bird-like nose, were fine-hatched.

The men. Jo, almost grey, lean, his skin greyish, still attractive. The sharp features would not change, nor the clarity of the light-green eyes. Clement, a sizeable bulge over his tightly belted trousers, hair now much paler with the white admixture, but flopping like a boy's over his coarse and pleasing features. Charles Nesbitt, quiet as usual, greying as elegantly about the ears as if a make-up expert had been to work on him: no eyes for anyone but his wife. A nonentity, but not for her. Piers? She could not see him as perhaps he must appear to others. His body was trim, alert. She thought of the bliss it gave her.

Georgina, blandly smiling, a weather-eye on Paul, thought of other things. A few months ago Clement, aged only forty-seven, had begun to fail her demands upon him. One night, after a week containing two disasters he had been unable to conceal, he had said: "Old girl, I'm sorry for you, but I'm through. Early, I know. But I can't stand this sort of thing repeatedly, and don't pretend you don't understand. It's too much of a strain on me. But you— what will you do?"

"Oh," she had replied, deliberately letting her eyes stray, like a contented mother, in the direction of her son, who was in the next room, playing a game called L'Attaque against himself, "I shall simply think of something else."

Forty-three, and her sexual life at an end. Well, it was fun

374

while it lasted. Memory took her back to charming orchestras, the hypnotic shine of ballroom floors, the amorous breath of men upon her cheek, the smell of their washed and amorous bodies.

"Anyway," she had added, "I like being with you. Wild oats all gone. Gone away-way."

She had steeled herself: she would not betray him.

Fay wore grey Swiss cotton, and was no longer lady-like but like a lady. She had grown to Charles, was completely of his world. Only the glorious tail of hair gave her away: it was this that her husband admired, and would not let her change.

Jo could view her now without emotion. The progress of his illness had been arrested, and he felt as well as he had done for some years. His life was becalmed, only a few boats upon it: among the sails, he could see Alison's—faintly—and Davina's, even paler. Since Davina, in a passion of desire for consolation, had sought out Kit, and Kit had married her, she hardly seemed real at all. Jo was content enough with his humdrum life at home—what was the matter with it, anyway? At least it was quiet. He had been shaken only once, when his firm, to mark the completion of his twenty-year service, had presented him formally with a bed-side clock in leather case, tooled and gilded.

Kit had taken him twice on tours of the U.S.A., requiring him to act as male-nurse and policeman. Davina he would not take, insisting that he was fonder of her when they had something of a life apart. In fact, he did not like her to see him when the alcoholic fugues were overwhelming. Jo felt like a travelled person baffled by inability to see anything at all: he had spent his whole time in America sobering Kit up, or extracting him from engagements likely to prove ruinous. The country was for him no more than a green and brown relief map seen from the air.

Alison watched him, as he talked idly to Clement and Nesbitt. Piers and Fay were chatting like old friends, with an old warmth between them pleasant to them both, but never likely to flare up again.

As a child Alison had painted splashy water-colors, always too wet, and had dried them out on sheets of green blotting paper which, when she saw their like today, rushed her back in time. The dresses of the women were like blobs on that familiar paper: her blue, Georgina's pink, Fay's delicate, ruffled grey.

Lucy came running across to her. A neo-Victorian child, she wore her hair in a long, thick fair plait, with a scarlet bow at the end of it. "I'm hungry!"

James came behind Alison, affectionately ran his hand down the nape of her neck. "Hasn't it occurred to you that we all are? It must be nearly one o'clock. You forget I'm a growing boy."

"You can't have much further to grow," Piers called across to him, "so don't give your mother such a nice line in pathos."

She called them all to the meal. Fay put a frilled pinafore over Lucy's dress.

"Oh, Mummy, I don't want it!"

"When you're less of a messy eater you needn't have it. Perhaps that will be very soon now. Anyway, you want to enjoy all these nice things, don't you, and not have to worry?"

They drank to James's success, and he responded gracefully, adding, "But we must drink to Christian, too."

"Why?" his brother asked, "What have I done? You know I'm a dope."

"No, you're not. We'll drink to what you're going to do."

They drank to Alison, also, as founder of the feast.

Afterwards all the children, except James, went into the trees to play some war-game invented by Christian, who was ingenious in such matters.

"Oh dear," Fay sighed, "all of us so old!"

"You're a death's-head at the feast," Alison retorted. "You all look wonderful, and if anyone is old, I am."

James said, "Don't be so woeful, Mother. I never think of you as any age at all."

Clement said he did not know whether that was a compliment or not.

"It is," Georgina replied, "and I wish Paul would take the same attitude towards me. Only the other day I caught him scowling at me covertly because he thought my new dress was kittenish."

"I didn't feel old till the day they gave me a clock," Jo brooded. He had been scooping up some fallen blossom into a little heap of white and brown fluff.

"A *clock?*" Fay exclaimed.

"For all my years of service. There was an office party, with a formal presentation. Photograph of me, too, receiving gift with humble and grateful smirk. Thank God it wasn't a watch and chain."

"When did I begin to feel old?" Georgina, clasping her hands behind her head, gazed up into the kaleidoscope of sun and leaves. "Last year, I think, after Suez and Hungary. I couldn't get the wind up over the first, or worry about the other, awful though it was."

"I did," said Clement, "I worried like stink. Morally, in both cases. But no, I didn't expect a war."

Piers said that once the decision to seize the canal had been taken, wrong though he believed it was, it should have been carried through.

They protested loudly.

"I dislike being told what to do by John Foster Dulles. I know Alison doesn't agree. She thinks the wrong can occasionally be right."

"Kit doesn't grow old," said Georgina, "only fat. He is like a stout cherub. Not that I have any right to criticize excessive *embonpoint*."

"Davina's good for him." Jo tried to ease any underlying tensions by speaking her name first. "Polly only looked calm, but Davy really is. And she never interferes with him, just shrugs her shoulders."

"Don't you think someone ought to interfere with him?" Alison demanded.

"Nobody can," said Jo, "at least, not if he notices it. And he always does. Belphoebe tried, and you know he stands in awe of her: but his only response—marked—was to stay away from her for a couple of months. She understood all right."

James, not much interested by all this, lay comfortably back on the grass. He had many reasons to be happy, and one of them was secret. Two years ago he had gone through a difficult emotional period, unable to prevent himself from being attracted by other boys. He never translated this into action and indeed was loud in disapproval of those who did. But there had been a dark, flirtatious, long-lashed boy called Kinglake who had haunted his dreams in the uncomfortable hour before sleep. Too sensible not to realize that this was no uncommon phase in the development of most youths, he had nevertheless been deeply troubled, dreading what Alison might say if she knew. Then, at the Eton-

Winchester match, he had met a girl, the sister of one of his friends, and had known at once that it would be girls for him, for the rest of his life. Kinglake's sly tartishness seemed, these days, to be merely ridiculous, and he had to fight against his own intolerance. He would have liked to kick the object of his former passion, whom he now realized to be a seducer of the most persistent order. But fighting intolerance was much better than fighting the horrible suspicion that his nature might have gone astray. Meanwhile there was the joyful thought of Penelope, whose photograph he kept in his breast-pocket.

(Since he was careless in leaving it there, and since his clothes had to be examined before being sent to the cleaners, Alison knew of it and had heaved a sigh of relief. But of this he was not aware.)

Oddly enough, the subject had been discussed by his parents only the previous night.

"You don't know how relieved I am!" she had exclaimed, when she told Piers about the girl. "I don't mind confessing it now, but I was terrified when he was always casting lubricious glances at that terrible little boy."

Piers only laughed. "For a sophisticated writer, you really can behave like an ass! Jim is all male. At his age, I was still mooning over a boy called Ashbourne who, by the way, gave me not the slightest provocation, which makes me far inferior to Jim. I have never had the slightest worry in that direction over our son."

"What saved you from that distressful state?" she had asked, sounding affected, because he had for the moment embarrassed her.

"A girl, of course, plain and not at all virtuous. It was a blessed revelation."

Now, as Alison neatly packed up the remains of the meal, she looked across the field to where Paul was pursuing Lucy with loud cries of warfare that had an undertone of something else. She fancied he was one of those rare children who did not pass at all through the homosexual phase.

Georgina followed her glance, and laughed aloud. "Yes, she is far too young for him. But he's like that. He looks at women's legs in the tube. Don't worry," she added to Fay, "your daughter is perfectly safe from him. But in three years she won't be, and she knows that already, bless her."

Paul came back to them, flushed, pretending he had had enough of playing games with children. "I won't say," he added, "that Lucy hasn't a nice turn of speed."

"I had a nice turn of speed once," said Georgina innocently.

James rolled over, and began to ask Paul about Westminster.

"Have you got your futures mapped out?" Nesbitt asked the boys.

"Not me," said Paul, still pretending breathlessness. "I'm not a flyer. I shall probably go into public relations, or something sinister like that."

"After university," James replied, "I hope to do a bit of donning. I shall devote all my time to someone even dimmer than Manilius, if I can dredge one up. Can you beat poor old Housman, working on somebody he didn't even like?"

"Well, he was a poet," said Alison, "and may have felt that to work on anyone good might have affected his style. When I'm writing, I never read the great influentials, only detective stories."

Lucy and Christian emerged from the wood, faces gilded with sweat. They demanded something to drink.

"This is like heaven," James said, thinking of Penelope. To his mother he added, "Thank you. It's a great success."

"You thank your Maker. We might have had a downpour." But she was very pleased.

The magic of the afternoon was such, the charming weather, the children in flower, that even Jo felt entranced, his home a long way off, never, perhaps, to be revisited. Anyway, he could scarcely imagine such a thing.

"Dear Jo," said Alison, "they may present you with clocks, but you are still very personable. Are you aware of it?"

"I am very personable," Clement remarked, "but nobody comments on the fact. Perhaps it is all too self-evident."

Georgina prodded his stomach. "I know what is."

Nesbitt smiled at his wife. "Do you find them all a bit morbid?"

She said no, but that the past always was, and Alison had resurrected it.

"Poor Polly Perkins," Clement murmured, "wish you were here."

Fay said, "Don't."

"Why not? This is so nice, I want to pretend she's sharing it."

"So do I," said Alison, "but Clem—please—not ghosts."

The afternoon softened into sunset. Dreaming, James watched the colors change in the sky, deepen first, then pale under a wash of rose.

When his mother asked him to help her pack the picnic litter into the car, he jumped up like a gluey-eyed soldier to the sound of a bugle. They walked away, burdened, together.

"I don't want it to be over yet."

"It won't," she said. "They're all coming back to us for dinner, and the young ones can sit up all night, if they please. Do you think I'd plan a day especially for you, and then chop it off at six p.m.?"

He put his arm around her shoulders, flattering her by his height. "What do we eat?"

"You wait and see."

They drove off in cavalcade, Alison and Piers with the boys in her car, the others with their parents.

When the evening was over and they had all gone, Lucy sleeping on Fay's shoulder, Alison was elated by her triumph. Ten people, on a beautiful afternoon, had been happy.

"It was a good day?"

"A wonderful day," said James.

"Not too much like an Old Girls' get-together?"

"They aren't old girls," said Piers, "and neither are you. Do you realize it's past midnight?"

"I suppose it's got to stop," James said, "if we've already started a new morning."

Chapter Two

BOBBY PRICE, NOW LIVING IN MOSCOW AS CORRESPONDENT FOR A Communist paper in London, had not forgotten old acquaintances. He arranged for Kit to visit the U.S.S.R., and alerted all writers and teachers of English who would be interested in him.

Jo watched, with misgivings, the preparations for departure. "I want to meet Mamonov," Kit said feverishly, eyes glittering in the lights strung around the bar, "he's a great man. If Bobby's right, and they're holding roubles for me, I can get down to the Don."

"I wish you were taking Davina."

"Damn it, she hasn't been asked, and I can't raise enough sterling here to take her. Besides—"

"Oh, I know 'besides,' " said Jo.

Kit smiled, then dropped his lashes, like a shy girl.

He came back three weeks later, disturbed, excited, much the worse for wear, and telephoned Jo. "Come and see us. I'll tell you all about it."

Alison was quite wrong in thinking that it would be embarrassing for Jo and Davina to meet. He was used to the marriage, used to their ménage: and if he felt an outsider, that was precisely what he would have wished to feel.

"They sold scads of my Spain novel, seventy-five thousand copies, and when I went to see my publishers, they brought me in a bulky, badly tied brown paper parcel full of roubles. Good God, I felt like Ali Baba in the cave—of course, they're pretty big notes. Then I had to count the lot, or pretend to, and then Innokenti— I'll come to him later—took me down in a cab to the bank, where I had to count them again, and a very old lady cashier counted them twice more. I felt ghastly embarrassed, because there was an enormous queue behind us and I was holding everyone up. I talked to some huge type behind me in a taxi-driver's hat, and said I was sorry, and he said something that sounded pleasant. I asked Innokenti what, and he translated: 'Money has to be counted.' "

Kit was lying on the couch, looking white and tired.

"Half of all this will keep for another time," Davina warned him. Her manner towards her husband was concerned, yet detached: she might have been a paid nurse with a high sense of vocation.

"Innokenti's my interpreter, he always will be. He's a wonderful fellow, a big blond with a beautiful flat face, and small eyes like aquamarines. He's about twenty-four. He even gets my jokes over—I know that because people laugh. Oh—I never got to see Mamonov, he had flu. But I will, one day."

Jo asked what Moscow was like.

"The Kremlin's beautiful, in a sugar-candy, Hansel and Gretellish sort of way. The rest isn't so much ugly as dull, but all the lilacs were out, and there's so much green space. And it has the most peculiar smell everywhere—I don't know whether it's petrol or disinfectant. One hates it at first, and then one wants to bottle it to bring home. But Russia—so much is broken, so much is destroyed. If I ever take you, Jo, don't talk about our war, because they think it was piddle compared with theirs. It's maddening, but they're right."

"Were people restrained? Afraid?"

Kit was more than commonly slow in replying. "Yes, no. Probably not. The fact is, I don't know. I only got into a couple of *dachas*. The music's so loud in restaurants, one never really hears what anyone is saying. Perhaps one isn't supposed to. It's only fair

382

to say that people told me how much better things had got since Stalin's time."

Davina crossed her legs suddenly then switched them again, as if she had lost patience. Jo knew a flight back in time to a jolting train, the harsh light beating down on them both. How could he feel so remote from her now? But he did.

Kit added, "Private talk isn't entirely easy. I was always squirming deliberately in its direction, and usually getting found out before I got there. They do read, though: if they've read you at all, it's with inconceivable thoroughness. I got very vain, I tell you."

Davina rose and went out. When she returned she was carrying a tray with milk, scrambled eggs and stewed apples.

Kit said: "Christ, no."

"Yes. You haven't eaten all day."

"I'll be sick."

"Perhaps you will be. But that must come afterwards."

As if exhausted, he lay back and permitted her to feed him, sip by sip, spoonful by spoonful. To Jo, for a terrifying second, it looked like punishment, something out of the arcana of the nursery, that shameful second womb where all comfort is and all humiliation, of which no one, grown up, ever speaks. The second passed. He saw Kit seize onto the plate of fruit himself, pour cream on it in a great white dollop and eat greedily.

"Better?" she asked.

He nodded gratefully, and when she had pushed the tray aside, took her kind face between his hands and kissed it.

"I was frightened there sometimes," he said to Jo. "One asked for people one wanted to see, but they were often somewhere else, everyone vague about where. Then, damn it, some of them simply turned up, as right as rain. But it's a haunting place. Much more Dostoievsky than you think." He smelled the air like a dog: as if he could still detect the petrol fumes and lilac of the great streets.

When Jo left, Davina saw him downstairs to the door. "Don't worry too much about him," she said. "Of course he had a terrible jag in Russia, but I can get him over that."

"Listen, you ought to try harder about his drinking."

"And if I do," she said, "he will hate me. He quite likes me now, but I've never been Polly, you know."

"You're content with that?"

"Oh yes. I married in haste but I haven't repented at leisure. He makes life exciting."

"I couldn't have done that for you." For the first time he referred to their old love-affair.

She said nothing for a moment, then: "What was the matter with you? Because you're all right now?"

"Yes. But I got the wind up about something."

"Tell me."

"No."

"I've forgiven you for everything else but that."

"Ten years," he said, "it's a long time."

"You simply got tired of me." She did not speak with animus, even with reproach, but as if stating a fact.

"No. But don't question me, Davy." He kissed her. "Do what you can for him."

"If I could have given him a child, I'd be in a stronger position. But I seem to be no good at that, though I go on trying."

He noticed something he had missed: when kissing her, the hair from the mole had not flicked with its tiny wire at his cheek. Catching the direction of his glance she laughed.

"Kit cut it off."

Kit would.

All the same, Jo returned home in a mood even to him inexplicably jaunty. Did he really want more than what he now had out of life? The seasons passed in pleasant evenness: there was always some girl around, when the flesh was hungry. He was loved, housed, fed—and better fed, these days, since Mildred had begun to take a genuine interest in the subject. It was a hobby for her, and a source of agreeable surprise for him. Whether the house was ugly or not, he had ceased to care. It was the place he lived in, fitting him as comfortably as an old shoe. The sight of Alison still fretted him: but he was no more in love with her than with Davina. And he had abandoned his green-stick ambitions long ago, shutting them in a drawer with the untidy manuscript of his rejected novel. As for his health, it looked as if it were unlikely to worsen, as if the remissions were now becoming of longer duration. He hoarded his energies carefully, and it seemed to him that they were even accruing.

In place of Alison's photograph, he had hung a print of John

Donne, the Lothian portrait. A face to which the gallant poetry belonged—"She is all states, and all princes, I." Sometimes he thought that face a little like his own: but no, his own nose was sharper and not so long, his mouth was thin, and his eyes pale. Still, still . . . Jo found much solace in literature.

His mother was even now able to walk a little, with the aid of the aluminum dock. She hardly knew a day's illness: the rounded face was full of color, the peak of nose, between the two ruddy bays, sharp as a rosebud. When her arthritis was not paining her, her spirits were high, and Mildred's had risen a little to match them. By no means so bad a household to live in, whatever outsiders might think. And he was still in touch with his friends. He felt that to them he had become a sort of father-confessor—no bad role, all said and done. Behind his grille, he heard their interesting secrets.

One day, in the spring of the following year, Georgina telephoned him. Clement was away and she needed to talk. "You're a wise man. The point being that you are a man. Alison wouldn't understand this."

In the quiet of her flat, she brooded over a rather affected, dreamy-looking photograph of her son.

"When Paul is through school, I'm going to get him married off, somehow."

Jo suggested this would be a little early.

"No. I love him, but I'm not blind to the fact that in one respect he's abnormal. That boy is a young ram. I've had to hush up two scandals already—or rather, I've managed to abort them without Clem knowing."

"Not a bad abnormality as things go," Jo said uneasily.

"Not when it gets to Paul's pitch. If you knew how I've wished he'd contented himself for the past two years with a crush on the Captain of Games! Now I've almost stopped seeing Fay, whom I quite like, because I feel Lucy's not altogether safe with him. Jo, I mean that. Have you ever come across anything like it?"

He asked, diffidently, whether she supposed the boy had had any sex experience.

"Ordinary sex? Good God, no. What chance would he have? My view is that he'll be better when he does. But he's not seventeen yet, and in the meantime . . . ." Her voice trailed away. "A very peculiar complaint, coming from me. Jo, it sounds awful to say it, but there are times when I'm sure that, for want of anything better, he even finds *me* attractive. I've seen him appraising me with that lop-sided smile of his, and it makes me squirm."

Father-confessor or not, this was quite outside of Jo's experience. He said, however, "Can't he finish his education in France? He'd probably find a crowd in Paris where all that was no more than the accepted thing."

"You mean, and Mummy would know nothing about it."

"Partly, yes. Damn it, he'll soon be too old for you to worry about, anyway. Give him a year, and what earthly business will it be of yours?"

"I don't think," Georgina said, "that you really know what I'm talking about. Is there such a thing as infant satyriasis?"

He made a movement of distaste.

"Oh yes, you may flinch. Do you seriously suppose *I* don't?"

"A psychologist," he murmured, not hopefully.

"As if he'd see one! As if I could tell him why I'd like him to! Besides, I don't want Clem to realize, ever."

He wondered, looking at her as she lay like a Rubens woman, pink, soft and satiny, on the sofa, whether she was transferring her own sexuality to the child, and it made him wish he were somewhere else. "You're only guessing."

"Oh, am I? We've got a girl of twenty who does a bit of charring for us in the afternoons. During the last holidays, she came to me and complained about him. I paid her off handsomely, and told her to find another job. That's my young son, if you please."

She spoke so bitterly that he felt he had to do something of a practical nature. Should he take Paul out, one weekend? Was there any chance he might be able to talk to him?

She seemed to clutch at this straw: but in the event, it proved useless. Jo took the boy to tea and to a cinema, and afterwards they walked in the park. Paul was quiet, demure, almost exaggeratedly well-mannered. When Jo, in desperation, attempted to edge him into a man-to-man conversation, he shied like Daphne pursued by Apollo, and his neck reddened.

Jo comforted himself by recalling that the fears of devoted mothers were almost invariably ill-founded. He had been touched by Georgina's fear, battened down, but evident none the less, that

Clement should learn anything ill of the boy he had so flamboy-antly shouldered as his son; she was afraid whom he might blame. Jo was relieved when his advice was taken and Paul was des-patched for a year to the Sorbonne.

A less worrying companion was James Welford who, in Lon-don after his first term at Oxford, sought him out apparently spon-taneously, though Jo guessed the idea had been Alison's. He knew she was perpetually sorry for him. He took the young man to din-ner in Chelsea and was pleased with what he saw. Since their last meeting in Richmond Park, the latter had undergone one of those peculiar changes of resemblance, in this case from father to mother, which are more common with boys than with girls. Jo saw Alison in the bright, attentive face: he could even fancy a broken vein in one of the clear grey eyes. This was her directness, and, he fancied, there might be much here of her fighting spirit, if occa-sion for it arose. But James seemed to take life easily.

He was interested in contemporary writers, especially in Kit.

"Is he really so good, or is it all done on personality? I never know. I read his books and I'm fascinated, but next day there's only the glitter left. Do you suppose that's because I live in Lucky Jim days, and don't really understand his?"

"I think he's damned good. But then, ours was a different world."

"I might have enjoyed yours," James said, "when it wasn't horrible, which I imagine it must have been, most of the time."

"It wasn't all horrible." Jo smiled at successive flashes of memory, passing with the speed of a lighted express train by night.

"At least you knew where you were."

"Don't you know where you are?"

The boy hesitated. "Not really. Everything's so uncertain. And in some ways, so dull."

Jo felt depressed. What hopes they had all had, in the nine-teen-thirties, for just such a world! A war won, unemployment and starvation (in his country, anyway) pretty well defeated, no marchers with sick and ruined faces straggling from the north in the drenching rain, no terror by night, no. . . . And the young looked at this fulfilment, and found it dull. He asked if James were worried by the Bomb, now written with a capital B.

"Of course, I suppose one is, but in an abstract sort of way."

He raised his glowing eyes. "I haven't yet started to believe in my death."

"One doesn't till one's in one's forties. Sometimes not even then. Have you any religious beliefs?"

"Oh yes, quite strong. It's odd, really: it may be a hangover from infant instruction and church-going, but somehow I don't think so. Mother doubts more than I do, and Father certainly. Kit's a believer, isn't he? He says he is."

Reply was not easy. Kit certainly thought himself a believer, but Jo imagined that his faith stemmed out of a kind of mystic aestheticism, a revelation of golden pavements and towers of pearl, the easily evoked shock of delight in the natural world, and as easily evoked a shock of delight at a manufactured vision beyond it. "He seems pretty sure."

James smiled at the dish of fruit and ice-cream set before him. Thoughtful he might be: but he had a boy's appetite. "I envy him having you, you know."

Jo was startled. "Why?"

"Oh—friendships which last like that. I don't make intimate ones very readily, I don't think I ever shall. But when I get round to falling in love seriously, I fancy that will be all right." This was spoken with the kind of confidence which makes a future seem quite certain.

"You envy me having Kit—"

"I didn't quite say that, you know. I put it round the other way."

"Well, I envy you your sureness."

"Am I so sure? I expect I just sound so."

"Any time you want another dull evening in a dull world with a dull man," Jo said on parting (he had enjoyed himself immensely) , "give me a ring."

"Mother said you were masochistic," the young man murmured, face sparkling and sly, "so I won't dispute anything you say. I'll simply call you again."

On his way home across the starry river, Jo realized that this was the first time he had been sought out by anyone so much younger than he, and he was greatly moved. He had little to give, though he wished it were much. He understood, and feared, the growing gulf between the generations, the young who regarded their elders not simply as people with more years upon their shoulders, but as if they were creatures of quite a different species. He had felt the division, even among the workers in his own firm, and it had chilled him. But James Welford, clever, gentle, assured, appeared to be untouched by it. Not once that evening had he made Jo feel an animal different from himself.

He stood above the stream as it poured beneath the bridge. If the bridge had stood for the war, should the water have been blue on one side, yellow upon the other? He felt that Alison's son would have the power to heal time, first to suture the fragments, then watch them knit together, strong, as if the wound had never been.

Chapter Three

"KIT!" JAMES WAS CALLING TO HIS BROTHER.

"That's not his name," Alison cried, on a note of high irritation. "Call him Chris if you must, but not that."

"Why not?"

"Too many Kits around the world. It makes for confusion."

Piers, hearing this exchange, was worried, not by its tenor but by the strain in his wife's voice. She had been edgy lately, doing things uncharacteristic of her: and he knew the reason. It was the reappearance in their lives of Tim MacHaffie.

He was working in London now, for a travel agency, and had looked them up. They had asked him in several times for drinks, twice for dinner. At forty-six, he was as lithe and boyish as ever, good-humored, warm, amusing. But after his last visit Alison had suddenly stated that she felt stifled, and needed a walk. At midnight, she had roamed the streets for over half an hour.

She was, Piers knew, at the beginning of an early menopause, and had been thrown out of kilter. He realized that her early and fleeting fancy for Tim had gone deeper than she knew: she was suffering now because she was afraid of falling in love.

Tim seemed to notice nothing of this. As charming, as impudent as ever, he continued the process of making himself into a family friend. Both the boys, Christian, in particular, liked him immensely.

"In my firm," he told Piers, "there is a grisly man called Dobson, a mass of decorations and *idées reçues,* who says he knows you."

"Oh Lord," Alison exclaimed, her face flushed and animated, "please don't give him the slightest idea that we should like to see him again!"

"He leaps before he looks. When he found out that I hadn't seen much of the war, he instantly assumed I was a conscientious objector and praised my moral courage."

"What did you say?" Piers inquired.

"Nothing. I accepted the tribute with nods and becks and wreathèd smiles."

Alison giggled.

In bed that night, it was a long time before she slept. Piers knew she was lying on her back, staring at the refracted rays from passing cars; they streamed across the ceiling from a gap between the curtains.

He spoke to her. Turning to him, she embraced him hotly, muttered something he could not hear. Her cheek felt damp, whether from sweat or tears he could not tell.

In the following week the Nesbitts and Maclarens came to dinner, and Tim also. As usual, he was the last to leave, savoring the after-party gossip over the final whiskey, sitting on the hearth-rug, long legs athletically crossed.

Immediately he had gone Alison said, "The smoke in here is awful. The place smells like a tap-room. I must get a breath of air, just for twenty minutes."

"Darling, it's getting on for one!"

"I won't be long."

As soon as she had left the house, Piers followed her. He found her leaning on the parapet of the Embankment, opposite Rossetti's house, chin in her hand, cigarette glowing in the half-darkness.

When he spoke to her, she jumped violently. "What do you think you're doing? Spying on me?"

He nerved himself. The Alison of ten years ago would never have spoken like this.

"Well?" The shock had made her tremble. "Did you think I'd crept out to *meet somebody?*"

He put his hand on hers. "Quiet. Just for a little while." Below, in the murky water, a fish plopped. "You'd think the oil would poison them, wouldn't you?" He added, as he felt her growing calmer, her pulse-rate lessen, "No, I didn't. But my darling, I am not going to be a *mari complaisant.*"

"I don't know what you mean."

"I mean to deal with this in good time."

"God, God, God. You know I love you. There's never really been anyone else for me, not since Kit. But—"

"Tim troubles you."

"Don't touch me, I'm ashamed enough already."

"No reason why you should be."

"It's all mad!" she cried, so loudly that a passing policeman stopped for a second before continuing on the rest of his echoing round. "Piers, I don't want it to be like this. It will pass, I know it will. But yes, he does trouble me, and I feel sick with it, so I have to walk it off. Or to fantasticate it. That's worse."

"I do not for a moment believe," he said, struggling to regain his control over her, "that you have the faintest intention of divorcing me and going to Tim."

"The children—"

"Oh, not because of them. It might be rough on Christian for a bit, but Jim can ride anything. Leave them out of your calculations."

"For Christ's sake, I have no calculations! Please stop. You're making me feel disgusting."

She made as if to break away from him, but he held her arm.

"Try not to feel anything of the kind. This is, if you'll forgive something which sounds insulting, something to do with your time of life."

In the weaving lamplight, he perceived a faint smile.

"I'm not at all afraid of you leaving me. You're going through a difficult patch and Tim isn't helping, though I must add, chivalrously, that he seems quite unaware what he's doing."

"I know that."

"All the same, my girl, he's got to go."

"Yes," she said, "yes. But it will be difficult—"

"Not very. Just invitations lessening, degree by degree."

"He'll be hurt—"

"I'm afraid I'm far more concerned for myself than for him."

"He's so nice—"

"I agree. But there are many more homes where the Mac-Haffies of the world are welcomed with open arms, so I think he can dispense with mine."

"He's perfectly innocent. It's only me."

"This is an extraordinary conversation between husband and wife in the middle of the night. Innocent? Well, not entirely. He has great sexual charm, and he can't help enjoying it. He sees you look at him, as I have seen it."

She said then that she could bear no more. "Give me back just a little self-respect and let's go home."

"There's no reason why you shouldn't respect yourself. This will pass, and damned quickly, too. Listen, love." Another fish jumped. "I told you, when I went abroad, that there were going to be no women, that I was going to keep our marriage good. Well, there weren't. But do you seriously imagine I was never attracted by a girl, now and then?"

She said she supposed he had been, but her voice now held a note of retrospective jealousy, and he was glad of it.

"Certainly I was. But if I found the idea of one single girl beginning to grow like a mushroom in a damp cellar, I upped and went. Tim must up and go. By the by, when you want bed again, let me know. I'm not going to trouble you now."

In two months, she had returned to him completely.

Christian, in the summer holidays, complained, "We hardly ever see Tim these days. I like him."

She said, not even feeling a sense of betrayal, "He's the sort who comes and goes. I like him, too, but he gets tired of people."

James, more perceptive and abnormally forthcoming, spoke to his father. "I miss Tim more than somewhat, but I think you were right."

Piers was startled. "What on earth do you mean?"

"I imagine you put him out. He was obviously drooling over Mother."

"Well," Piers lied, "she wasn't over him. And your mama is a very attractive woman."

393

"Even I, in my raw youth, can see that. Do you suppose I shall go by the book, and seek her image in every girl I bring home?"

"Jim, you have something of a cheek."

"I'm only joking." (He was still young enough to need to explain himself.) "No, when she grows up I shall probably cast a lecherous eye on Lucy Victoria, though she'll have to be a lot less stuffy. All the same, the Tims can be rather disruptive influences."

"I often wish I were," said Piers, "it must be a glorious thing to be."

Paul Maclaren was in trouble, though not in trouble so severe that Paris could not conceal it. Overly sexed, mature in appearance, he had performed a feat that Georgina, in what she called her "unregenerate days," might have greeted with high amusement and a degree of pride. He had impregnated two girls who had discovered their plight within a month of each other.

But Paul was wily. One girl presented no problem. The daughter of a rich family, who would have done anything to save her from disaster, she had gone at once to her parents, confessing all, but naming no names. They had despatched her to an expensive nursing home in Neuilly, and no child was born. Liliane, however, appeared to pose some difficulties. For one thing, she was a practicing Catholic, and abortion seemed to her abominable. To Paul she swore fervently that the child should be the outward and visible sign of their love: with it they would out-front the world.

He had been studying her carefully, believed she was rather sickly. He could not marry her at once, he said, since he was too young: but when the baby was born they would both look after it, and marry as soon as possible. He drew charming pictures of a little *atelier* all their own, up among the stars, a beaming concierge who would be a friend to them both. Meanwhile, he assured her that exercise was the best possible thing, and took her on an energetic hiking holiday in the Dordogne. At three and a half months she lost the child (though he had to pay out Georgina's money for nursing purposes) and all was well. He went back to England, announcing that France had done all it could for him, and settled into Cambridge to study Modern Languages.

Good wombs have borne bad sons.

At thirteen and a half, Lucy Nesbitt was a radiantly pretty little girl and rather stupid, spending her holidays watching television or walking around the house clutching a transistor radio.

"Well," said Charles cheerfully, "I was never an intellectual myself, Fay, and though you're extremely smart in your fashion, I shouldn't call you one. Indeed, I'd never have married an intellectual. A horrible thought."

Lucy went to a girls' boarding school in Sussex, where lessons were dutifully given, but horses were of paramount importance. Bird-like face, flashing grey eyes, golden tail of hair bouncing on her back, she took her fences beautifully: she would have a future, her riding-mistress thought, in show-jumping.

"Expensive," said Charles.

It was a morning of bright-blue sky and white frost. Along the banks of the Isis the trees sparkled as under a weight of blossom, not a twig untufted.

James Welford, in his first year at Oxford, was in love. Her name was Dorothy Ford. She was a small, brown-haired girl, with large brown eyes in a triangular face; a freshman at Somerville who meant to be an actress, and was likely to succeed. She looked school-girlish in her thick navy coat and hood of white wool. "I wish you'd grow up a little," said James, "I'm always expecting to be arrested for taking a minor from the parental roof."

"Oh, isn't it beautiful! Look at the ice under the banks, like blue glass."

"And cold."

"I never feel the cold." But she jumped up and down several times, clinging to his arm. They walked back into the town for coffee. It was a morning of bells; a car went by on the way to a wedding, white ribbons twittering in the breeze.

"For us, one of these days," James said, pointing through the window.

"I hope so," she said solemnly, "but it seems a long time to wait."

"We shall enjoy ourselves while we're waiting, and all of it will be wonderful."

"If I have a career, will you mind? I do feel—though it sounds pompous to say so—what's called 'dedicated.' "

"I shan't mind at all," he replied, "and I shan't be jealous of all the people you act with. If you do marry me, you'll be sure of yourself by then. But you must take time off to give me heirs."

She smiled. "How many?"

"We'll cross that bridge when we come to it."

She blew on the pane, and watched her breath congeal in a silvery blot. "I don't think you'd have to be jealous of me. I fancy I'm going to be one of those actresses who love the work and somehow don't like the life. I'm not stage-struck at all in that sense." She mocked him: "But how did you learn to trust so, and you so young?"

"From my father, I think. I'm sure he was jealous of my mother sometimes, but he never showed it."

"Had he cause to be?"

James was thoughtful. "No. But she often attracted people."

"I don't wonder. I think I'm going to be scared of her, though. She's famous, too."

"She's well-known. Not more than that, she would never say so herself. But nobody's ever scared of her." He really believed this, having had no experience of the quelling eye Alison could turn upon an offender when she chose. He took Dorothy's small hands, the nails still childishly bitten, in his long ones. "Say something lovely for the day."

"People will stare."

"There's no one near us."

She considered, then spoke in her soft, clear voice, naturally high, but flexible within her wishes:

> "Some say that ever 'gainst that season comes
> Wherein our Saviour's birth is celebrated,
> The bird of dawning singeth all night long:
> And then, they say, no spirit can walk abroad:
> The nights are wholesome; then no planets strike,
> No fairy takes, nor witch hath power to charm,
> So hallow'd and so gracious is the time."

He regarded her in the calm of adoration, raised her hands, kissed them. "We shan't forget this morning."

A flurry of frost came down like white chestnut fluff from a tree, blueness flashed from the wind-screens of passing cars. From yet another spire, bells rang out.

" 'So hallow'd and so gracious is the time,' " she repeated, her eyes searching his face as if she were asking some question.

James, understanding, answered it. "I am pretty sure this is going to last."

It is impossible to lose touch forever with the Dobsons of this life.

He appeared suddenly to Kit who was sitting, remote, drunk, surly, in a corner of the Lord Nelson, a pub he did not usually frequent. Dobson was now very stout and quite grey: but the thick glasses had gone, and in their place were contact lenses, very visible when he looked sideways.

"If it isn't Mallings! What a lot of water has flown under the bridges! Mind if I sit down?"

"Yes," said Kit.

The other took this for permission. "Well, well, well! Tell me all the news. I hear you got married again."

"So it's said."

Dobson blinked, took out one of the lenses, polished it, and replaced it beneath a stretched and blood-shot lid. "I'm sorry about your loss."

"My loss," said Kit, "nobody else's. And I don't talk about it."

"Forgive me. Anyway, may I congratulate you on your success? Now, I did say you were going to find your own style, didn't I?"

"I don't remember much of what you said."

"How's your friend Upjohn, who always used to pull my leg? Married too, by this time, I suppose."

"No."

"I'm not, either. Just an old bachelor. Too many flowers in the field, I suppose."

He fetched more pints of beer.

"I say, Mallings, who do you think works with me? Chap called MacHaffie, great friend of the Welfords."

"I've met him."

Dobson removed the other lens.

"Christ, no," said Kit, "I can't bear it!"

Dobson's reply was mild: they were difficult, at first, to get used to, one needed to rest the eyes from time to time.

"Yes," he went on, "Tim MacHaffie. Seems very much taken with Alison, as he calls her."

"It's her name."

Dobson gave a sudden, swift glance round the room, then lowered his head conspiratorially. "Look, a word to the wise. You're an old friend of hers. What I say is, Mallings, if a word out of place can save trouble in the long run, it's got to be said."

"I don't know what you're talking about. You're tiring me."

"Now, don't you start pulling my leg, too. Listen: if she were my wife, I'd be grateful for a word in my ear—"

"Words, words, words, what are you talking about?"

"You know them well. Quite well enough, if you felt like it, to drop a word—"

"I shall scream."

"—to Welford, just for safety's sake. I wouldn't have Mac-Haffie around my house, if I had a wife who was still very pretty—"

Light dawned upon Kit, and the fuzziness of drink fell away from him. He was furiously angry.

"Dobson, if you don't take that mug and clear away from me, you're going to get it right in your bloody contact lenses!"

Dobson backed in his chair, which skidded and squeaked. "You know I never meant—"

"You've never meant any of your bleeding interference or your crapulous advice or your slug-like condescension, have you? Don't you dare meddle with any friends of mine! If Piers had one of your little words dropped into his military ear, he'd kick you down six flights of stairs, with a refresher at every landing. Get out of here!"

Dobson began to bluster. Neither of them were boys: they were middle-aged men—"Speak for yourself, you fat ponce!"—who ought to face up to things. Not to speak of something that might do harm, because the speaker was afraid of giving offense—"You have given it!"—was mere cowardice. He was not imputing anything to Mrs. Welford, only that he regarded MacHaffie as a dangerous type.

398

"I know MacHaffie, and if I gave you away to him, he'd kick you downstairs too. Now will you clear out?"

Dobson rose with dignity. After this, he said, he felt there could be no more friendship between them. He regretted this deeply: it all seemed so unnecessary. Honesty had always been his policy, at no matter what cost to himself, and—

Kit rose.

Dobson fled, forgetting his beer, which Kit drank.

Chapter Four

KIT WALKED DOWN THE COVERED WALK OF ALBANY, WHERE BEL-
phoebe now had chambers. Sparrows flitted among the penum-
brous laurels, gauzed by London dirt. It was a cloudy day.

He had not seen her for over a year, since she had been living
in Pembrokeshire, but she had written to him often: long, affectionate, arrogant letters, rich with incident heightened by her
comic fancy.

He found her in her usual chair, a grass-green rug over the
knees of her golden dress, and asked her how she was.

" 'Old, old, Master Shallow.' But that's in the natural order of
things."

Yes, she was old, and so frail that the light seemed to shine
through her, making an X-ray of her skull. Her hands, lying on
the arms of the chair, might have been lengthened through the
years by the weight of rings upon them.

"I see that our friend Mr. Baynes," she continued, as if no
time had elapsed between their last meeting and this, "has turned
to ornithology and is making quite a reputation in that field.

Could it be because of flagging success in another one? Oh dear, what fun I had with him, and how angry he used to make me! It all seems so silly now."

"You are high above the plateau on which the Bayneses of this world can touch you. You look down on them from the golden bar of heaven."

She praised him, that he was still an accomplished courtier. "But, my dear boy, you are getting very plump. Can it be good for your health?"

"Probably not. It's the beer wot does it."

She called out, "Jeanie! We have some beer for Mr. Mallings, have we not?"

"We certainly have," said the secretary, putting her head in at the door. "Only we've been waiting for him so long that it may have gone flat."

"Flat or ebullient," said Kit, "it's all the same to me. I have lost my palate."

"How is Davina?"

He said she was well, that she took care of him like a mother, that she was the kindest girl he had ever known.

"It doesn't," said Belphoebe, "sound altogether exciting."

"I think neither of us expected that. But we're happy together."

"Make *her* happy. She deserves it. You can have no real idea whether she is or not. You are very self-sufficient, dear Kit."

"Aren't you?"

"Certainly I am. But then, I have no responsibility for anyone else. Tell me, why is today's poetry so low-toned? One is never offered a color lighter than pewter. And it is so hard to remember. Luckily Mr. Baynes does not write poetry, or things would be so much the worse."

He sipped slowly at the beer Jeanie brought him. Belphoebe drank gin and lime-juice.

"You have had a hard time, my poor Kit," she said. "You remember it, so I mustn't pretend that I don't. But you have had the success I hoped for you. Is it dust and ashes?"

"Not really. I enjoy it, and Davy enjoys it for my sake."

"Everyone does things for your sake, don't they? Even I do."

"Are you scolding me, Belphoebe?"

"I don't really know," she smiled, and her eyes, light as the bed of a stream in sunlight, danced. "Do you remember how I made you wash your hands?"

"Do I not! And here I am, tamed like a hooded falcon, using pumice stone on my fingers and a scrubbing-brush on my nails whenever I come to see you."

"Kit," she said earnestly, "when you are an old man, or even an elderly one, be a little grandiose. Rebuke the young, stand no nonsense in your imperial presence. It is a great shield, the assumption of grandiosity. You'll be astonished how many people will really come to believe in it. Only have fun behind the scenes, love the people you do love very much indeed, and let just a few of them see you as you really are. There is not the slightest need to be kind to your enemies: only Our Lord could postulate that and get away with it, and anyway, look what happened to Him. But treat your friends as delicately as egg-shell china, and be kind to them always." She added, "I am very tired."

Taking this for dismissal, but startled by it, he rose.

"No, I didn't mean that. I do tire easily, of course. I am an old woman. But I feel a cosmic tiredness, and sometimes it weighs me down. Come and see me again, very soon."

Jeanie saw him to the door. She whispered, "She's far from well. Don't leave things too long."

A month later Belphoebe was found dead in the day-bed, her hands folded on the green rug. The rings shone like flowers on some idyllic bank of springtime one dreamed about but never before beheld. Her face was not like that of a woman, but of a Plantagenet king cut in yellowed marble. Kit sent an enormous wreath of golden broom; he had scoured London to find a florist who would make it. It blazed and sprayed like a bonfire upon her coffin.

On Wednesday evenings, Davina went to work at the local Labour Party. Kit spent the time by himself, or sometimes dropped in upon the Welfords. He was there on the night James brought Dorothy for inspection.

Kit liked the look of her, small, trim, obviously nervous but courageously keeping up her end of the conversation. It amused him to see how friendly and easy Alison was to her, yet, whenever the girl looked away, how watchful. Piers was not watchful at all, but as pleasant to Dorothy as he would have been to anyone else. If James were nervous, he gave not the slightest sign of it.

402

"I'd like to see you act," Alison said. "When shall we get the chance?"

"I'm playing Rosalind with the O.U.D.S. next June. I should love you to come, if you won't be bored."

"Certainly we'll come, won't we, Piers?"

"The only thing that puzzles me, Dorothy," he said, "is where you're going to find a midget Celia. For a woman you aren't really 'more than common tall,' are you?"

"Well, I've got a very slightly smaller Celia: but it seems to me that I'd do best to turn the whole thing into a joke." When she spoke of her acting, nervousness left her. She explained to them earnestly just how she would speak the lines. "Luckily, Orlando's rather small, too. It would really help me if we had a midget cast, but I'm afraid that's past praying for."

"She's going to be remarkably good," James said, confidently, as if passing critical prophecy on someone he did not personally know.

"If I ever thought I should be as good in my line as Mr. Mallings is in his, I'd be over the moon." Dorothy said to Kit, "I do love your books, but I don't at all know how to talk to you about them. It would seem impudent."

Kit told her that an expression of love was quite enough. "When anyone does talk to me about my writing, I always find myself squirming, saying Ooh, how nice, or Come, come, it's really too *much!*" He transformed himself into an amateur reciter congratulated after the garden fête, and she laughed aloud.

"Yes," he said, "I've always thought I wouldn't have been so bad in your line, either."

He knew he was relaxing the atmosphere for them all. Alison never permitted herself to be possessive of James: yet even she was going to feel that only the best was good enough for him—was Dorothy the best?

When the boy and girl had gone off together, Kit said, "She's a delight. Count yourself lucky, Allie, and pray that it lasts."

"He's so young to be serious. Do you think he is?"

"I think," said Piers, "that he's deadly serious. You know what an octopus grip he keeps on anything he's made up his mind to. On the whole, my verdict is the same as Kit's."

Alison said she would be scared if Dorothy really did become an actress. The life would part her from Jim, she would always be in contact with other men, professional charmers at that.

Kit said that James, as a charmer himself even if non-professional, would not be beaten easily.

"Theatrical marriages always go on the rocks." Alison frowned. "Anyway, the idea of them marrying is implausible really, I suppose. It will be so long before they can."

Piers said she must not deceive herself. Did she remember when Jim was a small child, how he had wanted so little, had been so abnormally undemanding, yet when he had set his heart on something would persist in his grave, dogged courtesy until he got it? "That is how he is going to be about little Dorothy."

"Alison," Kit said, "you are the only person refusing to accept this. I didn't expect silver-cord stuff from you. You should be ashamed of yourself."

"No, no, I do like her! I could love her easily. But I did want him to range about a bit before he thought of settling down—"

"Range around, making you anxious by coming up with all sort of unsuitable types? I can't see much fun for you in that."

He thought how pretty Alison was still, how youthful, and for a moment something old, which was deeper than admiration, stirred in him, like a bird in a thicket. "You'll never think anyone's quite good enough for him," he teased her.

"No," she retorted, "and no mother worth her salt would ever think anything so cold-blooded."

Kit felt a touch of depression. Once upon a time, they had all talked about themselves: now they talked of their children, and he had none. How old would Ruth have been, had she lived? Nearly twenty. And how beautiful! That would have been inevitable. At five, the lovely bones of her face had promised beauty. He wanted to talk now about himself. He felt, at this moment, frustration because he hardly knew how to introduce the subject.

Of his work and hers, he and Alison rarely spoke together. Her outward preoccupations were domestic: but she was writing well enough to suggest that her inner ones were otherwise.

Piers said he had to go out for half an hour, and Kit at once offered to leave.

"Don't," said Alison. "Stay and talk to me."

It was, curiously enough, the first time they had been alone together (for more than ten minutes) in over twenty-five years. He fought the inner knowledge that it was more. He knew a desire to establish an intimacy undeserved. Sitting with his back to the window—Polly's boat and his had been below it—he wondered where to start.

It was she who began it. She said, "Kit, I often feel—perhaps absurdly—that I am 'getting on in years,' as they say. I want you to know that, though we had our troubles—good God, again, 'as they say!'—I can't really remember much about them. I want us to be friends without the thought that there was anything between us."

"Oh, but there was, Clytemnestra," said Kit, "and I don't forget all that easily. You were the first most important thing in my life."

"Well, now I'm no longer of any importance to you, and nor are you to me."

"What a brute you can be!"

"You saw that quite early, and that's why you came to hate me."

"Hate?"

"Oh, I choose my words, as you do yours. But the break had to come, and you were remorseless, and I was an ass, so it all evens out."

"You think that, over one solitary evening, I still feel guilt?"

"I think you have done. But there's no need. I love you, Kit, and I always will, but in a remote fashion that wouldn't please you at all."

"Still a bitch."

"I hope so. I should hate to go soft, like a rotten apple."

"All right. I behaved to you abominably. Is that what you want, an admission?"

She was walking restlessly up and down, the movement only below her spare hips. "No. No admissions. I only want you to know that *it's all right*. It always will be."

"You and I, and all the others?"

"All of us. How quick you are! We are a sort of blend, and we've strung our blending out over the years. If none of us ever meets again tomorrow, the past is smoothed out for us all like a well-tacked carpet. Wall to wall."

He thought of many things to say: that even through her choice of simile, the bitterness of the past had crept in: that her attempts to reconcile past and present had failed: that despite her obvious married happiness, the blood of youthful rejection was

405

pulsing like the clot of cells at the temples of a migraine sufferer. But he was wiser than that. He said, "All gone. All over. In a sense, you will be the first always. May I have another drink?"

Then she laughed, and the spell was broken—a good thing, for it had been an uncomfortable spell.

"Ought you to?"

"No. But I am set in my ways."

"Will you stay for supper? Piers will be in soon."

"Certainly I'll stay, if I'm not expected to eat too much."

Perhaps she had not altogether failed in what she had meant to do (i.e., give absolution), for they sat in peace while, above Chelsea reach, the twilight descended like an iron safety-curtain behind the four chimneys.

Kit said, "Don't ask me how I know. The answer would sound too ridiculous. But were you ever fond of Tim MacHaffie?"

She looked at him, with the derisive face of a fresh girl. Only the slackening of the cords in her neck betrayed her age. "Sporadically, yes. But it was only a fretting after something else."

"Do you know that he's going to be married?"

Her response was a simple one. "No. How splendid! Who to?"

The answer was of no importance. "You don't care?"

"Of course not. The best marriage has its bouts of silliness, especially if you're a long time alone, as I've been. Don't you know that?"

"Rhetoric," said Kit, "never moved me. By nature, I'm as monogamous as a swan."

He heard the old man crying, down the length of the stream, "Swan! Swan! Swan!"

He began—"Allie—"

"Why do you call me that? You know I hate it."

He thought about this. "Once upon a time, because I wanted to write you down a bit; I suppose I did so in order to salve a guilty conscience. Did you never realize how much in awe of you I was, and how envious? A little later, too, because I wanted to antagonize you, hoping you might show antagonism first. Now, I suppose, because I feel we are friends, and friends needn't be especially respectful to each other."

She nodded. "I accept that." Though she had her reservations. She could think of friendships that had been based on mutual respect, on the surface, almost courtly: beneath that surface, naked and deep.

He began again, without premeditation, "Allie, this may be the last time we're together."

At this, she flared up. What the hell did he mean? Strong drama. Why?

He spoke more slowly than usual. "I didn't mean it literally. But in a way, it's true."

He had intended to imply that they might never speak together in such intimacy, even though this was a difficult intimacy, with the sores of the past still raw between them.

She did not fail him. "Yes, it could be."

Released, he got up from his chair and put his hands upon her shoulders. "May I kiss you?"

"I'd like it."

For a second they kissed almost like lovers, warmth flowing, and love. "Dear Kit."

"Many thanks. Fierce, dear Alison."

Chapter Five

ONE EVENING, TOWARDS THE END OF THE YEAR, DAVINA TELEPHONED to Jo at the office.

"Can you meet me somewhere? I want to talk to you."

Her voice, normally as soft and talkative as a stream, sounded brittle.

"Of course."

"Kit's lecturing in Oxford. Would you like to come to the flat?"

When he arrived, he found her strung-up, news about to burst from her as steam from a boiler. She had lost what looks she had, only her eyes remarkable. If she and Kit had had a child, Jo thought, what incredible jewels it would have had in its head! She had always been lean and now, at thirty-five, she was scrawny. She managed to get through the preliminaries—the drink, the cigarette—smoothly enough, and to make forays into the kitchen to see that all was well with dinner. In fact, her news did not erupt till food was on the table.

"The Union of Soviet Writers has invited him over for next June. He wants you to go with him, and you must."

"Look," Jo said, "I'm too tired. I can guess what such a trip would be like. Anyway, he ought to take you."

"They invited us both. But I can't go. I don't want to."

She stared at him almost accusingly: accusations for the past and for the present. It was a miracle to him that he had ever wished to marry her. Gone, dead, flat. He was forty-seven, a man in advancing middle-age: Kit two years younger. But he could not resist, in his heart, making the debit of the six wasted years.

"You ought to. You never go with him anywhere."

"That's because I can't bear to watch him drinking. For God's sake, Jo, do you realize how bad it is?"

"Sporadic," he murmured.

"Not sporadic. Steady. And every night of my life, I could kill him. Oh, he tries to pretend: a couple of long ones, then nothing. But he sneaks to the bottle. Do you suppose I can't hear the floorboards cracking?"

Jo said she should go to Russia with Kit. She had never been on one of his foreign tours: it would be exciting for her: and if anyone could be of help she could.

"You don't understand. It is always worse on his trips, and I couldn't bear to watch him. But I would watch him, I couldn't stop myself, and that would make him worse. You're far better for him than I am."

"I don't think I could stand it. How long's he going for?"

"Three weeks. Two in Moscow and one on the Don, with his hero Mamonov. Can you begin to imagine what it will be like?"

Jo felt weariness in his skeleton, making him feel as if his spine, the bones of his legs, were made of soft plastic tubing. "Look, I don't think I could get leave."

She brushed this off. He could take his annual holiday then.

"I can't nurse-maid Kit again. It's not my job, Davy, it's yours. I won't take it on."

She put her face in her hands, so cutting off the chin that it looked like a fox's mask. Her eyes glowed and were steady. "You care for him, you always have. And he's only really cared for three people in his life, you and Polly and Ruth. When his father died last year, he didn't bat an eyelid."

"Damn it, don't you care for him?"

"Not all that much. It's faded away, most of it. But it's up to me to take care of him for other people. He's not only our prop-

409

erty, Jo. He's a famous man, though I find that hard to believe. And the best way I can look after him is to throw him back on you."

"You don't love Kit any longer?" Jo was stunned. He knew that Kit's love for her had long since turned into a sort of distrait kindliness: he could not believe that this had happened to her love also.

Now she did not answer so readily. After a while she said, "I don't know. Sometimes I believe I don't care. At other times I want to shout at him, to make him notice me; to tell him, damn it, I'm his wife! Oh, I don't suppose anyone who was ever involved with Kit cuts entirely free from him. I know I can't. Sometimes I wish I could. But, look—I didn't want to tell you this. I *can't* go to Russia with him."

Jo looked up at her sharply.

"We're going to have a baby. Oh, yes"—she stopped him, when he tried to speak—"it's silly at my age, isn't it? Not that I'm a hundred, but still. . . . And he doesn't even know yet. I was only sure this morning."

He was shocked into excitement, then into delight. "Davy, it's wonderful! It's going to mean so much to him."

"I wonder. But anyway, I shan't be taking any undue risks. So you'll go?"

"I suppose so."

"Good." She spoke briskly, as if she had settled a business deal. "Now get on with your dinner." Her face brightened and seemed younger. "There's one person who's pleased, the only one I've told before you. My father. He's in a sentimental lather about the baby, you could hear him over the phone, barely controlling his tears. He's thinking of dandling his grandson on his knee."

She spoke ironically, but her eyes had softened. She had always loved her father. "And if it's a boy, of course it will have to be Prime Minister when it grows up. Poor chap, what a long row he'll have to hoe!"

Another child, Jo thought, come into the circle that had grown up almost thirty years ago. How many of them were there? Alison's two boys, Fay's girl, Paul Maclaren. This one to come. (Also, a child who was dead.) Five in all. Not many. Not much to pass on to the future. If James married early, there might be the

410

first grandchild. Alison would like that, and be proud of her youthfulness. Grandchildren, good God! He felt a small run of chill along his spine.

Davina chattered on. Of course, if he turned into a writer, like Kit, nobody could touch him: or if he became (which was unlikely, considering the genes) a mathematician. But if he had no particular gift, her father would be prodding him steadily towards politics from the dawn of his understanding. "I think it must be a 'him.' Not a girl, I hope. She's unlikely to be a beauty, and that would make Kit hark back to Ruth all the time. I do have to live with his ghosts, you know."

Jo, returning home, spoke to Mildred and told her what he would have to do.

She snapped at him that it would be crazy.

"Well, Davina won't be able to."

"Then let him go by himself! You're always saying how fagged you are. Do you imagine you'll be able to stand up to Kit's antics?"

"He can't go alone."

"Oh, for Pete's sake, aren't you the perfect 'Charles, his friend?' "

"If that's the role I'm cast for, I suppose I have to play it. How's mother tonight?"

"All right. The vicar came in, and they had a marvellous hour of soppy comfort. She sat there inventing spiritual problems for herself, and he adored every happy moment. She'd better get her glasses changed, by the way, her sight isn't what it was. She says she can't thread a needle."

"At her age," said Jo, "I don't expect to be able to see a needle, even Cleopatra's, much less to thread one."

"Is that you?" Bessie called from the bedroom. She was doing now what she had not done for twenty-five years: she was waiting up for him. No, she could not sleep till he was safe at home. These awful road accidents, anything might happen.

He told her about Davina's pregnancy, at the idea of which she burst into silvery laughter.

"How silly of her! She must be nearly your age, like Sarah in the Bible."

"If you remember," Jo said patiently, "she was much younger than me. She's only in the middle thirties."

Bessie's peal grew more mellifluous. "Is that what she says she is? *Women!*"

"She's twelve years my junior. Puzzle that one out."

"Well, if you say so."

"Damn it, I do say so!"

"Don't swear, dear. It grates on me."

He did not tell her about the projected visit to Russia. Time enough for that.

He bent down to give her the usual quick goodnight kiss, but she locked her fingers at the back of his neck, forcing him to sit beside her on the bed.

"There, I didn't mean to be cross with you. But I don't suppose I have very much more time left, and when I'm sitting alone for hours I can't help brooding on it."

"Rubbish."

"What with my eyes going, and my hearing not what it used to be—"

"You can hear the grass growing, and you know it."

"You've missed so much, Jo. But I do like to think that wasn't my fault."

He reassured her, feeling a sudden warmth of pity for her age, her invalidism and now, for what had become a real physical ugliness. The two kittens (the old cats had died long ago) snuggled close into her side, as if loving her old, hot, sweetish smell. They were Siamese, giving to their surroundings an exotic touch. Curled up into each other, they looked like a bunch of white violets.

"I did want you to marry Davina," she said.

She released his neck and fell to picking at the pink woollen blanket. One finger caught in a strand, and the nail split: she bit it down to evenness. Bessie's hands: pink as the blanket, as the light, to Jo disembodied, moving objects that seemed to bloat and to shrivel, to bloat again: plump hands, but the skin wrinkled over the backs and the little blotches of mortification just beginning to show beneath the silk-screen of flesh. Her wedding-ring was sunken deep between two engorged cushions. He wondered if the constriction ever hurt her.

"Give me an emery-board, dear, there's one in the dressing-table drawer—no, the right one, not the left."

He watched her as she filed her nails.

412

"Yes, I wanted you to marry her. I wanted to see my grand-children. You weren't a very faithful gallant, were you?"

"Not very."

"Of course, it was Alison you liked best."

"Old history," said Jo. "I'm going to bed."

"Millie was a fool, she should never have married that man. I never liked him."

"Poor old Frank."

"Just dirty," said Bessie, luxuriant in her world-hating, "just a dirty old man. I always saw through him. But of course, she was so keen to get married, she'd have taken Crippen if he'd asked her."

"I'm tired. Goodnight."

"You never let me have those nice little chats I used to enjoy so much once. You know what it means to me, just family gossip with my son. Are you eating enough?"

"Why shouldn't I be?"

"You look peaky. You're not constipated, are you?"

He told her he was a man nearing fifty, and that the state of his bowels was his own affair.

She gave one of her rare Rabelaisian laughs. "Well, well, go to bed, if you must. I'm not going to have you thinking I'm an old bore, or not thinking so more than you do already. You take some syrup of figs, it always did the trick for you."

He went out into the kitchen, where Mildred was making some pastry for the next day.

"Kept you a long time," she said.

"Concern for my health. She's badgering me about syrup of figs."

"And discussing me, I expect. Wouldn't you think I'd have palled as a topic of conversation by this time? She was mulling my affairs over with Mrs. Thatcher yesterday. I could hear her through the open door. God, she wrings the last drop out of her darling daughter's humiliation! But I can't honestly bring myself to care."

Jo said he wished there might still be someone else for her. She laughed. What, at her age? She folded the pastry and rolled it for the third time, carefully pinching the edges together.

"Somebody lost a good cook," he said, to please her.

"On the contrary, somebody gained one. You."

She pushed the hair back from her tired face, flouring it as she did so. She was hardly grey at all. She muttered, "Me, with another man. Wonders would never cease." Then: "Anyway, I've reacted quite strongly against the lot of them, believe me."

Yet he knew that it was still in vestigial hope that she attended church socials, whist drives, musical evenings.

"Jo, you've had something out of life, haven't you?"

He answered cheerfully, "A hell of a lot, all said and done."

"No shortage of girls, anyway. You're a bit of an old stallion, always have been."

He grinned at her.

"But I'll never understand why you wouldn't marry Davy, and why you were so mysterious about it."

"I just couldn't face it, that's all. I was never really in love with her, I suppose."

"But Alison—" She stopped. "Damn it, I forgot to tell you! She telephoned earlier on. That boy of hers is getting married, and he's not twenty yet. Isn't it crazy?"

Jo said it was not unexpected. Already he had dreamed of Alison as a grandmother. But crazy? Perhaps, if it had been anyone else but James. He brought a difference to all things.

"You must bring that paragon to see us sometime," said Mildred, "you never have. If, of course, you think he could stand it. Good grief, Alison must be—what?"

"Forty-five. And looking ten years younger."

"Yes, she'd have been the one for you."

"Let the past," said Jo, "bury its dead."

Next week, he took James to dinner. The boy was proud and excited. "Yes, I know it sounds rather absurd. But look at it this way. I've got some money Dad settled on me, and Dotty has a little of her own. We're both steady enough to go through our university work to the end and be happy at the same time. You know how I always want things to *begin?* Anyway, I do. Neither of us wants to sleep together and be furtive. It is"—he smiled—"unseemly. Or so I think. And I rather think Mother does, despite a lot of brave progressive sentiments. I do love to see her keeping up with the times, despite the fact that she doesn't really like the look of them."

"I think we're going to be formal and drink champagne," said Jo.

414

James said simply, "It costs the earth."

"I've nothing much else to spend my money on."

They became festive: and James, not used to drinking very much, spoke his mind.

"Jo, I want to ask you something. Was mother ever in love with Kit?"

"Yes, long ago."

"I thought so. What happened?"

"Oh, they just drifted."

"I see. Actually, I don't like him much. I'm sorry—I know he means a lot to you."

"It was all over long before she and Piers met."

"You were in love with her," James said, twisting the stem of his glass and studying the whirling bubbles. "Weren't you?"

Jo replied promptly: "Certainly I was. And to an extent, I still am. But that is not to be repeated."

James's eyes widened. "I never repeat things. I am a model of discretion, as even Mother admits."

"So you'll understand why I have a certain interest in you."

The boy answered slyly, "I did wonder why you've always stuck so much of me. I say—"

"What?"

"Was the life really wild? Mother gives that impression."

Jo said it had seemed to them very wild indeed: some of them had been poor, all more or less unknown, and all of them wildly ambitious. They had needed to race through life at top-speed, since it was rushing by them at so terrifying a pace. "It was a matter of keeping up, keeping on the run, to get everything one could out of it all before the night came. I dare say your generation is as wild as ours, and probably going to be worse. I sometimes suspect that our orgies were of a pretty tepid order, now I look back. Mostly too much beer. Alison never cared about the pub round."

"I haven't much taste for being wild," James said, "though of course I could be, if it became necessary. But somehow, I feel there's a lot of time ahead, and that it's not rushing so very quickly. I don't feel I have to be its pacemaker."

"But you're marrying damned young, all the same."

"That's because I'm absolutely sure of myself, and as sure of Dotty as comes within the bounds of modesty. You like her, don't you?"

415

"I like her immensely."

"I'm very slightly tight," said James carefully, "so if you snub me for saying something that's none of my business, the drink will take the edge off it. Snub away, if you have to." He hesitated. "Mother told me you nearly married Davina Mallings, then suddenly pulled out."

"That's true."

"And refused to tell anyone why. Will you tell me?"

The agate eyes were steady. *Gravitas* sat on the young man and became him.

Jo said, to this surrogate son, "Yes, I will tell you. And you are going to tell nobody else on earth."

"I shall tell nobody else on earth."

PART EIGHT

Wormwood on the Steppes

Chapter One

"THE RUSSIAN LAND," KIT SAID IN DELIGHT. UNDERNEATH THEM miles of birch and pine spread featureless, except for the out-croppings of buildings, from the air like hen-coops, which were the farms.

Jo tried to interest himself, but felt desperately tired. The journey had seemed endless: and he knew that, to spur himself to the trial ahead, he had been drinking too much. Kit, like most alcoholics a poor drinker, was nevertheless showing far less signs than he of the whiskey consumed. They were on an English jet, and they were coming down.

He heard Kit bumbling under his breath, "Whirlwinds of Danger" (so long ago, the marches through London under the blowing banners, the angry faces and the bright!) and then, more appropriately, "The Song of the Red Cavalry."

They were asked to put out their cigarettes and fasten their seat-belts. In a few minutes they would be landing at Vnukovo Airport.

The plane rushed along the runway, gave a huge withdrawing roar, then began to trundle towards the long building. Kit

419

looked down, his face shining. "Reception committee. No—let the others get out first. We need to make an entrance."

So they were the last. Kit preceded Jo out of the cabin, and on the top step clasped his hands over his head like a boxer. Then he plunged down, to what seemed to Jo like a sea of faces. Without photographers, there were perhaps ten. But it looked like a crowd, each member of it bearing great bundles of drooping flowers from the *dacha* gardens. Hot and stuffy: humid: the smell of petrol and pines.

Kit yelled, "Innokenti!" He kissed the interpreter on both cheeks, hugged and swayed with him.

A tall man, in his middle thirties: flat Slavic face, uncommonly blue eyes with the whites baby-clear: butter-colored hair.

"Innokenti! I thought you wouldn't come."

"But of course. How strange of you. How could I be anywhere else?"

"This is Jo Upjohn, my great friend."

"You are very, very welcome."

Then there was the greeting from the old writer, Nemenov, broad and bear-like, and from the poet Versilov, whose presence was creating a stir all over the airport: this one, also a big man, wore a little flat cap and no necktie. Kit's publisher. A representative from the Gorki Institute. All very exciting.

The excitement, in fact, did much to clear Jo's head, though he looked nervously at the array of bottles set up in one of the lounges, awaiting them. They would have to wait for clearance.

"But not long!" Nemenov thundered, in his great, Chaliapin voice, "I will see to that." He strode off.

"He will now harangue them for forty minutes," said Versilov, his tiny eyes twinkling, "and keep us much longer than we should have been kept without his intervention."

Jo understood all this perfectly, and in his tired and fuddled way was surprised that he should. It was not until later that he realized how effective a first-class interpreter could be, Innokenti's voice—the man self-effacing—like a purling stream in his ear.

He found himself, as time lagged on, drinking again. Somehow he had to pull himself into a state of vivacity: this seemed the only way.

Yet, when they were all at last in their cavalcade of cars, he felt less vivacious than in an agreeable dream-state. He smelled the

420

curious odor Kit had described to him, unpleasant at first, yet he thought it would come to mean Moscow for him eventually. He saw the wooden houses, Tolstoyan houses, soon to be destroyed, flaunting their faded fretwork behind the hedges: the purple lilac was in full swag, sometimes triumphing with its scent over the petrol.

At last the city: roads of enormous width where there was small traffic, except for the thunder of the lorries. Everywhere, the skeletons of flats arising.

"We need," Innokenti said to him (he was sitting between Kit and Jo), "the country to come into the towns. But it is, you understand, like the Sorcerer's Apprentice. As fast as we build, even faster they come. We shall catch up in—I suppose—ten years."

Jo felt it would be more like twenty.

Now the grandiose skyline, the shops with their tiny show-windows. Not much attempt at display—pyramids of canned meat or fish, a few ceramic or wooden goods. The embrace of a great hotel, all foyer. Upstairs to magnificence, a suite: a sitting-room painted blue with a piano in it, pictures of birch-trees and lakes: a bedroom hung with green brocade, embossed, a prodigious wardrobe.

"Good God, Seryosha," Kit exclaimed to Nemenov, "we haven't enough clothes for that!"

Nemenov laughed. Here there was a cold collation: slices of sturgeon, sausage, salads, pickled cucumbers, cold chicken, hard-boiled eggs, jam, an imposing quantity of bread. And vodka.

Oh no, Jo thought, who had just managed to keep his feet down the interminable corridor.

Nemenov said, "We do not welcome you for your sartorial accomplishments, my dear Kit." He turned to Jo. "You are a writer, too?"

"Failed."

"Which of us is to say that he is not?"

Then, at last, solitude: and Innokenti. "You would like to sleep, I expect, so I shall leave you. I will come at half past seven, and we will go out to Peredelkino for dinner. Mr. Versilov has invited us."

"Half a tick." Kit, still keeping his feet, still lively, rummaged in a suitcase. "Present for you. Not a souvenir, just nice. You don't want Scotch thistles, or the Tower of London all over scarves and ties. Look, lovely whiskey!"

Innokenti gave his child-like grin. "Thank you, that is a very nice present. There is nothing quite like whiskey. In return, we shall give you vodka. You will take an enormous amount home with you, and caviar as well."

"What's the time?" Jo asked him. He realized that he could not read his watch.

"Five o'clock. So you have two and a half hours."

"Are we bugged here?" Kit demanded.

Innokenti hesitated. "Of course not." Then, as an act of trust—"I don't really know. I don't think so."

Kit shouted to the ceiling, "If we're bugged, bugger to you!"

"Kit, you need to sleep."

"No, I don't. I'm fine."

But Jo left them and went to lie down. After the long remission, he was afraid again: he had a good supply of tablets, but knew he must go for three weeks without a comforting visit to the doctor, and it unnerved him. He lay quietly, his eyes upon the green wall, trying to focus the pattern. Thank God there was no press conference until the following morning. Kit was in no condition for one now. He heard the click of the door as Innokenti left the suite.

Then Kit began to strum upon the piano, and to sing at the top of his fine voice, "The Song of the Volga Boatmen." Jo put his fingers in his ears, but the noise still beat in his head. Groggily, he rose and went into the sitting-room.

"For Christ's sake, stop that! I'm drunk and I'm tired. So are you."

"No, I'm not. I'm going for a walk. I want to breathe it all in, the lovely stink, the 'broad nature.'"

"Come and lie down. We've got an awful evening ahead, and a damned heavy day tomorrow."

"Marvellous, marvellous evening!" But at that point Kit reeled smiling to his own bed and fell asleep almost at once.

They woke simultaneously, half an hour before they were due to be called for, and Jo felt fresher than he had anticipated. It was Kit who still staggered slightly as he washed, and changed his jade shirt for an orange one.

Innokenti with the car, and a drive through the vast streets of the vastly spreading city, into smaller streets, into birch forests, down sandy roads to the gate of Versilov's house. The poet and his small round wife Nadya were waiting for them in the ragged garden, now filled with flowers which had struggled to great heights to free themselves from the long grasses, so they might catch a breath of air. Lilacs, mauve, white and pink, tumbled low over the paved walls: the men had to stoop beneath them. The evening was sultry, heavily scented.

"You are both refreshed?" Versilov inquired, adding at once, "No, how can you possibly be? Here we work our dear guests very hard, a strange manifestation of our affection for them. But there are few ills a little vodka will not cure, and it is said that Nadya is the best cook in Moscow."

"He is a flatterer," said Nadya. "There are many better. But I would not call myself a very bad one."

Versilov's *dacha* was of brick, not of wood: he was a rich man. The furnishings were modern in the Swedish style, there was indoor sanitation and a bathroom of some splendor.

"Please be at home here. Having some idea that our English friends might be tired, I have asked nobody else: only you. There are countless children running about—"

"Countless, Alyosha! Only five."

"Innumerable—but then, they always run away again. Here is the smallest."

They were sitting on the porch now, vodka and brandy and *zakuska* before them. Through grass higher than himself came a child of two or three, with bullet head and flax-blue eyes, clutching a vast spill of flowers of his own picking. These he solemnly divided between Kit and Jo.

Versilov introduced the little boy.

Jo said daringly, *"Bolshoi spessibo,* Petruchka!" and Kit, looking faintly put out, echoed him. Kit had never troubled to learn a word of Russian. Jo had learned fifteen words.

Two other children appeared from the circling woods: a tall boy, twelve perhaps, and a girl of eight, who also brought flowers. Nadya took the smallest ones upon her knees and caressed them.

Encouraged by Jo's linguistic gifts, the older boy said in English: "How do you do."

"He goes to the English school," Nadya explained.

There was a hint of thunder in the air which gave to this

family ambience a closeness, perhaps a secretiveness, all the more pleasing because of its vague oppression. The lilacs hung deadly still, there was no breath among the tulips, the blue iris.

Jo, somewhat to his surprise, found he was hungry, and attacked the cold table with a vigor that brought to Nadya a smile of delight.

Kit whispered, "This is only the first course. For God's sake keep that in mind," and signed to Innokenti (who had no intention of doing so) that he must not interpret this.

"Now Kit," said Versilov, "your book here has been discussed widely at Readers' Conferences in the branch libraries. We have planned for you to make an appearance at a library in the Baumann district, to meet your public."

"I do wish," said Kit, "that you'd publish more of my books. I've almost forgotten that one."

Versilov made a gesture which, in a Spaniard, would have been construed as *mañana*. "Things," he said, "take time."

Here Kit became vivid. Why did they take so much time? In England and America, things moved far more quickly. "After all," he added, "I've written better books since."

"With us," Versilov repeated, "things take time." A grin irradiated him, diminishing his eyes, widening his mouth, in some extraordinary way brightening his hair.

For the first time since his dazed arrival, Jo felt strangeness: which was all the more strange because of the illusion of familiarity. Far away behind the pine-trees lightning flashed pale as a moth's wing, with no following thunder. The grass darkened. Rain would come first.

But now Nadya made them come into the house and be seated round the long table at which two other children had appeared, a boy of fourteen, abnormally tall, a little round girl with a black pigtail, thick as her own wrist, hanging down her back. Both greeted the visitors in slow, precise English.

Partridges were served, brown and tender, without accompaniment. Jo, still hungry, ate his to the bones, while Kit talked about poets and the problems of translation.

"In my country," said Versilov, "I am well-known. In yours —by a single short story, the only one I ever wrote, and certainly it will be the last."

Jo believed for a moment that Innokenti was missing. But no, of course he was there, interpreting with brilliant rapidity. Had he not been, no conversation could have taken place. It was the second time he had noticed this, but it seemed to him as surprising as at the first.

Kit was asking about Stalin. Jo saw Nadya's eyes fill as she put a round chocolate cake, large as a cartwheel, upon the table.

Versilov said, "For us, of course it was a dreadful shock. We knew there had been terrible things, though not so much as we know now. But in the war, you understand. . . ." He paused. The children had gone away, were eating cake elsewhere. "For the young, it is very different, a liberation. In time to come, what will history say? That he was like Ivan the Terrible, or Peter the Great, a man who did much evil but made his people strong? Oh, it was a shock, a shock. But for me . . . well, I had friends who went away and I did not see them again. This is a new day for us, I think. I hope. But the shock—yes. I cannot describe it to you. And besides, there were good things that people of my generation will never forget."

"*Nyet*," Nadya murmured, "*nyet, nyet.*"

Versilov changed the subject. He pointed out of the window, where the rain was pattering lightly on the leaves. The light was lurid, gold and parrot-green. Did they know who lived there, over the wooden fence? Boris Pasternak. And a lane away, Leonid Leonov. He was a great gardener, a true horticulturalist. "Most of us, we do not care about neat lawns, neat flower-beds, we just like the flowers to grow. But Leonov's garden—you must see that."

The brief transition made, Versilov began to tell jokes. He had the full, conscious charm of the Russian clown; he was both wise and cunning. As he and Kit laughed till laughter began to be painful, Jo remembered that this was a brave man, one of the bravest in the land, and had been sage and shrewd in his bravery. Deeply respected, of true peasant stock, he had been careful to make himself virtually untouchable: and in his strong position, spoke as much truth as he could, and saw to it that it was written. He was in every sense a patriot, but, like the best patriots, believed in the necessity for constant improvement. There had been bad things, yes. He believed there were to be far fewer. He believed in beautiful things to come.

He said suddenly and compassionately, "Jo, do you feel so far away?"

Jo started. "Why?"

"For a moment you looked lost, and very tired. I know you are very tired, and it must all be very strange."

"No, I don't feel lost. At the moment, found."

Versilov beamed. *"Khorosho."*

"Pay no attention to him," said Kit, "he often goes off into dream states. Anyway, perhaps we should be getting back. No early start tomorrow, Innokenti?"

"No, and I have ordered breakfast. You will find it at nine in your room. At ten, the press. That's not too early?"

"One for the road," said Versilov, filling glasses, *"Pasashok!"* They drank.

All the family came to the gate to wave good-bye, even the baby, wading in rain and dew, his fists full of dandelions.

Then the journey back through the woods, the fitful lightning, the heavy scent of lilac and pine. Kit began to sing drunkenly,

> "It's a long way from Clapham Common,
> It's a long way to go. . . ."

Innokenti joined in with "Tipperary."

Just as he was leaving them in their room, having made sure in an aunt-like way that they had fruit and mineral water, he said, "You must know how much all of us who are younger admire Versilov. All of us."

"I know," said Kit.

"You are tired now, and I have a strong suspicion that neither of you could really see to read a letter I have translated for you. It is from Mamonov. Everything is fixed up. You shall see it tomorrow."

"You are dead right that we are too drunk to read."

"Now, Kit, Kit!" Innokenti looked shocked. "I did not mean drunk. Only fatigued."

"We know damned well what you meant, you old fraud. And you were right." Kit gave an enormous yawn and stumbled backwards, losing control of his legs. Jo caught him.

"Jo, I will help you get him to bed."

Jo said this was quite unnecessary, but Innokenti persisted: in Russia they understood these things. "And I will see you into bed, too, because you are very pale and I want you to be happy tomor-

426

row. There is the House of Friendship after the journalists leave us, and in the afternoon the Kremlin Museum and the Tretyakov, that is if you wish, and in the evening we go to Vnukovo to dine with Mr. and Mrs. Nemenov. Their *dacha* is wooden, more old-fashioned, but very nice."

Kit woke his friend in the middle of the night. "I love these people. I believe in these people. But I believe in friendship everywhere. Everyone has got to trust."

"Oh, shut up!"

"And I believe in God. Jo, do you believe in God?"

"For Christ's sake, go to sleep."

Chapter Two

NEXT MORNING AFTER BREAKFAST KIT TELEPHONED DAVINA, HAVING found out that this was a more reliable form of communication than letter-writing. He reported that she was cheerful but rather tired, since the baby kicked her all night: she thought it was going to be a footballer. "Oh, and I asked her to ring Bessie up and give her your love. I thought that would save picture-postcards."

At the age of forty-five Kit, who, despite his fat, looked ten years younger, had become more considerate of others. Jo was grateful to him.

There were four journalists at the press conference, a man from Moscow Radio and a photographer. Jo, who had retired modestly to the back of the room, was brought forward again by Kit. "No. I want you in the picture, too."

He dealt with the little conference surprisingly well: if what he said was basically platitudinous, he managed to sound as if it were not. They were pleased with him.

"Mr. Mallings," said a young man from one of the literary magazines, "I would like your views on some contemporary English writers. The Angry Young Men, for example."

428

"Journalistic tag," Kit grinned, "they've really nothing whatsoever in common. Don't you be caught by that."

This seemed to disappoint the inquirer. He asked about three or four English novelists widely translated in the Soviet Union.

Kit, who held no brief for more than one of these, and no very enthusiastic brief for him, dodged neatly. "You ought," he said, "to publish more of our writers who may say things you don't like, but are telling you more of what England is really all about."

The reviewer mentioned large editions of Kipling and Conrad.

"Dead," said Kit. "Not that it isn't splendid, but dead they are."

Asked about Soviet writers, he poured praise upon Mamonov and announced with pride that he and Jo were going to spend three days with him next week, on the Don.

"And what do you think of us? Of our people?"

"Before I came here," Kit replied promptly, "I used to think Dostoievsky wasn't a realistic writer. Now I know that he is."

"Tolstoy—" A hint of protest from one man, a fleeting smile from another.

"Oh, he's true, too. But I don't meet so many of his characters around."

He was told that the Moscow Art Theatre was to present an adaptation of *The Brothers Karamazov* in the following year, and Kit wished he could be there to see it.

"Well, why not?" Innokenti asked. "You know you are welcome here always."

When the press had gone, the telephone rang. A man spoke in good English, but with a heavy American accent. His name was Sasha Popov, he was a research student in English Literature at Moscow University. He was downstairs in the hotel lobby. Might he pay a call? He admired Kit greatly.

"We have only half an hour," Innokenti murmured.

"We've only got half an hour," said Kit, "but we'd love it. Come along up."

There appeared a scowling young man with fair crew-cut hair, wearing a tweed jacket, grey flannel trousers and a westernizing tie. Innokenti made a tactful excuse and left them.

"Please, you must call me Sasha. My English is not perhaps

what it should be, because I have never been out of Russia, but it will serve. Your books are very fine, Mr. Mallings. I particularly admired the last. We would publish it here if we had any sense, which our editors have not, the half of them."

It was evident at once that Sasha, twenty-four years old, felt his country had certain shortcomings in the field of aesthetics, and these he began to enumerate at the top of his voice. Jo slipped to the window and opened it, thinking the roar of the traffic would militate against hidden microphones. Sasha, with a look of scorn, said he had a cold and shut it again. He went on with acute and noisy criticism. Either he is doing it because he knows we aren't bugged, or knows we are and doesn't care, Jo thought muzzily. He suspected the former explanation.

"So why," Sasha demanded, "do we not read Robbe-Grillet? Evelyn Waugh? Ivy Compton-Burnett?"

"Perhaps not much social content in two of them, and too much of the wrong kind in one," Kit answered.

Sasha said Pah! Literature was literature, the world over. He asked an aesthetic question of some complication.

Not knowing quite what to reply, Kit was silent for a few minutes. Jo noticed that Sasha's scowl had darkened, that his lips were trembling a little.

He said, "What's the matter?"

"You do not like me. Mr. Mallings does not like me. I feel it. I have said something wrong, something you do not like."

Kit was on his feet at once. "My dear chap, it's not that! Only your question was so interesting that I had to think about it seriously. We like you very much, honestly we do!"

At once Sasha was radiant, his eyes shining like brook water in the sunshine. "You do really? It is all right? I haven't put my foot in it?"

Innokenti returned to tell them the car was waiting and Sasha left regretfully, making them promise that he might come to see them again.

On the way to the House of Friendship Jo, who was full of vague suspicions, asked Innokenti whether he knew the student.

Innokenti smiled. "Popov? Everyone does. He is one of the very brightest. At present he feels a sense of restriction, he pines to travel, he believes all the Americans are like Hemingway, he wants to 'swing.' But he is a brilliant scholar, and may be an Academician someday. Do not think all our young men are fossilized, Jo, or that they all talk the same way. There are many different views on many different things. Kit will tell you I am not totally conformist myself."

But he was. Like Versilov, like Popov (as it transpired), he not only accepted the régime but whole-heartedly believed in it. Unlike them, he was secretly satisfied (since the Twentieth Congress) with everything about it, except—for this touched him closely—its incapacity to deal as efficiently as it should with a rapidly growing tourist industry. He much disliked young female guides in Leningrad, escorting a group of American scholars, who would begin brightly with the statement, "Some of you may perhaps have heard of Lenin." They made him writhe with embarrassment.

The day passed in its charmed exhaustion, the new faces, the collations of cakes, oranges, chocolates, fruit and wine, the candied Kremlin, the dazzling gold of churches, the drive into the country and the long, long dinner, host, wife, and more children bobbing among the flowers, playing on seesaws and swings. The thundery weather had gone and it was pure soft summer. Jo noticed with relief that Kit, though still drinking far too much, was not drinking in a fashion they had nervously termed Homeric. The day passed, and the days.

On the sixth, the one before they were due to fly south to Rostov, Jo could not get up. He said he must at least spend the morning in bed, otherwise he would be unfit to travel any more. No—to Kit's anxious inquiry—he had not been more drunk last night than on the one before. He was just dead tired.

"Look, you'll be all right the moment you've had a shower. I'm O.K., and I've talked far more than you have. Besides, you can't lie here all day on your own."

"Yes, I can. Anyway, till lunchtime."

"I hate going around without you."

"Well, you'll have to."

"You know you'll feel fine after the first vodka."

"I'll feel fine this afternoon, I promise."

Innokenti, when he called, took one look at Jo and said, "Of course you must rest. I'll see they send your lunch in, and then you

431

can sleep for the rest of the day if you want to. Dasha will call" (a girl from the Writers' Union) "and see if there's anything she can do. No one will bother you, but you won't be alone."

"If Jo stays where he is he'll get stuck like it," said Kit, still cross, "the only thing on this sort of game is to keep going."

"I shan't want any lunch."

"Well, then," said Innokenti, "you needn't eat it. But they will bring you some consommé and perhaps some eggs."

They went away at last. Jo slept. He did, in fact, wake at lunchtime, was able to eat a little food and get dressed. At two o'clock Dasha came, a girl with the grey eyes of Minerva who needed, he thought, no more than an owl on her shoulder.

"Will you sleep again?"

"No. I'll just lie on the bed and read."

"I will sit quietly out here. If you need me, you will call."

By an effort of will, he was strong enough to go out with Kit that night, and he thanked God that his will could still operate. He had had something of a fright. To know that he could pull himself together stimulated him. At the party, at the Aragvi restaurant, he found himself almost as loquacious as Kit, and was pleased that people responded to him. Throughout the trip, so far, he had felt something like a superior sort of valet, a Dandini, a Jeeves. Now, for the first time he felt like Jo, someone in his own right, whatever that right might be. All would be well: a miracle had taken place. He had wanted no more than a few hours of sleep, a reasonable demand. Well, he had had them. He felt fine. He ate fried cheese, and bread hot enough to burn the pulling fingers.

Before they left Moscow, he borrowed some of Kit's roubles to telephone to his mother.

"Well, well," said Bessie, "you might be in the next room! Having a good time?"

He said he was.

"I can see you dancing that dance where they sit on their behinds and fling their legs out. I hope you're not drinking too much."

"No."

"Do you realize, I'm eighty next year?"

"What on earth made you think of that right now?"

"Well, it's a thought, isn't it? Eighty. Fancy! Don't stay too long away. I shan't last forever."

"You know perfectly well that you'll see me at the end of next week. How's Millie?"

"Oh. That's a bit odd. She's going out with a schoolteacher quite ten years younger than she is. It's made her all girlish. Not that it means anything. Listen, I can make the pussies talk to you. Wait a minute."

"For God's sake, Mother, you're not going to squeeze them?"

Apparently she was, for after a moment's delay, Siamese howls penetrated across two thousand miles of Europe.

"Put them down at once!"

"They don't mind. Isn't that like home? Do you miss your home, Jo?"

By some freak of the exchange, they were cut off. He did not bother to reinstitute the call.

They flew in an Ilyushin 18, a reliable aeroplane, but on this occasion a singularly noisy one, and the upper air was turbulent. Kit, submitting for once to weariness, slept all the way. Jo could not. He tried to read, but the leaping print disturbed his eyes and made him feel giddy. They were in the back of the plane in seats that were roomier than those further up, but where the bucketing was worse. Nearby, a young woman was being competently sick into a paper bag, at intervals of fifteen minutes. Jo averted his eyes, tried to stimulate some interest in the unvarying landscape, the interminable square miles, hundreds of square miles that had finally swallowed up a frozen German army. They could not be so far from Stalingrad. He remembered a story told by a German commander: his troops had been expecting a supply train, bringing comfort, food, surcease from the horrible cold. When it came, it was filled with one thing only: bottles of red wine, frozen. When they were lifted out, most of them exploded.

Stalingrad and suffering: the twenty million dead, or more, in the whole of the land. One reason why nobody in Russia wanted to listen to his bomb-stories, Bessie and Miss Pease in the passage, himself upon a roof, even the death of Polly and her daughter. Suffering is relative, except to the sufferer, and these people were haloed by it, set apart in the pride of their own destruction.

433

Then, coming down: rather rapidly, since the weather conditions were not so good. Kit, prodded, woke up and was at once sparkling. They fastened their seat-belts and put out their cigarettes, while many of the Russians did no such thing. One old woman, who might never have been in a railway train but regarded an aircraft as a kind of bus, was gathering together a mass of groceries in string bags. The woman who had been sick let the last container slip from her knees, where it burst all over the floor, just where Jo and Kit would have to step.

Kit gagged, then said, "Oh, not *now!*"

Innokenti held them back till all the other passengers had left the plane and then, with iron arms, steered them over the pool of vomit. At the head of the stairs, he stepped back. So, knowing his place, did Jo.

Kit, radiant, moved downwards to the waving and the flowers, his friends behind him. Cumulus clouds were enormous in the warm air, but the tarmac was sunny.

The Rector of the university and his wife. The Professor of English and his. Party officials and their wives. Pressmen crowding, cameras clicking.

"God," Jo murmured, "and all for one book!"

"Two," Kit retorted, injured. "Or almost."

This was a different country, southern, the streets far more like streets in Genoa than anywhere else. Pretty girls in light dresses, streets with roses planted between the traffic lanes. Jo wondered about Mamonov, what he would be like, how far they had to drive.

But it seemed they were not to meet him that night, but to have a party with university and civic figures in one of the hotels. Tomorrow, Tikhon Sergeivitch Mamonov. *Mañana.* Kit, Jo thought, looked a little put out.

Innokenti whispered, "He is only just back from Finland. He is exhausted. Tomorrow. . . ."

Fortunately for Kit and Jo, the party ended at no very late hour, and they were able to retire to a high, pale room where to stumble carried hazards, since contact with the wall spread whitewash over their clothes. It was a comfortable, a friendly hotel, but rougher than the one they had known in Moscow.

"And now," Kit said, "even I can sleep like the crack of doom. God, I nearly puked in that plane! I would have done, if I

434

hadn't known I had to make my usual grand entry. The show must go on."

He lay down and slept at once. There was a bedside lamp, but Jo could not find the switch: so he turned off the overhead lamp by the switch at the door and blundered his way through the dark to bed. He lay awake for a while, pleased at his recovery: he was obviously in rather better shape than Kit. He thought of his friends, of Alison and her son, of Clement and Georgina. Of Davina, not at all. He wondered that they were so far from home. His pleasant weariness was such that this place seemed home to him, he could be content there forever. What other home could there be? His mother, her eightieth birthday (with all concomitant festivities, no doubt) approaching: Millie, harmlessly making a fool of herself with a young schoolteacher. Privets on the West Side, the island in the pond, the Sunday speakers on their rostrums, the gritty feel of the Cinder Path under foot. Bobby Price: where? In Moscow, as a correspondent. They had forgotten to look him up. They must do so before their return. What had happened to Sybil Rainey, so stern, so ardent, so much the Party Biddy? Still in Ireland, probably: now elderly, training horses. Jim Welford would be—was? Jo had forgotten—married now to his little earnest actress. A grandchild for Alison soon. Good God! They were old, old, Master Shallow. Belphoebe had said that, Kit had told him so.

Through the open window came a lovely scent, impossible to name. The scent of space, of the loneliness of plains where no animal, no plant, nor busy insect, felt loneliness at all. Must ask about it tomorrow. What is it? Sweet, a little musty?

A long way from Clapham Common.

Chapter Three

IN THE FIRST TWO CARS, LAND ROVERS, THE RECTOR, THE CIVIC leaders: this time, no wives. In the second, besides the driver, Kit, Jo and Innokenti. They drove for hours, as it seemed to them, over the romantic steppes, they bumped through scrub and bush, skirted ravines where the wolves were, though they did not emerge in summer. Once they all stopped to drink of a beautiful pure spring, the water itself of a curious visual loveliness, more like quicksilver than water.

"It is quite safe," Innokenti whispered.

"What's that smell?" Jo asked.

"I don't know. This is a foreign part of the world to me." Innokenti asked the Rector, who turned with a smile, and broke off a sprig from a little low plant, grey, fluffy, dry, fragile.

"It is wormwood," the Rector said, "the perfume of our steppes."

They were off again, jolting over rough ground, Jo happy, exhilarated. He was doing very, very well. They came at last to a bluff above the river, and into a sanded courtyard. Above them, beyond a flight of steps, was a splendid wooden house, painted white, jade and apple-green. In a paddock, handsome hawk-faced

436

men were exercising horses. Pressmen again, and hordes of interested strangers. They stood and waited.

Down the steps, like a king made of silver, came the old man, seventy-six years of age, short-statured, his figure trim as a boy's, his back like a ramrod. He had a face like the face upon a silver coin, and the last of his silver hair swept curling away from a tanned forehead. Hawk's nose, hawk's eyes: silver eyes.

Tikhon Sergeivitch Mamonov.

He caught Kit to his breast and kissed him on both cheeks: did likewise with Jo.

Behind him came his stout and handsome wife, all in black, walking like a queen. Nearly twenty years younger than he, Darya Matveyeva. A thick plait of black and silver was bound round her head. Her eyes, like her husband's, were light.

"For one moment," he said, "you must see my river."

He led them to the wire fence, below which a mud-track zig-zagged to the edge of the water, a broad sweep, islanded, now filled with sunset the color of rose-campion. "One day, dear Kit, for I shall call you that, I will take you fishing. We will camp on an island, and catch and cook sterlet for our breakfast." He laughed as a gaggle of geese came up the hill, and in single file scuffled their way under the fence. "Come now, we will sit down and drink together, and you shall tell me what you want to do."

They sat on the porch, where Darya and an elderly woman served them. Beyond the gate, a crowd of villagers watched them still, as if they were actors in a play—Mamonov, Jo, Kit, the Rector, the functionaries. Kit began to praise Mamonov's trilogy, written thirty-five years ago, still the source of his fame. He had written little else.

"It is about my people, about this land, these Cossacks. There is the church, which you may remember. But this house, of course, and the school, and the hospital, they were not there then. Just the church remains, which the Germans did not burn. Otherwise, all was destroyed. But tell me, you are my guests. How will you like to amuse yourselves? For I sleep every afternoon, till suppertime."

"I should like," Kit said, "to ride a horse over the steppes."

"You can ride?"

"Of course." Kit was lying: but he would have risked exposure for the sake of a romantic idea.

However, Mamonov smiled and shook his head. "That is one request, my dear young friend, that I must refuse. You have not ridden horses like these. They are not used to the saddle."

He called something to a brown-faced, handsome man walking a mare in the paddock. The man smiled broadly with a flash of teeth, the front three made of steel. He sprang up onto the horse straight from the ground and it leaped away with him, as he sat erect upon the bare back, his hands in his pockets.

"He will not break his bones, Kit, but you would do so, and I could not send you back to your own country in anything but perfect health."

Kit expressed understanding, and some disappointment: but he was relieved.

He said, "Why do you call me young? It's pleasant, but it's not true."

"To me you are young. To me everybody is, but you in particular. Youth is in you like a lamp, and will be shining across the waters even at your end."

It was all very grand, Jo thought; this was the way a great man should talk. But as they moved in to supper, in a vast room full of green plants, Mamonov began to show another side to himself. He could be extremely funny, with a sly, sarcastic wit that on occasion amused Innokenti so much that he could barely interpret for laughing.

People were straying in all the time: there must have been twenty round the table, with places for twenty more.

"Tikhon Sergei'itch hates to eat alone," his wife murmured, "even at breakfast-time, there must always be nine or ten. And our people come and go as they please, knowing they are welcome."

Mamonov was like a patriarch among a tribe, or a king among subjects. He had done so much good in his village, Innokenti rapidly explained to Jo, that the whole population delighted to serve him.

"No staff problems," Jo muttered in reply.

Innokenti smiled.

"This is our great fish soup," said Mamonov, "it is *ukha*. I hope you will like it. The sterlet was caught this morning off the nearest island that you saw."

Ukha: vast platters of sturgeon, chicken, ham, bowls of caviar, tomatoes, cucumbers, cheese. Vodka, cognac, red cham-

438

pagne, apricot-colored wine from Georgia. Mamonov pressed these drinks upon them. "Come, they will do you no harm. Champagne is not even an alcoholic drink!"

He signed to the man who had ridden the horse.

"Yuri Ivan'itch!"

Yuri Ivan'itch drummed with his knuckles on the table in imitation of a horse's hoofs, and everyone began to sing.

"It is one of our Cossack songs," Mamonov said, "we have many."

Jo thought, Valhalla must have been something like this, and since it is going on for hours, we shall have to keep steady. He looked apprehensively at Kit, whose face was hot and wet, whose eyes were glowing like coals. It was not going to be easy getting him to bed that night.

Kit, however, when they rose at two-thirty in the morning, managed well enough, with a supporting hand from his host.

He and Jo shared a large, white-painted bedroom with rugs tacked to the walls, and yellow furniture highly polished. Just outside was a lavatory and a small wash-room: no hot water. Mosquito-netting at the windows, open to the scent of the dark miles.

Innokenti awakened them at half past nine with cups of coffee. "For breakfast," he explained, "isn't as you know it, and you'll get nothing hot to drink till the end of it."

"You are a good chap," Kit said gratefully. "My God, I've got a head! I could almost do with the hair of the dog."

"Then you do not know," Innokenti replied with a cunning smile, "what is coming to you."

What came to them was breakfast on the same scale as supper, with much the same food, and certainly the same drink.

Jo, after shuddering at the first mouthful of vodka, was grateful for it. Mamonov, at the head of the table, now wearing the Cossack uniform in which he spent most of his days, looked fresh and spruce, the morning light sparking the ends of his small moustache. As Darya Matveyeva had predicted, there were about ten persons present in addition to their own party. Toasts were drunk. Mamonov made a speech which had Innokenti doubled up with laughing, and flushed with a kind of embarrassment: it was extremely bawdy, and Darya made clucking noises of pretended disapproval from time to time.

They rose from the table at one o'clock. Mamonov announced that now he would sleep. The rest of them were to drive through the village, then picnic on the steppes. This time there were three Land Rovers, laden with apples and champagne.

The village, as Innokenti had translated the word *stanitsa*, surprised Jo on two counts: one, that it was more like a small town, with a population of nine thousand people: two, that the houses, deep in their gardens, protected by wooden palings, looked as though they had been there for a century. And yet, fourteen years ago, there had been nothing here but the church: scorched earth and rubble, death's desolation, the stink of rotting flesh.

Sitting on the high side of the Don, looking down over a vast plain flooded in the winter, they opened the crates and drank. Thank God, Jo said to himself, only two more days of this. Yet he felt exhilarated by the beautiful air, the only fresh air, he felt, that he had ever taken into his lungs. He believed that if he lived in it, he would be perfectly well. Sunflooded cliff-sides and tufted islands, sparked the wormwood to silver as it had sparked Mamonov's moustache.

"Have an apple," he said to Kit, but Kit was blissfully asleep on his back, his face towards the crystalline sky.

Chapter Four

AT SUPPER ON THE LAST NIGHT, THERE MUST HAVE BEEN FORTY people present: throughout, people came and went, sat down to eat and drink, were filled, and departed. At the far end of the table a group of women, all in dark-colored suits, overweight, hair plainly dressed, sipped red champagne. The glittering cloth, the cutlery, the bottles, the now familiar plates of fish and meat, the patties filled with meat or vegetables, the cheese, pickles, fruit, seemed to Jo to stretch out in exaggerated perspective to where some sort of darkness began, as it might have been the interminable, foggy corridor of a dream.

It was nearly midnight, and he was exhausted. They were to return to the hotel afterwards, too, in order to catch the morning plane. How he was to endure the longish ride, he did not know.

Kit, who was now very red in the face, had begun to slump sideways onto Mamonov's shoulder. Innokenti unobtrusively straightened him in his chair, but Mamonov smiled, and touched the younger man gently on hand and cheek. I have got to keep alert, Jo thought, or it will be hell getting him home. When nobody was looking, he tipped his vodka into a glass half-full of water and turned his face from the growing dark beyond the table, in which great spiky circles had now begun to wheel and dazzle. He whispered to Innokenti, "Don't let Kit drink any more." The interpreter shrugged. "How does one stop him?" "Just slide the bottle away." But Kit, seeing this maneuver, brought the bottle back again with a curious serpentine movement, and slopped more brandy into his wine-glass.

Mamonov was on his feet, toasting his English friends.

When he sat down, Kit struggled up. He had taken off his tie, opened the neck of his orange shirt. His hair stood up in clotted curls, as if with fright.

"I wan' propose toasht."

Everyone applauded.

"To propose toasht." He gulped, as if he might be sick, but recovered himself. Now he looked gravely about him, eyes focussing again. Mamonov glanced up at him as if in protection; but curiously.

"We love oneanusher tonight, don't we?"

Innokenti rose to stand by him.

"All love, brothershunder God. I believe in God, you don't, whashit matter? All goesh the same way home. Toasht, then. To the forgiving of all our enemish, in all lands. No more enemish. To the Forgiven!"

There was a silence. Then glasses were raised, one by one, to the lips: but no lips touched them. He looked wildly round. "Whashamatter with you all? Have I done something I shouldn't?" He dropped back into the chair, steadied by Innokenti. The separate conversations went on. Someone asked Yuri Ivanovitch for a song, and several of the men began to drum on the table, gallop-a-gallop-a-gallop.

But the song did not begin. Mamonov rose to his feet, arched his back till it was like a strung bow, then stood vertical, silent. He spoke.

"My dear friend Kit. My dear friend Jo. Once I went to Rome. In the Sistine Chapel I saw that great painting of the life breathed into Adam. I do not share my friend Kit's religious beliefs, though I respect them. But this picture moved me, for it was about something more than God: it was about the almighty spirit of man."

442

Innokenti's translation raced level with Mamonov's voice, a steady flow, clear as the running of a stream, but no more disturbing than the stream's voice.

"Adam stretches out an arm, his forefinger offered to God, who comes down from heaven to touch it with his own, thus conveying mind, breath and spirit into the perfect body of his creation. So, when I was young, did I believe that all men must touch, that even in death, a man might stretch out a finger to touch the finger even of his enemy, that both might be healed and neither, in that hour which must come to us all, and in which none of us is really able to believe till it is upon us, might be alone."

Jo looked around him at the intent faces, open-eyed, lips a little parted. Even Yuri, at first sad at being deprived of his song, had lost his animation, his superb physical restlessness, and no longer swivelled about upon his chair.

"You must understand my feelings, dear Kit, writer of beautiful words, about this land of mine, and especially about this particular vast stretch of it, where we sit tonight as in a lake of light with a great, beloved darkness beyond us, to which the deepest core of my heart is given. We have known miseries from our enemies, both within and without, that to you can be no more than the imagination derived from our own poor words."

Jo heard Kit mutter something Innokenti ignored: "Well, we were alone. For munsh and munsh. Our citiesh burned. Our children died. You had your bloody pact with the beasht."

Mamonov looked at him fleetingly, as if he understood, but did not ask Innokenti to interpret. He raised his voice. "Anna! Anna Avramovna!"

She came out of the kitchen; huge, old, she wiped her hands upon her apron.

"Here is Anna, precious to me, to my wife, to my life. Anna, will you tell them what happened to your brother?"

A flush suffused her dour face, turning it to the color of an aubergine.

"No, Tikhon Sergei'itch, I can't. You must tell."

She bore with her the smell of cooking, of basted meat, fish, and garlic.

"Ah, but try!"

443

"You will excuse me," she said, "I'm not good at talking."

She returned to the kitchen. Through the open door Jo could see her, bustling about the stove, preparing for tomorrow.

"Anna Avramovna is shy," said Mamonov, "and also, to speak to many people would give her pain."

His wife said something.

"What's that?" Jo asked Innokenti.

"She said, Anna would never speak of it before more than two people, perhaps three."

Darya looked at Mamonov with more than a touch of anger, then glanced through the kitchen door. Pans clattered. There was uproar from a newly stoked fire in the range.

Kit sat steadily now, but with his gaze on the far wall. His eyes were wide open, as if propped up by match-sticks.

Mamonov continued.

"When Denikin's armies were ravaging our land, Anna Avramovna and her family tried to hide away. Anna, her husband, and her children, left all their possessions and fled over the steppes to friends who might shelter them. It was her brother who stayed too late in the village, trying to salvage, from their home, the precious things—they had little that was precious of gold or furnishings, they were poor peasants. But he wanted to take with him his mother's portrait, a change of clothing, a bird carved in wood at school by his dead son.

"While he was still in the house, Denikin's men broke in. He hid in the wardrobe. It was such a small house, there was nowhere else. In the wardrobe, at eye-level, there was a little pane of glass."

Glasses tinkled, renewed. Yuri once more fidgetted in his chair, and his black brows came down above full lids.

"The soldiers went everywhere, sticking their bayonets through chairs, sofas, bedding. Then they came to the room where Anna's brother was, and of course, since it was so foolish a hiding-place, they saw him at once. The white face, the black eyes full of terror, behind that little pane of glass. They dragged him out, and before they left him, they cut off his nose and his lips."

"For Chrissake," said Kit loudly.

Mamonov spoke to Innokenti.

"Yes, for Christ's sake," he went on. "They believed themselves the soldiers of Christ. And when the last war came, we were again ravaged by these Christian soldiers. They hanged children: they herded men and women into churches and burned them alive. When we were their prisoners, they treated us as if we were not men but lower animals. Worse. These were people who loved their cats, their dogs, who carried photographs of their children close to their hearts."

Suddenly Kit began to cry. He half-rose in his seat. Mamonov caught him, and kissed him on both cheeks.

"No, no, it is all over now. But you understand that we cannot put out, to these people, the forefinger that might touch their own." He lowered Kit gently into place. Kit's tears ceased. He wiped his face on his napkin and was quiet, though Jo heard him mumble, "But *we* were alone. *We* were alone."

Now Mamonov's tone changed. He was talking not so much to Kit, or to his guests, as to the darkness outside the brilliant lake, a darkness full of the veiled faces of the world.

"Let no one speak to us about the reunification of our enemies. It is only we who understand. Keep them apart, keep them apart! Together they will come back. Do you understand this, our terror? Our hatred? We do not want to hate. But so much has been done to us that we shall never be able to touch the finger-tips of our brother-enemies, men in corporeal essence like ourselves, whose veins break beneath the flesh when they are old, whose eyes cloud over, who say 'What? What?' when they are spoken to, who suffer private griefs as we do, whose wives and children die of sickness, who are tender, tender, in the flesh as we ourselves. But we shall die with them, side by side, and there will be no touch of comfort from the soft pad of the finger, the last human contact, the conveyance, through the pores of the skin, of comradeship. Yes, we shall die, each in a place apart.

"And so, dear Kit, our friend, respected writer and good man, I will now offer a toast to forgiveness, to yours of myself, because I could not drink as you wished. Forgive me."

He raised his glass. Everyone rose to his feet, some unsteady, all bright-eyed, the women, still with their glasses of red champagne scarcely touched, steady as rocks.

"To our guests' forgiveness of myself."

They drank. Kit slopped vodka into the wine-glass, on top of the dregs, and drained it. One of the men began to sing, knuckles to drum. Two Cossacks, Yuri and a younger man, broke away from the table to dance, balanced on their buttocks, legs cracking out and back. Kit had slumped once more, had fallen against Innokenti, who cradled him as a mother a child.

"Change places," said Jo, "I'll take him."

"Better leave him as he is."

Kit was droning feebly something which sounded like "Whirlwinds of Danger," but his eyes were open again. Jo felt relieved. Also, since the darkness at the end of the room and beyond the rows of pink and white faces opposite seemed to be thinning, he believed he had drunk himself sober, which was all to the good, with the prospect lying ahead of the long drive and of putting Kit to bed. His imagination jumped the next tiresome hour or so, and he clearly saw Kit huddled beneath the eiderdown, breathing peacefully, chubbiness returned to him as it does to children when they sleep.

The party began to break up, one face disappeared, then another. There was a scraping of chairs. Mamonov, radiant, military in his olive tunic, was smiling, hugging, embracing.

"Come on, old man," said Innokenti, and brought Kit to his feet. Jo rose too, and the floor was level under him. He took Kit's other arm, but it was wrenched away from him. A hand went out to bottle and glass for another slop and swallow. "One for the road," Kit said clearly, then, remembering the word: *"Pasoshok!"* Obediently he moved between them, out into the hallway, Mamonov close behind.

"I can walk," Kit said. Pulling away from Jo and Innokenti, he turned, took two firm steps towards Mamonov's open arms, then fell flat on his face.

"Oh God," Jo said, "he's passed out."

Mamonov smiled. "He has had a good evening. He has enjoyed himself. Don't worry, my dear friend, Yuri Ivan'itch will help you to see him home."

The young Cossack, rock-like, hook-nosed and imperious, chestnut hair gleaming under the chandeliers, came forward to lend a hand to Innokenti. They spoke together and laughed. Together they hauled Kit up again, and half-dragged, half-carried him towards the door, Jo helpless in the rear. Mamonov opened the door onto the starlit courtyard, where the car was waiting. It had turned chilly and in the head-lamps the rust-colored roses round an ornamental basin shimmered in the wind.

"All will be well," Mamonov said, "tomorrow he will be as

446

fresh as the sterlet in the river. He hugged Jo, went to hug Kit. Then he stopped, and looked intently into his face.

He said *"Gospodi! On myortvyi!"*

Somehow, even had it not been for the sudden frightening change in the atmosphere, Jo would have understood. He felt an awful coldness, the coldness before panic.

Other guests, servants, had crowded about them. Mamonov waved them back. Yuri and Innokenti lowered Kit to the ground.

Jo dropped to his knees beside him, frantically feeling for the pulse. He was aware of silence. Then he saw, like pine-trees, two thick female legs, and, in the unnatural brilliance, a broad pink female hand in the palm of which lay a little round pocket mirror. He held it to Kit's lips.

At that moment Innokenti raised him up, thrust him aside, and falling beside Kit's body, lay with it mouth to mouth.

"The forefinger of God," Mamonov said, but this Jo did not understand. Someone had sat him in an armchair, was putting brandy to his mouth. He pushed it aside. He was seeing all that lay ahead, the doctors, the morgue, the return with the dead, the breaking of it to Davina.

He lost count of time. It might have been for more than half an hour that Innokenti's golden head and Kit's black one were so close together. The fingers of God and Adam did not touch, and in the meantime the doctor came, and took over.

Innokenti, with the air of a sleep-walker, rose to his feet and, coming to Jo, took his hand and pressed it. Mamonov stood like a sentinel by the body. He was weeping. The tears trickled down the silver ravines of his cheeks.

Dawn was breaking when Jo returned with Innokenti from the hospital. All things had been arranged. Tomorrow he would fly back with the body to Moscow, and from there to London. Telegrams had been sent to Davina and to Kit's mother·

The wide street was filling up with lavender light. Already the heavy lorries were on the move, and the lamps were paling. They went through the dim-lit lobby of the hotel, where a tired night-porter gave them their keys. They climbed the stairs and went along the thrice-turning corridor. The white stuff of the plaster brushed off on their shoulders and sleeves. Innokenti asked, was there anything he could do? He looked shaken at last, and very tired.

No, there was nothing.

447

"Remember, Jo, I am in the next room to yours. If you knock on the wall I shall hear, I sleep lightly. I do not think I shall sleep. So please, knock on the wall."

Jo did not draw the blinds, not wishing to see the day. In the bright bedroom, under the fancy lamp of rose and yellow glass, he looked across at the bed which was to be empty. He put his hands over his eyes to shut out a vision of the steppes in their awful loneliness, hundreds, thousands, of miles softened by the grey and aromatic wormwood, which clung to the dry brush like the grey fluff which he had, for one moment, seen between the lips of his dead friend.

The Turning World

Chapter One

DISPERSED ARE WE.

For years later, sitting under the apple-trees on a hot after-noon, Alison thought of her lost friends. She had just passed her fif-tieth birthday; since Piers's retirement, they had lived in Sussex. She felt her life becalmed, and was glad of it. She wrote little; she had had what rewards she desired, and she had little more to say. She watched her son Christian, now sixteen, handsome, amiable, trimming a hedge under his father's instructions. He was, at the same time, listening to Thelonius Monk on his transistor radio. Tomorrow James and his wife would be returning from America where Dorothy, already coming to fame, had been touring with the Royal Shakespeare Company. She had not completed her uni-versity course but had gone straight to R.A.D.A. She was ex-pecting a child, a thought Alison found both delightful and troub-ling.

"So very old," she said to Piers, as he came by her on his way to the garden-shed.

"Who?"

"Me. I am to become a grandmother."

451

He touched her cheek. "An excellent marriage." It was theirs he meant, not James's. Though James's seemed a good one. She kissed his withdrawing hand.

She never heard from Jo, had not done so for over a year. How odd it seemed that the death of Kit, the most self-absorbed of them all, had finally broken the circle maintained since they were young men and women! Clement had been in Washington for the past three years, as a political correspondent. He and Georgina had ceased to write. Fay and her husband were living in San Francisco. Davina, since the birth of her son, had evaded invitations for a long while, then had written frankly to say that she could not bear to be reminded, even by seeing Kit's friends, of what had been.

All so long ago, and the world so changed. Alison had tried to "go back," once or twice, had even joined in an Aldermaston March, but had felt out of place, separated from these boys and girls by the glass shell of time. The guitars, the sleeping-bags, the general holiday air, unaccountably depressed her. Yet none of her political convictions had changed, and she still felt old wounds. Also, she felt new ones. Nearly twenty years, now, without war. An encouragement. But how long, O Lord, how long? Under the earth's crust, the fires must be spreading. She envisaged the glowing core, the expansion of the fairy flames, all the colors of all the jewels, but fluttering like shot-silk blown by an electric fan. Fear, yes: the world lived with it; but not all the time. To live all the time in conscious apprehension of destruction would be like living, as mediaeval man was supposed to do, in moment-by-moment fear of hell. And she did not credit that mediaeval man had done this. He baked, he cooked, he worked at the forge, he had women, he married, he sired. Presumably he laughed. To live with fear in her own times had become a moral discipline: and, like other matings, the more relaxedly it was done, the less danger there would be in the relationship. Sometimes she felt that the only death she really believed in was her own.

She sang to herself "Riego's Hymn." "O joyous and fearless!" The lovely flag fluttered down from the mast, and men and women wept.

The sun came slantwise, gold as brandy, through the dark shimmer, and made a shifting pattern on the grass. The scent of the limes was heavy, the sweet chestnut was already in flower. The lovely "Tree of Heaven," Piers's particular pride, sang like an

452

aeolian harp as the breeze blew through its enormous leaves: bunches of fruit, pale-green, tinged with red, swayed on the ends of the branches.

After so cold a winter, what joy! She thought of her mother, long-dead, happily embattled with the summer weeds.

She picked up the newspaper, put it down again. The long, sad, squalid trial of Stephen Ward was drawing to an end, leaving behind it a kind of spiritual litter, the mind rubbish-strewn. All for so little, all for nothing, so parochial, so petty.

Christian came to her and flopped at her side. "Is there any lemonade?"

"In the larder."

"Too hot to go and fetch it."

"If that's a hint that I am to go and fetch it, you may think again, my boy."

"And my legs are younger than yours, isn't that right?" He smiled at her craftily.

"It is *quite* right. However many times I may have told you. You imply that I'm repetitious."

"All old ladies are."

"Now I'm damned if I'll fetch you any lemonade!"

"Game, set, and match. All right, I'll go. Shall I bring some for you?"

"Please." She watched him as he went towards the house with his buoyant stride. Not so clever as James, he had been for some eighteen months passing through a bad patch, almost relishing a sense of inferiority. Now, however, he knew what he wanted to do, and it would not be within his brother's range at all. He was to be a farmer, and when he left school next year would be going to an agricultural college.

As he rejoined her he said, "Do you remember that chap Paul Maclaren?"

"What on earth made you think of him?"

"I don't know. I just did. Wasn't he promising to be a bad lot?"

Her relations with both her sons had been singularly without constraint. Christian, even more than James, would discuss anything with her.

"Yes, he was. But he may be a reformed character by now."

"Oh, I know what made him pop into my mind. Do you remember a picnic one day? Was it in Richmond Park? I must have been about ten."

Alison nodded.

"I thought of it as a day rather like this one, the sun is the same color."

"Do you remember things by color?"

"I think I do. Don't start on Proust though—you will at any moment. He's for the likes of Jim, not me."

"I'm not so sure about that."

"Didn't Paul get some girl into trouble?"

"I believe so. I know Georgina was worried about him."

"I remember him chasing that stuffy little Lucy Nesbitt, she was only a kid. There was something awfully remorseless about it."

Piers joined them. "What are you talking about?"

"Oddly enough," said Alison, "Paul Maclaren. We were wondering what happened to him."

"Oddly enough, I can tell you. Georgina's got him safely married off: it was in *The Times*. He can't be more than twenty-two."

"Well, think of Jim—"

"Not at all the same thing," said Piers.

Christian finished his lemonade and lay on his back. "Aren't you both awfully glad I've turned out so well?"

"We're glad that you appear to be doing so," Alison said sternly.

"Oh, rely on me. The moment I start farming I shall marry a rustic beauty, a bit fat and a bit red in the face, only I shall call it apple-cheeked, but a marvellous cook. You need never know a moment's anxiety."

"Do we underrate this boy?" Alison wondered aloud, to her husband.

"You always have," said Christian, but he added, out of the gladness of his new-found confidence, "nevertheless, we shall see what we shall see."

When he had left them, she said: "He really is rather remarkable. He remembers things by tricks of the light, and he invents lovely fat girls for himself."

"I always knew he was remarkable," Piers said comfortably.

454

"There are times when I wonder whether farming is altogether right for him. He likes pictures. Suppose he studied the history of art and became Director of the National Gallery? He might get tired of separators and form-filling."

"What that one wants to do," said Alison, "that he will do."

Dispersed are we. Perhaps all for the best. There was no pain in the past now, and so it had ceased to be desirable. In the amity they had created, in this garden world, they found infinite interest in analyzing their children.

The weather remained fine on the next day, when James and his wife came home.

"We just made it in time," Dorothy said breathlessly, as she hugged Alison, "because I am beginning to *show*." She was rich with happiness.

"By the time our infant is born," James said, "and has been weaned, Dotty will be just about ripe for her first Juliet."

"Oh, I shall make a mess of that. I want to do Lady M., but I'm rather small."

James and his father had one old-fashioned custom, which, that night, they continued to pursue. After dinner, they went off for half an hour to Piers's study.

"You know, Daddy," said James, who had not chosen to put away childish forms of address, "things are working out surprisingly well. Not being a saint, I did have pangs of anxiety when it was obvious that Dotty was going to be a considerable actress. I was so afraid that neither of us might be able to stand up to endless partings. But I think it will be all right. She's set for Stratford next season, so we can live there and I can commute to Birmingham. Naturally, I shall continue to watch her handsome leading-men like a hawk. One would be a fool not to do so."

"Why Birmingham?" Piers asked him.

James replied that he had been offered a job at the university, and that he was pleased not to be separated from his wife. "Mother isn't dreading her new status, is she? Her forthcoming new status, I mean."

"Alison has always been arrogant," said Piers, "but never conceited. No, she's delighted."

"Were you ever sorry that I never had any hankering after Sandhurst?"

"Certainly not. I only went there myself through pressure of events. Or of family. I could never have got to the top in that sort of world: I was always saying, just slightly, the wrong thing."

"I can't imagine you doing that." Obviously, James was musing upon this.

"Can't you?" Piers sounded a little sad. "You think I'm pretty stuffed?"

"I didn't mean that. Only that you seem to me, and you always will, a wise man."

"I used to make my colonel's hackles rise like quills upon the something porcupine."

"Fretful porpentine," said James. "In my new avatar I am expected to know such things."

There are suspensions in life, almost any life, when happiness seems present in totality and graspable for an infinite time to come. Alison knew this, and touched wood against the future. For the week that James and Dorothy were with them, both she and Piers had a feeling of contentment which, in the context of the whole world, the danger, the ferocity, the starvation, the befuddling silliness of nations, made them a little ashamed. She loved to walk over the downs with her husband and her sons. "If I were Ivy Compton-Burnett," she said, "I should call you my menfolk. How splendid!"

"But her menfolk were always at loggerheads," James said, "ditching their wives, pinching each other's property, plotting bigamy, or steeped in incest. Not at all like yours."

"I am not plotting bigamy," said Piers.

The suspensions of life. The blessed dispersals.

It was James who said, "What was it like to live in an age when one could have a nice time and not feel it was indecent to do so?" He added irrelevantly, or so it seemed to them, "Damn it, I must write to Jo."

"I suppose one could have done that from 1919 until 1933," Piers suggested.

"No," James said, "not really. Only if one was blind and deaf."

"Do you think so?" Alison frowned, and for the moment looked plain. She was still trim, still youthful-looking, showing age only in the creasing of her neck, the thickening around the diaphragm. "I had friends in the thirties who had a high old

456

time, till Munich came to startle them somewhat, and the war came as a stunning surprise. While I—to what good, I sometimes wonder?—spent nearly all my time, when I wasn't writing, making public speeches and carrying banners and marching round the scenery."

"It was good," Christian said suddenly. "It did do good. If all you've told us is true."

She looked at him. "All I've told you is true." They walked on for a while in silence. Then she said, "Why on earth was it Kit's death that dispersed us? He never cared all that much."

But no one could answer, because Piers had not been of them, and the others were too young.

"Jo should have been the lynch-pin," she said, as if to herself, "Jo should."

Christian said, "I can't remember Jo."

She cried out, "Not even by a trick of the light?"

"I must wait for the light to play tricks."

So much for joy, she thought, snatched for a guilt-laden moment from an ugly world, no more than a truancy. Yet surely a sin not to exploit it to the full, this scatter of sovereigns from God's hand, gold quickly spent? Give us this day our daily bread, we pray, and if we are lucky enough to be given it, should we be wise to throw it in the mud and starve ourselves? Man cannot live by guilt alone. He doesn't, so he shouldn't pretend to. Shouldn't make holy faces.

When they returned to the house, Dorothy came out to meet them. She had been lying down for an hour, as instructed by her doctor. Alison thought how childish she looked in her short dress and little white boots, the hair hanging glossy and straight to her shoulders. It was absurd to think of her as pregnant. What was Kit's son like? She supposed she would never know. Not even his name.

Later that evening, on an impulse, she showed her daughter-in-law a photograph. "That was Christopher Mallings at twenty-three."

The eyes, chestnut fire-coals, the mass of curling hair, black as coal, the full lips that might have been stung by mosquitoes, the small chin, the look of appeal: *Do things for me,* please do everything for me!

Dorothy took a sheet of writing paper, and carefully covered up half the face, showing first only the brow and eyes, then, only nose, mouth and chin. "Two people," she said. "Was he?"

"Yes, but one of them nobody knew but himself. I never knew. I don't believe Polly ever did."

"I don't think I could bear that; I mean, not to know James as well as any one person can know another one. Fancy living with a half-mystery! It would torture me. To have to probe and wonder!"

"It was a torture."

Something in her voice caught Dorothy's attention.

"After all this time—?"

"No. Not that at all."

"It was the way you said it."

"Histrionic, I think. I was miming an old emotion, as a sort of emotional indulgence. Or, perhaps, because I am rather ashamed to feel nothing at all. One *shouldn't* be deeply in love, and deeply hurt, and then forget completely. But I have forgotten."

Chapter Two

THE TWO WERE PACKING FOR THEIR RETURN TO ENGLAND.

"Thank God Paul's all right," said Georgina, but in fact her heart bled for the girl. The granddaughter of a Republican Senator, Emmy Wright was rich, wilful, had set her unflinching desire upon Paul Maclaren from the moment they met, and had married him with a scowl in the face of family opposition. She was a lean, parchment-skinned creature, smart but not pretty, and Georgina's prayers that Paul would somehow settle down and be kind to her were genuine. She had even steeled herself to take Emmy aside and warn her that the boy was wild, changeable, deeply selfish. The girl had shrugged this off as the attempt of a possessive mother to cling to her son.

"Pray God Emmy will be," Clement replied.

"Don't think I don't know how decent you've always been to him."

"We've both done the best we could."

Clement's first reason for returning to England was that he was fed up with Washington and, since the murder of John F. Ken-

459

nedy, he was frightened. Things weren't what they used to be. They would not become so again. His second reason, apart from a good job offered him in Fleet Street, was the book an American publisher had asked him to write, a biography of Kit. As usually happens, Kit's reputation had suffered a slump immediately after his death, despite the gothic circumstances: the publication of his Russian diaries, written on his first trip to the Soviet Union, had revived it. Jo, one of his literary executors, had found the scraps in a suitcase and pieced them together: he had believed they were imperceptive and wrong-headed, yet had known he had no right to suppress them. The diaries were strange, florid, wildly imaginative, shot through at times with descriptions of extraordinary beauty, bizarre flights of psychological fancy. Despite his claim to be afflicted with "Russian rheumatism," as an earlier generation had been afflicted with "French flu," Kit's attitude towards the country as a whole was far from friendly. In the United States the book was selling well.

Clement had heard no word from Jo for eighteen months and nothing about him. This was his own fault: he and Georgina, always rushed, immersed in a diplomatic life full of trip-wires, had cut themselves off from friends in England, had written few letters. The Atlantic could have been a century of time forcing friends away from them.

Winter was closing in on Georgetown, though the snow had not yet fallen. The weather was gloomy, the lights from the self-consciously cozy, old-fashioned shop windows shone like lighted jelly-cubes through the murk.

Clement straightened up from the row of suitcases and cabin trunks, lit a cigarette. At fifty-three he was thick round the middle, but otherwise had kept his figure well. The flap of pale hair was still bouncing and boyish. Georgina, forty-nine, had made a virtue of her stoutness. Her hair, carefully tinted every few weeks, rather more golden than it had been in the past, was brushed up in a lavish manner to the crown of her head.

"Shall we miss it here?" he asked her.

"I don't think so, much. A year ago, we might have done."

Though Clement, no hero-worshipper, had never subscribed to the cult of the dead President, he did feel that Kennedy had brought to Washington a sort of cultural emollience. The assassination had shocked them both to something like a three-day si-

460

lence, but Clement it had terrified. He did not believe in a single assassin: he believed in devils going to and fro on the earth and walking up and down on it, and more than one of them. He had scant knowledge of the new man. Such as they were, Clement's Washington days had been the golden ones, the days of hope and Walter Lippmann. He said to Georgina, not being original, "It stinks, and I am ready to depart."

Georgetown in the murk, the wall about Dumbarton Oaks, a scarlet trail of dry and rattling creeper which by this time had every right to be dead. The bleakness of Massachusetts Avenue, the chilly governmental center, minatory as Imperial Rome. The Washington Monument, the flagpoles around it at least twenty feet too low for the height of the obelisk itself, and the flags looking as tiny as those stuck into a military map.

"I shall miss Dick and Bob. John and Helen. Jim Thomson." He mentioned several of their friends.

"I shall miss you, in a way."

He turned. "What does that gnomic utterance mean? Have you decided to stay behind?"

"Oh no. Only there are so many you's, and I quite liked the Washington one. So placid, at least within the family circle."

"For Christ's sake, give over for a bit and have a drink. You look worn out. We can do the rest tomorrow."

Rising wearily, she agreed: yes, it would be soothing.

Later he asked her, in the peculiar intimacy of that time of departure, whether she had suffered much, since his early sexual failure.

She replied directly. "For a year or two, somewhat. But, as I believe I once said before, I could always think of something else."

"Stoical girl."

She quoted. " 'I've taken my fun where I found it. . . .' Or I did once. That was no fun for you. My apologies, however belated. Perhaps justice on me was pretty condign."

"Do you remember when I walloped you in Tedworth Square?"

She gave him a slow, lubricious smile. "I have always enjoyed it in retrospect. I'm by no means sure I did at the time."

"Poor Polly was so shocked."

"Ah, Polly. Such an odd girl."

"Well, I shall have to go home, look up Jo and winkle everything I can out of him. He knew Kit far better than the rest of us did."

She agreed.

Clement said, musing, "It was *after that* that you stopped running around with Tom, Dick and Harry. That's peculiar, really, when one comes to think of it."

Understanding him, she giggled. "I never knew a Harry."

"Then he's the only one you didn't."

Pain, betrayal, all dead: turned to an easy domestic joke. Consolations of growing old: the slow remorseless approach to the nearest understanding one person can have of another. The old small mysteries solved in the lightning-flash of a word casually dropped, a sentence unfinished. Solved to contentment: though long ago, when one had been trying to claw them out, as frantically as a cat claws a catnip mouse from under a sideboard, they would have been solved to pain. In age, in the aging of a marriage, most of the mysteries will be brought into a clear light of sympathy, love, even the companionable anger of mutual pity. If only you had told me before, how I could have helped you!

But if I had, you would have hated me.

They travelled home on the *Queen Elizabeth,* the household goods they had acquired during their American years crated up to follow behind them.

For the Maclarens, as for many people, a transatlantic voyage was one of the rare oases of peace in a turbulent life. Neither of them would have dreamed of being sick, though the waters, charcoal-colored as a smoker's catarrh, were tumultuous, the fiddles were up night after night in the dining-room, and waiters carefully spilled water on the tablecloths. Georgina went to the library for innumerable detective stories, Clement persistently won the morning quiz competitions, both listened to the hour of classical music and, without success, played Bingo. Georgina wore her best dresses, danced a little and flirted much in a matronly way which had behind it something sly, something sardonic. When they came into Southampton Water the skies were icily clear, and the sun dazzled.

They settled into a flat in Hampstead lent them by one of their friends: they could use it for six months, or until they found a place of their own. Clement went to Fleet Street, looked into the possibilities of the new job, and in El Vino's found old friends. It was near Christmas. He let the season go by (it had always bored him and Georgina) before he began to think of his book on Kit. Obviously the first thing to do was talk to Jo.

On the last day of the year, he made a telephone call: seven o'clock, high time for Jo to be back from work.

An old, sharp voice replied. "Miss Pease speaking."

"Why, hullo! I don't know if you remember me—Clement Maclaren."

"Yes, I do. You came here once or twice, some years ago. How are you?"

He said he was fine, and could he speak to Jo—

There was silence. Then: "You can't have heard—"

"—or Millie? Is she there?"

"Millie married again and went to Canada. They're out in Vancouver. Mr. Maclaren, I'm afraid this will be a shock to you. Jo died a year ago."

It was such a shock that Georgina, seeing his face change, cried out, "What is it? Clem! What is it?"

He steadied his voice. "I've been in America. . . . What of?"

She told him, sounding almost business-like: of chronic leukemia. He had been ill for years but had told no one, not even his sister. The last two months of his life he had spent in hospital, and the end was sudden. "So when they took him in, I came here for good. Mind you, I'd been coming in during the days, because of course the old lady was too much for him once Millie left. Not that you could blame her, Millie, I mean, it was never much of a life, and all that business with her first husband—"

"You mean to say old Mrs. Upjohn's still alive?"

"Hold on a minute, I'll just see if the sitting-room door's shut. She might hear."

In the pause, Clement said to his wife, "Jo's dead. You've grasped that."

"Oh no! For God's sake, what—"

"Tell you later."

Miss Pease was back on the wire.

"Yes, indeed she is. Eighty-three, and wonderfully fit for her age. Still reads without her glasses. Yes, she's very fit. Funny, isn't it, her being the last?"

"Look, do you think she'd see me or would it distress her?"

Miss Pease answered, a little drily, that Bessie would be delighted. She was long over the worst of it. She still loved a chat. Any Sunday, Sunday always seemed the longest day.

He felt he could smell, through the telephone, the stuffy scent of the house, cocoa, stale biscuits, cachous, lavender furniture-polish, age, sickness. Age and sickness. The hermetic world of which Jo had nevertheless managed to make so much.

After he had told the facts to Georgina, there seemed nothing for them to do but sit for a while in silence. She said at last, "And he kept it to himself. Incredible. But just like him. I suppose that's why he threw Davina over? Must have been."

"I can't believe he's dead. I feel even now that he'll ring up, say it's all a mistake and ask us round to the Six Bells."

The telephone rang. They jumped as if in terror.

It was Alison, who had heard they were back, and had traced their address. She added, "Is something the matter? Clem, you sound so odd!"

"We've just heard about Jo. Miss Pease told me."

A few seconds passed before she replied. "It seems so long ago now. But I'm sorry you had to hear it in that way."

Georgina snatched the telephone from him. "Alison? It's Georgie. Alison, I loved Jo. I truly did. He was the best of them all. I honestly feel, at this moment, that I can't bear it."

"I didn't feel I could, not at first. I'd let him drift, you know. He didn't write, and I supposed he'd got tired of us all. He didn't even answer James, whom he adored. But I should have got through to him, I should never have let him hide. The housekeeper says that when he was in hospital he wouldn't even have Millie told. In the end she took it into her own hands, but by then it was too late."

Jo in hospital, alone, drifting to death, not in pain but simply dead tired, as he had been for years. The dark razor-sharp face on the starchy pillow, the grape-green eyes turned upwards to the ceiling. At last, medical fingers closing them, as they might have closed windows at nightfall.

When he had put down the telephone, Clement thought of these things. But what had Jo been thinking in those last days? He hoped, of the little pub across the common, ruby light in the mul-

464

lions, the airy barmaid with a soft spot for him, the occasional visit with Kit sending his stock up in her eyes. Or even of the flat in Tedworth Square, the day he knocked Kit flying for Alison's sake, parfit gentle Jo, boundlessly astonished at himself. Or on the houseboat, celebrating the glory of his first published work: Kit had let him come first for once, he had allowed it to be Jo's night, and not his own. The joy, the pearly sunset, and the crying of the gulls. But he must have thought of Alison. There had been, there could have been, no one else for him. Sometimes Clement and the others had made a joke of it. (Why not? What can't be cured is far better joked about, unless it is a cruelty of the flesh.) Not joked about in front of Jo, though: O! his stockings foul, ungartered, and down-gyved to the ankle. Hamlet Jo! "Georgie, I have a very uncomfortable feeling that I am going to cry."

"Well, that seems to me a perfectly reasonable thing to do."

But he did not, for rage swept him. "To think that she's left, sitting in her damned chair! *She's* left behind!"

"Oh, shut up. She has a right to live. And in a sense she had a right to Jo, just so long as he was too weak to save himself. Or too strong: sometimes I think it was that. Even if she'd brought herself to make a sacrifice, she'd never have checked his dotty determination not to accept it. Start blaming him! You'll feel better if you do. We both shall."

Some few days after this, they had an unexpected visitor: James Welford, whom at first neither of them recognized.

He was very tall: he had, in fact, grown an inch since his twentieth year and now stood high-shouldered, very slightly stooped. He had Piers's luminous eyes, but they were graver than his father's, just as his mouth was more humorous. His cheekbones, like Alison's, were high and hollowed beneath, but there was no suggestion of ill health. The tones of his face were pale and very clear, as if there were a stratum of light beneath the first skin. A slender boy, conspicuously well-dressed, though quietly: the grey suit, with trousers fashionably narrow, white shirt, grey tie, had cost a good deal of money.

"Mother asked me if I would tell you something about Jo. I know you're writing about him. You see, I did know what was wrong with him when no one else did."

Georgina was diverted by a fleeting thought. If only I were

465

twenty-three again, or—come to that—thirty-three, how I should find myself wanting that young man! How lucky he is that I am not.

"I'm glad you've chosen to tell us all this," said Clement, sounding like a benign headmaster with a cane in his top drawer which, however, he did not use more than once in three years. "But why us, particularly?"

"Well, you are writing a book. And books must be as complete as possible—"

"Though they never are."

"Of course not," said James, with rather dismaying promptness, "but I suppose one gets as near as one can."

"You do *drink?*" Georgina said elaborately, swaying her behind a little, more like a ceremonial elephant than she would have imagined possible, as she went towards the sideboard.

"Please," James replied; "gin, with anything to hand."

Yet when she had filled his glass he did not at first touch it, but looked into it, as into a soothsayer's crystal.

"Your wife's going great guns," Clement said, hearing in his own voice a bluffness commonly associated with Henry VIII, and feeling ashamed of it.

James said simply, "She's doing well. But listen, I wanted to talk to you about Jo."

Georgina was irrationally shrill. "Why should you know so much about Jo?"

James's eyes rose to hers, and as they rose, light filled them. "I suppose, because he wanted me to. But if it's of no interest, I won't go on. In any case, I haven't much to say. Only, that I knew and he wanted me to know."

"Why?" Clement was sharp, the sharpness without obvious meaning.

James replied that they had been close, that they had met for dinner at least once a fortnight. "It was after Kit's death that he didn't seem to need people any more, even me. You mean, why did he want me to know? I think it was a comfort to feel that somebody did. Perhaps he felt less on his own."

"Surely you should have told someone?"

"He made me promise not to. Mind you, if there had been any hope for him I should have broken that promise. I went to doctor after doctor, I asked them about people in his condition.

466

And they all said there was no hope at all. So you see, I didn't feel quite so bad. And I knew there might be long remissions."

"It seems to me," said Georgina, sounding angry because she was so moved, "that you were taking a lot on yourself for a boy of—what?"

"Nineteen. But I had to."

There were stars in the clear cold sky beyond the windows. "Thank you," James said, accepting another drink. No, he didn't smoke. Then he added, "You mustn't sentimentalize Jo too much, I think."

Georgina was tart, resenting his youth while admiring him. "Is that what we do?" An interloper into a past in which he could have had no place.

"Everyone seems to, rather. He wasn't often unhappy. He was very good at coming to terms with things, far more than most of us are. In fact, I don't think I ever knew a man better at doing that: with him, it was a sort of genius. Even being so disappointed because he couldn't write—"

"And about something else," Georgina said, her eyes darkening as they always did when she was thinking of love.

"My mother. Yes. But that was something he liked to hug to himself: in the end it was a comfort, I'm certain it was."

Clement stirred restlessly in his chair. "Well, I'll have to go and see Davina, whether she wants me or not. I suppose Kit had a literary executor besides Jo, and she must be it."

"No," said James, "I am."

Georgina exploded. "There's trust for you!"

"It was what Jo wanted, he asked me to do it when he'd told me about his illness. Kit was keen on the idea, probably just because I was so young. He thought of it as a kind of insurance policy." He gave Georgina one of his steady glances, disconcertingly direct. "I don't think I shall be inadequate. Anyway, I shall do my best."

She explained she had not implied a trust misplaced in himself, but rather a distrust by Kit of Davina.

"I'll help Clement all I can."

When James had left them, Georgina said, "There was hostility in the air, I could hear it crackle. Not from him, from us. Why did we let that happen? He's a good boy."

"Well, we were all in the circle, 'the wild life,' ages before

James was born. Circles like ours are as possessive as jealous husbands and wives. We always let Jo play second fiddle, yet he belonged to *us,* and to nobody else. He had our names on his collar."

They stood together looking down the hill, where the young man walked with his graceful stoop through lake after lake of lamplight, neither fast nor slowly, but as one who has taken the measure of the speed of the earth, and is in harmony with it.